THE BOY WHO SAID NO

THE BOY WHO SAID NO
AN ESCAPE TO FREEDOM

HISTORICAL FICTION

Patti Sheehy

LONGBOAT KEY, FLORIDA

This book is dedicated to my husband, Robert Hunter,
and to my daughter, Patricia Larson, the bravest woman I know.

ACKNOWLEDGMENTS

I would like to acknowledge Frank Mederos for his brilliant storytelling and his depiction of people, places, and events that form the basis of this true-life novel. His ability to convey detailed information in a language other than his native tongue was truly inspiring. Without him, this story would have never been told.

Books on Cuba, too numerous to mention, informed this narrative, but two were particularly helpful: Hugh Thomas's weighty tome, *Cuba: The Pursuit of Freedom* and *Fidel Castro* by Robert E. Quirk. I highly recommend them to anyone wanting to gain a better understanding of Cuba's complex history and culture. I would like to credit both gentlemen for their contributions to the details that enhanced or clarified this book. Any errors regarding the history and politics of Cuba are mine, not theirs.

My heartfelt thanks go to Donald Gibson for his work surrounding this book. Thanks to my friends Barbara and Tom Gardner and to David Lenihan for introducing me to the fine folks at Oceanview Publishing. Thanks to the Haddon Heights Library for excellent customer service and to the Happy Bookers for their encouragement.

Finally, thanks to my wonderful family and friends for their suggestions and readings of *The Boy Who Said No,* especially my book-loving friends, the Israels, Joyce Herrman, Carol Larro, and Janice Stridick. And always, always, thanks to my dear husband and partner, Robert J. Hunter, for his love and support.

PREFACE

The Boy Who Said No is based on the life story of Frank Mederos, who was born and raised in Guanabacoa, Cuba. Through a number of childhood experiences and the influence of his grandfather, Frank grew to despise the policies of his government.

As Frank matures, he falls in love, is drafted into the army, and becomes a member of Castro's special forces, making him privy to top-secret military information and placing him in direct conflict with some of the most powerful people in the Cuban military. He becomes an Antitank Guided Missile operator, defects, and escapes from Cuba in the manner described.

After being introduced to Frank by his daughter, I began to write his story as part of his family's history. But after several meetings with Frank, I decided that this story was far too compelling not to share with a wider audience.

To advance the plot, I have fictionalized some descriptions and dialogue based on interviews with Frank and with information he obtained from his family, friends, and fellow soldiers after the fact.

Since these events happened several decades ago, and since Frank does not have firsthand knowledge of certain events and conversations that occurred during his absences, I am calling this a "true-life novel."

With the exception of the name of Frank Mederos, all names have been changed to protect the privacy of family members and individuals still residing in Cuba. The material is presented as well as Frank's memory serves.

We are an army of light
And nothing shall prevail against us
And in those places where the sun is darkened, it will overcome.

—José Martí
Cuban poet

THE BOY WHO SAID NO

CHAPTER 1

My grandfather loved to fish.

He fished for tuna, yellowtail, red and black grouper. Sometimes he'd catch octopi, pound them on rocks, and hang them up to dry before bringing them to his home on Pepe Antonio Street. He lived only two houses from my family's simple bungalow, the one my father supported on his meager wages from the fertilizer factory in Havana. *Abuelo* liked the solitude, the peacefulness of fishing. "Gives me time to think," he said.

Abuelo was always ruminating about something, his thoughts fueled by various radio broadcasts and his daily ingestion of news contained in the pages of *The Havana Post* and *El Diario de la Marina*. His was the only house in the neighborhood filled with books, fat tomes on history, philosophy, and religion that sat helter-skelter on tables, some opened to the page he was reading, some underlined and bookmarked with bits of paper, some coated in a thin layer of dust. The neighbors all looked up to him. He was revered as an intellectual by those who knew him.

By the time I was four, Abuelo had declared me his "official fishing partner." This made me feel very special. I was his oldest grandson, and he was my hero. When I was around him I felt safe in a way that was hard to explain. I think it was partly because he was a strong man with a soft heart and partly because I thought he was the smartest man in the world.

Abuelo and I fished off the shoreline of the small village of Cojimar, where Ernest Hemingway kept the *Pilar*, the famous writer's boat.

Sometimes we'd fish from the dock. And sometimes we'd hop into my grandfather's old fishing boat and head a little way out from the coast, gazing at the rum and sugar fleets in the distance and listening to the calls of seagulls and the waves lapping gently against the shore.

I loved the smell of gasoline and the white burst of smoke that appeared when Grandpa yanked the cord on his small outboard motor. I was fascinated with how the clear blue water churned bubbly white around the propeller.

Occasionally, Abuelo would take me for a walk along the Havana harbor, a place teeming with fish and clotted with lights, a place where painted ladies in fine fur stoles and glittering jewels teetered on spindly heels so high they could barely walk. These were the wives of rich Americans and Europeans who frequented Havana's lavish hotels and brightly lit casinos, not people we interacted with, not people we knew.

From there we could see the Havana Yacht Club where the wealthy Americans who ran the United Fruit Company entertained each other on their expensive boats. Nattily dressed men smoked Montecristo cigars and gulped shots of Dewar's White Label, while their women sipped daiquiris decorated with tiny paper umbrellas. Abuelo told me that Fulgencio Batista had been blackballed from that club because he was uneducated, a *mestizo*, and a former cane cutter. I thought it strange that the president of the country could be kept out of any club, even if he did have mixed blood.

Early one evening when the air was rich with the scent of jasmine and Abuelo's boat was bobbing beneath us, my grandfather put a hand on my shoulder and urged me to look up.

"I want you to get to know the sky, Frankie. And to learn about the wind."

"Why?" I asked, sensing his seriousness.

"Because if you pay attention to those things, you can predict the weather. And predicting the weather can be very important in life."

I nodded and trailed my fingers in the water. Abuelo ran his hand over the stubble of his beard, making a rasping sound. I liked that sound, the sound of a man. The back of his hands were furred with curly black hair speckled with gray and riddled with flat, white scars. But his fingernails were invariably clipped and filed. And impeccably clean.

Abuelo was always trying to teach me things, practical things, like how to tie different kinds of knots and how to sharpen the blade of a knife. We rarely engaged in idle conversation. It was as if he was trying to impart everything he knew to me before time ran out, before it was too late.

"Do you see those clouds, Frankie?" I looked up to see purple striated clouds in the gloaming.

"Look at how they're formed, how they move. Different shapes mean different things. I'm going to teach you about them, and I want you to pay close attention. And more importantly, I want you to remember what I have to say."

Abuelo looked at me, and I nodded to let him know I was listening. We sat in silence for a moment. I wasn't sure whether the conversation was over. I hoped it wasn't.

Abuelo coughed. "You'd be surprised what you can tell by watching the clouds."

"Like what?" I wanted Grandpa to keep talking. He looked at me and laughed at my earnestness.

"Like whether you and Gilbert will be playing baseball together tomorrow," he said.

I smiled. Grandpa always brought the conversation down to my level. It was one of his talents.

"Look. Do you see the boat drifting?"

I looked at the movement of the boat in relation to the shore. "The boat is moving with the current," said Abuelo. "You must know the direction of the current, how strong it is and how fast it is."

"Why?"

"Because the current will take you where *it* wants to go. If you want to go in the same direction, it's your friend. But if you don't, you must work very hard to defeat it. Nature is very powerful, Frankie.

Never forget that. But if you pay attention and know what you're doing, you can use the clouds, the wind, and the currents to your advantage."

I thought for a moment, feeling the breeze on my face. "What about the stars, Grandpa, what do they tell you?"

"The stars are very special, Frankie. You have to know the stars like the back of your hand. If you know the stars, you can tell direction, you will know where to go. In the olden days, men crossed the oceans by reading the stars. That's how Christopher Columbus found Cuba."

"Oh," I said, mightily impressed by the power of the stars.

"Do you remember what Columbus called Cuba?"

I thought for a moment, making sure I got the words right. "He said it was the most beautiful land that human eyes had ever seen."

My grandfather nodded, proud of me for remembering. "That's right, my boy."

We sat quietly for a while, and I knew Abuelo was hoping I had taken in what he had said. The water was very still, the way it sometimes got once the sun went down. A dragonfly skated by, its long, slender body barely creasing the water. In the fading light it took on a peacock sheen.

We looked up at the twilight sky suddenly darkened by a flock of wild ducks. They honked plaintively. My grandfather raised a finger skyward.

"Look, Frankie, do you see that constellation? That's Orion, the great hunter of Greek mythology. It is said that Zeus placed him among the stars. If you look carefully, you can see his bow."

I looked where my grandfather was pointing. I felt very grown up gazing at the stars that way. The boat rocked slightly, underscoring my excitement.

"Will you teach me the constellations, Grandpa?"

Abuelo chuckled. "I'll teach you all I know, my boy. Mark my words—someday it will come in handy."

•   •   •

From the time I was a small child, my grandfather would sit me on his lap, his breath fragrant with smoke, and read the Bible to me. His was a hefty book with a cracked leather spine and pages as thin as gossamer. He told me about Moses and the parting of the Red Sea, about the leper Lazarus being raised from the dead, about Noah building his Ark. He taught me about God and the lives of the saints.

In his living room was a picture of the Sacred Heart of Jesus. He was depicted with a loving face, wavy hair, and fire leaping from a red puffy heart. After a cup of rich Cuban coffee, Abuelo would hold his fist to his chest, look at the picture and say, "Dear Jesus, save me from this heartburn!" I figured heartburn was something Jesus and Abuelo had in common, and that's why Abuelo asked for His help.

When I got a little older, Abuelo regaled me with tales of heroes such as Antonio Maceo, José Martí, Calixto Garcia, brave and honorable men who had fought for Cuba's independence from Spain. His eyes glowed when he spoke of them. He told me incredible things, like how Cuba's national anthem, "El Himno de Bayamo," was composed from the saddle of a horse. It was my favorite story, and I pleaded with him to tell it to me again and again. When he described the 1868 Battle of Bayamo, I felt like I was there. When he was finished, we'd break into song:

> *Hasten to battle, men of Bayamo!*
> *That the homeland looks proudly to you;*
> *Do not fear a glorious death,*
> *Because to die for the fatherland is to live.*

> *To live in chains is to live*
> *In dishonor and ignominy*
> *Hear the clarion call;*
> *Hasten, brave ones, to battle!*

Then Abuelo would tickle me, and we would laugh.

•   •   •

When I started school, Abuelo helped me with my homework before we went out fishing. Sometimes he would try to tutor Gilbert and Luis. But they were not academically inclined. And Luis tried Abuelo's patience with his constant fooling around. After a while, he only helped me.

Three years my senior, my cousin Luis spent a lot of time at my house in Guanabacoa, a district of Havana. He was lively and fun and my family liked having him around. He and my cousins Tato, Gilbert, and Pipi spent so much time at our house when I was young I thought they were my brothers. Pipi was not his real name. It was just what we called him. Nicknames were common in Cuba.

Luis had his own way of thinking about things. When he got to the fourth grade, he just stayed there. For years. I told him he had to move on, but he stubbornly refused—even though he could.

"I like the teacher and I know the school work so it's easy for me," was his excuse.

"But, Luis, you can't stay in the fourth grade forever."

"Why not?"

"Because it's stupid, that's why."

"It makes me happy."

"You're happy being held back?"

"It's not being held back if you do it on purpose."

"Aren't you bored?"

"No. I know the fourth grade material so well now the teacher says I can help her teach next year. So I'll be smarter than you—I'll be a teacher."

"That's crazy, Luis. You won't be a real teacher. You'll just be a big fourth grader. If you know the material, why don't you just take the test?"

"Because I don't want to take the test, and I don't want to go to fifth grade. I'm happy where I am. I don't think that's stupid at all."

I just shook my head.

•   •   •

Gilbert had his own little quirks. For the first two years of school he rarely washed his feet. His mother would reprimand him. But nothing worked. Like Luis, Gilbert was stubborn.

Gilbert liked to take his socks off in school and show off his pitch-black feet as if they were a badge of honor. Then he'd scrape the bottom of his feet on the floor beneath his desk to scratch an itch.

The girls in the class would wail and complain, but that just encouraged him. I felt sorry for any girl who sat next to Gilbert. Not only did she have to smell his feet all day, but when he took off his shoes and the odor grew worse, he'd shamelessly blame the smell on her. Gilbert loved girls, and this was his way of getting their attention.

There was no end to our boyish pranks. Some days we got together with our friend Jabao and rigged the blackboard so it would fall down when the teacher touched it. Then we'd all laugh so hard, we'd be sent to the principal's office. Some days Pipi would bring his pet parrot— the one he had taught to swear—to school in a brown paper bag and hide it under his desk. When the parrot let loose with a string of expletives, he'd blame it on someone else. Then we'd all laugh so hard, we'd be sent to the principal's office. Some days Gilbert would put glue on the teacher's seat and blame it on some hapless girl. Then we'd all laugh so hard, we'd be sent to the principal's office.

We drove the principal crazy. He was a strict disciplinarian who demanded to know the perpetrator of these acts. No one would ever snitch. Except Antonio.

Antonio was a slightly built boy, a fearful kid, the type of child other kids pick on. To make matters worse, his older brother was always beating him up. Antonio often showed up to play with a swollen lip, a black eye, a bruised arm. He always claimed to have fallen down.

On warm sunny days when the sky was dotted with fat white clouds, we'd all play hooky and go skinny-dipping in the area's rivers, marshes, and streams. We would play tag, merrily skipping from one warm river rock to the next, our arms outstretched to keep our balance.

Jabao came up with the idea of playing hide-and-seek by using dry, hollow reeds that grew on the river banks to breathe underwater. For a while it was our favorite pastime. We would sneak up and scare the other boys, splashing and giggling until we almost drowned.

Since everyone in Guanabacoa knew one another, whenever we skipped school we had to figure out how to get back to our homes without being seen. Many limestone caves skirted the port of Cojimar, and a complicated warren of tunnels ran under the nearby *Rio Lajas.*

Always on the lookout for someone who might report us truant, we ran from one tunnel and cave to the next, hiding from prying eyes and enjoying the thrill of it all. Our fear of being caught was somewhat abated because no one knew the ins and outs of these hiding spots better than we.

Mostly I hung out with boys, but there was a special girl in the neighborhood who had stolen my heart. Miriam was sweet and shy and had hazel eyes. My mother said it was just a crush—but it lasted for years. Whenever I was feeling upset about something, I'd talk to Miriam. If I found a caterpillar, I would show it to her, and I was always looking for presents to give her, like shells I had found on the beach or bright butterflies that had lost a wing. On the days my mother made cookies, I would hide one in my pocket for Miriam.

Every night the people on my block would dress up and go for a *paseo*, a stroll around the park. The boys would walk one way and the girls would walk the other, accompanied by stern *dueñas* draped in black lace shawls. The boys would wink and wave at the girls, trying to get their attention without attracting the wrath of the women in charge.

They say a small town is like a big family. That's how it was on my block. The people in my neighborhood knew all the houses and everyone in them. We knew whose mother was mean and whose father was mad. We knew who was sick and who could come out to play. We knew whose aunt drank cane juice and whose uncle drank rum. We even knew the names of each other's dogs. That's just the way it was.

A lot was going on politically in Cuba while I was growing up, but I was too busy being a boy to notice. I was too busy playing baseball to know that Fidel Castro's poorly armed rebels had led a failed assault on the Moncada Barracks on July 26, 1953, an assault that landed Fidel in the Presidio Modelo Prison for two years, but gave birth to a revolutionary movement that would eventually topple the government.

I was too busy playing marbles to know that although Fidel's forces comprised fewer than two hundred men, they often caused Batista's army of forty- to fifty-thousand to cut their losses and run.

I was too busy sunning myself on alabaster beaches to know that opposition to Batista in Cuba had been growing like rice in China, due to his pandering to the American mobsters and big business interests who controlled most of Cuba's resources and wealth. I was even too busy to notice that the dictator had been forced to flee Cuba on New Year's Day 1959.

But eight days later, I got my first inkling that something was happening in my country. Something Abuelo didn't like. That day, after my grandfather and I went fishing together, we stopped in Havana so Abuelo could get some coffee. We were both very tired.

As we walked down the magnificent *Malecón*, the wide seaside walkway that circles half of Havana, a line of heavily armored trucks rumbled by. This was the first in a column of cars, lorries, and tanks that would carry Fidel's now five-thousand-strong victorious rebels into the city.

Fidel and his men had been traveling for days from their camp located six hundred miles away in the Sierra Maestra, stopping to speak to rapturous crowds along the way. I could hear shouts and cheering nearby. When we turned the corner, I saw thousands upon thousands of people lining the streets, smiling, laughing and hoisting placards that read *"Gracias Fidel!"*

Many people seemed beyond jubilant, almost delirious. As the chanting grew louder, Abuelo's face grew dark, and he quickly reached for my hand. A number of rough-looking men in olive-green uniforms jumped down from the trucks. They were a tough, dirty bunch with grizzled black beards, waists bulging with guns, and feet shod in mud-covered boots. A tank rolled by with Fidel sitting atop a pyramid of men. Abuelo placed his body partly in front of mine, as if to protect me. I tugged on his shirt.

"What's going on?"

"It's Fidel and his rebels," said Abuelo.

"What does it mean?" I was getting a little nervous, sensing my grandfather's unease.

"There's been a fight for control of the government," he said. "Batista's out and Fidel is in."

I looked at the men who had jumped off the trucks. "Are these the guys who won?" I asked. I could hardly believe that these scruffy, long-haired men could be the victors. But people on the balconies of the modern apartment buildings seemed to think so. They were waving red-and-black flags embroidered with a large white 26 *Julio*, throwing confetti and chanting *"Viva Cuba! Viva Fidel!"* Several of the men were drinking Hatuey, a fine Cuban beer. I had never seen anything like it.

"Yes," Abuelo said. "These are the guys who won."

A fleet of long, black Cadillacs drove by. The men in the cars were honking their horns, laughing, and brandishing their guns. There were a lot of machetes on display, a lot of knives, a lot of guns. I was eyeing the cars' whitewall tires.

"Where did Batista go?" I asked.

"To the Dominican Republic. Took his family with him. After that, who knows?"

I looked up as several airplanes thundered by. "Why are there so many planes?" We had to wait for a minute for the noise to die down before Abuelo could answer my question. I noticed some girls wearing tight red sweaters and short black skirts shouting "Fidel! Fidel! Fidel!" with the kind of enthusiasm young women usually lavish on movie stars.

"They're taking the Americans back to the States."

"Why?"

"Shush, Frankie. Not now. You are asking too many questions. I'll tell you when we get home."

Fidel approached the podium to address the crowd from the terrace of the presidential palace. He had a rosary wrapped around his neck and he was carrying a rifle. A bank of microphones amplified his voice so it could be better heard by us and by those listening to Havana Television and Cuban radio stations throughout the country. I stood on my toes, the better to see.

"Fellow countrymen—" he began. The crowd grew quiet. People looked mesmerized. A car honked in the background and then the sound died away. Fidel's voice rang out. "As you know, the people of Havana are expecting us on Twenty-Third Street—" The audience stood in rapt attention.

I looked up at Abuelo as Fidel droned on. His eyes had narrowed, and he was listening intently while still holding my hand. A few minutes into Fidel's speech, someone in the crowd released two doves into the air. We watched as they winged their way skyward. Then, as if by divine intervention, one swept down and settled itself on Fidel's shoulder—a symbol of universal peace. The crowd went wild.

Abuelo shook his head, and a cold chill ran down my spine. I was a little scared and very confused.

"Tell me," I said. "Are you glad Batista's gone? Was his leaving something good or something bad?"

Abuelo drew in his breath. He let go of my hand and rubbed my head. "Time will tell. Now let's go get you an ice cream cone."

But from the look on his face, I knew it was bad.

CHAPTER 2

It was a bright Saturday afternoon, warm and dry as old crackers. I had finished my chores around the house and was riding my bike down the road with Gilbert. Dust rose beneath our tires and clung to the hair on our legs. Occasionally I had to wipe it from my nose. A lizard darted near my tires, and I swerved to avoid it.

We were in high spirits, headed for a swim in the river, when Gilbert suddenly stopped his bike and waved me forward. I pulled up alongside him, dragging my foot in the dust to bring me to a halt.

"Why'd you stop?" I asked.

"I almost forgot to tell you." Gilbert took a breath and puffed out his chest the way he did when he had something important to say.

"What?"

Gilbert hesitated a moment for dramatic effect. "We don't have to go to school anymore." A smile lit his face, but a trace of concern filled his eyes.

At age thirteen, I was old enough to know that what he was saying was nonsense.

Still, there was something convincing in his tone of voice. I smiled and shook my head.

"Are you crazy, Gilbert? Of course we have to go to school. Where'd you get that idea?"

"Around," he pronounced mysteriously. "Fidel's got a new plan to eliminate illiteracy, so he's going to close the schools. Not just ours— all of them."

Gilbert was always coming up with strange and ridiculous stories, and I figured his imagination had run amok again.

"That's totally backward, Gilbert. If you want to stamp out illiteracy, you *open* schools, you don't *close* them."

Gilbert smiled smugly. "I know. But they say Fidel's going to use *us* to do it. We'll be working for him."

"To do what?"

"To wipe out illiteracy."

"How do you figure?"

Gilbert studied the ground for a minute. "They just passed a law closing all the schools."

"Why haven't I heard about it?"

"Probably because you weren't in school on Friday."

I looked up at the sky for a moment. A brown bird with a red breast settled lightly on a narrow branch and began pecking furiously at his feathers. He looked at us momentarily and then returned to his grooming.

"Well, I don't believe it."

Gilbert made a face. "It's true."

"What's the point?"

"They're going to get every kid to teach *una familia pobre* to read and write."

"What poor families?"

Gilbert shrugged. "How would I know?"

I laughed, dismissing the idea as sheer lunacy. "We're going to be the teachers? Us? You are loco, Gilbert."

"No, listen. Fidel is forming a literacy brigade. He says a million illiterates in Cuba need to learn to read and write."

"Literacy brigade? You mean like an army? What will we do? Shoot people with letters of the alphabet?"

"Have it your way. But you'll see when they send you off to some awful place to teach people to read."

When I got home from our swim, my mother met me at the door. "I just heard that they're closing the schools," she said.

"Gilbert told me. He says we're going to teach poor people how to read."

Mima placed her hands on her hips and tightened her lips. "I hear it's voluntary. Tell me you didn't volunteer for anything."

"No," I said.

She looked at me sternly. "Good, because you are to have no part of this, do you hear?"

"I said I didn't volunteer for anything."

Mima gave me a long, searching look and then waved her hand. "All right, go get washed up for supper."

The following week, soldiers showed up at our school demanding the names and addresses of all sixth and seventh graders. The school was in an uproar, and the teachers kept leaving the classrooms to confer with each other behind closed doors. Their voices were strained and their faces were starched with concern. I still couldn't believe the government would send us away.

Just after the bell rang, four soldiers marched into the classroom, telling us about the difficult lives of the peasants—how they never had a chance to learn how to read and write. They described their squalid living conditions and how they couldn't even decipher a food label. They told us to close our eyes and imagine how awful it would be to be illiterate. A wave of pity washed over me.

Two well-dressed university professors joined the soldiers to announce that all the boys were "volunteering" to join the brigade. Girls could also join if they obtained their parents' permission.

Our teacher stood at the back of the classroom looking skeptical. She held her lips together the way she did when she was displeased with our behavior. She questioned the officials about where we would go, when we would return, what we would eat, and where we would sleep. Neither the soldiers nor the professors provided her with satis-factory answers.

Within a week, signs started sprouting around Havana that read: *"¡No creer, leer!"* "Don't just believe, read!" The slogan signaled not only a new Cuban government, but a new Cuban society. Rumors filled the air about how Fidel planned to wipe out illiteracy in the whole country. People were lauding his plan as a noble gesture, the first step in making Cuba a world power. Newspapers proclaimed the elimination of illiteracy as Fidel's top priority.

Parents were put on notice that their sons had been selected to participate in the government's National Literacy Campaign and that any resistance from them—or their children—would result in severe repercussions. Peasant families were told that they would be given ten dollars to take boys into their homes to teach them to read—whether they wanted to learn or not.

On Saturday morning, my mother got up early to bake *pastelitos de guayaba*. She had just lined up the crescent-shaped dough on a cookie sheet and popped the pastries into the oven when Luis ran in the back door, red in the face and panting.

"What's gotten into you?" asked Mima.

Luis was so excited he could hardly form the words. "It's time to go," he said. "Everybody's getting ready—it's really happening. Gilbert says they'll take you so far away you can't escape—you can't get home. They're coming right now *¡Cuidado!*" Then he ran out of the house, the screen door banging behind him.

My mother looked at me in alarm and turned off the stove. She removed her oven mitts and slapped them down on the counter in an expression of rage. Neither of us could believe this was happen-ing.

My hand flew to my mouth as I considered what to do. The knot that had been growing in the pit of my stomach after I saw the soldiers at school exploded into a stream of bile that burned the back of my throat. I looked around, not knowing whether to run or to hide.

Our neighbors were standing in front of their houses, stretching their necks to see what was going on. Some people were whispering and mumbling to each other. A few women were crying.

A child being taken from their parents was something Cubans had never experienced before. We had lived under President Carlos Prío Socorrás, a man who hosted lavish parties where guests snorted cocaine and relieved themselves in bathrooms outfitted with faucets of gold.

We had lived under Batista, a dictator who hung dead revolutionaries from the limbs of trees and subverted the interests of his nation to those of the Mob. But the idea that children could be sent to some unknown place for the sake of the revolution was totally foreign.

The "volunteers" were ordered to go to the baseball stadium for processing before being taken to the train station in Havana. I looked out over the crowd and spotted my sisters and brothers. Theresa was holding my father's hand and sobbing uncontrollably. My brother, George, stood with his arms crossed, looking angry and rebellious. My mother was holding my baby brother Raúl.

Anguish filled her eyes. I was her oldest child and the fear of losing me haunted her expression. My throat constricted in grief as I read the sorrow creasing her face. She squeezed my hand tightly and kissed me before I left.

CHAPTER 3

The railroad station was mass confusion. Trucks were lined up like sentries to drop off more than five hundred boys and adult teachers from all over the city. Some of the younger boys were sobbing for their mothers. The older boys looked just plain angry.

A few scuffles broke out but, for the most part, everyone was too scared not to toe the line. We were herded into cattle cars for our three-day trip to the Sierra Maestra, the wildest, most remote part of the country. The mountains were six hundred miles away, the same mountains where Fidel's Rebel Army had made their headquarters and launched their guerrilla attacks. Most of us had never even heard of the place.

The train ride was long and tedious with the cars screeching and lurching along the tracks. There were no bathrooms that I could see, and kids were peeing and defecating on the floor. Many of the boys got sick. The stench was horrific.

Boys were pushing and punching each other. I was lucky to find a place to sit. I closed my eyes and thought about the long grasses fluttering in the slipstream of the train. I wished I were fishing with Abuelo.

When we got to Bayamo, heavily armed soldiers handed everyone a literacy ID card, a uniform, a blanket, and a canvas hammock. They issued each of us two books—*¡Venceremos!* and *¡Alfabetizemos!*

I tried thumbing through the books, which contained pictures of happy families proudly standing next to their animals and produce. One book contained phrases such as "The Revolution Wins All

Battles," "Friends and Enemies," and "International Unity" as a teaching aid. I scanned the glossary, but there was too much commotion to read. Soldiers distributed blue lanterns donated by China to be used during lessons.

None of us knew where we were going or how long we'd have to stay. Frightened and bewildered, I hoped I would end up somewhere near my cousins and friends. Luckily, Gilbert, Tato, Luis, and Antonio were still with me. We stayed in a small town in the mountains for two days, sleeping outdoors, drinking coconut milk, and wondering where we were headed. During the day it seemed like a big adventure, but at night I cried a lot.

On the morning of the third day, soldiers arrived to escort us to our assigned families. Fifty or sixty of us walked in single file up Turquino—the highest mountain in Cuba. We marched up a narrow path thick with cacti and then wended our way through hanging vines and dense guaguasi trees. Lizards slithered through the underbrush and colorful birds pierced the air with cries of alarm. We were told to beware of large mud holes that could suck you in so quickly you would drown in mud before you could escape.

When I stumbled on broken rocks, soldiers nudged me along with the barrels of their rifles. One of the soldiers allowed me to sip water from his canteen. A howler monkey narrated the scene.

Boys were dropped off at different towns along the way. When they departed, the soldiers smiled. It was obvious we were a burden they were eager to unload.

Below us, waving in the wind, were rows and rows of King Cane, harvested by the darkest of people, people who were considered too ignorant to make their own decisions and run their own lives.

Giant sugar complexes, mostly American, had either bought out or driven out all the small farmers and now ran their consolidated holdings with an iron hand. The families of those who oversaw the operations lived in nearby gated communities where they swam in crystal-blue pools, dined alfresco, and sent their huge profits home.

We passed under manchineel trees whose poisonous sap caused angry sores on our skin. I used my hands to slap mosquitoes from my sweat-drenched limbs.

Soon the blue lantern felt too heavy, and I threw it down the mountainside. It tumbled over itself and landed next to a fallen branch. Other boys had already discarded their lanterns, so the soldiers barely gave it a glance.

We walked the rest of the way in silence.

CHAPTER 4

When we got to our destination, I was delivered to a Haitian family that eyed me with suspicion. Two boys about my age sat on a dirt floor, while a barefoot girl glared at me from behind a banana tree. A fine layer of clay lightened their ebony skin.

A matronly woman with straggly hair and missing teeth clung to her husband, José, while three dirty-faced toddlers hung on her legs. The father stood tall, an onyx giant, with well-defined muscles etching his shoulders and back. His arms were stronger than his legs and his shoulders showed the results of years of hard labor.

Wiry black hair covered his chest and back. A "lazy eye" wandered around in his eye socket, making it difficult to tell whether he was looking at you or not. A rope hung around his neck and a machete yoked his waist. The carcass of an animal—I didn't know what kind— hung from a pole to dry. Its skin had been removed and its body was marbled with blood.

I looked at the children, feeling sorry that they had to live in such squalor. I figured the parents were former slaves brought to Cuba from Haiti to work the plantations, but I didn't ask any questions. That wasn't my job.

One of the soldiers, the taller of the two, stepped forward and said, "Frank is here to teach you to read." He spoke loudly and slowly as if that would help the peasants comprehend what he was saying. He butted me with his rifle.

"Show 'em the books so they understand."

I scrambled to hold up the books for them to see.

José shot me a look of disdain. He fingered the handle of his machete and grunted.

"Ain't no use for readin' here," he said. "Might as well send 'im back where he belong!" The boys nodded in agreement. Then the man spat on the ground and walked away. I wondered how long I would have to stay with these people.

The soldiers shrugged their shoulders and took their leave.

After the soldiers departed, José and I squatted on the ground opposite each other while the children busied themselves winding and unwinding a ball of twine. Neither of us knew what to say. He seemed content to just sit and look at me. He struck me as a man filled with subterranean emotions, one I would have to tiptoe around.

Not knowing what to do, I unlaced my boots and rubbed my feet, which were red and sore from the long hike up the mountain. My boots were heavy and stiff as cardboard, and I knew they would be difficult to walk in for any length of time. I fingered a plump blister, rolling the liquid beneath the skin. I was tempted to lance it, but I looked at my dirty hands and thought better of it. I felt a pang of longing for Mima. She was the one who tended to my scrapes and cuts.

José was still staring at me, and I figured I looked very young to him, far too young to teach him anything. An uncomfortable silence hung in the air. I lowered my head and studied the ground in an effort to look respectful. I knew I'd have to prove myself to him—and to everyone else.

My first order of business was to figure out where to bed down for the night. The two boys, Juan and Ernesto, showed me the primitive hammocks they used for sleep, and my hopes for a bed evaporated like smoke in the wind. I unpacked my own canvas hammock, and the boys indicated that I was to tie it between two trees.

I glanced at Ernesto who was eyeing my blanket enviously. I offered it to him, and he took it with a smile. I knotted the rope the way Abuelo had taught me and climbed into my gently swinging bed. I turned on my side, drew my legs to my chest, and listened to the insects hum in a minor key.

I missed Abuelo. I missed my parents. I missed the sweet smell of my sheets and the coldness of my pillowcase against my cheek. I missed my mother's pastries and the sound of her laughter. I missed the safety and surety of home.

I looked up at the moon and felt comforted that it was the same moon that shone on the roof of my home on Pepe Antonio Street. Then I cried myself softly, very softly, to sleep.

My life in the hills was very different from my life in Guanabacoa. The thatched-roofed hut that the family called home had no electricity, no stove, no refrigerator, and no indoor plumbing. Chickens pecked the hut's mud floor and pigs roamed the crowded living space.

The urine and feces of the two animal species melded into a smell so foul it made my eyes burn. Large black flies feasted on the scraps of food that littered the children's mouths, and ugly sores festered on their shoeless feet.

I figured I had to fend for myself to survive. Although I was an official "teacher" and was not required by the State to work, the only way to earn the family's respect was to pitch in and help.

Our routine was to rise early in the morning and wash our bodies in a nearby stream, the same stream where Maria did the family's laundry. José, Juan, Ernesto, and I then went out to work, while Maria stayed home to tend the younger children and to prepare the morning meal. Around ten o'clock she'd bring breakfast for us to eat in the fields.

The family wore rubber shoes made from old tires. I drew my knife and sliced off enough rubber to make shoes for myself. Maria, a large, powerful woman with a sweet smile, showed me how to sew the ends with a long curved needle and urged me to stuff the shoes with rags the way the family did. While serviceable, the shoes were slippery when wet, and I had to sit and slide myself over rain-slicked rocks to avoid an accident.

The family grew coffee, which required long hours of picking, sorting, and packing the beans into rough burlap bags. With no electricity and no machinery, all the chores had to be done by hand. The boys and I found a flat spot on the side of the mountain. We set up a large tray to spread the coffee beans. We spent hours pushing the beans back and forth to dry. Although I ached all over, my arm, shoulder, and leg muscles were beginning to ripple beneath my skin.

In addition to coffee, we raised red, black, and garbanzo beans, yams, maize, and other vegetables. We mostly ate dried corn, fried plantains, and boiled yucca, augmenting our diet with snakes, iguanas, and small animals. We roasted birds and guinea hens over an open fire. Juan, Ernesto, and I climbed trees for bananas, coconuts, and mangoes. I could smell a ripe banana a mile away.

Work ended when the sun went down. After dinner, by the light of the family's three candles, I tried to teach. The content of the two textbooks the soldiers gave us related to current issues facing Cuba. These books were very different from the ones I used to learn to read.

I tried teaching José and Maria some letters, but it was tough going. José saw little use for reading and usually pushed me aside. Maria followed his lead. But once a month or so I got her to sit and work with me.

Most of the time, my teaching was frustrating. I didn't know how to teach, so I did the best I could. I held up the letters of the alphabet over and over until the boys knew them by sight. I had to further drill them on a couple of letters such as *W* and *H*.

The times when the children sounded out a word were satisfying—even fun. But it wasn't enough to make me happy or to keep me from being homesick.

For after I blew out the candles, after the weary red sparks died on the wick, after the inky night swallowed the last curl of smoke, I was still a thirteen-year-old boy, alone. High in the mountains and very alone.

CHAPTER 5

Once a month, the authorities allowed us to go into the small village of *Turquino del Mar* to meet with the other literacy teachers in the area. Because of the danger due to rebel activity in the Sierra Maestra, José and Maria accompanied me into town. Besides, they needed to get their beans to market.

On those days Gilbert, Tato, Luis, Antonio, and I would sit on the bare ground watching the lines of mules, their backs burdened with bags of beans, snort and kick the dust. We entertained each other with tales of our mountain adventures. Gilbert and I discovered that we lived on opposite sides of the mountains, and we promised to send smoke signals to each other so we'd feel less lonely.

Several girls in the village tried their best to get our attention. They called us "The Havana Boys." Since we came from a city, they thought we were very glamorous. Some of them dashed back and forth behind the trees, shyly enticing us with their girlish laughs. Other girls flirted more unabashedly with us.

We had been told that the girls were hoping we'd fall for them and get them pregnant. Then we'd have to marry them and take them back to Havana with us. Once in a while Gilbert talked to a couple of the girls, but the rest of us wanted nothing to do with them. We had enough trouble as it was.

Living the same lifestyle as my "students," I wore next to nothing. Only when I wanted to shield my skin from the sun did I get fully dressed. Dirt gathered under my nails and calluses grew rough and thick on my hands and feet. My hair lay in oily tangles around my head.

I acquired a host of survival skills—hunting, cooking, farming. I even learned a new way to fish, flushing out trout with the strategic placement of rocks and then stabbing them with V-shaped prongs attached to a long stick. I couldn't wait to show Abuelo my newfound skill.

I still missed my friends, their laughter and pranks, and I thought about my family every day. I missed my long talks with Abuelo and my short talks with my father. I even missed helping my mother with chores.

Since not knowing when—or if—I would ever return home made me feel afraid and uncertain, I tried not to think about it. Instead, I found comfort in hearing Juan and Ernesto sing their ABCs and spell out words such as DOG and HELLO. At these times, José would cast me a glance of resentment tinged with pride.

Every couple of months, families from the area came to see Maria during an all-day spiritual event, the likes of which I had never seen. The day before the ceremony the family would busy themselves gathering food and making other preparations to welcome their guests.

José would erect an altar for Chango, the god of fire. He'd place upon it large black dolls along with bananas, mangoes, pineapples, and various herbs and potions to be used in healing. The dolls were strange, primitive things that served as vehicles for human hair, fingernails, and scraps of people's clothing. Some contained bits of colored glass, ceramics, or stones. People used the dolls to cast spells on enemies by puncturing them with pins and nails. They gave me the heebie-jeebies.

We would gather chickens and either a goat or pig whose throat would be slit in sacrifice. José would draw a long, sharp blade across its neck, slicing through skin and tendons. Maria would gather the animal's blood into a rough, wooden bowl and sprinkle it over the crowd in a blessing.

Maria always wore a long, white dress for the ceremonies. She layered strings of shells and beads around her neck and wrists to enhance her image as someone with special powers.

Maria would sit in front of the altar and enter a trance, her eyelids flickering and her thick throat emitting incomprehensible singsong sounds as competing spirits entered her body. There would always be a period of time—ten to fifteen minutes—when she struggled, dismissing the spirits she did not want to possess her.

Eventually, she would welcome the familiar spirit of a man into her body. At that point, her voice would sink to a lower register and her facial expressions would change so much that practically no vestiges of Maria remained—for all intents and purposes she had become another person. People would sit in a circle and ask Maria questions regarding their personal lives, and she would recommend spells and potions to cure their ills.

Once the advice was dispensed, she would stand like a man, spitting alcohol at people and smoking a fat cigar. Sometimes she'd crack a raw egg on her chest—I wasn't sure why—while attendees danced to the rhythmic beat of large, conical drums. A bonfire kicked sparks high into the air and served as a backdrop to the frenzy.

Meanwhile, men would saunter about opening and closing their shirts in front of people. Tobacco smoke wafted from their chests in great gray puffs that dissipated like fog into the cool night air. The smoke was used to heal people, but I was never sure where it came from. It was magic to me.

By dawn, everyone would be spent from drinking and dancing. Maria would collapse well before the ceremonies ended, exhausted from her encounters with the spirits.

Once Gilbert came to the event with his peasant family, and we watched the proceedings in wonder. The words *vodou* and *brujería* were bandied about. Neither of us knew what to make of the ceremony.

The next morning Maria would act as if nothing unusual had happened. Sometimes I wondered who the real Maria was.

•   •   •

One rainy day I was packing coffee beans and thinking about putting grass under my bed for the camels of the Three Kings to eat on the eve of the Feast of the Epiphany.

I was so immersed in reverie I failed to notice a soldier who had come up behind me. When he tapped me on the shoulder, I jumped, startled. I had no idea what he wanted. The soldier canted his head, indicating that I was to go with him.

"Your work here is done, Frankie," he said.

"What?" I asked, trying to take in what he was saying.

"The Literacy Campaign is over. Fidel says it was a huge success."

"So I can go home?" The news was almost disorienting.

"Yes. Get your things together. The train to Havana leaves tomorrow."

I was so happy I began jumping around and clapping my hands. I gathered my things together and bid the boys farewell, knowing I would soon be in the arms of my family. The boys seemed startled by the news. I sensed they would miss me, and I knew I would miss them.

We managed awkward smiles, and Ernesto wrapped his arm around my waist for a minute before bending over the dirt and spelling out the word GOODBYE with a stick.

Maria stopped cooking and hugged me farewell—we were almost family by now. There was something universal about maternal love. She had become a surrogate mother to me, and I had become her surrogate son.

I looked about for José, but he was nowhere to be found. I figured he was out hunting birds, something he did at that time of day. It would have been nice to see him one more time. It was a strange and bittersweet goodbye.

I laced my shoes and marched for a day to the historic town of Bayamo. As I walked through the narrow, cobblestoned streets of the "Birthplace of the Cuban Nation," I remembered my grandfather telling me about this place. It was where the Cuban national anthem was written. I was glad Abuelo had taught me this, and I was proud of myself for remembering.

From there I joined hundreds of boys to board the train to Havana. I had been away from home for nearly ten months. As the train panted for breath along the tracks, I thought about how much my brother Raúl must have grown. He was no longer a baby. I was eager to see my parents and to hold my brother in my arms. I was looking forward to seeing Miriam and recounting my adventures. But most of all, I couldn't wait to tell Abuelo that I'd been to Bayamo.

When I got home, there was a huge celebration in Revolution Square in Havana for all the *alfabetizadores*. Hundreds of people gathered to eat, drink, and wave gigantic pencils in the air. Music played over loudspeakers and people sang and danced in the street. *Fidelistas* made speeches about how important literacy was to the future of the country. I stood next to Gilbert, thinking about my stay in the mountains.

"Are you feeling proud of yourself?" asked Gilbert.

"A little," I said, shrugging. "But I never managed to teach the mother and father to read and write."

"But you taught the boys—Ernesto and Juan."

"Sort of."

"Well, that's something."

"I suppose."

"What about you? Are you feeling proud?"

Gilbert shrugged, ignoring my question.

"Have you heard about the *Bahía de Cochinos*?" he asked.

I modulated my voice to match Gilbert's. "No," I said. "What's that?" I was envisioning a bay of dead floating pigs.

"It happened while we were gone. The Americans tried to do Fidel in—but they failed."

"The *Americans* failed? Are you sure?"

"Yeah, it happened in April. It was a big deal. The Americans called it a fiasco, and Fidel ran around telling everybody how he'd beaten the Yanks."

"That's hard to believe!"

"Ask your grandfather. He'll tell you about it."

I jumped down from the seawall and put my arm around Gilbert's shoulder. "Let's get a Coke," I said. We walked through the park with the sound of bongos and maracas in the background. A cha-cha was being played and a couple was dancing under a banana tree.

"So what does it mean?"

"Fidel's now stronger than ever," said Gilbert.

"It's weird. Abuelo says he puts his pistol on the lectern before every speech just to show people who's boss."

Gilbert shook his head. "They say Fidel and his brothers were the biggest bullies at their school. The headmaster even tried to throw Fidel out."

"Abuelo said he actually did. Fidel's father was happy his son wasn't going to school anymore so he could stay home and work."

"That's messed up."

"Fidel threatened to burn down his parents' house so he could get back into school."

I laughed. "Sounds crazy."

We stopped at the refreshment stand and paid for a couple of bottles of soda. There was no Coke in sight.

"Where's the Coke?" I asked.

"Fidel closed down the Coca-Cola factory," said Gilbert.

Gilbert plucked off the ruffled metal cap with his teeth and then grabbed my bottle to do the same.

A group of young women marched by, carrying placards with a picture of Fidel brandishing his gun.

"I think Fidel's in love with that rifle of his," I said.

Gilbert shrugged. "Maybe he's looking at girls through his telescopic lens."

I laughed. "That's something you'd do, Gilbert."

The music died down and a voice again rang out over the crowd. A man sporting a 26 of July Movement armband was singing the praises of the nearly two hundred and seventy thousand people who had formed the literacy brigade. He said forty-two "Martyrs of the Revolution" had died in the campaign. I nodded slightly, understanding how that could happen.

We fell silent for a moment, remembering.

"It *was* an experience," said Gilbert, shaking his head.

I turned the toe of my shoe into the ground. "I really missed Abuelo," I confessed. "And my mother and father." I upended the soda bottle and took a long drink. The soda tasted funny, flat, not like Coke at all. I wanted the buzz, the fizz. For a moment I missed tracing the white Coca-Cola letters with my fingertip on the green soda bottles. "I never thought I'd miss my family that much, but I did." I gazed at the ground. Nothing seemed the same any more. Not even myself. I looked Gilbert in the eyes and said, "I even missed you."

Gilbert stood up, stretched, and started walking away. "Yeah, I know," he mumbled. "Let's go home."

I stood up thinking about how different I was now. Fending for myself in the mountains had made me stronger in so many ways. I had learned a lot of things. But I had the nagging fear that I had not learned enough.

Then a thought struck me: When I left for the mountains, I was a thirteen-year-old boy; now I was a man. A young man, but still a man.

CHAPTER 6

The very next morning two soldiers arrived at my house. After the celebration last night, I couldn't imagine what they wanted. My father led them to the living room sofa and extended his hand for them to be seated.

One of the soldiers opened a leather satchel containing official-looking papers. My name appeared on several pages. He spread the materials on the table, cleared his throat, and looked at my father.

"Our records indicate that your son conducted himself well in the literacy program. The government would like to honor him by sending him as a *becado,* a student scholar, to one of the government-run scholarship schools."

My parents and I looked at each other in astonishment. Cuba's scholarship schools had a reputation for providing an excellent education. But they were expensive—well beyond the means of my parents.

As if reading our thoughts, the soldier said, "This is a special honor, a gift from the government to recognize a select group of citizens who provided literacy services to the poor. Frank will be able to attend this school—all expenses paid."

Suddenly my skin felt warm, the way it did when something bad was about to happen. I was trying to figure out how I felt about this. I was looking forward to spending some time with my family and friends. The thought of having anything to do with the government left me cold.

The soldier turned toward me and asked, "Any questions, Frankie?"

"Where is this school?"

"In east Havana—Tarara—not far from here."

I knew the exact location of the school. The buildings and grounds were beautiful, but I couldn't imagine myself there. I wouldn't know anyone, and I wanted to be with my friends.

"When would I start?"

"Tomorrow. Fidel doesn't want to waste any time."

"But I just got home." I felt like someone had sucked the oxygen from my lungs. I looked to my parents for some kind of direction and support. I was hoping they would back me.

A moment of silence elapsed. My mother glanced at me before she stepped forward and said, "The government took my boy from us for almost a year. We had no idea where he was or what had happened to him. We didn't know whether he was dead or alive. Now you want to take him from us again? It's not fair—to him or to us. He needs to stay here."

The soldier looked at Mima with disdain. When he spoke, his voice was deep, resonant, and brusque. "With all due respect, señora, your son is no longer a boy. He's a young man, and his government is offering him a chance of a lifetime. I strongly suggest he take advantage of it."

My mother's face flushed. She was taken aback by the soldier's sharp rebuke. Still she pressed on. "But he will be away from home again."

"Señora, señora, the education Frank will receive will more than make up for his absence from home. Surely you understand that."

My mother bristled and crossed her arms in defiance. "If he attends this school of yours, how often can he come home?"

"Once a month. And, of course, on holidays."

The other soldier—the silent one—gathered up the papers. He turned and spoke to my father. "We are offering your son an opportunity to receive the finest education Cuba has to offer," he said. "Frank will learn things in this school that the public school does not

have the resources to teach. It would be a great disservice to him—
and to Cuba—for him not to go."

My mother turned to me, confused. She was as undecided as I
about what to do. "Frankie, what do you think?" Her voice was softer,
more resigned.

I didn't want to go. On the other hand, I thought about what
Abuelo had told me about the importance of learning. He had always
taught me to study hard and had stressed the value of education.

I was afraid that by not going to this school I would disappoint
him—and I didn't want to let Abuelo down. I needed more time to
think. But I had to make a decision *now*. I looked at the men standing
before me, men who seemed to have my best interests at heart. I took
a deep breath and reluctantly said, "Okay, I'll go."

To my surprise, life at the school in Tarara was like living at a resort.
It was totally fenced and an armed guard stood at the gate, providing
little chance for escape or interaction with the outside world. We
checked with the guard when we went home and when we returned.
We made our beds every morning, shined our shoes, and kept our
quarters spotless. But other than that, the school offered me everything
I could possibly want.

I was housed in a former mansion surrounded by towering royal
palms. Our rooms were more luxurious than anything I had ever seen.
I bunked with only one other boy, a boy I really liked. The food was
great and we had time to swim at the beach. We even had our own
baseball field and basketball court. In many ways it was a young man's
dream.

Our educational program was rigorous. The first hour of the day
was devoted to political science. Señor Gonzales taught us about the
benefits our government had bestowed on our people. We learned that
health care and literacy had improved, that the peasants were better
off, and that more doctors were graduating from Cuban universities.

We were lectured on the rampant corruption that fueled capitalist societies. We were told that the Cuban government promoted love and brotherhood. We learned that Fidel was a friend of the people, of the peasants, of the working class.

Sometimes we listened to Fidel's radio broadcasts, events that lasted four or five hours. His speeches seemed like gobbledygook to me, wild meanderings braided with production statistics, condemnation of the "lumpen"—whoever they were—and crazed calls to action against the "American imperialists."

We were supposed to pay close attention to these speeches, but many of the students had trouble staying awake. Señor Gonzales rapped his ruler on the desk of any boy who started nodding off, and those who actually snored were severely reprimanded for "counter-revolutionary" leanings. But on more than one occasion even Señor Gonzales had to stifle a yawn.

Much time was devoted to the corruption and abuses under the Batista regime: how the former president had cozied up to the United Fruit Company; how the American gangsters had drained millions of dollars from the Cuban economy; and how the American-controlled Havana Mob had used Cuba as a base for drug trafficking and money laundering. We learned that the United States had sucked hundreds of millions of dollars from the Cuban economy and had plundered the wealth and resources of Latin America.

When we were not discussing the writings of Vladimir Lenin and Friedrich Engels, we were absorbing the teachings of José Martí and Karl Marx. José Martí was the only Spanish hero Abuelo had taught me about whom Señor Gonzales mentioned. I thought the government was using the writings of this great poet to serve their own needs. There was no mention of Jesus, the Virgin Mary, or the saints.

Our other classes consisted of history, geography, science, and math, but always presented through the lens of the Party. I listened carefully, attentively. I attended all the classes, read the books, and studied the texts. But instead of becoming more convinced of the merits of these ideas, I was becoming anxious, rebellious, and angry.

When I returned home every month, I saw things more clearly, like you do when you meet people you haven't seen for a while. You notice that their hair is grayer, their waistlines thicker, their wrinkles deeper.

Conditions were not as rosy under this regime as the teachers at Tarara were telling us. Since Fidel had passed the Agrarian Reform Law in 1959, the government had seized all the farms, land, businesses, and companies owned by middle- and upper-class Cubans—millions upon millions of dollars in private property.

Political issues between the Cuban and American governments were making things worse. Fidel had defied the Eisenhower administration by nationalizing all kinds of businesses and industries, both foreign and national: department stores, distilleries, breweries, construction companies, paint manufacturers, and bottling companies.

They shut down flour mills, rice mills, even sugar mills. The list was endless. One weekend when I was home, I stopped to talk to a black boy who shined shoes on the corner of a well-traveled street in Guanabacoa.

Alcadio was polite, somber, and earnest. He was shy and pretty much kept to himself. None of us knew his last name, so we referred to him as Alcadio Negrito.

He would bring a small chair from home along with an old wooden stool and set up his "shoeshine shop" not far from his house. He owned two brushes that he cleaned carefully after each use. He had several tins of black, brown, and cordovan polish, and a couple of rags that he folded neatly beside his stool.

Alcadio was meticulous about his work and politely shined the shoes of anyone willing to pay five pesos. Alcadio's father had died in a fishing accident shortly after he was born, and his mother struggled to support a family of five. Alcadio was very proud that the proceeds of his business helped to put food on the table.

One afternoon when business was slow, I sat on the sidewalk to shoot the breeze with him. We started to play gin rummy while he waited for customers. I had a pack of candy cigarettes in my pocket and I offered him one. I had just sucked the cigarette to a point when a policeman approached, looking somber and stern.

"What's going on here?" His tone of voice was so sharp it could have sliced potatoes.

Alcadio and I scrambled to our feet, afraid that the policeman thought we were smoking real cigarettes.

I removed the candy cigarette from my mouth and extended my hand to show it to the officer. "It's just candy."

The man glanced at the cigarette and then knocked it from my hand. It landed on my trousers, sticking briefly to the cotton material before breaking on the sidewalk. I looked down, chagrined to have lost my sweet.

"I can see that," said the officer. "I don't give a damn about your cigarettes."

Alcadio and I looked at each other, dumbfounded.

"Did we do something wrong?" I asked.

"Whose operation is this?" demanded the officer, pointing to the shoeshine stool.

Alcadio looked alarmed. It took him a moment to gather his wits before he could answer.

"I'm the one who shines people's shoes."

The man looked at Alcadio and made an ugly hissing sound under his breath.

He pointed to me. "And him?"

"He's just a friend," said Alcadio, waving his hand dismissively. "He doesn't work with me."

The officer returned his gaze to Alcadio. "How long have you been doing this?"

Alcadio looked confused. "About three years. I give the money to my mother for food."

"Well, this little game is over." The officer dropped to his haunches and grabbed Alcadio's work items, tucking them snugly under his arm.

Alcadio looked panic-stricken. "What are you doing?" he said. Tears welled in his eyes. I was afraid he was going to start to cry in front of the officer.

"Private enterprise is no longer allowed. This business is closed. If anybody asks, tell them that your business belongs to the People."

"I don't understand," said Alcadio.

"There's nothing to understand. It is what it is. And if you give me any guff, I'll report you and your family to the authorities."

Alcadio looked down at his feet. "I'm sorry, I didn't know," he said. I watched the scene with a sense of horror, knowing how much his mother relied on his meager income.

The man shook his head and stared at Alcadio. "Where do you live?" he asked. His voice had a coarse edge to it, like he was talking to a delinquent in need of reprimanding.

Alcadio pointed in the direction of his house. The officer followed his finger with his eyes.

"Then run along. And I don't want to ever see you doing this again. Do you hear? Your shoeshining days are over."

"But—"

"No buts about it," said the officer, and he walked away carrying the tools of Alcadio's trade.

Stunned, Alcadio walked back to his house empty-handed. On the way he started to sob.

I put my arm around his shoulders. "It'll be okay," I said.

Alcadio didn't respond. He wiped the tears away with the back of his hand. We walked half a block before he spoke.

"I can't face her," he said.

"Her?"

"My mother. What's she going to do?"

"It wasn't your fault."

"But what if she doesn't believe me?"

"I'll go in with you to tell her."

"Would you?"

I shrugged my shoulders. "Sure."

When we got to Alcadio's house, his mother was washing laundry in the sink. She was a big woman with large upper arms that waved like flags when she wrung out the clothes. She looked up, surprised. Her expression darkened when she saw her son's face. She knew immediately something was wrong.

The woman looked back and forth, scrutinizing the two of us. I didn't know her last name so I didn't know what to call her.

"What's the matter?" she asked. Her eyes were bloodshot and her voice was weary. "Why are you home so early?"

Alcadio emptied his pockets and dropped a few coins on the table. Then he began to sob again, garbling his words so they were incomprehensible. His mother turned and looked at me for an explanation.

"What happened?"

"A policeman came by and took Alcadio's stuff."

"His shoe polish? His stool?"

"Yes."

She looked perplexed. "But why?"

"He said that all businesses now belong to the State."

Alcadio's mother turned back to her son and held him by the shoulders. "Is this true?"

He nodded and took a deep breath. "I didn't do anything wrong. I was just waiting for customers like I always do. I didn't mean to get into trouble. You've got to believe me."

Alcadio's mother thumped down on a chair and held her thumb and forefinger to the corner of her eyes as if she were fighting a headache. She gulped a breath of air and a tear trickled unchecked down her cheek. She sat in silence for a moment and then heaved a heavy sigh. Her arms fell to her lap in a gesture of resignation.

Alcadio's siblings ran into the room, noisy, curious. I looked at Alcadio and then back at his mother before she nodded for me to leave.

The sky was turning purple as I walked home, heart heavy, head down. The world seemed suddenly dark and foreboding, a place where anything could happen at any time. A feeling of dread spilled into my stomach. I tried not to think about it. I didn't tell my parents about the incident. I'm not sure why.

I never saw Alcadio shine another pair of shoes.

CHAPTER 7

It was obvious that things were not as they had been in Havana. Due to the American embargo on almost all commodities sent to Cuba, the market, once piled high with fresh flowers, fish, and tropical fruits, was now choked with irritable shoppers queued up just to buy a loaf of bread. Unemployment was high, morale was low, and people were struggling to make ends meet.

The local grocery store had been seized, and my mother had to shop at one of two thousand government-run people's stores, with their sparsely stocked shelves. The women in town complained bitterly about this, but only to people they could trust.

But our family heard all about it. "There's no soap, no toothpaste, no toilet paper," my mother groused. "I can't get chocolate to make dessert. Even sugar is in short supply. Who'd ever think you'd have problems getting sugar in Cuba? If this is what Fidel has to offer, God help us."

My mother wasn't the only one chaffing under the policies of the new regime. All of Havana looked older, wearier, shabbier. Well-tended parks were now strewn with litter and gardens once bright with flowers now bloomed with weeds. Many storefronts were closed, and peeling paint and crumbling buildings pointed to layers of malaise and decay. Lacking the incentive that came with owning their own property, people let things fall into disrepair.

Meanwhile, the government had seized many Havana hotels. The blue neon sign on the Riviera no longer defeated the darkness, and the name of the Hilton had been changed to *Hotel Habana Libre* since

Fidel had proclaimed it belonged to the workers. Glittering casinos still attracted the rich and famous, but their patrons now seemed too gay, their laughter too loud, their stylish clothes out of step with the mood of the city.

The faces of waitresses, taxi drivers, and street vendors told the real story. They were marred by a sullen defiance, like a heavy downpour on an old tin roof. They were the first to feel the life force being sucked from this habitually exuberant city. They knew something vital was missing—like poker minus the betting, showgirls minus the feathers, Coke minus the rum.

When I told Gilbert about my life at school—the chocolate desserts, the days playing volleyball on the beach—he accused me of having lost touch with reality.

"Things are bad in the neighborhood," he said. "Very bad. You're living like a king because they're grooming you to become one of them, while we're surviving on scraps and crumbs. You'd better wake up. There's something very wrong with that school. You're living in a dream world, Frankie."

I could hardly argue with that.

My grandfather's situation lent credence to Gilbert's contention. During the course of his lifetime, he had worked to acquire three rental properties that he believed would provide him with retirement income. He kept his houses meticulous, scraping and painting the interiors on a regular basis, pruning the bushes, and sweeping the sidewalks daily.

One afternoon while we were playing checkers, a police officer arrived and served my grandfather with notice that his properties belonged to the State. Abuelo's face went ashen.

"But I have the deeds. My properties are paid in full. They belong to me."

"Show me the deeds," said the policeman.

Abuelo shuffled to the bedroom to open the metal box where he kept his important effects. He retrieved the papers in question and gave them to the officer. His hands trembled slightly as he turned over the documents.

The officer wrinkled his nose, took the papers, and glanced at them briefly. I held my breath. Tension filled the air like a morning mist.

"These papers are worthless." The officer tossed the papers on the green chair next to the sofa.

Abuelo's eyes followed the papers and his back stiffened. He picked up the papers and smoothed them out. Pointing to the bottom of the documents, he said, "They are legal—signed and notarized."

The policeman shrugged. "It means nothing under the new law. Private property is now illegal. You should know that by now."

I figured Abuelo did know it, but he was not going down without a fight. Angry and red-faced, Abuelo waved his hand in a circle. "And what about this house—my own home? The one I built with my own two hands? Does it belong to the State too?"

"All property belongs to the State," returned the officer. "This place is no longer yours. If you want to continue to live here, you must buy the property back from the State, the legal owner. If you would like, we can discuss this matter at a later date."

My grandfather nodded, too angry and frustrated to speak. I had never seen him so agitated. He turned his back on the officer, not even opening the door for him to leave. When the man closed the door behind him, Abuelo sank into his chair and shook his head. Then, to my surprise, he leaned back and fell asleep. I watched him until he began to snore. I left the house quietly, not wanting to wake him.

That night Abuelo and I went fishing together. He was still in a foul mood, morose and distracted. Even I, his favorite grandchild, couldn't cheer him up.

As we approached the water, we were descended upon by a group of forty or fifty soldiers. A lieutenant approached us and demanded to know what Abuelo was doing with his torch. My grandfather was not amused.

"What do you think I'm doing? I'm using the torch to help me fish."

The soldiers huddled together and talked; the discussion was very animated.

Then the lieutenant turned to Abuelo and asked, "Are you sure you aren't signaling the Americans?"

"Signaling the Americans?" said Abuelo. "What are you talking about? Why would I do such a thing?"

"The Americans are sitting in boats offshore waiting to attack Cuba," one soldier pronounced.

My grandfather scratched his head. He pointed to the water and said, "Look out there, do you see any ships?"

The officer squinted at the horizon. "No, but that doesn't mean they aren't there."

"Well, if they were there, do you think they'd need to see my torch to attack? Use your head. The whole harbor is lit up like a Christmas tree. If the Americans want to attack Havana, they don't need my little torch to see where it is."

The soldiers huddled for discussion. One man agreed that other people in the area used torches to fish—and had done so for years. My grandfather looked at them as if they had lost their minds. They detained us for an hour or so, arguing back and forth, their voices rising like hot air balloons. Just before Abuelo reached his boiling point, they let us go.

The following week the road from Guanabacoa to Cojimar was blocked. When Abuelo tried to get through, the soldiers told him that everyone had to obtain a permit to fish. Our incident had prompted a host of new regulations.

You now had to register with the authorities to fish. You had to fish with a group and supply the authorities with their names and addresses. You had to state what kind of fish you were after and the type of bait you were using. And you had to tell the authorities the kind and number of fish you had caught.

That night my grandfather paced the floor of his house, railing against the government so loudly you could hear him down the street. My parents were afraid he would be arrested.

"Damn *Fidelistas* are ruining it for everybody. What good is fishing if you have to go through all that rigmarole? They've taken all the fun out of it. You can't even take your grandson out to fish without government intervention."

As the dichotomy between what I saw at home and what I learned at school became more pronounced, I knew I must decide what to do.

CHAPTER 8

Increasingly confused, I began to challenge the teachers at school, especially Señor Gonzales. The more he insisted on the benefits of the government's policies, the more I argued with him. I told him that people were suffering under Fidel, and he told me I didn't know what I was talking about, that things had been much worse under Batista. Batista had murdered and tortured people. He had siphoned off millions from the Razzle Dazzle, a high roller's casino scam, and he'd made millions more from kickbacks from the construction of luxury hotels.

Batista had supported the Mob in the heroin and cocaine trade and was involved in gambling, racketeering, sex shows, and prostitution. I was too young to speak with any degree of authority on these matters. But I did know things were bad at home.

One day Gilbert and Luis told me that communist governments forbade the worship of God. I went home and told my grandfather we had to talk.

"Okay, then. Get me my cane and we'll go for a walk." Strolling down Máximo Gómez Street, he asked me what was on my mind.

"I don't know what to think. Señor Gonzales says Fidel is a hero, a great thinker, a great leader. But Gilbert and Luis say he's an atheist—that he doesn't believe in God. Is that true?"

"The boys are right," said Abuelo. "He doesn't believe in God, and he doesn't believe in family."

"What do you mean?"

"Well, he can't believe in family or he wouldn't be taking young boys like yourself off to God knows where to teach people to read. He wants to separate children from their families so he can drum his beliefs into their heads without interference from their parents. Next thing you know, he'll forbid boys to visit their grandfathers!"

I grew quiet while I considered this for a moment. "Are the Communists evil?"

"Well, they want to destroy the Church and keep people from praying. They've seized everyone's property and they want to control how we think. You can't even see a good movie anymore. That one they're showing now—*Battleship Potemkin*. Old as the hills."

"Why would they want to control the movies?"

"They don't want us to see American films, Frankie. They don't want us to know how other people live—it may make people dissatisfied with their plight. The only movies in the theaters right now are from the Soviet Union and Eastern Europe. And the Russians haven't the foggiest idea how to make films that won't put people to sleep."

We continued walking. Abuelo was on a roll. When he got like this, he needed no encouragement to keep talking.

"That man's closed all the city newspapers—*The Havana Post, El Diario de la Marina, El Cristal*—all gone. The editor of *El Diario* asked the Cuban people to pray to *La Virgen de la Caridad del Cobre* to save us from the 'Red Antichrist.' That's what he called Fidel. So Fidel closed them down. There are only two newspapers left in Havana: *Revolución* and *El Mundo,* and both of them spout the Party line. Phat! Next they'll have us reading that Russian rag, *Pravda*. It's the same thing with the radio stations. All we have to listen to is *Radio Rebelde*— a big propaganda machine."

Abuelo took a deep breath as if he were calming his nerves, so I decided not to ask him any more questions. It sounded like he had been thinking about these issues for a while and was glad to be finally getting them off his chest. I picked at my nails and walked silently beside him. Then he started talking again, as if he were continuing a conversation he'd been carrying on in his head.

"And God help you if you thwart their plans—they'll throw you in jail at the drop of a hat. Without even a trial. Torture you. Shoot you in the back. Are they evil? You tell me, Frankie, whether they're evil or not."

I felt the hairs rise on the back of my neck. I didn't answer Abuelo.

On my way home I decided to take a stroll into the city. At this time of year Havana was always ablaze with Christmas lights that hung like vibrant gems from public buildings and plazas. Fidel had banned any depiction of Santa for reasons no one could fathom. But I was certain there would still be lights.

As I rounded the corner, I saw the public buildings shrouded in darkness as black as coal. No wreaths brightened the doors, no trees shimmered with lights, no crèches reminded worshipers of the birth of Christ.

In their place was a "Revolutionary Nativity," a scene painted on the marquee of CMQ-TV. The Three Kings—the ones whose feast was celebrated by the people of Cuba—were depicted as Fidel Castro, Ernesto Guevara, and Juan Almeida, all men with blood on their hands. The angel hovering above the crèche was the dead revolutionary hero, Camilo Cienfuegos.

I sat on a bench, trying to take it all in. I looked up at the stars and wondered whether God had taken offense at what was happening. I felt like someone had stolen my childhood, and I would never get it back. And that made me angry.

For reasons unknown to me, I started to cry. The tears trailed down my cheeks like silver tinsel off pine needles. I longed for the smell of Christmas trees, the sweetness of candy canes, and the sound of Christmas carols. I wanted to see the baby Jesus in the manger. I wanted the excitement and the joy of Christmas. And I wanted those lights, those gay, beautiful lights. It seemed very childish. But I wanted them anyway.

I went home to my room and lay on my back on my bed, my hands folded beneath my neck. Fine cracks in the plaster lead to a light fixture that hung from the ceiling. The opaque glass contained the bodies of insects, moths, and flies that had batted themselves against the hot white bulb, pitiful creatures that had been caught, struggled—and died. Their lifeless bodies looked thin and papery. They had morphed into nothing but bits of debris that would disintegrate into a fine brown powder when touched.

But I didn't want to consider that now. Right now I had some serious thinking to do. I needed to weigh all the things I'd been taught in the Tarara School against the things my grandfather had said. And I had to measure them both against the things I knew.

I thought about the great writings of Marx, Lenin, and Engels. I thought about the stern Señor Gonzales and the long-winded Fidel. I thought about the peasant family in the Sierra Maestra. I thought about the soldiers and the guns, so many guns.

I was trying to make sense of it all. Was Fidel a hero? A friend of the working class? If so, why were so many people out of work? Was he a brilliant lawyer, a great thinker, a renowned leader? Or was he the devil incarnate?

Should I stay at school and get a good education? Would that make me a better person? Was Fidel better because he was smart? Would staying at that school make me party to something evil? These were complicated questions. The ramifications were great. I needed to use my head.

I met my cousins at the corner of Maceo and Bertematti Streets to talk it over. It didn't take Gilbert long to get to the core of the matter.

"Are you a Communist, Frankie?"

"No."

"Do you believe in God?"

"Of course."

"Then, it's simple. If you're not a Communist, and you believe in God, then you shouldn't go to that school."

"But it's a good school," I countered, playing the devil's advocate. "I'm learning a lot."

"You're just learning to be a Communist, Frankie. That's what that school is all about. And if you stay there, you'll become a Communist, too. You'll begin to think like them, to act like them. Think about it."

I sighed deeply. "What would you do if you were me?" My stomach was roiling with anxiety.

"Escape!" said Jabao.

"Escape? I thought of that, but how?"

"We'll have to figure it out," said Gilbert thoughtfully. I could tell he was quite taken with the idea.

"I'll help you," said Luis. "You can't do it without help." Luis was not exactly the genius of the group, but I was glad for his support.

"I'll help, too," echoed Pipi. "I'll drive the getaway car."

"You've been watching too many old movies," I said. "Besides, you don't have a car, and you're too young to drive."

While I was inspired by their loyalty and audacity, I was also afraid. Very afraid. Who knew what could happen to them—and to me—if we got caught? My grandfather's words about being thrown in jail still rang in my ears.

I knew that people who opposed the Party had a way of disappearing, never to be heard from again. There was talk of torture. I didn't want to end up as one of Fidel's casualties. We'd have to make a plan—think it through.

"Seriously," said Gilbert, "we'll need a car."

"I guess," I said, wondering how that could possibly happen. None of us had access to a car or even had a sibling who did.

"We need someone who knows how to drive," offered Luis. "Someone older."

I nodded, starting to lose my nerve. "Maybe this is impossible. Maybe—maybe I should just stay at school and forget about the whole thing."

"No," insisted Jabao. "You've got to get out now. Otherwise, you'll become a Communist, and we won't be friends anymore."

"Okay," I said. "But I don't want to get killed trying. We really need a plan."

"Don't worry," said Gilbert. He patted me reassuringly on the back. "One way or another, we'll get you out."

A week later, while I was outside playing basketball at school, a small pebble dropped on the pavement in front of me. Then another one hit me on the back of my head. The wind was blowing, and I thought it might be a falling twig. I turned around to see Gilbert lying flat on his stomach on the other side of the six-foot fence. My stomach did a somersault.

I bounced the ball to a teammate and signaled that I was leaving the game. I walked to the fence, my heart skipping a beat.

"Hey, where are you going?" called a classmate, a short, smart-alecky kid who never failed to get on my nerves.

"Just *shut up* and leave me alone," I said. The boy shrugged and started to saunter away.

I got to the edge of the fence and peered through it. "What in God's name are you doing here?" I asked. Gilbert smiled at me mischievously.

"We're here to rescue you. Just like we promised. Hurry! I'll help you over the fence."

I looked around and leveraged my foot against the metal support. My classmate turned and yelled, "Hey, you'd better be careful. You know you're not allowed outta here."

I was scared enough without this kid mouthing off. "Will you be *quiet*," I said. My classmate smirked while Gilbert pulled me over the fence. I landed on the ground with a thud.

I looked around. "Where's the car?" I whispered.

"We didn't bring a car," said Gilbert, acting as if this were no big deal. My heart dropped like an anchor to the floor of the sea.

"No car? How will we escape?" My face froze in apprehension. This was feeling far too dangerous to me.

Gilbert nodded in the direction of the bushes, as if the answer lay therein. Suddenly Luis and Jabao popped up from behind the shrubbery, waving red baseball caps and pushing their own bikes—as well as Gilbert's—in our direction.

"What the—"

"Shush!" said Gilbert. "Quick, get on my handlebars."

"This isn't going to work," I said. "We can't escape this way. They're gonna catch us."

"Just *shut up* and get on," ordered Gilbert.

I hopped onto Gilbert's handlebars, and we started wobbling through the high grass. The ground beneath us was rutted, and it was difficult to stay upright. The tires on his bike were almost flat.

"What's the matter with you, Gilbert, couldn't you even put air in the tires?"

"Stop worrying about the tires, would ya? I got here, didn't I?"

"Yeah, but God knows if we'll ever get home."

"Oh, shut yourself up, Frankie. You have any better ideas?"

Luis and Jabao raced ahead of us, spewing a cloud of dust and pebbles into the air. The fender on Jabao's bike was so rusty it was about to fall off, and Luis's dirty shoelace was dangling dangerously close to the chain of his bike. I crossed my fingers that it wouldn't get caught. I could just picture them going head over heels into the dirt.

Meanwhile, I was hanging on for dear life as my cousin tried to steady his bike to keep it from keeling over. By now I was sure the guard at school had notified the authorities. They would be out looking for us, perhaps with dogs. I envisioned vicious canines chasing us and biting our legs.

Gilbert kept peddling, his face getting redder and redder as he huffed and puffed down the road. He kept mumbling things under his breath and wiping the sweat trickling down his forehead with the back of his hand. After we'd gone about a quarter of a mile, I began to laugh, a rip-roaring belly laugh.

"Don't get too happy up there," hollered Gilbert. "In a little while we're going to switch places, and you're going to have to peddle. Then we'll see how funny this is."

But I couldn't help it. The whole thing was classic Gilbert. We were miles from home, running from the authorities on a wing and a prayer. No adult knew where we were or what we were up to. And God knows what would happen to us if we ever got caught.

All I could think of was: This is it? My great escape? My stance against the Party? A bunch of crazy kids with worn-out sneakers and rusty bikes teetering down the road like crippled penguins on slippery ice?

It was too rich. Too reckless. Too much fun. *The Communists be damned!* I thought. I let out a whoop and a yell.

We peddled like wild men all the way home.

CHAPTER 9

I tossed and turned all night, trying to get some sleep. My sense of euphoria about having escaped the school was giving way to a feeling of dread about what would happen when the school officials came to get me—and I knew they would. Señor Gonzalez could not let my escape go unchallenged lest other boys in the school follow my lead and try to run away. I had no idea what my punishment would be, but I knew it would be stiff. I was going to have to face the music.

The next morning my mother prepared breakfast, and we talked about "my great escape." Mima laughed with me when I told her about riding on Gilbert's handlebars. Still, I could tell her nerves were on edge. A hint of fear colored my voice as I talked about my adventure. I was hoping she wasn't sensing my apprehension.

Since my experience with the literacy brigade, I no longer felt like I had control over my life. I had frequent nightmares about someone forcing me to do something I didn't want to do. I would awake in a cold sweat, and it would take me a couple of hours to get back to sleep.

On my last visit home I told my mother about my dreams, and she confessed that she'd been having nightmares, too. Not knowing where I was—or what had happened to me—when I was away in the Sierra Maestra had been very painful for her.

Before she cleared the table, she stood up, pulled me to her bosom, and kissed me on the forehead. She stroked my hair and held my head to her chest for a little while as my body began to relax. Her mouth quivered, and I knew she was happy to have me home.

My brother, Raúl, began to cry, and my mother went to tend to him. I turned and looked at my father, who was sipping his coffee and eyeing me curiously. He lifted his spoon and stirred his coffee to release sugar sitting at the bottom of his cup. He studied my face for a moment, knowing full well that something was weighing heavily on my mind.

A man of few words, my father cleared his throat and said, "Tell me what's bothering you, son."

I took a deep breath. I didn't want to burden my father with my fears, but I had to talk to someone. "What if they come to get me?"

"Who do you mean by *they*?"

"You know who I mean," I said, almost afraid to speak the words out loud. The expression on my father's face turned dark with a disturbing thought. He shook his head and pushed his chair away from the table with enough force to rattle the dishes. He stood abruptly, threw down his napkin, and said, "You're not going anywhere." His face wrinkled into an accordion of rage. He was in no mood for discussion.

Later that morning there was a loud knock on the door. My father opened it to find Señor Gonzales and two soldiers standing on the front steps.

I was in the kitchen helping my mother prepare lunch. An old checkered apron hung around her neck and was tied at the small of her back. We could overhear what was going on, but Mima held me back from entering the living room. I felt her warm arms encircle me and watched a red flush creep up her neck. I took a deep breath as a ribbon of fear danced up my spine.

"Can I help you?" I overheard my father say.

"We're here to take your son back to school," said Señor Gonzales. "He left without permission, which could be construed as counterrevolutionary activity—a very serious offense."

My siblings wandered into the living room looking wide-eyed and fearful, and a crowd of neighbors started to gather outside my house. In my neighborhood, like in many others in Cuba, whenever soldiers showed up on anyone's doorstep, it was cause for alarm. The front door remained open, leaving little to the imagination.

"There's nothing to be discussed," said my father. "Since he doesn't want to go to your school, I must ask that you leave my house. *Now*."

"That may be so," said Señor Gonzales, "but I still need to speak with Frankie."

The soldiers mumbled something to each other that I couldn't understand. I peered through the kitchen door to see my father's shoulders stiffen with determination. Knowing my future was at stake, I squirmed away from my mother's hold and marched into the room. Mima followed, alarmed.

My father glanced at me and said, "These men want to take you back to school, Frankie." His gaze held mine knowingly, and I got the impression that what he was saying was more for the benefit of the soldiers than for me.

"Do you want to go back?"

I glanced warily at the soldiers, then back at my father. I knew this was no time for hesitation or cowardice. I pursed my lips, shook my head and said, "No. I hate that school and I don't want to go back."

Señor Gonzales stepped forward, looking somber and all puffed up. He had a job to do and he was determined to do it.

"Frank, you are making a big mistake. You are a very talented young man. You were doing very well at school. There is a future for you in the Party if you return to school. But if you don't—" He shrugged. "Who knows?" I took this as a thinly veiled threat. I didn't like being threatened.

I mustered my courage and said, "I've been to your school. I gave it my best shot, and it's not for me. I'm staying here with my family."

Señor Gonzales looked appalled. If we were alone, he would've handled the situation more forcefully. But with my parents present, he took a more conciliatory approach.

"The teachers hold you in high regard, Frankie. You are doing well in sports—everybody likes you. Think about your future. You will regret it for the rest of your life if you don't go back to school."

I wrinkled my nose and shook my head, wondering whether I was old enough to have any rights. I sensed that something was going on that was more ominous, more threatening than just disobeying a teacher. But I couldn't define it.

Fear lifted the hairs on the back of my neck. I glanced at my mother and realized that some cultural factors were at play that might work in my favor. Mima looked at me and stepped forward, wiping her hands on her apron. Lips tightened and eyes blazing, she looked like a woman possessed.

Like many Cuban women, my mother was sweet and good natured, but when it came to her children, she was a force to be reckoned with. She had her own mind and she didn't shrink from telling anyone what was on it. I had a pretty good idea what she was going to say, but I had no idea how it would be received. Mima placed her hand on her hip and pointed a finger at the men. Beads of perspiration erupted on my forehead.

"Didn't you hear my son?" chided Mima as if she were scolding a group of small children. "He doesn't want to go back to your school. He wants to stay right here. And what's more, *I* want him to stay right here. Do you hear me?"

My father turned to the soldiers. He set his jaw the way he did when a discussion was over. I started to say something, but my father raised his hand—palm out—to stop me. I knew enough not to disregard his gesture.

I glanced at my mother and held my breath, awaiting the men's response. They looked at once angry and confused. It was clear they wanted me back, but it was also clear that tradition dictated that they respect the wishes of parents in their own home. Parental control of their children was well honored in Cuba, and although under Fidel the concept was quickly disappearing, it still had a firm hold.

The crowd outside began shouting and chanting, "Leave the boy alone. He doesn't want to go. Didn't you hear his mother? Why are you bothering him?"

The muscles bunched in the back of my neck. I held my breath, not knowing whether the support of my friends and neighbors would make things better or worse.

I looked out the front door and saw Jabao pointing at Luis and Gilbert who were hiding behind the bushes, afraid they'd be identified as the culprits who helped me escape. They repeatedly shouted, "Let him go," and then quickly ducked down so they couldn't be seen. I had to smile, despite myself.

Finally, one of the soldiers signaled to the other that it was time to leave. They turned and stomped out the door. I heaved a sigh of relief.

Señor Gonzales was the last one out. He left with this parting remark, "You are not living up to your duty, Frankie. Don't think you are getting away with this. We'll be back."

But I sensed that he was all bluster. My mother had prevailed in the discussion, and I figured I'd never see him again. At least that's what I hoped.

I talked to Abuelo the next day about whether what I had done was right. I wanted his approval and was afraid he might scold me for giving up the chance for such a good education.

"Did you do your best at that school?"

"I did more than my best."

"How so?"

"I didn't want to go to that school, but I went anyway. I completed all the homework. I studied and studied, but I never felt like they were telling me the truth." I hesitated a moment. "I didn't want to become a Communist, so I left."

"When did you come to that conclusion?"

"A while ago."

"But you stayed anyway?"

I sighed. "Yes. It took me a long time to sort it out. And I didn't want to let anyone down."

"Who were you afraid of letting down?"

"You, mostly."

"I see. Not yourself?"

"No."

"So you were doing more than your best for me?"

"Yes," I said. I got the feeling that there was something more to Abuelo's questions, but I wasn't sure what.

"Maybe you shouldn't have done more than your best," said my grandfather softly. I looked at him, startled and confused. I thought Abuelo always wanted me to do more than my best. I couldn't believe he was saying this.

"What do you mean?"

"Well, Frankie, there are three things you can do in life: less than your best, your best, or more than your best. Doing your best is usually the right thing to do. Doing less than your best is always wrong because you cheat yourself—and others—by failing to live up to your potential."

"I understand," I said. "But what about doing more than your best?"

"Ah, that's the tricky one, Frankie. Say you go fishing. You've caught six fish and you're very tired. You've met your goal for the day, but you press on to do more. Your wife is home waiting for your help with the baby. She's counting on you. When you get home she's angry. She doesn't even care that you caught more fish."

"So you're saying it's bad to do more than your best?"

"I'm saying that doing more than your best always comes with a price."

"And the price is sometimes too high?"

"Most of the time."

"Are there any times when it isn't?"

"Yes, but only under three circumstances: when it is a matter of life and death, when it is a matter of principle, and when it is a matter of love." Abuelo looked me straight in the eye. "Always do more than your best, Frankie, when it comes to matters of love."

That summer rumors circulated that Fidel was buying oil from the Kremlin, that he was on the side of the Soviets, that he had thrown hundreds of people in jail.

Some people believed these rumors while others did not. Many of the neighbors had been listening to Fidel's frequent radio broadcasts, and some were praising *El Comandante* as if he were a savior.

Antonio's brother had swallowed the bait. To the horror of his mother and father, he had left for the Sierra Maestra to join the Rebel Army. This didn't surprise me. Like many others, he had read—and believed—too many articles that appeared in *Granma*, the Communist national newspaper.

He worshiped Fidel as a brave strongman who was righting the practices of the corrupt Batista. He wore an armband of the 26 of July Movement to prove it. It gave me the creeps. But Antonio was still on our side, and my cousins and I openly discussed our hatred of Fidel with him.

At the same time, Fidel was working on ways to suppress any dissent and to limit Cubans' freedom of expression. The days of speaking our minds regarding the country's leader were quickly drawing to a close.

CHAPTER 10

Afraid that the people would rise up against him—or join the thousands of people who had already fled the country—Fidel instituted Committees for the Defense of the Revolution or CDRs. Their motto, "*En Cada Barrio, Revolución,* In Every Neighborhood, Revolution," struck fear in the hearts of Cubans.

These groups were responsible for reporting and squelching any suspicious or counterrevolutionary activity. CDR members reported people suspected of being CIA agents, homosexuals, and readers and writers of antirevolutionary materials.

Each block had a warden charged with keeping tabs on everyone in the neighborhood—their friends, their contact with foreigners, their work habits, their travels.

The CDRs were also authorized to find and detain anyone trying to flee the country illegally. Pictures of "fugitives from justice" were posted on telephone poles and in other prominent public places. All citizens had to report suspicious behavior to a member of the CDR. Fear of reprisal for not reporting such activity assured compliance.

Everyone had to show their ID card to the block warden to get permission to go from one town to another. Given Fidel's efforts to improve education, the whole thing seemed counterproductive to me. I wondered how people could learn if they were forbidden firsthand experience of the world.

The position of block warden rotated from week to week, and from house to house. Because we lived in such a closely knit community, the warden was always someone we knew. The warden for the week had to stay up all night to watch and report anyone who ventured from home.

When the task fell to my father, he passed the time smoking and shooting the breeze with a neighbor. He believed that the CDRs were violating a basic human right—privacy—and he had no interest in turning anyone over to the authorities. The CDRs were powerful snoops who made everyone edgy and wary.

Our sense of community was being systematically eroded. Fewer people were willing to share what was happening in their lives or to openly air their political views. People no longer sat on their stoops or gathered on the street corners to pass the time of day. Those who did dispersed quickly when approached.

Meanwhile, I was spending as much time as possible with my cousins and friends. With it getting so complicated to get around, we whiled away the hours talking about girls—who we thought they liked and how we could get their attention.

Gilbert had taken up weight lifting to build his muscles. By now he was the "leader of the pack," a good sportsman, and a self-proclaimed ladies' man. My cousins and I followed Gilbert's lead to work out. We measured our biceps weekly. Jabao and I tied for best biceps. Pipi came in second.

Jabao was girl shy, while Gilbert was always "in love" with this girl or that. He was forever trying to impress us with stories of how he had touched some girl's hand. Gilbert's ulterior motive was he liked to eat and drink. With a bunch of siblings at home, there was never enough food to satisfy his needs.

Hospitality dictated that a young man calling on a girl be served refreshments. So he would go to a girl's house, introduce himself to her parents, and gain permission to visit.

Gilbert was handsome and charming. All the girls liked him, as did their parents. But as soon as he had finished eating, he'd abruptly excuse himself to hang out with his buddies, leaving the girl and her parents befuddled. He broke many hearts with his boorish behavior.

My cousins, Antonio, and I would loiter outside the windows of the homes of these trusting, young girls, waving our arms in the air, jumping around and making a general nuisance of ourselves. As soon as Gilbert came out, we'd collapse in gales of laughter. But, much to our chagrin, Gilbert always insisted that he had managed to touch the girl's hand. Touching a girl's hand was something the rest of us could only dream about. We never knew whether he was telling the truth, but his stories were enticing, and we all wanted to believe him.

By the time I got back to my old school—the one I attended before I became a *becado*—I was the talk of the town. Many of my friends hadn't seen me for a very long time. They greeted me warmly and peppered me with questions. The girls wanted to know what it was like in the mountains, and the boys wanted to know if I had a girlfriend. I felt like I was finally home.

On the morning of my first day of class, I saw Miriam and Antonio standing on the school steps talking with the most beautiful girl I had ever seen. Miriam was now dating Antonio. My old friend softened Antonio's hard edges, and they seemed to be very fond of each other.

The two girls were engaged in an animated discussion. A surge of excitement coursed through me as I studied this girl. She had a regal carriage, a fall of lustrous black hair, large dark eyes, and a smile that could light up a city. Not wanting to appear too interested, I brushed my hair back from my forehead and casually approached.

Since our puppy love days, Miriam and I had nurtured a very close friendship. She was so excited to see me she squealed with delight and kissed me on the cheek. After inquiring about my parents, she introduced me to her girlfriend, Magda.

It didn't take a genius to know that Magda was special. Her refined mannerisms. Her full red lips. Her perfectly proportioned face. Her brilliant smile. I was transfixed. Magda was clearly a different breed from the rest of us. I could tell from the way she dressed—her fine leather shoes, her strand of cultured pearls, her silk scarf—that she enjoyed a very privileged life. I stepped forward, enchanted.

"I'm very glad to meet you, Magda," I said, extending my hand in greeting.

"Glad to meet you, too," said Magda. She spoke in a softly modulated voice that reminded me of lemon chiffon. Silly, but it did.

After we shook hands, I coughed, mustered my courage, and said, "Any friend of Miriam's is a friend of mine."

I immediately second-guessed my words. They sounded simple and hollow to my ears, and I hoped I wasn't being too forward. I wanted to appear nonchalant, although that's not how I felt. But Magda shot me a megawatt smile that sent a thrill down my spine. I had never felt that way around a girl before. I stared at her in relief and my whole body relaxed.

We smiled at each other and made small talk for a while. She told me she was new at school, and I promised to introduce her to my friends. Then I asked, "Do you have a boyfriend, Magda?" She laughed, displaying a mouthful of perfect, white teeth.

"No. Do you?" She giggled. "Do you have a girlfriend, I mean."

"No," I said. She nodded and smiled.

"Would you like to have a boyfriend?" I asked hopefully. I moved a little closer to her and smelled a light touch of Jean Naté.

She looked embarrassed and confused, and I was afraid I had spoken too soon. I didn't want to scare her away. A crimson rush crept up her neck. She didn't answer my question.

When the bell rang, Magda and I walked down the path to our class together. I felt happier than I had felt for a very long time. I had great hopes that something would come of this meeting. I looked up at the sun filtering through the trees and imagined what it would be like to hold this sweet girl's hand.

CHAPTER 11

Magda's parents *were* well off. She had attended Lancha, a private school owned and run by her Aunt Sophia. A brilliant woman with a doctorate in education, Sophia was horrified when Fidel closed all private and parochial schools in Cuba, forcing Magda's parents to send their daughter to the public school.

I was now entering the second half of eighth grade, and I felt like I'd been away from my friends for a very long time. I was trying to figure out the lay of the land socially, while attempting to ingratiate myself with Magda.

I soon realized that the government-run school had been far superior academically to my old public school. I was almost a year ahead in my class work. Although I did not excel in English, I was at the top of my class in all other subjects. I was especially good at math, and my classmates were amazed at how quickly I could solve difficult problems.

Three weeks after I got to school, I was nominated for a seat on Student Council. I was elated, mostly because I thought it would impress Magda. Shortly thereafter, I was elected council president. Gilbert, Jabao, and I went out after school to celebrate. We walked around the park, eating tamales from one of the street vendors, and talking about the upcoming year.

The next day I met with the council to come up with plans for the students—dances, sporting events, and outings of various kinds. We drafted a school calendar, making sure nothing conflicted with fiestas and holidays.

The school had limited space for sporting events and social gatherings, and things had to be carefully orchestrated to meet conflicting demands. I worked very hard on the schedule and was pleased with the work of the council.

But Fidel had his own plans for the school. Shortly after my election, he announced the establishment of a Communist Youth Council to oversee what was called "government-related student business." The Student Council would oversee student activities, and the Youth Council would oversee the promotion of communism. There would be two separate student governing bodies—with two different agendas and two different leaders.

Our experiences with the CDRs had taught us that whoever occupied this position would wield much power, and there was great speculation as to whom it would be. Student support for Fidel was split pretty much down the middle.

I was very sure where I stood. My stay in the mountains, my stint at Tarara, and my talks with Abuelo had dispelled my former confusion. These experiences had sharpened my views regarding the Party into stark-white clarity: as bad and corrupt as Batista had been for Cuba, Fidel was worse. Under Fidel, freedom was quickly becoming a casualty and, despite his claims to the contrary, he was well on his way to usurping all our liberties. The writing was on the wall for anyone who chose to read it.

Magda and Miriam shared my views. So did my cousins.

It was a bright, sunny Tuesday when a general assembly was called into session at the school. There was more than the usual commotion with students conferring and whispering about whom they thought would be president of the Communist Youth Council.

The principal stood in front of the auditorium looking very serious. He was a short, stout man who worked hard to maintain control of his students. He ran his fingers through his hair, straightened the microphone, and tapped it with his finger, sending a piercing shriek around the room.

After conducting some minor administrative business, he announced that the position of president of the Communist Youth Council had been awarded to Antonio. An excited murmur ran through the gathering as students began nudging and whispering to each other. There was scattered applause. Antonio stood, looking quite pleased. He walked to the center of the stage to receive an armband that proclaimed his position. The principal asked him if he wanted to say a few words, but he declined.

My cousins and I looked at each other with unease. Since we'd been so open in discussing our anticommunist views with Antonio, I didn't have a good feeling about his appointment. I feared we were in for big trouble.

It didn't take long before Antonio and I began to disagree. Much to my chagrin, Antonio had started picking on Magda, mocking her behind her back because her parents were wealthy. To him, anyone who had any money was suspected of being a counterrevolutionary. I told him that Magda's parents were good people, but my arguments bounced off him like a ball off a wall.

Conflicts also arose over student activities. Antonio cancelled dances and sporting events so students could attend Fidel's speeches and rallies. He tried to get Miriam to accompany him on these outings—but she seldom complied. When she did attend, she returned looking depressed.

One day after school she confronted Antonio. "Are you out of your mind, Antonio? We don't know Communists. We don't know Fidel. We grew up together. That's where our loyalty should lie—with each other, not with some wild-eyed radical whom none of us ever met."

"You don't understand," said Antonio. "Communism is not a fad, it's not an idea dreamt up by Fidel. It's an international movement to shift power to the People. It will help save the world."

"I don't want to save the world. I just want to have some fun with our friends."

Sometimes when Miriam and Antonio argued, he would just turn his back on her. He pretended not to care what she thought. But whenever she scolded him, a muscle danced on the side of his jaw.

The Communist Youth Council quickly gained an alarming amount of power. They helped with the collection and destruction of textbooks and the distribution of ones espousing the communist cause. Books about politics were pulled from stores and library shelves. Even books that had nothing to do with these topics disappeared from view. In short order, history was rewritten. Falsified. Censored.

The list of forbidden books changed frequently, and you were never quite sure whether what you were reading was banned by the Party. Many books were considered subversive—a corrupting influence—especially on the youth. But the definition of "subversive" was strange, subjective, and ever-changing.

Culture—as well as freedom—was being decimated, disbanded, discarded. You could feel it in the air. It was so palpable you could almost taste it.

At least once a week Antonio arranged for buses to transport students to hear speeches by Fidel and other *Fidelistas*. Behind the school, trucks lined up like crows on a wire to take students to see movies about Lenin and the Russian Revolution.

One day Antonio announced that the Youth Council would issue communist report cards that would coincide with the distribution of academic ones. Students would receive a "citizenship score" that reflected their attendance at political events and rallies. We would also be graded on our knowledge and views about Fidel, communism, and the revolution.

Antonio and I went head-to-head on this issue, while the teachers remained neutral, seemingly reluctant to speak up. I eventually lost this battle, and the report cards were issued. Since everyone was afraid of not getting a good citizenship score, it drastically increased the number of communist events students attended. The political complexion of the student body was changing—and, to my mind, not for the better.

Magda put herself at risk by agreeing with my position on the report cards. Although two years my junior, she was mature for her age. Having received an excellent education at Lancha, she was very knowledgeable, had strong opinions, and served as an excellent sounding board for my ideas.

During lunch break, Magda and I would walk in the park together. Sometimes I was so taken with her beauty that I failed to concentrate on what she was saying. I would look at her hands, her long slender fingers, and her pretty, polished nails and would wonder what it would be like to hold them in mine. I was often tempted to reach for her hand but I was too afraid. What if someone saw us? What if she didn't like it? What if she pulled her hand away?

I longed to touch her, but I decided to let it be for a while.

CHAPTER 12

Although Magda and I saw much of each other during the day, there were few opportunities to be together at night. We waved to each other during our *paseo,* but our strolls around the park were hardly enough—for either of us. Some evenings she would sit on the second-story balcony of her parents' beautiful Spanish villa, her hair backlit with an amber light and her body framed in a classic Spanish arch, while I walked up and down her street.

When her parents weren't looking, I'd wave to her. Then I'd saunter to the bottom of the street and walk back again, hoping to see her once more. To me, she was like a princess in a fairy tale. Her home was the castle and the golden light that spilled from her window was a glittering promise of things to come.

My cousins would tag along, laughing, joking, and making snide remarks. After a few months, Magda and I tired of this charade.

Unbeknownst to me, Magda had decided to ask her parents for permission for me to visit her at home. While I assumed her father was the power broker in the household, I later learned that her mother ruled the roost. Magda had lobbied her mother for months to see me, regaling her with stories about how nice I was, how smart I was, and how much she cared for me.

After much discussion, she persuaded her mother to receive me in their home. Magda took me by surprise one day by asking me to approach her father for permission to call on her.

"Really?" I said, not believing my good luck.

She nodded, knowingly. "Don't worry. It'll be okay."

Now I had to talk to my parents about Magda. The next day after school I walked into the kitchen where Mima was peeling potatoes. The heat in the room was oppressive, rising from the linoleum floor like a morning fog. Mima looked up and smiled while I pushed past her to get a glass of water.

I glanced back and said casually, "I'm going to ask Magda's father for permission to see her." Mima narrowed her eyes and shook her head slightly. She rinsed the potatoes and dried her hands on a dish towel.

"Then we have to talk," she said. She nodded toward the living room, waving her hand for my siblings to go outside to play. They scattered like starlings at the look on her face. She closed the door behind them, lowered herself onto the sofa, and gestured for me to sit.

Concern filled her eyes. "What?" I asked. I was afraid she would object to me seeing Magda.

"Before you go calling on a girl, there are things a boy your age should know," she said.

I squirmed in my seat. I had a suspicion where this conversation was going, and I wanted no part of it. Mima studied me briefly.

"To ask a young woman's father for permission to see her is the first step toward marriage," she said. "I want you to think long and hard about what you are about to do, Frankie."

I sucked in a breath. "I'm not doing anything yet. I just want to spend time with Magda—do homework and stuff. I'm not about to marry her."

Mima pursed her lips. "Maybe not yet. But at your age one thing leads to another and the next thing you know—"

I stood up abruptly. "This is loco, Mima. I'm only a teenager!"

"Precisely. Now, sit down, young man."

I sat back down and looked at the floor. She began again, "The teen years are a very dangerous time for a boy."

"What do you mean, *dangerous*?"

Mima waited for me to regain my composure. She started to speak again in a softer voice.

"You are very smart, Frankie, and your father and I want you to go to college—to the University of Havana. You would be the first Mederos to go. You know how much this means to us. It's been our dream since you were born." She stared at me with eyes full of alarm and conviction.

I sighed in relief, hoping that this was her only concern.

"Don't worry, Mima. I'm going to college. My grades are good, I'm doing fine."

"That's not what I'm talking about."

"Then, what?" I said a little too loudly. I gulped down my anger.

"What? What?" mocked Mima. The pitch of her voice matched my own. "You act like this is a trivial matter. You have no idea how easy it is to ruin a dream."

"How would I ruin it?" I said, my voice wavering. I felt wounded at being accused of ruining her dream when I hadn't done anything wrong.

"By getting too involved. Getting carried away."

I did not respond. We sat in silence for a moment, each of us lost in our own thoughts. This was a difficult conversation for both of us. Mima coughed and turned toward me again.

"Frankie, how fond are you of this girl?"

I pursed my lips, wondering whether it would be prudent to tell her how crazy I was about Magda.

"She's pretty," I said. "And smart. And nice."

Mima's brow furrowed, and she rearranged her body on the sofa. "Frankie, you have always been a good boy. But there's a bit of the rebel in you."

I nodded, thinking about my skirmishes with Antonio, but I wasn't about to admit my shortcomings.

"Rebelliousness can get you into a peck of trouble," she said. "Trouble that can last a lifetime."

I stared silently out the window, trying to bring my emotions to heel.

"Now, about this girl—"

"Magda."

"Magda," she repeated, turning the word over in her mouth as if she could get a sense of my girlfriend by tasting her name. "You must respect her."

"I do."

When my mother spoke next her voice was fiercer, like the words had been burning a hole inside her and she was forced to expel them. "There are places on a girl's body that you are never to touch. *Never*, Frankie. Not until you are married."

I nodded in embarrassment.

"Look at me, Frankie. Am I making myself clear?"

I looked at her eyes and saw a trace of fright in them, not something my mother often showed. It scared me.

"I understand."

"No, you don't understand," said Mima. "That's the problem. Boys your age never understand—"

I sighed in exasperation. "I do understand," I said as convincingly as possible. "I would never—"

Mima studied me carefully before standing up. "Enough," she said. Her expression signaled that a headache was blooming. I knew it was best not to press the issue.

"You are not to call on Magda until your father speaks with you. Go with him to work tonight. Help him out while you talk it over." She waved me away. "Finish your homework so you're ready to go."

I stood and left the room while Mima expelled her breath.

• • •

When Pipo and I entered the factory where he worked that evening, hundreds of bags of fertilizer were lined up for inventory. Pipo handed me a clipboard and told me to start counting. The smell pervading the building made me sneeze and my eyes began to water. After a couple of hours, Pipo and I sat down for a break.

"I understand you want to call on a girl," he said.

"I do."

Pipo tapped a cigarette out of its pack and struck a match against a wooden plank. He inhaled deeply, threw his head back, and blew the smoke high into the air.

"This job," he said circling his hand around his head. "This is not easy. Standing on your feet all night, away from your mother, away from you kids." I nodded. "I want something better for you, Frankie. I don't want you to have to work this hard."

"I know," I said. And I did. I knew how tired Pipo was when he got home in the mornings, sinking into bed like his life depended on it, his clothes stinking, his eyes puffy and red from the chemicals that fouled the factory air. I looked at him in appreciation. He smiled and patted me on the knee.

"This girl, do you love her?"

"I think I do. She's—"

"It doesn't matter what she is," he said.

I was a little hurt that my father had cut me off so abruptly. I wanted to talk about Magda, to tell him about her thick curly eyelashes, about how her eyes sparkled when she laughed.

"What matters is that you go to college. No matter what, you must go to college."

I nodded. We sat staring at the bags of fertilizer for a couple of minutes.

"Things are getting crazy, Frankie."

"How so?"

"People are disappearing. Like Carlos. You remember Carlos?" I nodded. "I used to see him every day at the coffee shop. For years he was there. Now, gone. "

"Where do you think he went?"

"Who knows? Maybe to America. Maybe one of the CDRs got him. Maybe he's in jail—or dead. You have to be smart to survive today—and educated. Do you know what I'm saying?"

"I know. Mima says the same thing. So does Abuelo."

"It's important. I can't stress it enough." Pipo sat silent for a moment before adding, "It's okay to be in love, but you still need to get an education. Promise me you'll go to college."

"I will. Don't worry about it."

"It's a father's job to worry, Frankie. That's just how it is. Now about this girl..."

"What about her?"

"There are limits as to what you can do with a girl. You know about limits, don't you, Frankie?"

"I know."

"Do we need to talk some more?"

"No, I think we're good."

"Okay, Frankie. Just don't let anything you do with this girl keep you from going to college."

"It's okay," I said. "I get it."

The next evening, before the sun went down, I went to Magda's house and rang the bell, requesting to speak with her father. As if on cue, Señor Hernández appeared at the door and led me up the stairs to his study. A crystal chandelier hung from the ceiling, and a Persian rug cushioned our feet. A silver vase held a profusion of flowers, and a portrait of Magda's mother stared down at us from a gilded frame.

Men of Señor Hernández's status were larger than life in Cuba. They rode about in chrome-laden cars, cutting dashing figures in white linen suits. They frequented bars, casinos, and nightclubs and oversaw their sugar, coffee, and real estate holdings with great authority and panache. But it was all theater. In real life—in the home—women held all the power. This was no less the case in the villa.

When we entered señor's study, he left the door slightly ajar. It crossed my mind that he might have done this so Magda's mother could eavesdrop on our conversation.

I straightened up as Magda's father struck a match to light his cigar. He bit off the end, then slowly turned the cigar in his mouth as he inhaled. I mustered the courage to speak.

"I was wondering, señor." I cleared my throat and started again. "I was wondering if—"

"If what?" he said, eyeing me with curiosity. He smiled slightly as if he found me amusing.

"If I could have permission to see Magda here—to study, señor."

Magda's father looked me up and down. "To study," he repeated in a gravelly voice.

He blew out his match and dropped it into an ashtray as he settled himself in a mahogany chair behind his desk. "What are your intentions, then?"

I looked around, confused. I didn't know what he meant by "intentions." I felt like he had sprung a trap.

"Señor?"

"Your intentions, young man," he said in a louder voice.

"My intentions, señor, are to study with your daughter—if I have your permission, that is."

He thought for a moment. "I suppose that would be all right." His eyes twinkled briefly. For some reason, it crossed my mind that he was playing with me, and I wondered why he might do that.

He interrupted my thoughts. "But there are rules: You can only come *one* night a week for *one* hour—to study. And you can't overstay your time. You can't meet my daughter on the street. And you can't touch her—*ever*. Do you understand?"

"I understand, señor. Thank you, señor."

I backed out of the room giddy with delight. I met Magda on the staircase and whispered the good news to her. I was beaming, hardly believing my good luck. She seemed happy, but not too surprised.

I showed myself at the window and gave a thumbs-up to my cousins who were waiting below. When I left the house, they descended on me like a pack of hyenas, laughing and jumping around. Pipi wanted to know what Magda's father had said, and Luis wanted to know what kind of cigar he smoked.

Gilbert had only one question, "Did they give you anything good to eat?"

The next night I showed up at the villa, and Magda and I went off to study together. Whenever I visited, Magda's mother, Estel, would bring us cheeses and meats on a silver tray. After placing the food on the table, she'd spend some time chatting with us before retiring to a corner of the room to sew.

I could see a strong family resemblance between Magda and her mother. Estel was quite a beauty, slim and raven-haired with a dazzling smile.

After a short time, my once-a-week visits turned into two, and two turned into three. Before I knew it, I was visiting Magda almost every night. I was in heaven. Magda and I studied and talked, talked and studied. I still had not touched her hand, but it was a thrill just to look at her, to be with her.

Señora Hernández busied herself with her needlework while chaperoning us, but I sensed that she was taking in our every word. I complimented her on her appearance and took an interest in her sewing. She told me about her job at city hall in Havana, and I told her about sports and political issues at school. Little by little, she was starting to warm to me. Little by little, I was becoming part of the family.

Señora Hernández also told me things about the family I never could've guessed—about Magda's grandfather's involvement in politics under the Batista regime, about the family's stakes in luxury hotels, about family businesses being seized by Fidel.

Slowly I was becoming privy to the trials and tribulations Magda's family had endured under this regime. I was beginning to understand that, despite the vast differences in our social standing, our political beliefs and philosophy were perfectly aligned.

And this was cementing our relationship in a way that transcended everything else.

CHAPTER 13

The summer between my eighth and ninth grades, Castro made it a graduation requirement for all boys to spend their summer vacations helping poor farmers harvest their crops. The idea was to help us to identify with the revolution by giving us firsthand experience of the peasants' lives and pain.

Gilbert, Jabao, Pipi, Luis, and I traveled with many other students to the hills of Oriente Province in the Sierra Maestra to do our part. We helped various families harvest coffee, tobacco, and other crops during the day, and we slept in their barns at night. We were required to do a good day's work, and the farmers were required to feed us.

I was assigned to a farmer named Manuel, a friendly man in his mid-thirties. His wife and six children all worked the fields. It was a two-month stint of tedious, backbreaking labor, but it was work I was used to, work I had done.

Oriente Province was rugged and beautiful, filled with towering royal palms that provided palm oil, lumber, and roofing material. The Cauto River offered water for drinking, bathing, and laundry. My cousins and friends met there every Sunday to swim. We even managed to catch some fish for Manuel during the height of a hurricane.

Although working the fields was not the way I wanted to spend my summer, my biggest concern was that I was unable to see Magda.

Before I left, I told my favorite aunt about how much I cared for Magda. She went to her old, wooden jewelry box and retrieved a ring—a trinket really—inset with small fake diamonds. I looked at it and pictured putting it on Magda's finger one day. The thought took my breath away.

"Take it," urged my aunt. "Someday you might want to give it to Magda. Regardless of its worth, a ring is a symbol of love. A circle has no beginning and no end—just like love. Keep it in your pocket, Frankie. You'll know when the time is right to take it out."

I took her advice. While working, I would sink my hand into my pocket and finger the ring as if it were a magic charm that would allow me to touch Magda's cheek, to run my hands through her hair, and to eventually win her heart.

When I went to sleep at night, I would place the ring safely under my pillow and picture Magda's body lying next to mine in bed. When I awoke, the first thing I did was slip my hand under the pillow to retrieve the ring. If my fingers didn't find it immediately I'd panic, afraid it had been lost or stolen.

I thought about things that might make Magda happy. She was always thrilled with the smallest tokens of affection. I thought about being able to do things for her every day of the week.

During the summer of 1963, I did not see Magda, but I held her gently in my heart. And, for the time being, that was enough.

CHAPTER 14

When I saw Magda on the first day of school, she looked more beautiful than ever. Over the summer her features had become more defined, her legs longer, her body more curvaceous. She seemed more poised, more elegant, more self-assured. When she spoke, her voice was warm, soft, and refined.

Magda drew people to her. She charmed them with her infectious laugh, the kind that made others join the fun. When I was near her, my spirits were lighter. I felt smarter, happier, like a cat luxuriating in the afternoon sun.

Magda employed her quick wit to soften the edges of angry remarks students sometimes hurled at each other. She soothed their fears about rumors that the *Fidelistas* were beating, torturing, and kidnapping people who disagreed with their views, fears that filled even the most level-headed students with angst. Magda was not only my darling, she was becoming the darling of my entire school.

In some ways, the lives of Cuban teenagers in the early '60s mimicked the lives of our peers in America. We partied, danced, and had an occasional beer. We learned new dances—the Frug, the Monkey, the Twist. We talked about famous singers and movie stars, and we assuaged our fears with the rhythms of rock 'n' roll.

My cousins and friends visited Magda's home, and her parents often drove her to my house. We double-dated with Miriam and Antonio, spinning our 45 rpm records and dancing the jitterbug in Magda's living room. We listened to the melancholy lyrics of "Silhou-

ettes on the Shade" and danced to the romantic strains of "Put Your
Head on My Shoulder." Posters of the Everly Brothers, Bobby Darin,
and Paul Anka were taped to our bedroom walls.

While Magda, Miriam, and I disagreed with Antonio's political views,
we thought it was just a phase he was going through. Besides, we had
a lot of history together. But when school started in the fall, the political tensions emergent last year now blossomed profusely.

Although Antonio and I still remained friends, the feelings between us regarding politics were reaching a boiling point. Having
known everyone in school for most of my life, I felt confident to freely
express my thoughts and views. Perhaps, too freely. I gave short shrift
to the fact that I was bucking a powerful force, one more dangerous
than I could've imagined.

I was not the only one expressing anticommunist views. Arguments
between pro- and anti-Castro factions were frequent, boisterous, and
rancorous, partly because we were so young and partly because we
knew the stakes were so high. Due to my leadership position at school,
I often found myself smack in the middle of these disputes.

Meanwhile, Antonio was spending most of his spare time in an office
the Party had opened in Guanabacoa. He attended lectures on socialist
history and philosophy, becoming more entrenched in his views by
the day. Occasionally, senior officials would visit our school and ap-
plaud Antonio's efforts on the Party's behalf, praising his success in recruiting new members to the Cause. His role as an ardent Party
supporter was providing him with a new sense of power.

Our disagreements regarding student policies were now becoming
weekly events, with Antonio and me arguing our points on opposite
sides of the table in the principal's office. Some battles I won. Some
battles I lost.

Antonio wanted our sports teams named after heroes of the revolution, a fight I won. He wanted to carve out half an hour from every

school day to lecture students about communism so he could recruit them into the Party, a fight I lost. He wanted to replace the school flag with flag of the Party, another fight I lost.

But when Antonio announced that the students should sing "The Internationale," the international song of communism, instead of the national anthem at school events, I hit the ceiling. I had too many fond memories of singing "El Himno de Bayamo" with Abuelo to allow that to happen.

"Do you have some problem with the revolution?" taunted Antonio. "Do you have some problem with China, with Russia? Aren't they big enough countries for you, Frankie?"

"What are you talking about, Antonio? We don't live in Russia. We've always sung the Cuban national anthem, you know that."

Antonio's style of arguing was to bob, weave, and parry my attack. I never knew where an argument would take us.

"Are you forgetting what Batista did?"

"What does Batista have to do with it?"

"Batista was an enemy of the People."

"But, Antonio, that's irrelevant. Nobody wants to sing this song. We don't even know the words."

"It's not what the students want that counts, it's what the Party wants that counts."

"Maybe so, but it's not something I want."

"Well, times have changed, Frankie. The Party doesn't care what you want. If you know what's good for you, you'd better get on board."

I closed my eyes for a moment to steady my emotions. This argument was headed in a dangerous direction. I didn't want to blow up at Antonio. On the other hand, I didn't want him to walk all over me either.

"Is that some kind of a threat, Antonio?"

Antonio shrugged. "Take it any way you like."

I studied my friend's face. In the past few months the light had fled his eyes. His remark made me feel sad, disconcerted. I felt like I had lost something I could never recover. I inched closer.

"Look at me, 'Tonio; it's me, Frankie. What are you trying to do? I'm your buddy, your lifelong friend." I lowered my voice. "Let's not do this to each other."

Antonio's gaze narrowed. He shot me a look I'd never seen. "I don't need you, Frankie. I don't need friends. I don't even need family. I have the Party; that's all I'll ever need."

When my cousins heard what Antonio had said, they could hardly believe their ears. They didn't want to think that one of us had turned into a Communist. It was almost unimaginable.

While I felt sad, hurt, and confused, Gilbert, Luis, Jabao, and Pipi teased Antonio about his views. Luis was the worst.

"Antonio, come here. Is it true you're a Communist?" asked Luis.

Antonio threw back his shoulders and expanded his chest. "Of course, I'm a Communist. Communism is the future. And you better watch out what you say—or else."

"What are you going to do, report us as 'Enemies of the People'?"

"Maybe," said Antonio. "Or maybe I'll do something that will make your life truly miserable."

I urged my friends not to cause trouble. I told them Antonio could call the police and accuse us of anything, including counterrevolutionary activity.

But they had known Antonio too long to fear him. To them he was still the shy, reclusive kid who showed up at baseball games with black-and-blue marks. They just wouldn't lay off.

Believing he was following the advice in billboard proclamations that read, "The Working Day Is Sacred!" and "To Be Communist Means to Sacrifice!" Antonio began recruiting students to work for the Party on weekends.

He wanted students to volunteer to clean the streets and sidewalks.

He also arranged for buses to transport students to an abandoned drug company to collect old prescription bottles so they could be recycled by the Party.

Most students had no interest in these activities. When they didn't show up at his events, Antonio blamed me for sabotaging his efforts.

Fired with enthusiasm, Antonio distributed communist pamphlets at sporting events and gave out tickets for communist parties and rallies. He told the students they served free food and drinks at the rallies. People were hungry. He was gaining support.

Meanwhile, Miriam was becoming more and more disgusted with Antonio's behavior. Rather than support him, she took my side in all our disputes. So did Magda. Which did nothing to endear any of us to Antonio.

The good news was that my relationship with Magda was developing nicely. One day during one of our walks, I reached for her hand. I had thought about how I would do this for days, and when I finally slipped my hand in hers, it seemed like the most natural thing in the world. Sometimes we would entwine our fingers. At other times, we would hold each other's hands as if they were enveloped in an old woolen mitten. When I removed my sweaty hand to wipe it on my pants, it felt naked and cold, like a child abandoned on the side of a road. I thought about how it felt to hold Magda's hand every night before I went to sleep.

The only problem I had with Magda concerned an occasional bout of jealousy. Being on Student Council meant I had meetings to attend and problems to solve.

Because I was two years her senior, Magda feared I would tire of her and find a girl my own age, someone who was more sophisticated. We had several long talks about this, and she voiced her concern about the attention being paid to me by other girls. She clung to the fear that I would make a fool of her by dating someone else. I thought this was something she would eventually outgrow.

One day, some students were discussing politics in the back of a classroom. In the heat of the argument, a beautiful young woman grabbed my arm. A look of anguish crossed Magda's face. Her hand flew to her mouth as tears gathered in the wells of her eyes. She looked like she was about to be sick.

Magda stumbled out of the classroom with me close behind. She wandered around the hallway for a minute as if she had no idea what to do. Tears streaming down her cheeks, she opened the heavy metal door to the stairwell and began stumbling down the concrete steps. I followed her. The door clicked behind us as the metal bar fell into place. A window was open and sun poured in, casting a parallelogram on the wall.

Magda's back was to me, and I called for her to stop. I wanted to reach out and grab her, but I wasn't sure how she'd react. I ran down the stairs, calling after her.

"Magda, Magda, what's the matter?" I had no idea why she was upset with me. I racked my brain for something I might have said to offend her.

"You know what's the matter," she said. Her voice was laced with anger and a very deep hurt.

"No, what?" I asked, confused.

"That girl touched you." Her voice rose an octave. "She touched your arm. I saw it."

"Magda, please don't be upset over that."

Magda turned her face to the wall, not wanting me to see her cry. I placed my hand on her shoulder to make her turn around. She moved away from my hand and mumbled something into the wall.

"I'm sorry. I can't hear you. What is it?"

Magda hesitated a moment before facing me. "It's nothing."

"That's not true. Tell me what's bothering you."

Magda took a deep breath. "That girl likes you. I've seen her try to get near you before. She wants you for her boyfriend."

"She was just trying to get my attention, that's all."

"Yes, she does. I know it. I've heard her talk about you. You don't know anything about girls. What I'm saying is true."

"But Magda, even if it *were* true, what difference would it make? I don't care about *her*. I care about *you*."

"Then why did you let her touch you?"

"She touched *me*, Magda. I had nothing to do with it. Besides, it didn't mean anything. It was nothing—nothing at all."

"Nothing for you," said Magda, her voice cracking. "But not nothing for her."

I looked at Magda's face, so fragile, so beautiful, and I thought my heart would break. Never, *ever* would I do anything to hurt Magda. She was the girl I went to sleep thinking about, the girl I woke up thinking about. She was the only girl I *ever* thought about. How could I make her understand?

Suddenly I was possessed with an overwhelming desire to take Magda in my arms, to soothe her fears, to tell her how much I loved her. I didn't care whether it was proper, whether her parents would approve, whether my parents would approve. I just didn't care.

I took Magda by the shoulders, pulled her toward me, and hugged her tightly. As I did, some tension drained from her body. I held her for a moment, relishing the feel of her body against mine. It almost made me dizzy. This was the beginning of a sea change in our relationship. I took a half step backward and reached for her hands. I was brimming with emotion.

"Magda, I want you to know something."

"What?"

I hesitated just a moment, hoping she wouldn't laugh—or reject me. I drew in my breath, mustered my courage, and said, "You are the most dear and precious person in the whole world to me. And there is no way on earth I could ever care for anyone else."

Magda looked up, surprised. "I am?"

I smiled at her. "Yes, you are. I'm sorry I haven't told you that before."

Magda sighed and tried to blink back her tears. One large teardrop drifted down her cheek, and I brushed it away with my thumb. I pulled her toward me, lifted her chin gently with my finger, and kissed her on the mouth.

It was the first kiss for both of us, and one I had dreamt about for a very long time. I couldn't believe how soft her lips were, and I was suddenly hungry for more. I hoped our kiss felt as good to her as it did to me.

Magda looked startled at first and then I kissed her again, nibbling her bottom lip while gathering the back of her neck in my hands. My heart beat faster, and the rest of the world disappeared. There were only two things that existed at that moment: her lips and mine. This time Magda eagerly returned my kiss. I pulled away and looked at her. I could hardly believe this was happening.

"I'm crazy about you, Magda. You know that, don't you?" She nodded briefly. "I've fallen head over heels in love with you." My voice cracked a little and I blushed.

"You have?"

"I really have," I replied with a smile.

Magda nodded twice to indicate her understanding. She looked very happy. She drew in her breath, and to my surprise, she replied, "I love you too, Frankie."

My heart was thumping in a way I had never felt before. Her response confused all my senses. Suddenly I couldn't think. I couldn't hear. I couldn't speak. I hugged her for a long minute, and I then pulled away so I could see her beautiful eyes. She looked angelic.

I took out the ring I had kept in my pocket all these months, the one my aunt had given me, and pressed it into her hand. She looked down at it.

"It's fake," I said. "But I want you to keep it until I'm old enough to get you a real diamond—one you can be proud of. But it would make me so happy if you would wear this one for now—as a sign of my love."

Beaming, Magda closed her hand around the ring and drew it to her heart. "I will be proud to wear it," she said. "I will wear it for the rest of my life."

I took Magda in my arms. "And I will love you for the rest of my life."

Magda hugged me so hard I was sure she could hear my heart beating through my shirt. I squeezed her hair in my hand. It felt just the way I had imagined: thick and silky to the touch. She handed the ring back to me, confusing me momentarily. Then she held out her hand, her fingers outstretched.

"Please put it on for me," she said. She looked jubilant.

"Which finger?"

She laughed and wiggled her ring finger, and I slipped on the ring. She stretched her fingers upward to view it. A beam of sunlight caught one of the stones and it sparkled, throwing a burst of color against the wall. I had never seen Magda look so happy.

"I want you to make me a promise."

Magda looked at me quizzically and nodded. "What, Frankie?"

"Promise me here and now that you will never, ever doubt my love. No matter where we are, no matter what we do, no matter what happens in the future, we cannot doubt each other's love."

She nodded again.

"This is very important to me, Magda."

Magda looked up to me and smiled. "I promise," she said. Her words reassured me.

"Say the whole thing."

Her eyes twinkled. "I will never doubt your love, Frankie. No matter where we are, no matter what we do, no matter what happens in the future."

I saw her shoulders soften, her whole body relax. Her skin was flushed, lovely, radiant. I looked at her, black eyes searching golden brown, in a silent communion that celebrated and fixed our love for each other as surely as the planets were fixed in their orbits. I took her in my arms and kissed her again. I knew at that moment that someday I would make Magda my wife.

I almost floated home that night, replaying in my mind what had happened. I could still feel the warmth of Magda's body against mine, the curve of her waist, the smell of her cologne. My mind could hardly grasp what my heart knew so well: I loved Magda. And she loved me.

I wanted to stand in the bell tower of the *Catedral de San Cristóbal* in Old Havana, to pull the rough cord and ring out our love to everyone walking the cobblestoned streets. At the same time, I wanted to keep what had transpired between us to myself.

It felt like I was holding a sweet and fragile secret, like a delicate bubble that might dissipate with exposure, leaving nothing behind but a memory of what had been. That night I fell asleep with a happiness and warmth suffusing my heart that I had never known.

The next day word was out. Evidently, Magda had told Miriam what had happened, and Miriam had told Antonio. All the tongues were wagging. Everyone at school knew we were in love.

CHAPTER 15

Speaking to a gathering of young Communists in August 1963, Fidel announced that the country would implement a program of compulsory military service. His brother Raúl, whom *el líder máximo* had named minister of the revolutionary armed forces, cited the need for a disciplined adjunct workforce as the main reason for the draft.

Cuba had the most modern and powerful army in Latin America and had little use for more recruits. But Fidel had signed a trade agreement with the Soviet Union and had failed to meet the sugar quota, a great political embarrassment.

The lackluster harvest was mostly due to the dearth of spare parts for sugar mills as a result of the American blockade. But Fidel blamed it on the poor work ethic of Cuba's young people.

With the need for more hands to harvest the cane, he launched a campaign to "rehabilitate" the "lumpen and lazy" through military service. These included kids who played hooky, frequented bars and billiard halls, and swooned to the songs of Elvis Presley.

Fidel claimed that the army would cure these "economic malefactors, loafers, and parasites" of their "deviant behavior" by providing them with productive work.

All males aged fifteen through twenty-six had to register for three years of compulsory military service. No one subject—or soon to be subject—to the draft was permitted to leave Cuba under any circumstances.

Fidel labeled those wanting to leave the country "scum, worms, and antisocial elements." Worm was one of his favorite words, and many of his followers had begun to use it.

To make it more difficult to leave Cuba, the government demonetized the nation's bank notes, making Cuban money worthless outside the country. The notes were replaced with ones that boasted pictures of revolutionaries. To me the new currency represented a form of imprisonment—another way to keep us under the thumb of the Party.

The draft was designed to provide young people with a "respectable trade" and to serve as a punishment for incorrigible youths. Soldiers were enlisted to harvest sugarcane and coffee. Raúl estimated the cheap labor would save Cuba hundreds of millions of pesos each year.

As second lieutenant of the Communist Youth Council, Antonio was responsible for turning over the names of all draft-eligible boys in our school to the proper authorities. He prepared the paperwork, processed the transcripts, and recommended the order in which young men would be called up for service. I feared we were in for trouble.

Among the initial groups to be drafted were criminals, school dropouts, and those who had received black marks against them from the CDRs. Because Luis was still in the fourth grade—and now sporting a moustache—Antonio identified him as a "slacker" who should be one of the first to be drafted. But we suspected that Luis was chosen more for taunting Antonio than for being an "incorrigible."

It was a very sad day. Luis was heartbroken and frightened, and his whole family sobbed at the news. I was losing my cousin and friend. I sensed that it signaled the end of an era. I was angry with Antonio and Fidel for the sorry state of affairs.

Gilbert was the next to be called up. Fortunately, he was too flat-footed for military service. We rejoiced at this news, but wondered who would be next.

It was Saturday night and Magda's parents had agreed to allow her to attend her first teenage party. Her father was to drop her and Miriam off at Gilbert's house, and I was to watch over them until he picked them up.

I got to the party around seven p.m., and the girls arrived shortly thereafter. Magda wore a blue organdy dress and Miriam a yellow seer-sucker one.

The party was held in Gilbert's parents' living room. His parents were nowhere to be found. Someone said they had gone for a walk in the park. Close to thirty kids were there, including Tato, Pipi, Jabao, and Antonio. Everyone was dancing, laughing, and telling funny stories. Bottles of beer were passed around.

There wasn't enough beer for anyone to have more than a swig or two. When I offered Magda a sip, she made a face. She knew if she went home with alcohol on her breath, it would be a long time before she'd be allowed to attend another party.

Jabao walked over to the record player and turned on "The Twist." Miriam and Antonio started to dance, swinging their arms and legs back and forth, lost in the music of Chubby Checker.

I sat down next to Magda and took her hand in mine, happy to be with her. I put my arm around her shoulder and pulled her close to me, burying my nose in her hair. It smelled fresh and clean, like Johnson's Baby Shampoo.

Magda and I sat out the first song and then started to dance to the pulsing rhythm of "Duke of Earl." The party was in full swing. Several couples snuggled on the sofa while others were busy talking. Suddenly, the music stopped and someone turned off the lights. The room went black as ebony, and a scattering of nervous laughter broke out. This had never happened at a party I had gone to before. A sense of adventure was in the air.

I blinked my eyes against the darkness and grabbed Magda's hand. She giggled. I laced my fingers through hers and pushed her gently toward a corner of the room. She pressed her body close to mine, and I felt an immediate rush of heat. I wrapped my arms around her waist and she laid her head on my shoulder. My heart was pounding wildly, and I tried to quiet my rushing pulse.

I knew some of the boys would take this opportunity to kiss their girlfriends, and I desperately wanted to kiss Magda. I even thought of touching her breasts. But I was on edge, afraid a fight might break out.

The laughter died down and the room grew quiet. I could feel Magda's heart beating against my chest. The top of her head was nestled just beneath my chin. I stroked her hair with my hand.

I felt for the back of her neck and pulled her face toward me. A moment later her warm lips were on mine. I nibbled her lower lip and she sighed, almost imperceptibly. I kissed her again, hoping the lights would stay off forever. She opened her mouth and my tongue sought hers. It was the first time we had French kissed, something I had only heard about recently. My breathing quickened and I pulled Magda even closer. My hands roamed her back, feeling the architecture of her spine and the soft curve where her waist met her hips. I pushed my pelvis into hers, and we moved together, swaying back and forth like a swing.

A moment of sheer bliss elapsed. I wondered what it would be like to make love to Magda. Out of nowhere someone whispered, "Communism sucks!" It was an angry, startling remark and it was impossible to know who said it. In the dark, you couldn't tell.

An electric current ran through the crowd. There was a moment of pregnant silence and then, as if on cue, the entire room erupted in chants: "Communism sucks! Fidel is a pig! Power to the People!"

My heart leapt into my throat. I immediately sensed danger. This was no place for Magda. Anyone could mistake the scene for an anti-communist rally. Magda stepped away from me and started to chant along with the others.

I grabbed her hand, pulled her toward me, and whispered "don't" into her ear. Her body stiffened like a mannequin. I could almost envision the expression on her face as it dawned on her why I had cautioned her to remain silent.

With Antonio present, I knew enough to keep my own mouth shut. Someone close to Antonio hollered, "Socialism stinks!" and Antonio took a swing at him. Whoever it was swung back. I heard the sound of knuckles connecting with bone.

Antonio screamed, "I'm hurt, turn on the goddamn lights." But no one paid attention. Instead, the cheers grew louder, bolder, more intense. Several kids started yelling in unison, "The hell with Fidel! The hell with Fidel! The hell with Fidel!"

The chanting became so loud I was afraid we'd be overheard, but there was no stopping it. Anger and frustration raced through the room like a renegade train. I wasn't surprised. If Magda and Antonio weren't there, I would be chanting too.

A few minutes later, I heard the wail of sirens in the distance. My heart leapt into my throat, and I squeezed Magda's hand. The chanting slowly died down as the sirens grew closer.

"One of the CDRs must've called the police," Magda whispered. I knew she was right.

"Get the lights back on. Quick!" someone hollered.

The lights flashed on, and we all squinted against the brightness. Jabao coughed and a couple of girls rubbed their eyes.

Six green jeeps filled with police screeched to a halt in front of the house. We looked at each other in terror. I grabbed Magda and put her in back of me. Ten policemen broke open the door, stomped into the house, guns drawn as if they were looking for any excuse to shoot.

A burly police officer, his arms knotted with muscles, stepped forward. His face was beet red and his green uniform was stained black with perspiration.

"We got a report about counterrevolutionary activity," he said. "What's going on here?"

We stood in silence as thick as a jungle. No one dared utter a word. The officer looked at us one by one, studying our faces for signs of subversion. He waited a minute and then barked, "Somebody better tell me what the hell happened here or you are all going to jail."

A murmur ran through the group. Miriam started to whimper as Antonio stepped forward to take charge. Blood was running from his nose like rain down a gutter. He shook his head and wiped his face with his shirtsleeve, tilting his head back for a moment to stanch the flow of blood. The veins in his neck stood out like vines on a tree. Someone handed him a handkerchief, and he blotted the blood. I took a deep breath.

The room remained silent as a tomb. Gilbert shifted back and forth on his feet, his face pinched with fear.

The policeman regarded Gilbert suspiciously. "Is this your house?"

"Yes," admitted Gilbert.

"Where are your parents?"

"They aren't here."

The policeman turned to Antonio. "What's going on here?"

"We were partying and—"

"And what?" snapped the officer.

"Someone turned off the lights." Antonio gathered his courage and thrust out his chest, playing the dual role of leader and victim.

"Go on," said the officer, fingering his sidearm.

He looked at all of us. "Someone hit me in the nose. I hit him back, but he hit me first." He hesitated and looked around the room accusingly. "People were screaming and cursing, saying things against the Party. Against Fidel."

Everyone looked at each other in terror.

"Who?" demanded the officer. "Name them."

Antonio narrowed his eyes. There was no way he could positively identify anyone, but it didn't matter. As long as he pointed the finger at someone—anyone—his standing would rise in the eyes of the Party.

Antonio scanned the room. A feeling of foreboding cramped my throat. The last thing I wanted was to have Magda involved in something like this. I had worked very hard to gain the trust of her parents. I couldn't imagine their reaction if we were taken to jail.

Antonio's eyes darted around the room. He held my stare for a moment and looked away.

"Him, him, and him." He pointed to Martino, Tomás, and Roberto, three boys I didn't know very well.

"They walked into the party, uninvited. They were cursing Fidel."

"Anyone else?"

"Oh, there are plenty of worms here, that's for sure. I'm not certain who they are right now. But I'll figure it out soon enough."

"Well, keep us informed. This kinda thing is going on all over Havana and it won't be tolerated." The officer shook his head and mumbled, "You'd think people would know better by now."

Antonio nodded triumphantly. "I will," he said. He scowled at us in warning. Magda closed her eyes and shook her head, almost imperceptibly.

The policemen grabbed the three boys, put their hands on their heads, and pushed them to their knees. The boys' faces were ashen. A couple of girls began to cry. Tomás struggled, blushed, and wet his pants. His urine puddled like spilled milk on the linoleum floor.

The heavyset officer stepped forward, looking bored and disgusted. He pulled the boys' arms behind their backs. Tomás and Roberto struggled to no avail before we heard the sickening snap of handcuffs.

The boys' faces turned pale as the officers pushed them toward the front door. When the door slammed behind them, we climbed on the sofa, parted the curtains, and watched them duck into the jeep.

Kids were pushing each other aside in hopes of getting a glimpse of the action. Tomás looked back at us with a pitiful stare. It was as if he were hoping that someone would come to his rescue. Nobody moved.

The car doors shut and the motors jumped to life. We watched the jeeps' red taillights fade into a star-filled night.

CHAPTER 16

Beginning after the Bay of Pigs, Fidel created panic in the country with repeated announcements of a coming American invasion. No one knew whether Fidel truly believed this. Some people thought it was all a sham to gain support for the draft.

The government frequently sounded sirens in Havana, claiming American planes were ready to bomb the city.

Now that Fidel controlled the country's television channels, he broadcasted his speeches twenty-four hours a day, often predicting an imminent attack.

Several times a week Cubans ran to their homes for cover. Many lived in constant fear of annihilation.

That summer I joined other boys for my third stint helping poor farmers in the Sierra Maestra. This time I was accompanied by Antonio. I spent my days harvesting yucca, coffee, and sugarcane and my nights listening to Antonio extol the virtues of communism. Not a day went by when we did not argue.

Once a week, Antonio lectured the locals about the Bolshevik Revolution. Most of them had difficulty understanding what he was saying. Cubans were considered well educated if they had completed sixth grade. Many inhabitants of the Sierra Maestra were still illiterate—despite the efforts of the literacy brigade.

By now Fidel had declared that, with the help of the Soviet Union, Cuba would become a great military power. Cuba would cease to be a "puppet" of the United States and would command worldwide respect. He needed young men to help him accomplish this mission.

In early October 1964, I received a telegram stating that I was to report for military duty at six a.m. on October 31. I had just begun eleventh grade, and the news took me by surprise.

My family was furious at the government for disrupting my life. Their dream for me to be the first in my family to graduate from college was squashed like gum on a sidewalk. My grades were excellent, and I was well on my way to achieving their dream—until now.

I blamed myself for having to go into the service so soon. With top grades, I should not have had been called into service until I graduated from high school. But Antonio had labeled me a troublemaker in need of redemption. He said the army and I would "do each other good."

I was devastated. I didn't want to serve in a communist army. I didn't want to be separated from Magda. I didn't want to interrupt my education. And I didn't want to disappoint my parents by not going to college.

Taking these factors into consideration, my skirmishes with Antonio now seemed petty and foolish. I recalled Antonio's parting remarks during our last argument, "Frankie, don't mess with me or I will get you. And believe me, you will be sorry."

I thought about the price of speaking my mind and the more I did, the more disillusioned I became with Antonio, with Fidel, and with the whole system of government.

When I told Magda I had been drafted, she was beside herself. Neither of us knew where I'd be stationed, or when we'd see each other again. Given the circumstances, Magda's parents eased their rules regarding my visits.

For the next three weeks Magda and I visited late into the evening, kissing, hugging, and planning our future. We discussed when and where we'd get married and who we'd invite to the wedding. We talked about making a home together, how many children we'd have, and what they might look like.

We even talked about trivial matters regarding running a household—chores, furniture, and paint colors. I told her she'd be the boss regarding anything that had to do with the household. That seemed to please her.

But the joy that usually accompanies such plans was tempered by the knowledge that our days as young lovers were drawing to a close. It was a bittersweet, tender time, filled with hope, promise, and pain.

As the date of my leave-taking grew nearer, Magda became despondent, her feelings of grief exacerbated by the fact that she'd never been separated from anyone she loved. I tried to temper her melancholy with love letters and small presents, but nothing seemed to console her.

The only thing that provided either of us with any comfort was holding each other. We touched each other in tortured pleasure, our caresses a blend of bliss, hunger, and a stabbing ache. I dreaded our last day together, not knowing how I'd manage life without her. I hadn't even left and I was already missing her. Not knowing what lay ahead, I felt like we were dancing to the first strains of "Boléro" and the final strains of the "Moonlight Sonata."

While I was feeling sad, I was also feeling guilty about leaving Magda. I knew she shouldn't be sitting home waiting for me, although if the truth be known, the last thing I wanted was for her to date someone else. The very thought of it filled me with jealousy and dread. I wrestled with the idea for days. I knew I'd be taking a chance of losing Magda if she dated other boys. Still, I wanted to be fair to her.

One evening, while walking in the shadows of the ornate mansions lining *El Malecón*, I took her hand in mine, playing with her long, slender fingers and tracing her polished nails with the tip of my thumb. We sat on the seawall and listened to the waves lap the riprap for a minute before I turned to her and said, "What would you say if I suggested you date other boys while I'm gone?"

Magda looked at me askance and shrugged her shoulders. "I'm sorry, Frankie, but I can't do that." Her voice was calm and serene as if she had already given this issue some thought.

"But I have no idea when we'll be able to see each other again— it might be months, even years. I could be stationed anywhere, and who knows how often I'll get home."

I took Magda in my arms, thinking she might cry. But she didn't. She was determined and feisty—and she wasn't about to let this get her down. She pulled away from me and gazed out at the water.

"It won't be that long," she said. "Fidel will eventually be toppled. Cubans are too smart to keep him around. Sooner or later people will see through him. This can't go on forever."

"I'm not so sure about that. He's gaining a lot of power. You may be engaging in wishful thinking."

A moment of silence elapsed before Magda said, "I don't think so."

"What would you want to do if he's not overthrown?" I asked. I needed to test the waters—just in case.

"If he's not overthrown, and you have to spend three years in the service, so be it. I'll gladly wait for you." From the tone of her voice I knew she was serious.

"But this is the time in your life when you should be having fun, meeting new people—"

"So what exactly do you suggest I do, Frankie?" She sounded a little annoyed that we were even discussing the matter. "Go to parties without you? Dance with other boys? Kiss them? Think about it—is that what you really want?"

I gazed into her eyes. Her irises were a lovely brown flecked with gold and surrounded by a darker brown circle. They reminded me of the color of mink. I wished I could look at her face forever. I dragged my eyes away from hers and looked at the water slapping the rocks. I shook my head.

"No," I admitted.

"Then what?"

"I just thought—"

"Well, think again, Frankie. Because I have no interest in any of that. I will wait for you as long as it takes."

My spirits lifted with her words, despite myself.

"Are you sure?"

"I've never been more certain of anything in my life." Magda searched my eyes and laughed mischievously. "Besides, I know what you're up to, Frank Mederos. And you aren't getting away with it."

"What might that be?" I asked, amused at her enthusiasm.

"You're trying to do what's best for me."

I took her hand in mine. Her palms were warm, almost sweaty.

"Is that such a bad thing?"

"No, it's not a bad thing. But I'm not a child, Frankie. I know perfectly well what's best for me."

"And what's that, Magda?"

Magda poked me playfully in the stomach. "In case you haven't figured that out yet, what's best for me is you."

I laughed. "But Magda—"

"Shush, Frankie. You once made me promise that I would never doubt your love."

She held up the ring on her finger for me to see. I nodded, knowing exactly what she meant. "Now it's time for you to promise that you will never doubt *my* love." I chuckled and slapped my leg, delighted at this pronouncement.

"Okay."

"Say it."

"I will never doubt your love."

"C'mon, say the rest of it. No matter—"

"No matter where we are, no matter what we do, no matter what happens in the future, I will never doubt your love."

"Promise?"

"Of course, I promise," I said, laughing.

We stood and embraced tenderly before I kissed Magda long and hard on the lips. She parted her lips and my tongue met hers. My arms encircled her waist, and I felt her breasts pressed against my chest. The instant I felt them I became aroused. I longed to reach up and feel them, to cup them in my hands.

My need for Magda was almost overwhelming, but I knew we had to wait for marriage to consummate our relationship. Our culture, our religion, and our families would never allow otherwise. Still, it did nothing to stifle desire.

I pulled back and looked at Magda. I felt the length of her body against mine, thinking about the days when all I wanted to do was to touch her hand.

CHAPTER 17

On the morning of my departure for the army, just before dawn purpled and pinked the horizon, Magda's parents arrived at my house. They had promised to drive me to Havana, and I was looking forward to holding Magda's hand while we rode in the commodious back seat of her father's black Buick.

I embraced my mother for a long time before leaving, knowing how difficult it was for her to let me go. She looked very vulnerable in her pink slippers and her white cotton bathrobe with the big plastic buttons.

Her eyes were red and puffy and her hair was tangled from sleep. A bobby pin clipped a tightly wound curl on the side of her face. I assured her that I would take care of myself and would come home as soon as I could. She nodded, sniffled, and put on a brave face. Mima didn't deserve any of this and my heart went out to her. My father put his arm around her shoulder as she waved goodbye.

Hundreds of boys were milling around Havana's sports arena when we arrived. This modern, round building had been the talk of the town when it was first erected. For years it had been the center for Cuban sporting events, concerts, and celebrations.

After Fidel came to power, it was used as the site for the series of public "purge trials" that resulted in hundreds of executions of *Batistiano* "henchmen."

It was here that bloodthirsty crowds shouted "to the execution wall" and where foreign journalists began writing about "a blood bath" in Cuba. It was not lost on us that it was now being used as a place to press young men into military service.

I waited for hours for my paperwork to be processed. Around noon, I was trucked to Rancho Boyeros, a boot camp located not far from the airport. It was a sea of army tents with thirty to forty boys assigned to each one.

Loudspeakers were positioned in front of each tent and hung on poles situated every few feet around the camp's perimeter. The speakers blasted a speech by Raúl Castro about the importance of military service. His voice sounded almost effeminate.

His speech alternated with a deafening rendition of "The Internationale," complete with orchestra. The tape was set on a continuous loop that played day and night. I tried plugging my ears with cotton and placing a pillow over my head to drown out the sound, but without success. There was no way to escape it.

We lined up to swear an oath to the flag of Cuba and to sign a formal declaration never to disclose any information regarding Cuba's military operations or intelligence. The consequence of doing so was certain death.

We stripped to our underwear for a medical exam. The doctors checked our height and weight, our eyes and feet, our blood pressure and teeth. The sergeants shaved our heads, leaving hunks of black hair on the rough cement floor. Then we lined up at various stations to receive our clothes, gear, and tent assignments.

Boot camp was brutal, a steady stream of physical, verbal, and emotional assaults. The training was designed to break our spirits—and for many it did. The first day we ran for two straight hours and then did calisthenics. Then we ran again. And again. And again.

We jumped fences, scaled walls, and climbed ladders. We did hundreds of push-ups, sit-ups, and chin-ups. We broiled in the sun, jogged in the rain, and crawled in the mud. Many boys sobbed and vomited—or dropped from exhaustion. The sergeants punched and kicked us, called us names, spat in our faces. We received no time off and were forbidden to communicate with family and friends—no mail, no visits, no phone calls. The outside world ceased to exist.

At night, when I climbed into my bunk, I was almost too exhausted to think of Magda. Almost.

Thirty days later, an unfamiliar man appeared at camp. He was tall and lean with shrewd eyes and finely wrought features. He exuded an air of confidence born of competence. He looked like a man who would brook no nonsense, a man who was used to getting his way. I wondered what lay beneath his calm exterior.

Unlike the unit commanders, he was smartly dressed. His clothes were clean and well tailored, his shirt ironed, his shoes shined, his pants well pressed. There was something about the way he spoke, the way he moved, that I thought suggested years of study, perhaps abroad.

The unit commander introduced him to the troops as Lieutenant Pino—the first names of officers were never revealed to us. Several lieutenants accompanied him on his rounds. The commander paid him great deference.

Unit commanders had strong personal ties to Fidel. These were loyal supporters who had stayed with the rebel leader when he was fighting Batista from his camp in the Sierra Maestra. But they were mostly illiterates with little or no formal education. Their years in the hills made them well suited for their job: to command the sergeants and corporals, to show off their muscle, and to instill fear and discipline into the troops. But Pino was a man of a higher rank, a man of a different stripe.

The lieutenant made his way from tent to tent, questioning the sergeant major who provided him with the names of three or four boys from each location. The lieutenant busily reviewed charts and took notes. I wondered what all the fuss was about.

•   •   •

The next morning I learned I was among thirty-three young men who'd been selected for a special military assignment. We were chosen from the larger group of four hundred because of our academic stature and our contributions to the revolution. We did not know the nature of our mission.

All the selectees were either in their last two years of high school or their first two years of college. With so many illiterates and so many school dropouts in Cuba, the army was hard pressed to find soldiers with more than a grammar school education. I was chosen because I was an eleventh grader who had served in the literacy brigade, had attended a government-run school, and had spent three summers helping poor farmers to harvest their crops.

No mention was made of my escape from the Tarara School or my dealings with Antonio. I had to assume these things had not been noted in my record or had been overlooked due to my other qualifications. I wondered whether Lieutenant Pino had investigated my background—perhaps he had made a mistake. I tried not to think about it.

The following day the sergeant major announced that Manny Cadiz, "Lazo" Lazaro, and I had been assigned to a military base in Santa Maria, a town located on the outskirts of Guanabacoa. I knew these soldiers from our time at boot camp, but only slightly.

Lazo was a well-educated, sophisticated mulatto from Guanabacoa—tall, handsome, and crazy about his girlfriend. He was a well-muscled sportsman who used his cultured voice to teach me about classical music.

Manny was just the opposite. A brilliant young man from Regla, he could figure out the most difficult theoretical problems. He was an abstract thinker and a whiz at math, which greatly impressed Lieutenant Pino.

A high school junior, he was also frail and sickly. Although he was very good with his hands, he had difficulty doing anything physical. He didn't have a girlfriend and, as far as I could see, had little prospect of getting one. I was amazed he had survived boot camp.

Although this base was less than ten miles from my home, I had had no idea it existed. It was located on approximately seventy-five acres and screened by heavy foliage. Fidel had ordered this facility— and others like it—to be built in densely populated areas to protect it from bombing by the Americans. He figured they would not dare bomb a camp in an area with a high civilian population.

The camp housed ten barracks. It had paved roads and parking lots, housing facilities, and a state-of-the-art command center. A columned rotunda with the feel of an old Spanish mansion served as the officers' quarters. A large obstacle course occupied the center of the facility and guards regularly patrolled the perimeter. "Do Not Enter" signs were ubiquitous.

Manny, Lazo, and I looked at each other, astonished. It was clear this was a highly classified operation, and we would be required to do something important. But we had no idea what. We showered and were issued starched, pressed uniforms. We never looked so good.

Around one p.m. Lieutenant Pino introduced himself to the group in a polished, eloquent voice. He informed us that he was the political commissioner, and explained that he would be very active in the political life of the unit.

After welcoming us to the base, he told us that we had been hand-picked to join one of the most prestigious military units in all of Cuba's Revolutionary Armed Forces: the Elite Counterattack Force. We were about to become the most highly trained and skilled military personnel in Cuba. The soldiers' voices buzzed with excitement.

The lieutenant told us that their military intelligence indicated that it was likely that the United States would invade Cuba the way it had invaded Vietnam. With the help of the Russians, a careful plan had been drawn up for the country's defense. Our job was to protect Havana, the nation's capital, against an American attack at the city's six most vulnerable points. We would undergo a long and difficult training process and, for the sake of our country, we must give it our all.

The lieutenant apologized to us for the brutality of boot camp, but said it was necessary to instill discipline into the troops. Then he did something surprising. He told us we would be immediately issued our six-pesos-per-month military allotment and given a seventy-two-hour leave. We were elated.

We were trucked to the outskirts of the base, and I grabbed a bus home from there. My first priority was to see Magda. As I walked down her street, one of her neighbors approached me, telling me how lonely Magda had been and how much she had missed me. The middle-aged woman accompanied me to my girlfriend's house and stood beside me when I knocked on the door. Magda was home alone, wearing a white eyelet blouse, a delicate gold cross, and a red satin ribbon that tied back her hair. She was so surprised to see me she broke down in tears.

"I can hardly believe my eyes. Is it really you?"

She was literally jumping for joy. I took her hand in mine and noticed she was still wearing the ring I had given her. I wanted to hug her but was hesitant to do so in front of her neighbor. Finally, the woman said, "Go ahead, young man, and give your lady a proper kiss."

After I kissed Magda for a while, she said, "I didn't mean for it to go on *that* long. I can't be responsible for this." We all laughed merrily.

CHAPTER 18

During the Missile Crisis of 1962, all nuclear weapons had been removed from Cuba. The country now relied on high-caliber 57-millimeter cannons and Anti-Tank Guided Missiles (ATGMs) for defense. This expensive, high-tech equipment was supplied by the Russians and housed in top-secret locations in each of Cuba's six provinces. As part of the Elite Counterattack Force, we were told we would be trained on this equipment—and we must die to protect it.

Captain Martinez commanded the operation in Santa Maria. He made all military decisions up to the point where they became strategic and political. Then he relinquished control to Lieutenant Pino, giving the lieutenant considerable power. Pino was very knowledgeable about political issues in Cuba and in other countries. But he had limited knowledge of military operations and tactics. That was the purview of Lieutenant Brown.

During our first few days of service, we were assigned to a unit and issued an instruction manual on military rules and regulations, the proper way to address officers, and so forth.

There were two barracks of infantry, a brigade of one hundred seventy-five troops who guarded territory up to a mile from our position. They served as the first line of defense against the enemy.

Serving as the second line of defense were four batteries of 57-millimeter cannons that could shoot down low-flying aircraft. They consisted of units of sixty men each.

The most important, expensive, and lethal weapons were the ATGMs, which cost upward of one million dollars each and could hit targets two miles out—ships, aircraft, helicopters, tanks—just about anything the enemy could throw at us short of a nuclear bomb.

The ATGMs required a driver, a trained operator to fire the rockets, and personnel to supply food, ammunition, and other support services. Manny, Lazo, and I were to be trained as ATGM operators.

Lieutenant Brown, a black Haitian graduate of the Military Academy of Cuba, was in charge of our thirty-man unit, which included fourteen ATGM drivers, fourteen ATGM operators, and two support personnel. The lieutenant was an excellent instructor, hell-bent on turning us into superb "killing machines." He drilled us early, often, and relentlessly. The word "failure" never parted his lips.

Our focus was defeating the American marines, the finest fighters in the history of man. The good lieutenant taught us to anticipate and overcome any move a marine might make by engaging in hand-to-hand combat with other platoons. We practiced how to kill with a kick, a punch, or a knife to the throat. We mastered how to snuff out life with our own bare hands.

We were instructed on how to track the enemy by studying footprints, the lay of the grass, and the breakage of twigs. We became expert in escape tactics in case we were captured by the Americans. We studied the best practices of other armies. "Learn this or die," was the lieutenant's constant refrain.

Brown also oversaw the daily rigors of the obstacle course, draining us of our last ounce of energy. Navigating the course was easier for me than for some other men because so many exercises were similar to things I had done as a kid.

Climbing rope ladders was akin to scaling mango and banana trees. Maintaining balance required the same skills as skipping from rock to rock on the *Rio Lajas*.

Long marches were similar to climbing the hills of the Sierra

Maestra. My muscles were already well developed from lifting weights with Gilbert and my other cousins, which made the course easier to complete.

Brown watched my every move, liked what he saw, and used me as an example for others to emulate. He soon made me leader of the platoon.

Every morning, Pino—or one of his four minions—provided us with political instruction and indoctrination. Those with any issues regarding their personal or army life were individually counseled.

We were all required to read the daily newspapers, including the Cuban and foreign press. We were taught about economic and social problems in the United States, about injustices inherent in the capitalist system, and about the suffering the American Negroes experienced under segregation. We were repeatedly told that Cubans enjoyed more equality and freedoms than people living in Europe and the United States.

Current events in Russia, China, and Vietnam were dissected and discussed at length. Occasionally, a consultant from Vietnam instructed us on military tactics the Americans had employed in his country— and how to combat them.

We saw films of burned-out villages, napalmed children, and other atrocities perpetrated by the Americans on the Vietnamese. I found them fascinating, but I was also very aware that they were propaganda tools to gain more support for Fidel.

With the help of a translator, a Russian commander named Mikhail trained the operators on various aspects of the equipment— how to fix our target in the crosshairs, how to operate the radio at frequencies that wouldn't be intercepted by the enemy, and how to use the joystick to launch the three 150-pound rockets that sat atop each tank.

We learned to make the complex calculations required to determine the rockets' trajectory and the amount of time needed to hit both stationary and moving targets under normal and extreme weather conditions.

To keep information from falling into enemy hands, we were required to memorize all military procedures. For security purposes, no instruction manual existed.

All our training so far had been theoretical, simulated. No one had yet seen the ATGMs. Naturally, we wondered where they were. Many thought we would be transferred to another facility when it came time to engage in live operations.

Meanwhile, we were being carefully watched to make sure no mistake had been made in our selection for this critical work. In addition to our loyalty to the communist cause, we were being judged on our physical prowess, our reaction under fire, our technical proficiency, and our ability to learn and to survive. Anyone giving any hint of not fully subscribing to the Party line soon disappeared, never to be seen or heard from again.

We worked for six months before we learned that the rockets were hidden in a bunker right in our own camp—smack under our noses.

I was ordered not to discuss our assignment with anyone. Nor did I. Not with my parents, not with Magda, not with Abuelo. I did tell Gilbert and Jabao that I was working with very dangerous weapons, but that was all I said.

My grandfather did not want to know what I was doing and advised me to keep my own counsel. He was horrified that I was even in the army, and a communist army at that. He thought it was the worst thing that could have ever happened to me. One day when we were sitting in his living room sipping coffee, he said, "You are a pawn on the chessboard of freedom, Frankie. Make no mistake about it."

"What do you mean?" Whenever Abuelo talked like this I paid careful attention.

"Fidel is taunting the Americans with this military build-up. He's saying we have Russian military equipment and support, so come and get us. The man is a born bully, and he's playing the Americans like a fiddle. But don't underestimate the Yanks. They're on the side of freedom—always have been. They won't let us down."

"What do you think will happen?"

"Sooner or later the Americans will invade Cuba again. They can't let the Bay of Pigs stand. It was a big embarrassment."

"So they'll invade Cuba to save face?"

"It's bigger than that. America can't allow a communist nation to remain on their doorstep. They're afraid communism will spread like a virus through the entire continent."

"When do you think they'll invade?" This talk was making me nervous.

"I have no idea, Frankie. And neither does anyone else. But if they do invade, you will have three options: to take the side of the Americans, to fight the Americans, or to flee Cuba. You will have to choose between losing your life to the Communists by refusing to fight the Americans, or fighting the Americans, the very people who have come to liberate your country."

"Those are my options?"

"Or you can try to figure out a way to leave your family, friends, and country behind."

"Not great choices."

"They're terrible choices, Frankie. But you need to think long and hard about them because that's what it's likely to come down to."

CHAPTER 19

Despite all their drilling, training, films, and propaganda, the army was failing to turn me into a Communist. I felt very alone in my convictions and wondered if anyone in my unit shared my views. I couldn't imagine that everyone else was a Communist, but the problem was to figure out who was—and who wasn't—without drawing attention to oneself.

It was far too dangerous to openly voice anticommunist sentiments. We could face torture or an execution squad if we did. But occasionally, if you paid close attention, a soldier might provide subtle clues regarding his political views.

I had suspected that Manny was religious and might not be sympathetic to the communist cause. When he first came to boot camp, I thought I glimpsed the cord of a brown scapular around his neck. But the next day it was gone, and I began to wonder whether I had even seen it.

While marching with Manny one day, I complimented him on how well he could handle a knife. He lowered his voice and said, "Thanks, but I'm not sure I could slit anyone's throat if it really came down to it." My eyes widened in surprise. I smiled and nodded, knowing full well what he was saying.

On Good Friday, a day Catholics were forbidden to eat meat under the threat of mortal sin, Brown got us up before dawn and took us on a long march. He worked us very hard that day, harder than ever before. We had missed eating both breakfast and lunch. By late afternoon, we were all tired and hungry, but poor Manny looked like he was about to faint. To make matters worse, we had not been given a scrap of meat to eat for weeks.

That night we were served a big, juicy steak for dinner. Nothing else. No potatoes, no vegetables, no bread. Just steak. I looked at the tantalizing slab of meat sitting like a solitary diamond on my plate. Pino was watching me intently. I made an instant decision, firmly believing the Good Lord would not punish me for what I was about to do.

I stared back at the lieutenant, picked up my fork, shoveled a big slice of sirloin into my mouth, chewed it thoroughly, and swallowed it with a gulp. I took a few sips of water to wash it down. The lieutenant nodded his approval and looked straight at Manny, who was toying with his meat.

"Mederos, what's going on there?" he barked. "I don't see Cadiz eating his steak."

Manny looked up with alarm.

"Nothing's going on, sir. Everything's under control."

Pino nodded. Manny severed his steak from the bone, sliced off the fat, and forked a bite into his mouth. As soon as the lieutenant walked away, he spat the steak into his napkin, placed his napkin on his lap, deftly dropped his plated steak into it, and slipped the bundle neatly into his pocket, all the while chewing a phantom piece of steak for everyone to see.

I watched in amazement at the rapidity and dexterity of his move. Had I not been staring intently, I never would have seen it. There was more to Manny than met the eye.

By now our military training had become both more rote and more sophisticated. We had performed our routine exercises so often they were becoming second nature. We also had the benefit of Russian, Vietnamese, and Czechoslovakian technical experts instructing us on advanced skills needed to shoot down American helicopters, blast vessels far out at sea, and conduct various nighttime maneuvers that required a complex set of skills.

After dinner we were allowed an hour of socialization with our fellow soldiers. We got to know each other slowly, carefully, reluctant to reveal anything that could be ever held against us. At first we discussed baseball: the batting averages of men playing for the Chicago White Sox, the New York Yankees, the Detroit Tigers. We talked about Joe DiMaggio as if he lived next door. Occasionally, one of the officers allowed us to listen to part of a game on the radio or simply updated us on the score.

It was weeks before we talked about girlfriends, mothers, fathers, siblings. It was weeks more before we opened our wallets to reveal snapshots of those we held dear. I carried a picture of Magda dressed in her Sunday best. Standing next to Estel, she wore a beguiling smile, white cotton gloves, and a straw hat with a grosgrain ribbon cascading like a waterfall down her back.

The picture was dog-eared and wrinkled because I had held it so often. But I never showed it around, thinking it would be disrespectful to Magda. She was no passing fancy, and I was afraid that that's how she'd be viewed. I wanted to keep our relationship private.

As I became friendlier with Lieutenant Brown, however, I revealed the nature of my feelings toward *mi novia* to him. Being older, he seemed to understand. He often inquired after her and occasionally granted me permission to go into town to call her from a public phone.

Every Friday was court day, the day it was decided whether your performance warranted any demerits. Demerits were issued for dirty boots, forgetting to salute, failure to keep your quarters clean, etcetera. A soldier's monthly leave could be cancelled or reduced by days—or hours—depending on the severity of the offense. I was sure to mind my business so I'd be able to see Magda and my family. And, while Brown might berate me for infractions, he seldom kept me from leave.

One evening Manny, Lazo, and I were talking about him over a game of hearts.

"That guy's a good instructor," I said, sorting my cards. "He drives us hard, but he seems to care."

Lazo lead with the deuce of clubs. "Yeah, I've learned to do things I never would've believed possible."

"Is that good or bad?"

Lazo laughed. "It depends on how tired I am."

We played out the trick, and Manny took it with the ace of clubs. He breasted his cards and squared the trick. "The good thing is he lets me slide on doing chin-ups." He hesitated a moment. "Of course, you don't have to be a genius to know I can't do very many." We all laughed.

"He's no dummy," I said. "He does it because you're a whiz at firing rockets—better than any of us." Manny smiled shyly at the compliment.

"Thanks," he said.

We sat in silence for a moment while Manny lead a low spade. He was trying to flush out the queen, which I held in my hand. I took a sip of coffee and tapped my fingers on the table. There was a moment of silence while I appeared to ponder what card to play. I fingered my cards and followed suit with the ten.

"I can't figure out why he hasn't been promoted to captain," said Lazo.

"Good question," said Manny. He lit a cigarette and dropped the match into a metal ashtray. "Pino respects him, that's clear."

"It's probably just a matter of time," said Lazo. We all nodded. I glanced at my watch to see that our recreation time was over. I had managed to escape without playing the queen of spades on my own trick. I gathered the cards and slipped the deck back into its cardboard box.

* * *

While my life at the base was evolving nicely, life in Guanabacoa was devolving into chaos. The combined effect of high unemployment, low productivity, and the American blockade were staggering. You just had to walk out your door to see the results.

Every month an estimated seven thousand motor vehicles broke down for lack of spare parts. Streets were littered with abandoned cars that sat on the curbs like roadkill. People waited in vain for inoperable buses and rail cars no longer in service.

The government handed out scarce consumer goods at distribution centers with no thought given to consumer needs. Some months there was no toilet paper or soap. Some months shoes were distributed without shoelaces. Some months there was toothpaste but no toothbrushes. Some months the reverse.

One week the government distributed clothing supplied by the Soviets. Boys between the ages of ten and fourteen were issued one pair of pants, one shirt, and one pair of shoes. The next day the boys all showed up at the park wearing the same thing: red shirts, black pants, and black shoes. We dubbed them the "ladybug brigade."

Food was also in short supply. My father now had a *libreta*—a ration card—and a number—ninety-four—that he used when he went to the distribution center to pick up our family's two-week allotment of food. One day he took me with him. I was appalled. My father waited for hours in an endless line before his number was called. Everyone was cranky and irritable, just wanting to get their goods and go home.

"Number ninety-four," the food distributor screamed. This infuriated my father since he had known Roberto for years. He lived down the street and he knew Pipo's name full well. My father was a proud man, and it sawed on his nerves to be reduced to a number.

"You get one pound of rice, one pound of flour, one bag of tea, and a half cup of sugar," said Roberto. "Do you have twenty-five pesos for payment?"

"What about beef? Or beans?" asked my father. "My family hasn't had protein for months."

Roberto glared at him. "Stop grousing, number ninety-four, or I'll write you up for counterrevolutionary leanings."

"I'm no counterrevolutionary, Roberto. I just want some beef."

Roberto smirked. "Are you unhappy with the revolution, number ninety-four? Are you unwilling to sacrifice for a better life for everyone?" My father's back stiffened.

"Right now, I'd just like a better life for my family." Pipo fixed him with a baleful gaze. Roberto extracted a cigarette from his pack of Populares, lit it, and dropped the match on the grungy floor. He inhaled deeply and blew the smoke in my father's face.

My father's lips flattened into a thin angry line while Roberto called several other food distributors to his side to confer. They huddled and whispered among themselves. When they emerged, Roberto scribbled something on my father's chart. My stomach turned to gelatin. Roberto looked at my father with eyes of a zealot.

"No beef and no beans," he grunted. Roberto handed my father his groceries before saying, "You'd better watch yourself, number ninety-four or I'll have you tracked as a troublemaker. Then you can tell your problems to the warden in jail."

My father crossed his arms and worked to steady his emotions. A line of perspiration dewed his forehead. He mumbled something under his breath. He was struggling to contain his frustrations until he got home. But I knew he would. He had seen less circumspect men handcuffed and tossed like sacks of flour into the backs of trucks by Fidel's secret police. And he was too much of a survivor to allow that to happen to him.

But the experience helped me understand why the black market was thriving. Even the threat of five years of hard labor could not deter some people from avoiding the distribution centers to buy what they needed.

•   •   •

The economy was now so bad that Fidel was sending young girls to the mountains to pick coffee. With no one to protect them, they were often molested, raped, and abused. When they left their homes, they were innocent señoritas. When they returned, they were hardened, coarse women, wearing torn, dirty clothes, and using language fit for the gutter. Scorned by society and often rejected by their families, some turned to prostitution to eke out a living.

I watched all these developments every month when I was on leave. While peddling my bike through the neighborhoods of Havana, I'd endure hateful stares from lines of people waiting for bread, for soup, for fuel. People I'd known for my entire life regarded me with disdain. I was a soldier. I wore a uniform. I was one of *them*.

Whenever I went home, I'd go for a walk with Abuelo. We were routinely stopped by the CDRs whenever we stepped out the door. I asked my grandfather how often that happened. "Every day, every day," he said, biting back his bitterness.

We discussed Marxist philosophy, the Bolshevik and Cultural Revolutions, and the economic problems in the Soviet Union. One day the idea of a classless society came up in the course of discussion. Abuelo scoffed at the notion.

"The Communists talk a good game," he said, "but I don't see them living it."

"What do you mean?"

"I see Party officials driving fancy cars and living in beautiful homes, while the rest of us try to scrape up enough to eat. That doesn't sound like a classless society to me."

I shook my head. "But that's what they're teaching us in the army."

"Make no mistake about it, Frankie, communism equals wealth if you are selling it and poverty if you're buying it."

"So you think the idea of a classless society is—?"

"Pure poppycock. It's against human nature." As if to add emphasis, Abuelo kicked an empty tin can down the street. It rattled, echoing its hollowness.

"So you don't think Cuba is a classless society?"

"Not only that, I don't think such a thing is possible. We'll always have different classes. That's how people are wired. Humans are social creatures, and we rank ourselves according to who's smarter, richer, more talented, more beautiful. Even the animals have a pecking order."

I thought about this for a while.

CHAPTER 20

My relationship with Magda and her family was growing closer every time I came home. I had always enjoyed her mother's company, her keen sense of humor, and her ability to put me at ease. Now I was enjoying the company of her father.

Since the night I asked permission to visit Magda at home, Señor Hernández and I had developed a relationship as close as father and son. He had even asked me to call him Sergio. A warm, generous man who was eager to please his daughter, he readily gave me permission to take Magda to social events, dances, and parties.

One weekend I fixed Manny up with Magda's cousin, Carmen. Manny was thrilled, even if Carmen wasn't. Carmen tolerated Manny's company on several occasions, and Manny was grateful that I had arranged for him to see her. After every date, Manny would ask me what Carmen had said about him. I hated to hurt his feelings by telling him the truth.

Whenever I came home on leave and Magda was home alone, I'd tell her I'd have to come back later—when her parents returned. I respected her, and I didn't want to tarnish her reputation—a fact not lost on her father.

On warm summer days, Sergio allowed me to take Magda to the beach. We usually hung out with my cousins and friends—sometimes with Lazo and Manny—swimming, chasing the waves, and playing volleyball in the sand. Afterward, Magda and I would lay on the beach blanket together, my arm draped around her waist, our legs touching, our feet entwined. Sometimes I'd read a novel to her while she closed her eyes and covered her face with a hat. Occasionally, I'd rub her back with suntan lotion, my fingers lingering longer than necessary on her soft, supple skin.

The first time I saw Magda in a bathing suit, I could hardly breathe. Her skin was a toasty brown and as taut and as smooth as ripe mangoes. The suit was two shades of pink with a V-neck that revealed the top of her breasts. I thought about how she looked in that suit for weeks.

Sometimes I'd playfully chase Magda around the beach. We'd run back and forth, kicking up sand before splashing into the gently cresting waves. I would hold her against me, her body supported by the water, her legs wrapped around my waist and her cheek pillowed snugly into my shoulder. She would lean back and float, her back arched, her long black hair gently moving with the rhythm of the water and her legs firmly gripping my buttocks. Those were the times when I was most tempted not to return to base.

When we got back to Magda's house, we would shower and change into dry clothes before the Hernándezes would serve us dinner. After dinner we'd stay up late talking about the situation in Cuba, the fate of the Church, and the role of the Party.

On Sunday nights, we often went to Havana to dine with Magda's Aunt Sophia and Uncle Rigo. They lived in a large brick home with a wrought iron fence located in a lovely section of Havana. Stone fountains misted the bougainvillea and other tropical plants that bloomed in their garden, and large paddle fans cooled their tiled floors. Ever gracious hosts, they welcomed guests to their home with the fragrance of roses and lemon oil and the promise of coconut shrimp and generous *Cuba libres*.

Sophia was a lively, vivacious conversationalist, never reluctant to express her opinions on education, politics, and sports. An elegant woman, she liked to dress in long graceful skirts with blouses trimmed in lace. Her fingernails were always manicured and polished a bright red and her feet were usually cosseted in fine leather sandals.

Her husband, Magda's Uncle Rigo, was a warm, welcoming man. He was less talkative than his wife, and tended to get flustered and nervous. Still, as a successful business owner, he frequently voiced his disdain for Fidel, at least among family members.

Rigo, Jr., was friendly, polite and respectful. He looked up to me like a big brother. We listened to music together, discussed The Beatles, and talked about baseball. Occasionally, I'd take him to the park. He had the open, curious, and engaging manner of a thirteen-year-old boy who was pampered and adored by his parents.

He and his cousin, Sergio, Jr., liked to question me about my life in the army. They were very curious about what I did and how I did it, and I told them what little I could. Sergio was a year younger than Rigo and both sets of parents lived in fear that their sons would be drafted.

On Sunday nights Sergio would drive me back to the army base so Magda and I could spend an extra hour with each other. It was a gracious gesture that Magda and I appreciated.

I looked forward to our rides in the car. It was one of the few occasions during the weekend when Magda and I got some privacy. We would snuggle in the backseat and exchange an occasional kiss when we thought Magda's father wasn't looking. I'm sure Sergio knew what was going on, but he was too polite to notice. It was so wonderful to feel the warmth of Magda's body next to mine, to bury my nose in her hair, and to dream of the day when I could make her my wife.

In early 1965, Pino was sitting in the front of the class next to a portrait of Che Guevara. The Cuban flag hung to his left and Brown was seated to his right. He began to lecture us on how poorly minorities were treated in the United States.

He berated Americans for relegating Negroes to the lower class and for making them attend segregated schools, ride on segregated buses, and drink from segregated water fountains. He had shown us pictures of the "Coloreds Only" signs posted on public restrooms in

America's southern states and used this as an example of the problems inherent in the American way of life.

"In Cuba everyone goes to the same schools, we ride the same buses, we all have the same opportunities. There are no classes in Cuba. We live in a classless society." He said this as a matter of fact and it irked me. I squirmed a little in my seat.

Pino looked directly at me and said, "Mederos, Fidel says it is the duty of every revolutionary to make revolution. Having lived in a classless society in Cuba, would you become a revolutionary to fight segregation if you lived in America?"

I don't know what possessed me. I just couldn't stifle my views one minute longer. I hesitated only a second before saying, "I agree that the Negroes are not treated fairly in the United States, but I don't agree that there are no class differences in Cuba."

Lieutenant Brown sucked in his breath and shot me a withering stare, while Pino looked totally baffled. All eyes were suddenly upon me. Alfredo, a fellow ATGM operator, kicked me under the desk in warning.

"Would you care to elaborate on your statement, Mederos?" Pino's eyes were spearing me like swords, making me feel even more belligerent.

"Well," I said, warming to the subject, "if everyone is treated the same in Cuba and everyone is so happy, why have a million Cubans left the country? And why have two hundred thousand more Cubans been sent to jail for trying to leave?"

The class grew deathly quiet, knowing full well that I had overstepped my bounds.

Pino tightened his lips and glanced around the room, looking for someone to call on. He was silently challenging anyone to come to my defense.

"Lazo, would you like to answer the question posed by your friend here?"

Lazo looked up, startled. He was none too happy about being put in this position. I watched him carefully. His face froze for a moment while he thought about what to say.

He straightened up and said, "I can't answer your question because what Mederos says is true. A million Cubans have left this country and a whole bunch of nice people are now rotting in jail."

Pino looked unruffled, like he was chastising unruly boys. But despite his cool exterior, I knew he was rattled by our remarks. It was unheard of for a soldier, especially a member of the force, to publicly disagree with a tenet of the Party. A thin line of perspiration erupted at his hairline.

"You are mistaken, Lazo, in calling these people Cubans. We don't consider those who have left this country to be Cubans. They are worms, subversives, enemies of the revolution."

Lazo shot the lieutenant a challenging look. Pino turned to Manny.

"What do you have to say about this, Cadiz?"

Manny stood tall, squaring his shoulders. He had grown much less timid since he had joined the force. I think the physical training had given him a newfound confidence. He looked at Pino and said, "I don't understand, sir. If they were Cubans before they left the country, why aren't they Cubans now?"

Pino wrinkled his nose. The class had grown so quiet you could hear the leaves rustle in the trees outside the window. Somewhere nearby a bird trilled a mating call. The lieutenant squinted as if trying to bring the conversation into focus. He shook his head.

"We don't need to go into that subject right now," he said. He glanced at the class. "What you must understand is that we do not consider anyone who has left the country to be a Cuban citizen. Nor do we consider anyone in jail to be Cuban. These people are our enemies. They are scum, parasites, worms." His voice rose an octave and he repeated the word worms. "Do you understand?"

Lazo, Manny, and I nodded and sat back in our chairs. When class was finished, Pino demanded to see the three of us in his office. A coil of fear gripped my throat. We marched in together, saluted, and looked straight ahead. Manny was breathing heavily. I wondered whether his asthma was acting up.

"What is wrong with you men? You seem confused," said Pino. He walked back and forth in front of us, seething. "You must be talking to worms when you go home on leave because only worms could have filled your heads with such poison. I want you to give me a list of everyone you speak to about politics when you are on leave." He looked me square in the eyes.

"I don't speak to anyone," I said. There was no way I was about to give him Abuelo's name—no matter what the consequences.

"Are you telling me you speak to no one? Not to your father? Your uncles? Your friends?"

"I don't talk to anyone," I insisted. I was afraid I didn't sound too convincing. Lying was not something that came naturally to me. But despite my Catholic upbringing, I knew I'd have to get a lot better at it to survive.

"You must be talking to someone. Where else could you get such radical ideas?"

"With all due respect, sir," I said, "José Martí said it's the first duty of each man to think for himself. That's what I do—I think for myself." The lieutenant closed his eyes for a moment. He was aggravated at my response and quite unconvinced. He turned to Lazo.

"What about you, soldier? Has your friend here been filling your head with poison? Or has it been someone else?"

"No sir. I also think for myself."

Pino crossed his arms in front of his chest, signaling his contempt.

"What have you to say, Perez?"

"The same thing, sir. My ideas are my own—nobody else's."

"Mederos, you know that Cuba is the finest country in the world, do you not?"

"Yes, sir."

"You know you owe total allegiance to the Revolutionary Armed Forces, do you not?"

"Yes, sir."

"And you know you must defend Cuba with your last ounce of energy, do you not?"

"Yes, sir."

Pino sat down in his chair and leaned back, tapping his fingers. His eyes shone with anger and impatience. Lines of frustration bracketed his mouth. He sat quietly observing us for a moment while we stared straight ahead.

After what seemed like an eternity, he leaned forward and said, "I can see I'm not going to get anything out of you men right now. But I'm telling you for your own good that this kind of thinking—this kind of behavior—will not be tolerated from any member of the special forces. You have sworn allegiance to the revolution. You have signed a statement to that effect. This is a very serious matter. Do you understand?"

"Yes, sir."

Pino looked at me and saluted. "*Patria o Muerte!*"—Fatherland or Death!"

I saluted and repeated, "*Patria o Muerte!*"

Pino dismissed us, saying, "Consider this a warning, men. I never want to hear this kind of talk from any of you again. You are not to discuss these topics with each other, not with the other troops, not with anyone. Am I making myself perfectly clear?"

Lazo, Manny, and I said, "Yes, sir" in unison. I caught the look on Manny's face out of the corner of my eye. He was resolute, not sorry. Lazo looked perturbed. I wasn't sure whether he was angry at me, at Pino, or at the whole situation.

We saluted and marched out the door. The lieutenant sighed heavily as we walked away. I wondered whether he thought he had made a mistake in selecting us to join the force.

CHAPTER 21

When we got back to the barracks, my fellow ATGM operators be-rated me for my behavior. And even though Lazo took part in our little fiasco, he was mad as a hatter. He knew the stakes involved, and he thought I was taking unnecessary risks.

"What's wrong with you, Mederos? Have you lost your mind? Why did you have to antagonize him?"

"I just couldn't take it anymore," I said. "Whatever happened to freedom? I'm sick and tired of swallowing my beliefs. Sometimes you just have to speak up."

Lazo glared at me. "Well, speak up to me if you have to, but don't speak up to him. I thought I was going to fall off my seat when you said what you did. Just watch your mouth from now on, will you?"

"All right," I said, peeved at his reprimand. "But I could've gone it alone. You didn't have to defend me."

"I wasn't going to leave you hanging like clothes on a line. Of course, I was going to defend you. But it doesn't mean I liked it."

Lazo thought for a moment. It was obvious from his expression that the thought didn't agree with him. "Christ, they throw people in jail for twenty years for doing nothing. We could get forty for what we just did. Pino could have us in front of a military tribunal tomorrow."

I considered for a moment, weighing the merits of his argument. He was right. It was a rash move, one that could've landed us in a heap of trouble. "I know," I said.

Lazo sat down on his bunk and began removing his shoes. He

lined them up together on the floor. The bed creaked beneath him. "I backed you up this time," he said, "but there's no way I want to be put in that position again. Do you hear?"

"I understand," I said, duly chastened. "And, by the way, thanks for your help."

At three a.m. the following day we were awakened by a piercing siren, warning us of an enemy attack. It was a reconnaissance exercise. We were told that half of the troops had been captured and needed to be "rescued" from the marines. For the first time ever, we got to practice on real equipment.

The infantry was sent on a fifteen-mile march away from the base, while our Russian commander had us work loading and arming the rockets. We were informed of multiple strategic supply bases that had been established in case of an attack, and we were given their names and locations. This was top-secret information, never to be disclosed under any circumstances. We were to guard it with our lives. It made me nervous just knowing about it.

Brown assigned me and the rest of my platoon to rescue two operators and drivers who had been "captured" by the Americans. We'd spent several hours surveying the "enemy's" position when the lieutenant announced he was taking me on a scouting mission—alone.

We marched away from base and circled the "enemy's" position. I was lying on the ground next to the lieutenant when he said in a low, serious voice, "Frankie, I need to talk to you."

I turned to Brown, stunned that he had addressed me by my first name. This was a breach in military command, a gesture of familiarity that would never be tolerated. I looked at him, astonished.

"We need to talk about what you said to Pino." I nodded and lowered my binoculars.

"Your comment made sense, but you can't say things like that. Pino doesn't tolerate dissent. You should know that by now."

"I do," I said, feeling contrite to have put Brown in a difficult position.

"Whatever possessed you?"

I sighed, not wanting to engage in this conversation. I wasn't sure how honest I could be with Brown, but I was still feeling aggravated and was willing to chance it.

"I am just fed up with not being able to say what I think. After a while, I feel like I'm choking on lies."

"You can't say what you think, Frankie. You know that."

I placed the binoculars on the ground and looked the lieutenant in the eyes. "It's sick."

"What's sick?"

"The whole country—Cuba."

"Sick?"

"Yeah, it's sick when you can't speak your mind without being thrown in jail."

Brown sighed. "That's just the way it is, Frankie."

"But it doesn't make it right."

"Right or wrong, speaking your mind is a luxury no one can afford. Least of all a member of the force."

I nodded. "Lazo has already given me hell about it."

"Good. Because a remark like that could cause a lot of trouble—for you, for me, for everybody. You're not just challenging Pino with your words, you're challenging the government. You're saying no to Fidel."

"I understand."

Brown nodded. I could tell he was hoping I really *did* understand.

"We are not playing games here, Frankie. You're playing with fire. It could mean life or death. I'm going out on a limb talking to you about this. I'm doing it because I don't want you to die. Do you understand?"

"Yes, sir."

"It can't happen again. Are we clear?"

"Perfectly clear."

Brown looked at me for a long minute, and then patted me on the back as he moved out of position. I lay for a moment, thinking. I could have my own thoughts and opinions but I dare not voice them. I just wondered whether I would be able to do such a thing for any length of time. It was against my nature.

I thought about what Brown would do in my place. Suddenly it struck me: he was no more of a Communist than I. He had joined the army before Fidel had come to power. He had a job to do. And, like me, he was doing what he needed to survive. That's why he hadn't been promoted to captain.

Two weeks later, Pino lined up the entire platoon against the wall. We were standing at attention, anxious to see what would happen. I had no idea what it was all about. I hadn't said a word about my discussion with Pino to anyone, nor had I spoken of any forbidden topics with my fellow soldiers.

Pino marched up and down in front of us and cleared his throat. "It has come to my attention that certain soldiers in this unit are talking about things they shouldn't. I believe you know what I mean."

I looked at Manny, alarmed. Pino fixed me with a stare that nearly halted my heart.

"What do you have to say about this, men?" The silence was as thick as a baker's waist. You could taste the fear in the air.

"I will ask you again. Can anyone tell me something about this?"

"No, sir," we answered in unison.

Pino folded his hands behind him. "It is my understanding that some soldiers in this unit are questioning the freedoms we enjoy as Cubans. Is that true?"

"No, sir," we repeated. Our voices were loud and clear but many throats were dry with angst.

"Some men are asking why their mothers can't shop where they want. Others are questioning why they have to get permission from the CDRs to travel about. Does this sound familiar?"

It was so silent I could hear the breathing of the man standing next to me.

The lieutenant stopped in front of me. I cringed at the thought of another confrontation. He looked at me with contempt while I combed my brain for anything I might have done to anger him. A lattice of fine red lines etched the whites of Pino's eyes. They were bulging slightly.

"Mederos, have you spread any counterrevolutionary poison lately?"

"No, sir."

"I think you have, Mederos."

I didn't respond. Taking this as a possible admission, Pino moved his face closer to mine. "Are you that stupid—that irresponsible?" I looked at the gathering clouds as the lieutenant inched even closer. "Answer me, Mederos. Answer me. *Now.*"

"I haven't talked to anyone, sir."

"No counterrevolutionary ranting?"

My back stiffened. "No, sir."

Pino regarded me with disdain for a long moment and moved to the next man.

"Gonzales, have you spoken to anyone regarding these matters?"

"No, sir."

"Lazo?"

"No, sir."

"Cadiz?"

"No, sir."

The lieutenant sighed in exasperation. When he got to Alfredo—the last man in line—he said, "Have Mederos, Lazo, or Cadiz been poisoning your mind?"

I broke out in a cold sweat, not knowing what Alfredo would say.

Someone had crossed the line by saying something they shouldn't, and I would serve as a perfect scapegoat. So far, I'd been lucky that no one had pointed a finger at me. I had faith in Alfredo, but one could never be too sure when it came to matters like this.

To my relief, Alfredo responded, "No, sir."

Pino's questioning took a surprising turn. "I understand you were complaining that under Fidel your brother doesn't have shoes to wear. Who told you to say that? Mederos?"

"No, sir."

"Cadiz?"

"No, sir."

"Lazo?"

"No, sir."

Pino's pupils contracted. They glinted with rage. "If I hear any more counterrevolutionary talk from any of you, there will be hell to pay. Do you understand?"

We all responded, "Yes, sir."

Pino shot me a sulfurous look, spat on the ground, and walked away in disgust.

That night I spoke with Manny. "I haven't talked to anyone about our incident. Have you?"

"Not a word."

"What do you think happened?"

"You started a fire, Frankie. And Pino fears he can't put it out. That's why he's afraid of you."

I blinked, wondering what Manny was talking about. "Afraid of me? He has all the power. Why would he be afraid of me?"

"Because he depends on you as a leader—there aren't many around."

"So?"

"So he needs you, but he fears you'll lead the men in the wrong direction. You've got him in a bind, and he hates it."

I grew quiet for a moment. "I never thought of it that way."

"Well, think about it. The men are following your lead and saying things they shouldn't. Pino is worried. He doesn't want things to get out of control."

"He doesn't seem worried to me. He seems angry."

"He's worried—and angry. The last thing he needs is a revolution within a revolution. His neck is on the line. He's angry because the situation is dangerous. You are a threat to his authority."

I smiled at Manny, thinking how similar he was to Abuelo. Same measured manner, same sound advice. I thought about my dealings with Antonio, disgusted with myself for not learning my lesson back then. I seemed to have a primal need to speak my mind, and I was afraid that someday it would get me in real trouble. My thirst for expression was not easily slaked.

I sighed heavily. "I'll be more careful," I said, wondering whether I could really live up to this promise. *"Lo siento."*

CHAPTER 22

It was a warm, windy day in June 1965 when we engaged in our first military exercises. All the top brass had gathered for the event, including generals, representatives from the Soviet Union, and Raúl Castro.

Raúl Castro had completed an advance course in military studies taught by Soviet experts and was highly familiar with our Soviet-supplied equipment, its capabilities and performance. Pino was just as knowledgeable, having been trained on the equipment himself.

After preparing for this event for months, my platoon was secure in our ability to handle the situation. We had been drilled and redrilled on every aspect of the ATGMs. The most sophisticated military equipment in Cuba was in our hands, and the knowledge regarding how to operate it was firmly fixed in our minds.

More than just demonstrating our individual skills, our performance would prove to the world that Cuba was the new center of Soviet-backed military power in all of Latin America. Cuba, the Soviet Union, and the entire communist bloc was invested in the outcome of these exercises. Lieutenants Pino and Brown had done all they could to prepare us for the event. So had Mikhail, the Russian commander. The reputation and future of these men rested squarely on our shoulders. It was now up to us.

A fine mist fingered the treetops as we made our way to Playa Bacuranao, about twenty-three kilometers east of Havana. I was so excited about the event, I had only gotten a couple hours of sleep the night before. There had been a lot of speculation among the ATGM operators regarding the exercises. We had no idea what our target would be or where it would be located. We hoped it would be a land target. A sea target would be more difficult to hit due to the motion of the waves, especially on a windy day such as this.

When we got to the beach, the infantry was lined up, all polished, starched, and ready for inspection. A band dressed in white gloves and military uniforms played a spirited march, while Cuban and Soviet flags flapped briskly in the wind. Members of the press were on hand to cover the occasion. It was difficult for me to imagine myself as part of such a high-profile event.

Raúl Castro marched back and forth, inspecting the troops and stopping occasionally to make a remark or to question a soldier. The expression on his face was sober and stern. The band completed its piece with a flourish, the last note dying softly in the breeze. Everyone clapped.

The 57-millimeter cannons arrived with much fanfare. People were waving and cheering wildly. When the applause died down, Pino walked to the bandstand and adjusted the microphone to accommodate his height.

"I want to thank our honored guests, especially our Minister of the Revolutionary Armed Forces, General Raúl Castro, for joining us here today." A loud roar rose from the crowd. The lieutenant reached for his hat to keep it from blowing off in the wind. "We are deeply honored by his presence and that of the other officers of our great military establishment."

The lieutenant turned toward his right, away from the buffeting wind. "What you see before you are the finest soldiers of the Revolutionary Armed Services: The Elite Counterattack Force." The audience cheered again and waved small, plastic Cuban flags that made sharp clicking noises in the wind.

"You are about to witness a demonstration of the most technologically advanced Soviet-made military equipment ever to be seen. This is the finest military equipment in the world, and it will keep our great country safe in the face of an attack from the imperialists. When the Americans come, they will be no match for our Elite Counterattack Force and the equipment supplied to us by our great comrades in the Union of the Soviet Socialist Republics." The crowd gave its full-throated approval.

"I direct your attention to the barge on the horizon." Everyone turned toward the sea, squinting against the wind and pointing at the barge that was bobbing in the distance. "The barge is two miles out at sea. Make no mistake about it—this is a very difficult assignment. Three of our highly trained ATGM operators will demonstrate the effectiveness of our military training, the depth of their skills, and the power of our rockets by destroying this target. Please join me in congratulating them in advance on this successful demonstration."

When the applause died down, the audience turned their attention in our direction. I was sitting with my driver in the last of three tanks. I was trying to process what I had just heard. I had been trained for months for this moment. Still, I had to tell myself: *focus, focus, focus.*

"Do you see the target?" I asked my driver Milton. He scanned the horizon for what seemed like a long time, while I tried to locate the barge through the small, rectangular lookout inside the tank.

"There it is. I can see it."

I wiped some condensation from the lookout glass and followed his pointer finger to a gray barge in the distance. It appeared and disappeared from view as the waves rose and fell. I blinked my eyes to gain a clearer view.

"It won't stay still," groaned Milton. "It's too windy out there. I think you'll have a tough time hitting it."

I took a deep breath and steadied my hands. I waved him away. I didn't need someone telling me what I could and couldn't do. "Just let me do the calculations," I said.

Manny's driver pulled his tank into position. I didn't envy him having to go first. I bowed my head slightly and said a silent prayer for my friend. A short time elapsed before I heard the roar of the rocket. The ground trembled beneath us. The rocket quickly rose into the air, arched, and splashed into the ocean without leaving a trace. The crowd moaned as a dull ache settled in my forehead.

A few minutes went by before we heard the launch of Manny's second rocket. Again the crowd groaned—another miss. Acid gathered in the pit of my stomach. I wiggled my shoulders to relieve some tension and crossed my fingers that Manny wouldn't blow his last attempt.

Manny launched his third and final rocket without success. He had struck out on all three tries. My heart went out to him. Scattered applause rewarded his efforts, but I knew this was no consolation. Manny was our best rocket launcher, and I was afraid if any of our efforts would succeed. I felt disheartened.

Lazo was up next. His driver pulled the tank swiftly into position, and I hoped against hope that Lazo would hit the target. His success would mean I would not be required to perform—the difficult mission would be completed.

I held my breath as the first rocket left its launcher. A whizzing sound hung in the air. Then the rocket fizzled and hit a stand of trees on the far side of the beach. I waited, expecting an explosion, but none came—the rocket was a dud.

This whole exercise was turning into a disaster. I didn't want to think what would happen to us when we got back to base. Lazo made two more futile attempts at hitting the target, with both rockets dropping like lead pipes into the sea. The crowd remained mute, and the wind kicked up, blowing sand in front of my lookout glass.

"It's up to us," I said to Milton. He gave me a wan smile and maneuvered our tank into position so the crowd could see us. I said a small prayer to St. Jude. I began calculating and recalculating the distance to the target. I turned to the blinking red lights on my control panel. The rockets were ready to launch.

I scanned the horizon for the target, but it was suddenly enshrouded in mist. I waited for a minute for the fog to dissipate. After what seemed like an eternity, the barge reappeared only to disappear from sight below the waves. I waited for the wind to die down and the sand to stop blowing.

Milton was getting flustered, fidgeting in his seat. "C'mon, shoot," he urged. I found his nervous energy to be distracting.

"Gimme a minute," I snapped. I didn't want to let down my platoon in front of Raúl Castro. And if I didn't hit the target, Pino would come down hard on Manny, Lazo, and me. And also on Brown.

I gathered my wits, recalculated for the wind and distance, and concentrated on the task at hand. The acid in my stomach began to gurgle, and the hairs on the back of my neck stood straight up. I hit the launch button and heard an explosion so loud I feared my eardrums would burst. The tank shifted and shuddered. It was as if a violent volcano had suddenly erupted above my head. I sealed my eyes from the light and the sparks while Milton and I coughed back smoke.

I opened my eyes to see the rocket's trajectory right on course. I held my breath while the rocket sped steadily ahead. It was almost too good to be true. Suddenly there was a tremendous blast. We heard the screams of the crowd before we knew what had happened.

I saw a giant blaze in the distance. Flames arose as red as fire engines and as yellow as butter. Scraps of debris—wood and steel—littered the sky like giant matchsticks. Ragged shards made their way upward and then dropped helter-skelter into the sea. Clouds of black smoke billowed forth, suspended for a minute in the air before drifting downwind. It took Milton and me a minute to realize that we had hit the target.

Milton and I looked at each other, amazed at our accomplishment. Lieutenant Pino ran toward us and helped us out of our tank. We emerged to thunderous applause. I never expected such a reaction. People were cheering and jumping up and down in the stands. Milton and I smiled shyly and waved at the crowd as Raúl Castro made his way toward us. He was beaming from ear to ear. We stood at attention as he approached. We saluted him and he congratulated us, shaking our hands vigorously in gratitude, and telling us how well we had performed for our country.

Lieutenants Pino and Brown quickly followed suit, holding up our arms like victorious boxers after a match. The band struck up a rendition of "The Internationale" as confetti and streamers filled the air. Milton and I were lifted onto the shoulders of our platoon and carried like heroes through the cheering crowds. They were screaming, *"Viva Fidel! Viva Cuba! Viva Fidel!"*

There was a huge celebration when we got back to base. Our platoon was jubilant. We were instant heroes. Champagne bottles were popped and beer was downed. Platters of food were placed before us. Much was made of the fact that Raúl Castro had witnessed our performance and had congratulated us by shaking our hands. Pino and Brown praised Milton and me for a job well done. The fact that Manny and Lazo had not hit the target was all but forgotten. Everyone was happy.

I smiled and accepted the accolades, secretly hoping that I'd never have to use my skills against the Americans.

CHAPTER 23

Unbeknownst to me, Magda's family had been engaged in serious discussions about leaving the country for good. This was a momentous decision that would put the entire family at grave risk.

Their main reason for leaving was that Magda's cousin Rigo and her brother Sergio, Jr., were quickly approaching draft age. Neither set of parents wanted their boys to serve in the army. As soon as Rigo and Sergio registered with the Revolutionary Armed Services, they would be forbidden to leave the country until they had completed their three-year tour of duty.

Obtaining a visa was not easy. Reams of paperwork were involved and it could take upward of a year, maybe two, maybe three, to obtain permission to leave the country. Making matters worse, the government could rescind your visa at any time. Nothing was certain. If the family wanted to leave, they needed to plan far ahead.

A decision to leave Cuba was irrevocable. Once you applied for a visa, you were automatically considered a traitor, a subversive, a counterrevolutionary, the scum of Cuban society.

It was common for young Communists to hold "Meetings of Repudiation" at the homes of these worms to scream obscenities and to hurl garbage. To avoid this, the Hernándezes's plan had to be kept secret for as long as possible.

Once you applied for a visa, everything you owned automatically became the property of the People. It belonged to the revolution, and you were forbidden to sell, barter, or give it away.

To determine the extent of your possessions, members of the militia visited your home—often accompanied by representatives of the CDRs—to inventory everything you owned, right down to your shoes, your clothes, and your silverware. When you received permission to leave Cuba, the militia conducted a second inventory to make sure nothing was missing.

Anything you broke in the interim—glasses, cups, plates—had to be kept and shown to the authorities as proof that it hadn't been sold or given away. If any item that originally appeared on your chart was missing, the police placed a cross on your application, and your visa was voided. Once you left Cuba, you could never return, not for a visit, not on business, not to see family.

Magda's relatives had spent many hours discussing their options. In addition to their son being drafted, the Hernándezes had little financial incentive to remain in Cuba. Uncle Rigo's restaurant, hotel, and dry cleaning business had been nationalized, and Lancha had been long since shuttered. The family believed that conditions in Cuba—the shortages, the rationing, the lack of freedom—would only get worse. Unlike Abuelo, they thought the Americans would not intervene to save Cuba, especially in light of the Missile Crisis and the disastrous Bay of Pigs invasion.

Making matters more dangerous, Magda's grandfather had been active in politics under the Batista regime—he had been elected councilman in Guanabacoa—and was now regarded with suspicion by the *Fidelistas.* He could be rounded up as a counterrevolutionary at any moment.

After weeks of deliberations, Sophia and Estel decided to discuss the family's plans with Magda. It was a little after seven p.m. and Magda had just gotten off the phone with me. She was sitting cross-legged on her blue bedspread, reading a book. She looked up curiously as her mother and aunt entered her room. She glanced at their faces and knew that something was wrong.

They told Magda that they needed to talk to her about an important issue. Magda nodded, put her book aside, and smoothed her bedspread, making room for them to sit. Estel took her daughter's hand in hers.

"Magda, you aren't going to be happy about this, but the family has decided to leave Cuba—for good." Magda took a deep breath and held it for a minute. She pursed her lips and then let her breath escape in a puff.

"But why?"

"For several reasons," explained Sophia. "But mostly because we don't want Rigo and Sergio to be drafted."

"When would we leave?"

"Not right away. We'll need time to obtain our visas. But we've got to act quickly so we can get out while we can."

Magda's eyes grew wide. "The Communists have made it impossible for everyone."

"They have," said Sophia.

A look of alarm crossed Magda's face. "But what about Frankie?"

"What about Frankie?" echoed Estel.

"He's in the army. He can't just leave," said Magda. Panic grated her voice.

"Of course," said Estel. "He'll have to stay and finish his military service."

Magda looked up, distraught. A sinking feeling gripped the pit of her stomach. "But he has more than a year to go in the army, and then he has to serve in the reserves until he's twenty-eight. It'll be years before he can leave the country."

"We know this is difficult for you," said Estel. She put her arm around Magda's shoulder. "We *all* love Frankie. He's like a son to us. But it's an impossible situation. It's hard to know what to do."

Magda thought for a moment, turned her head to the side, and said, "I'm not going anywhere unless Frankie goes."

Estel sucked in her breath. "This is ridiculous. What do you mean you're not going?" Her voice was an octave higher than normal. This was a development she hadn't anticipated.

"It's simple," said Magda. "If Frankie goes, I go. If he stays, I stay."

"You can't stay here alone, without your family," said Estel.

"What else can I do? I love him."

"But Magda, darling, there's no way for you to support yourself here. What would you do?"

"I can work. Take in laundry—do something."

"Honey, you're not ready. You're too young to work, and no one would hire you anyway. Unemployment is sky-high. Besides, you have to finish school."

"It's more important that I be with Frankie. He's the man I'm going to marry, the man I'm going to spend the rest of my life with. I can't just leave him." Magda looked at her mother for comfort, knowing she had no real answers to give her. Estel took her daughter in her arms and Magda began to cry. As she thought more about it, her sobs became louder.

"I know this is terrible for you, darling, but you're going to have to come to terms with it."

Magda stiffened and looked up at her mother. "But if I leave without Frankie, I'll regret it for the rest of my life. You don't know what it's like."

Sophia and Estel looked at each other, remembering what it was like to be young and in love.

Magda's aunt stepped in. "I'm sorry, but you've got to think of the rest of the family," she said.

Magda hugged her aunt. "It must seem to you like I'm being self-ish, considering what might happen to Rigo and all. I don't want the boys to have to go into the army. But I just can't go without Frankie." She sighed and her shoulders sank in desperation. "Please understand. I can't do it. I can't!"

Sophia and Estel traded worried glances. They understood Magda's concerns, and they were sympathetic to her predicament. But this seemed to be a problem with no solution.

"Isn't there some way we could get him a visa?" asked Magda.

"Magda, honey, Frankie's privy to important military information. They'd never grant him a visa," said Sophia.

"Couldn't we sneak him onto the plane?"

Estel shook her head. "No, Magda. They'd shoot him on sight. You can be sure of that."

Magda was grasping at straws. She looked at her mother. "There must be another way," she said. "We just have to find it."

The family discussion about leaving for Miami went on for two months, but I was unaware of it. Sometimes Magda was sad and distracted, but she never told me why. And while I tried to be sensitive and attentive, I was a little distracted myself.

Although my dealings with Pino had improved since my successful rocket launch, my antennae informed me I was still under suspicion. My fellow soldiers continued to challenge him about political issues. I tried to remain above the fray but, on occasion, I too gave in to the urge to speak my mind.

Pino was a man who was used to being in control, and his frustrations with us—especially with me—were palpable.

It was Friday night and I was home on leave. Magda, Manny, Lazo, and I had just lit a bonfire on our favorite spot on the beach when my skin began to crawl. As part of our military training, we learned to be hyperalert to our surroundings, and my senses were telling me something was amiss.

"Manny," I whispered, "do you feel that?" Manny stood up and casually looked around. Then he knelt beside me, poking the fire with a stick. A handful of sparks jumped into the air.

"Like someone's watching?" he asked under his breath.

"Yeah."

"Uh-huh, I've felt it for about an hour now."

"Have you seen anyone?"

"Just shadows. I think someone's hiding in the underbrush."

Manny nodded to Lazo. "Let's go for a walk," he said. The two men sauntered casually down the beach, and I knew Manny was telling Lazo about his suspicions. When they returned, we started talking about baseball, while I snuggled with Magda. I wrapped a beach towel around her to keep her warm in the chilly night air. She had no idea what was happening.

This wasn't the first time I had felt this way. I wasn't sure whether I was being watched on Pino's orders or whether I was imagining it. Nothing would surprise me. I made a mental note to be especially careful about what I said and did while on leave.

While the Hernándezes were concerned about Magda, they were also worried about me. They loved us both and the thought of leaving either of us behind was horrifying. Having come up with no answers, they decided to talk to me about the problem.

On Sunday night after dinner at Uncle Rigo and Aunt Sophia's house, the adults sent young Rigo and Sergio outside to play so we could have a serious conversation. I sat next to Magda on the living room couch and rearranged the pillow behind me. A cool breeze rustled the silk drapes as we sat drinking Cuba libres. My eyes fell on the slice of lime perched on the rim of my tall, frosted glass, and I thought about how fortunate I was to be with Magda and her family. Despite the conditions in Cuba, when we were together we usually had fun.

Señor Hernández startled me out of my reverie. "Frankie, we have a problem." He had a very serious look on his face, more serious than I had ever seen. I straightened up.

"What's that?"

"The family has decided to emigrate to the States so young Rigo and Sergio don't have to go into the army. We need to apply for our visas very soon." He hesitated. "As you can imagine, this is very privileged information."

"I understand," I said, although my mind was reeling with the implications of what he was saying.

"I have the feeling we are being watched, and I don't want to draw any attention to the situation," he said.

My mind drifted back to the day at the beach. Maybe it was Magda who was being watched instead of me. There were so many strange things going on in the country, one could never be sure. I looked at Magda in shock. Her eyes were glazed, and she wiped a tear away with her fingertips.

"Where would you go?" I asked.

"To Miami first. Then to New Jersey."

I nodded, never having heard of New Jersey. I was too shocked at the news to ask where it was. "I see," I said, trying to suppress my emotions. "When?"

"As soon as we figure out what to do," said Señor Hernández. He looked anxious and a little perplexed.

"I'm sorry. What to do?"

"Magda says she won't go with us." Sergio looked at his daughter with sympathetic eyes and then turned his gaze on me. He coughed and cleared his throat. "Which puts us in a very difficult position."

I was speechless, trying to absorb what he was saying.

"I'm confused," I said.

"It's pretty simple. Magda's says she loves you and she's not going anywhere without you."

I looked at Magda. Her jaw was set and that stubborn look I knew so well was etched like chalk on her face. She was one determined young lady. I took her hand in mine and placed it on my knee. I was feeling sad and befuddled.

"Of course," I said. "I love her, too. We've even discussed getting married someday. But the army would never let me leave. I'm sure you all know that."

Everyone nodded their heads in the affirmative. We sat in silence for a moment, thinking.

Estel coughed before she spoke. "We were wondering—" I tilted my head in her direction and looked into her deep brown eyes. She licked her lips and cleared her throat. "Would you be willing to take a chance to escape Cuba?"

I blinked at this unexpected turn in the conversation. "You mean by boat?"

"Yes, by boat."

I looked at her thoughtfully and rubbed my forehead, gauging my response. I was in great physical shape, the best I had ever been in my life. I had been well trained in escape tactics in case I was ever captured by the marines. And if anyone was worth risking my life for, it was Magda. On the other hand, I was in a top-security facility and escaping would be difficult, if not well-nigh impossible.

"I don't know," I said thoughtfully. "It's not something I could promise right off the bat. I'd have to do some investigating." Magda squeezed my hand tighter and beamed at me. I thought my heart would melt.

The room grew quiet as everyone mulled over what could happen. Sergio shifted in his chair. "Believe me, we understand what we're asking," he said. "And we would certainly understand if you said no. Thousands of people have died trying to escape this country."

Magda took a sharp intake of breath as the color drained from her face. "How exactly do they die?" she asked in a strangled voice. I could tell she wasn't sure she wanted to hear the answer.

Sergio paused for a moment, regarding his daughter with concern as he decided how to address her question. Since there was no way to sugarcoat the answer, he came down on the side of candor. His voice was soft, but his message was anything but. "The coast guard riddles escapees and their boats with so many bullets everything sinks. What's left of their bodies is devoured by sharks. No evidence is left of their defection so Fidel isn't embarrassed."

Suddenly it felt like all the oxygen had been sucked from the room. Magda covered her mouth in horror and let out a gasp. Her body recoiled and a tear rolled down her cheek. I put my arm around her shoulder to comfort her. My mind was trying to block the picture her father had so vividly painted.

A minute went by before Sophia spoke up. "We've talked it over and over, and it seems to be the only possible solution."

The thought of never seeing Magda again suddenly became very real. I was surprised at how devastated I felt. I looked at my sweetheart, my eyes hungry for her, like she was an ice sculpture melting in the noonday sun. Magda squeezed my hand and looked at me. "I can't live without you, Frankie," she said in a small, anguished voice. Her bottom lip quivered and a fine sheen of tears clouded my eyes.

"I can't live without you either, Magda."

I cleared my throat, sighed deeply, and looked at Magda's family, these dear, sweet people who had embraced me so warmly. I was filled with an insufferable sadness that I'd never see them, or Magda, again. I couldn't let that happen. Yet there were so many obstacles to overcome.

I leaned back on the couch and closed my eyes. Magda's hand was warm in mine. Strange thoughts raced through my mind. Visions of dead, bloated bodies. Pictures of red, bloodied water. Images of skeletal remains. I shivered slightly and forced myself back to reality.

"There's no good alternative," I said, thinking out loud. "If it's at all possible, I can do it. But first I need some time to talk to someone."

Sergio looked startled. He was a thoughtful, cautious man and he didn't want to take unnecessary chances. His body tensed and more than a trace of fear lined his voice.

"Who?"

"My grandfather," I said.

"I don't think you should talk to anyone about this. It's too dangerous."

"I can trust him. He's always been there for me."

"I'm sorry," said Sergio. He sounded apprehensive, nervous. "I don't know your grandfather. What if he tells your grandmother, and she talks to someone else and it gets out? We don't need a crowd of thugs throwing eggs at our doors. Or worse."

"My grandfather knows what to do and what not to do," I assured him.

Señor Hernández emitted a small, involuntary grunt. "We could all be killed."

I cut him short. "I'm perfectly aware of that. But if I'm going to do this, I must talk to Abuelo. He's a fisherman. He knows things…"

I rose and Señor Hernández followed suit. He put his hand on my shoulder and looked at me with such love I was afraid my voice would falter when I started to speak. I waited a moment to regain my composure.

"There's no time to talk to Abuelo tonight," I said. "Which means I can't talk to him until I come home on leave next month."

"We can't wait that long." Señor Hernández shook his head. "Is there some way you could talk to him sooner?"

My mind was racing, wondering how I could engage Manny and Lazo to help me get off base to talk to Abuelo. "Let me think about it. I may be able to work something out."

Sergio nodded. "Okay, you do that. Now let's get you back to base."

Magda and I climbed into the backseat of his car as the sun sank below the horizon. Magda wrapped a long scarf around her neck, and I pulled her to me, smelling her hair, kissing her gently on the mouth, and hoping her father wouldn't drive too fast.

When I got back to the barracks, Manny immediately sensed that something was wrong.

"You seem preoccupied. Is everything okay between you and Magda? Did you have a fight or something?"

I looked at Manny, glad for such a kind, loyal friend. "I'm going to need your help," I said.

Manny put his hand on my shoulder. "What is it?"

I looked around and lowered my voice to a whisper. "Magda's family is planning to leave the country."

Manny whistled softly. "Jesus! That's big."

"I know."

"How can I help?"

"I need to talk to someone, and I need to do it quickly. It can't wait until I go home on leave next month."

"I won't ask you who," said Manny. "I don't want to know."

I nodded. "We have night guard duty together this week," I said, thinking out loud.

Manny got my drift. He shook a cigarette from his pack, lit it, and inhaled deeply. "It shouldn't be too hard for me to cover for you. If we time it right, we can pull it off." He blew a smoke ring. It wobbled as it rose in a wavy circle above his head and then dispersed into nothingness. I thought about how easily things could disappear into thin air, never to be seen again.

"That's what I thought," I said. "If I leave after patrol around midnight, can you cover for me until six a.m.?"

Manny nodded. "That should work." He sounded optimistic. I was grateful for the sentiment. I needed all the optimism I could get. He cupped the palm of his hand and tapped a long cigarette ash into it.

"Next week?"

He nodded. "Okay. Next week."

CHAPTER 24

The following night, I asked Lieutenant Brown for permission to call Magda from town. As usual, he promptly agreed. When I got to the phone booth, I picked up the receiver to call *mi novia*. I didn't know who might be watching or listening. I was going to have to talk in code. I hoped Magda would be able to decipher what I was trying to say.

"Hi, Magda, it's me," I said, trying to drain the anxiety from my voice.

"How are you?"

"Fine. I'm looking forward to our time together."

"Me, too."

"It might be fun if you picked me up in your new car on your next visit," I said, hoping she'd understand that I didn't want her parents to pick me up in their car, which could be easily recognized.

"That would be fine. I'll come with my aunt and uncle."

"Great!" I said, knowing she had picked up my implication. "We'll go for a midnight stroll when I get home."

"How romantic."

"By the way, there's a full moon next Thursday. When I look at it, I'll think of you."

"I'll think about you, too," said Magda.

"Remember that night we saw the full moon through the trees near that big curve in the road?" I asked.

"Yes, it was such a beautiful night."

"Almost as beautiful as you."

"Can I do anything for you before I see you?"

"Just think about me on Thursday night."

"I understand. I'll put Thursday on my calendar."

"Okay. I've got to go now. I love you."

"I love you, too," said Magda.

I held the receiver against my cheek for a moment before I hung up the phone. I looked around surreptitiously, relieved that there was no one in sight. My heart was pounding and my throat was parched. I straightened my shoulders and walked down the road, keenly aware of my surroundings.

Back at base, my skills as a rocket launcher had improved to the point where Brown had asked me to teach classes on the technical aspects of the ATGMs. He also gave me more authority over the unit, a development that irked Pino to no end.

But Brown oversaw nonpolitical military matters, and Pino was in no position to challenge him. It created a great deal of friction between the two men. I wasn't sure how it would all play out.

Working together as much as we were, Lieutenant Brown and I were getting closer. Since that day when he had warned me about not crossing Lieutenant Pino, Manny, Lazo, and I had come to understand why he had not been promoted to captain. To rise to that rank, you had to join the Communist Party, and it was clear to us that Brown was loath to do so.

One evening I had a long conversation with him that shed some light on his views. He told me that three generations ago his family had been captured and shipped from Haiti to Cuba and enslaved to work the coffee plantations. Since then the Browns had labored to gain their freedom, obtain an education, and become landowners.

But under the Agrarian Reform Law, Castro had stripped the family of all their land. Many years of struggle and accomplishment were wiped out with the single stroke of a pen. The Browns hated Fidel with a passion, and the lieutenant had no stomach for the Communists—or their Party. It gave me some hope that he might not stand in the way of my escape.

The following Thursday I went on night patrol with Manny. I quickly made my midnight rounds so I'd be sure to be seen by all the guards. I smiled and waved to them, and then slipped out the gate behind the base.

Magda, Rigo, and Sophia were waiting in their car for me near the big curve in the road, a short distance from base. They dropped me off at my grandfather's house, saying they'd be back to pick me up at five a.m.

I turned the doorknob on my grandparents' house and quietly let myself in. My grandmother was asleep, but Abuelo was sitting up in his chair reading the Bible. He had on his bathrobe and his beat-up slippers. A light from a floor lamp shone down on his gray head. He removed his glasses when he saw me, stood up, and greeted me with a hug.

"Frankie, I'm so glad to see you. But what are you doing here at this time of night? Is everything okay?"

"Everything's okay. But I need to talk to you. It's important."

"Of course. Sit down. Can I get you a cup of coffee?"

"No thanks, I just need to talk."

Abuelo nodded. "Let's sit on the front porch then."

My grandfather wrapped his robe tightly around himself and we stepped outside. The screen door slammed behind us. The full moon lent enough light for us to see each other. A slight breeze waffled the evening air. Once he settled himself on the step, Abuelo nodded for me to continue.

"I've got a problem I thought you could help me with."

Abuelo adjusted his body on the step. "I'll certainly try."

"You know how much I love Magda."

"That's obvious," Abuelo said with a chuckle.

"It's not just a crush," I said. "She's everything I want in a woman, and I plan to marry her someday."

Abuelo smiled. "I figured as much. Is that what you want to talk about?"

"No, actually…" I hesitated, knowing this would be the beginning of a very difficult conversation for both of us.

"Actually?"

"The problem is her family is planning to leave the country. Her brother and cousin are approaching draft age, and the whole family wants to get out."

A flash of fear crossed my grandfather's eyes. He wrapped his arms around his knees, leaned his head forward, and groaned, almost imperceptibly. I watched him for a moment, suspecting from his reaction that he knew what I was planning. When he looked up, the lines in his forehead had deepened, his chest had shrunken, and his lips had drifted downward.

"Where are they going? To Miami?"

"To Miami first and then to a place called New Jersey."

"I'm sure you'll miss her."

"That's just the point. Magda says she won't leave without me."

Abuelo shook his head, took a deep breath, and exhaled slowly. "This isn't good, Frankie."

"I know. I can't leave Cuba for years because of the army."

"I'm aware of that. So what are you going to do?"

"I'm thinking about escaping," I said, watching for Abuelo's reaction. I knew my words would break his heart. He pushed out a sigh. His eyes looked so sad I had to turn away.

Abuelo blessed himself. "Dear God in heaven," he murmured. He looked up and down the street. It was as quiet as a cemetery after dark. A broken soda bottle lay on the sidewalk and a tabby cat tiptoed around it.

"I know it's a big risk."

"A big risk? It's beyond that, Frankie. Do you have any idea of the danger involved?"

I nodded solemnly. "I know," I said in a low, somber voice.

"No, I don't think you do," said Abuelo. "They'll hunt you down like a dog, shoot you in the back of the head, and leave your body to rot on the side of the road—if you're lucky. If you're not lucky, they'll sink your boat and your body will be ripped to bloody shreds by hungry sharks."

I shivered a little, and Abuelo wrapped his arm around me.

"I'm aware of the danger. I've talked about it with Magda's family." We sat in silence for a few minutes. Abuelo withdrew his arm from me and sat holding his head in his hands.

Finally, he looked up at me and said, "And they agree with this?"

"They're worried, of course. But, yes."

Abuelo regarded the moon with skepticism, and when he spoke again there was a hitch in his voice. "Have you thought about your parents, your siblings?"

"I've thought about them a lot," I whispered.

Abuelo looked at me. "You've had to leave them so many times already. Your poor mother—"

"I know and I'm sorry about that." I felt a lump forming in my throat just thinking about it.

"It's possible you may never see any of us again."

"Perhaps. But I have to take it one step at a time. There may come a day when, God willing, everyone can leave. Fidel could be overthrown. Who knows what the future may bring. But right now I have to follow my heart."

Abuelo nodded. "So you've thought it through? Slept on it? Explored all your options?"

"Yes."

"And you're willing to risk your life for this girl?"

"I am—as long as there's any chance of success."

Abuelo shook his head, "Let's go inside. It's getting chilly."

My grandfather and I walked up the stairs. I held the door for him while we stepped inside. I looked around the living room fondly, trying to memorize every square inch of it for posterity. This place held such poignant memories for me. Here was where I took my first steps, where I celebrated my birthdays, where I learned to read. Abuelo settled himself on the sofa, and I sat down next to him. He draped his arm protectively around my shoulder. He seemed more resigned to my leaving.

"Tell me what you're thinking," he said.

"Well, you have a boat—"

My grandfather withdrew his arm from around my shoulder. He closed his eyes and shook his head. "No, no, *no!*" Each no became louder and more pronounced than the previous one. I was startled at the intensity of his response. I looked at my grandfather in surprise. "Frankie, my boat is only fourteen-feet long. It's no match for the ocean. You'd die for sure."

I sighed. "But if you could just get me into international waters, I could hitch a ride with an international patrol boat—or hop aboard one of the big commercial ships."

"International waters are a long way out. I doubt my boat would make it. And even if it could, there's a matter of gas."

"Gas?"

"Yes, I'd have to have enough gas to get myself there and back. And buying that much fuel would alert the authorities. They'd be suspicious immediately."

"I understand if you can't help me." I shrugged. "I just didn't know where else to turn."

Abuelo looked almost angry. "You've put me in a difficult position, Frankie."

"How so?"

"I can never tell anyone about this, not even your parents. If the authorities get wind of it, they'll torture them for information." A slight shudder ran through my grandfather's body. Then it ran through my body. He thought for a moment. "What if you die, Frankie? How would I ever forgive myself?"

I straightened my back and patted Abuelo on the shoulder.

"I'm not going to die," I said in the most reassuring voice I could muster.

"The odds are against you, Frankie. You'll have to outsmart some very smart people. Do you think you can do it?"

"I'll do my best," I said and then thought for a moment. "Actually, I'll do more than my best." Abuelo looked at me wide-eyed. "Didn't you once tell me to always do more than my best in matters of love?"

My grandfather sighed and nodded. "Yes, I did. And that was good advice—still is."

"Well, I'm going to take your advice."

"You always have. I just never thought it would come to this."

My grandfather stood wearily. The conversation was over. "Let me think about it," he said. "Talk to some people. But don't *you* talk to anyone, you hear?"

"I won't," I said, a little heartened.

"When can you come back to see me?"

"Three weeks from tonight. I'll bring Magda's father."

"Okay, I'll ask around, come up with some ideas." Abuelo looked very sad. And suddenly very old. "Give me a hug."

I stood and took my grandfather in my arms. I could feel the muscles in his back. He raised his hand to my face, stroking my cheek with his thumb the way he did when I was a little boy. He wrapped his arms around me, and I hugged him tighter than I had ever hugged him before.

Back at base the time for another round of military exercises was fast approaching. I was now considered the force's best operator, especially in light of my last performance in front of Raúl Castro and the other high-ranking military officers. Lieutenant Brown decided that I would be the only operator to demonstrate the rocket launch. He didn't want to chance it with anyone else.

Pino vehemently disagreed with this decision, mostly because it would again provide me with high visibility among the top military brass. It was clear he didn't trust me, and he didn't want me to be viewed favorably by those to whom he reported. It could complicate matters if he needed to discipline me. But to Pino's chagrin, Brown overrode his decision. The two lieutenants were again at odds.

The military exercises were designed to mimic a real enemy invasion. As usual, Fidel closed all schools and work centers for the day of the event. It was a joint exercise of all the Revolutionary Armed Forces protecting Havana.

I was well prepared. To my surprise, I felt breezily confident in my ability to complete the task. The day of the event, the crowds cheered, the bands played, the infantry stood for inspection, and the 57-millimeter cannons displayed their power.

When it came time for me to perform, I was told to destroy a truck while it was pulling a trailer. It was a difficult assignment—a moving target—but one I was up to.

I turned to my driver and smiled, hoping this would be the last time I would ever complete such a task. I did my calculations, made a sign of the cross, and blew up the target on my first attempt.

The crowd roared its approval. I waved and smiled back at them. I saw a look of pride cross the face of Lieutenant Brown and a look of frustration cross the face of Lieutenant Pino.

Three weeks later Manny covered for me on guard duty again so Sergio and I could go see Abuelo. My grandfather was no more enthusiastic about my plan than when I first proposed it, but he did have some information for me. He told me about a fisherman who lived in Guanabo, a close friend of his by the name of Ralph. Sergio took out his notepad and wrote down his name and address.

"I've already spoken to him about you," said Abuelo. "He knows you are coming."

Sergio and I exchanged hopeful glances before we drove off in the middle of the night to meet with my grandfather's friend. I was very hopeful that something good would come of this meeting.

Ralph lived in a weathered, wooden house not far from the beach. Peeling brown paint clung to my knuckles when I knocked on his door. It creaked on its rusty hinges when Ralph answered it, rubbing sleep from his eyes.

"I'm sorry to disturb you. My name is Frank Mederos. This is Señor Hernández, *mi novia's* father. My grandfather sent me."

"Call me Sergio," said Señor Hernández.

"Yes, yes," Ralph said, holding the door open for us. "I've been expecting you. Come in."

Sergio and I went into Ralph's dimly lit living room. The curtains needed washing and the scent of stale tobacco permeated the air. He removed some newspapers from his tattered green couch to make room for us to sit. A cat was curled up on the armchair. Balls of her hair floated across the floor with the movement of air. She lifted her head curiously and then settled back down to sleep.

"Can I get you something to drink?" asked Ralph. He looked happy for the company.

"No, we can't stay long," I said. Ralph brushed the cat off the armchair and plopped himself down. Although he was thin, the springs creaked beneath him. The chair was in obvious need of repair.

"Your grandfather and I go back a long way," he said. "He has spoken to me about you many times."

"He's a good man."

"He is," said Ralph.

Ralph moved his neck side to side as if releasing a kink. He brushed a strand of hair from his forehead. Without preamble he said, "He says you want to leave Cuba."

"Yes. He thought you might be able to help, but I'm not sure how. Do you have a boat?"

Ralph groaned. "My boat was seized by the government," he said with more than a hint of anger in his voice. "So I have no boat, at least not one that would do you any good."

I heaved my disappointment. Ralph looked at me with concern. "Are you sure you want to do this?"

"It's not something I want to do—it's something I must do."

"Well, I don't want to discourage you, but many people try to leave Cuba and many people die. The coast guard patrols every half hour on the edge of Cuban waters. Your chances of survival are bleak."

"How far out is that?" I asked, knowing this was important information.

"Twelve miles," said Ralph. "Right at the point where you can no longer see land. After that, you're in international waters."

"As long as you remain within Cuban waters you're safe?"

"As long as you're in Cuban waters, the coast guard leaves you alone—unless they have reason to suspect you of something. But it gets very dangerous when you cross from Cuban waters into international waters. There are a couple of miles out there where you really have to watch out."

"What about radar?"

"The coast guard is fully equipped. They can pick up your engine on radar within a ten-mile radius."

"I see," I said, tucking this information safely away in my brain.

"Think this over carefully," said Ralph. "Don't make any decisions right now. I'm willing to meet with you again if you'd like."

"I've already made my decision," I said. "And I'm in the army, so it's very difficult for me to get away."

Ralph regarded me warily. "I see."

"So if you have any more information, I'd really appreciate it if you'd give it to me now."

Ralph shook his head and muttered something inaudible under his breath.

"Pardon me?"

Ralph looked at me, confused. "It's just that—"

"It's just what?"

Ralph thought for a moment. "I don't want your grandfather to hold me responsible if anything happens to you."

I nodded. "Of course, I understand. But Abuelo sent me here. I'm sure he'd be fine with any information you can give me."

Ralph studied us for a minute. I could tell he was not quite convinced to part with his information, but he wasn't sure what else to do. He sighed and said, "I know someone who can help. He's arranged for hundreds of people to get to freedom."

I breathed a sigh of relief. "What's in it for him?"

"He hates the Communists with a vengeance. I'm not sure why."

I brightened at this news. "Good. Where can I find him?"

"He's a barber in Cojimar, born and raised there. He knows everybody—who to talk to and who not to."

I nodded at Sergio to grab his notepad. "What's the name of his shop?"

Ralph waved me away. "Doesn't matter. He won't talk to you there. It's a business—too dangerous, too many people around."

"Then where?"

"He spends Sundays at a bar in Cojimar, La Terraza—where Ernest Hemingway used to hang out. He sits at a table overlooking the boats. You'll find him there."

"How will I know him?"

"He's about forty-five, five foot nine, medium build." Sergio scribbled the description on his pad.

"Anything else? Glasses?"

"No, but he has a little gray hair."

"You're sure I can trust him?"

"You can trust him. He's wary, but he needs to be. That's what makes him the best."

"Name?"

"Just call him Cuni."

CHAPTER 25

While I was on leave the next Sunday, Sergio and I went to see Cuni. We had had a long conversation with Magda's family beforehand regarding whether we could trust him, and we came to the conclusion that we had to take a chance.

Magda wanted to go to the meeting, but I insisted she remain home with her mother. I told her we would need privacy to conduct this conversation. She balked, but finally gave in. Naturally, everyone in the family was nervous.

La Terraza Bar had been a popular gathering spot for American and European tourists during the days of Batista, and it retained its elegant trimmings. Framed photographs of Ernest Hemingway lined the walls and polished brass accented the mahogany bar. It was also a comfortable place where workingmen could let down their hair and enjoy a few drinks with their buddies. As we walked in the door, the chatter of fishermen who had known each other for years filled the air. It was crowded and very noisy.

When we stepped inside, a hush fell over the bar. The men on the barstools turned to look at us. Sergio sported his usual starched shirt, and I had on my army uniform so I'd be ready to go back to base that night. Our clothes signaled that we were not one of them. For a moment we were a source of mild curiosity.

Sergio and I sidled up to the bar and ordered a couple of beers, while the men resumed their conversations. We looked around, but from Ralph's description, we couldn't identify Cuni. Several tables overlooked the marina, and they were all filled to capacity. The bartender smiled, placed our drinks in front of us, and wiped off the bar with an old, wet rag. I put some bills on the bar and caught the bartender's eye.

"I'm a friend of Cuni's. Please send him a drink with my compliments," I said. "I don't want to interrupt his conversation."

The bartender nodded, plucked a bill off the bar, and pulled a lever to fill a mug with beer. I watched as he carried the drink to a table of four overlooking the water. I had no idea which man was Cuni, but I was about to find out. The bartender leaned down and whispered something into the ear of a man who was eating a hamburger. He wore a red plaid shirt and met Cuni's description.

I waved when Cuni acknowledged my drink. He wiped his face with his napkin and motioned to me to come to his table. I extended my hand and introduced myself and Sergio to him and his companions.

"We have a mutual friend," I said.

"Who's that?"

"Ralph Huezo. He asked that I stop by and say hello. I'm Frankie and this is Sergio."

"Yes, yes," said Cuni. "Pull up some chairs. Here." He made room for us at the table and we sat down. Cuni took a sip of his beer and said, "A great fisherman, Ralph. We used to go to cockfights together."

"He's an old friend of my grandfather's," I offered, hoping this would impress Cuni.

"Well, any friend of Ralph's is a friend of mine." Cuni wiped off a line of foam dripping down his beer mug before lifting it in a toast to Ralph.

We all made small talk for a while and Sergio and Cuni seemed to be enjoying each other's company. Suddenly Cuni pushed his chair back from the table. He looked like he was about to leave. I realized I needed to figure out some way to speak with him alone.

"I parked my car around the corner," I said, looking down the street. "I'm not familiar with this neighborhood. Is that a safe place to park?"

"I don't know exactly where you mean," said Cuni. "I'll walk out with you, and we can check it out together."

"Great!"

We opened the door to the bar's porch. As soon as we stepped outside, Sergio took Cuni by the elbow and said softly, "I hate to take any more of your time, but we have a situation we thought you might be able to help us with."

Cuni stepped back and eyed us both cautiously. "What kind of a situation?"

"My family is leaving Cuba," said Sergio. "We have two boys nearing draft age, and we don't want them to go into the army." Cuni looked at us with a flat affect. I was not getting a good feeling about this conversation.

Sergio turned his head toward me. "Frankie is like a son to me. He's going to marry my daughter, and we don't want to leave him behind. We need to get him out of the country, and we were told you could help."

Cuni shook his head vigorously. "You have the wrong guy. My business is to cut hair. I'm a barber. Besides, what you're asking me to do is illegal. I wouldn't do anything like that. Who told you I would?"

The muscles in Sergio's face suddenly collapsed. This was not the reaction he was expecting. Sergio started to say something and Cuni cut him off sharply. "Quiet! Not another word."

We stood together in silence for a couple of minutes. I wasn't sure why. Sergio and I were feeling very uncomfortable. Cuni had not made a move. He was simply standing there staring at us. Beads of perspiration gathered at my hairline and trickled down the side of my face. Sweat broke out in my armpits, and I could feel my shirt getting wet. Sergio's face had gone pale. He wiped his sweaty palms on his pants before pulling the collar of his shirt away from his neck with his finger.

Cuni rolled his shoulders and leaned against the banister. He drew a lighter from his pocket and lit a cigarette, tilting his head back and looking up at the sky as if he were daydreaming. I watched as two men walked past us and down the stairs to the street. They nodded to Cuni as they passed.

Finally, Cuni's gaze turned toward me and he said casually, "I'm going to have to visit Ralph very soon. It's a shame he lost his leg in that fishing accident. All he can do now is sit. He's gotten so fat."

Sergio's face contorted in confusion. He had no idea what Cuni was talking about. I could tell what he was thinking. Perhaps we had knocked on the wrong door the other night and spoken to the wrong man. Perhaps this was a setup, and the man who claimed to be Ralph would turn us in to the authorities. Perhaps we would both end up in jail—or worse.

I smiled because I knew immediately what Cuni was doing. He had never met us before, and he wasn't about to take a chance. The stakes were too high. He was trying to determine whether we really knew Ralph and whether he could trust us.

"Ralph's doing great on two legs," I said. "And I guess he's been on a diet, because he's not fat at all. Perhaps you're thinking about another Ralph."

"Perhaps I am," said Cuni. He took another puff on his cigarette and eyed me with a little less suspicion. His shoulders relaxed. "Walk with me a little," he said. We walked the length of the porch. People were dining inside, but there was enough ambient noise that our conversation could not be overheard.

Cuni looked at me as if he were trying to resolve some half-formulated doubts. "Ralph is a great friend of mine. I would trust him with my life. But this is a very delicate business you bring me."

"I understand."

"If I'm to help you, you must follow the rules. If you aren't willing to abide by them, we can end this conversation right now."

"Tell me the rules," I said. The fact that Cuni had rules made me feel more confident about him.

For a brief moment fire danced in Cuni's eyes. "First, you are never to mention my name. Ever. To anyone. No matter what happens. Are we clear?"

"Perfectly clear."

"Second, you are not to talk to anyone about this. Not to your mother, your father, your sister, your brother."

I nodded and he continued, "In the last five years, more people have died trying to escape Cuba due to loose lips than to mistakes by fishermen, to bullets, to the ocean—to everything else combined. This is very, very serious business, Frankie. Do you understand?"

"I do," I said. I was getting butterflies in my stomach just hearing him talk.

"Remember: *Las paredes oyen*, the walls have ears."

I nodded.

"Third, this is a business, and it will cost you. Fishermen take you to safety. They charge by the passenger. No money; no escape. Everyone pays their own fare."

"How much is it?" interjected Sergio. He was looking nervous.

Cuni turned toward him and said, "Are you the one paying?"

"I am," said Sergio.

"Two thousand Cuban pesos," said Cuni. "And, just to be clear, I don't take a penny of it. I want you to know that."

"Why?" I asked.

"Why what?"

"Why don't you take any money? And why do you do it?"

Cuni shook his head slightly, as if remembering something. "The fishermen do it for money. I do it for my beliefs." I wondered whether Fidel had tortured or killed someone close to Cuni.

"Money is not a problem," said Sergio. I looked at Señor Hernández and took a deep breath, wondering how he would finance my escape. He had lost a great deal of money under Fidel, and now he had to pay the travel expenses for his family to go to the States. And, thanks to Fidel, Cuban pesos were worthless outside the country. Cuni interrupted my train of thought.

"There's something else," he said as if he were hesitant to give us this information. "You probably won't make it to the United States. The fishermen will look for a cargo ship to pick you up. There's no telling what kind of ship will be out there, or if they will stop. If they do stop, you go where they go. You may end up in South America, Panama, Canada—who knows?

"If you get picked up by a Soviet tanker, they will turn you in to the Cuban authorities. There will be no mercy. You might get lucky. An American ship may pick you up, but there are no guarantees."

"I understand," I said. I hadn't considered these possibilities. They added a whole new layer of complexity to the situation.

"Do you still want to pursue this?"

"I do."

Cuni shook his head and turned to Sergio. "If we are to work together to get Frankie out of the country, from now on you must not call him by his real name. Someone may overhear. It's too dangerous. Tell me how you'd like him to be addressed."

"We'll call him Machin," said Sergio. "It's common enough."

"Machin it is," said Cuni.

Cuni looked at me. "You're in the army?"

"Yes."

"Can you swim?"

"Yes."

"Well?"

"Yes."

"All right. Now I must tell you this. If the police catch you on land, you'll get five to seven years in prison. Hard time. But if the coast guard catches you on the Cuban high seas, you're dead—you can count on that. The Cold War has made it too embarrassing for Cuba to have people trying to escape the country. It's all about propaganda. The United States wants to make Cuba an example of bad government, and Fidel wants the world to think he's the leader of a great nation. Both countries know a great deal is at stake, and the whole world is watching."

"I understand the political situation very well."

Cuni scrutinized me. "Make no mistake about it. The coast guard has orders to shoot people on sight—no questions asked. Deaths at sea are never reported in the press—or anywhere else. That way no one knows how many people are trying to escape. You just disappear. ¿*Comprendes*?"

"*Comprendo.*"

"Questions?"

"Do you have any idea when this might happen?"

"It depends on many things, including the weather. I have something coming up in twenty days, but I have to make sure there's room for you."

Sergio and I looked at each in alarm. This was much sooner than either of us had anticipated. The family's visa applications had already been made, but the Hernándezes were still awaiting the CDRs to inventory their possessions. If I left in twenty days, I would leave before the Hernándezes. What would I do when I got to America? Where would I stay if Magda and her family did not arrive before me? Still, it was a way out.

"One other thing," said Cuni. "I am your only connection. You are to talk to me—and only me. You are not to ask questions. Not where. Not how. Not who the fisherman is. Don't ask. Leave that up to me. That's my job—it's none of your concern."

"All right."

Cuni looked back and forth at the two of us. "I don't want you to give me your answer now. I want you to think it over carefully. I won't be responsible for hasty decisions."

"That's fair," I said.

"Then it's settled." Cuni smiled slightly. "We'll get together next Sunday. Same time, same place—to talk. Now I must go back inside. This is my only day off."

CHAPTER 26

Sergio and I left the restaurant in silence. The enormity of what we were about to do was suddenly hitting us. My stomach was letting me know it existed, and I was so nervous it felt like a swarm of hornets had embedded themselves under my skin. We walked to the car deep in thought. When we settled ourselves in our seats, Sergio turned to me and asked in a voice laced with concern, "What do you think of Cuni?"

"He seems okay. He's exactly what Ralph said he would be."

Sergio considered my response for a minute. "Do you think you can trust him?"

"My instincts tell me yes. Besides, we have no other options."

"That's not the point. The point is whether he's someone we can rely on."

"Who knows? We don't have much information to go on. But if I had to go with Cuni or someone else I didn't know, I'd take him."

"Fair enough." Sergio thought for a moment. "What will you do if you don't get picked up by the Americans?"

I heaved a sigh. "I'll just have to take my chances with that as well as with everything else."

"But how will you get to us?"

"I've memorized the address of the place you gave me in Miami. I'll make my way there from wherever I land—come hell or high water."

"Even if you're taken to Canada? Panama?"

I shrugged, pretending to be less afraid than I was. "It doesn't matter. I'll find a way to Magda—no matter what."

Sergio stared out the windshield before turning his gaze to me. "Look, Frank, it's not my life on the line here. I understand the magnitude of what you're facing. This is a very difficult choice. Everyone in the family would understand if you decided to back out. There would be no hard feelings."

I regarded Sergio for a moment, knowing he was in a bind. This was almost as unpleasant for him as it was for me. "Thanks. But I've given this a lot of thought and I've made up my mind. I'm not going to back out."

"The odds are against you."

"I know. But I'll chance it to spend the rest of my life with Magda." I hesitated to make sure my voice would not betray my emotions. "She truly means more than life to me."

"She means the world to me, too," said Sergio. "But I'm her father."

We both smiled.

"My options are clear. Try to escape and spend the rest of my life with Magda. Or spend my life in communist Cuba. It's not a difficult choice."

"I just want you to be sure."

I looked at my hands and thought of the scars that marked my grandfather's skin, knowing full well that he would fight for the woman he loved. "Don't worry," I said. "I'm sure."

Sergio patted me briefly on the back.

When we got home to the Hernándezes' house, everyone was anxiously waiting to hear what had happened. Estel was concerned about whether we could trust Cuni not to betray us, and Sophia was worried that he would just take the money and not deliver on his promise.

As the discussion progressed, blotches broke out on Magda's throat and chest. It happened whenever she got nervous. I watched her as we talked. She was becoming more upset by the minute. I took her by the hand and led her into the living room where we could talk in private. I sat down on a hassock. She sat facing me on the couch.

"Talk to me," I said.

Magda sighed, lowered her chin, and looked at her hands, twisting the ring I had given her around on her finger. She took a sharp intake of breath and said, "I'm beginning to think this wasn't such a good idea. I feel so selfish for even asking you to do this."

I took Magda's hands in mine, and we both looked down at the ring. "Is it selfish of you to want to marry me?"

"It is when it could cost you your life." The look on Magda's face pierced me to the core. I reached up and smoothed the lines on her forehead, wanting to relieve her fears.

"This is my decision, and I don't want you to feel guilty about it, no matter what."

"I'm just so afraid," said Magda. "I don't know what I would do if anything ever happened to you."

"Listen to me. I'm in the best shape I've ever been in my life. I've been trained in survival tactics, and I'm a damn good swimmer. I've got as good a chance as anybody of making it. Lots of people get to America. Why shouldn't I?"

"But it's so dangerous. Everyone says so. There's got to be another way."

I folded Magda into my arms and brushed a strand of hair back from her face. "Well, there isn't. We've been over this again and again. And I'm more than willing to chance it if we can have a future together."

"It just seems unfair that you have to be the one to risk your life. I'm so sorry you have to go through this."

I sighed. "It's just the way it is. And I'd rather it be me risking my life than you risking yours."

Magda fell silent for a moment. "Do you have faith in this man, Cuni?"

"He seems competent and careful. This isn't the first time he's done this, so he must be on the up-and-up. Besides, Ralph has vouched for him, and Ralph is a friend of Abuelo's."

I pulled Magda to me and could feel her head nod in agreement against my chest. But hard knots riddled her back. Tension permeated every cell of her body.

Suddenly, she pulled away and looked up at me as if she were thinking about something. She jumped up so quickly she startled me.

"Wait right here." She ran up the stairs and was gone for several minutes. When she returned, her hair was pulled back and fastened with a black satin ribbon.

"Are you going somewhere?" I was bewildered at her behavior.

"No," she said. "But just in case—"

"In case of what?"

"In case you get caught and killed."

"I don't understand."

"I wanted you to know how I would look at your funeral."

I sucked in my breath, trying to steady my emotions. I didn't want Magda to know how hard her statement had hit me.

"If I get caught, there won't be any funeral." I brushed the back of my hand against her cheek. "I'll just disappear."

"There will be a funeral with you or without you," said Magda. "If you don't make it back, I'll hold my own funeral for you—even if it's only in my heart."

I blinked back my tears.

"Oh, Magda."

She stood up and turned around. "I wanted you to know how pretty I'll look for you. I wanted you to know that I would wear my hair the way you like it." Her voice was strained as if she were trying to ward off desperation. Her eyes caught mine. "Do I look pretty?"

"You always look pretty—more than pretty. I think you are the most beautiful girl in the world."

"Pretty enough to stay alive for?" A single tear slid slowly down Magda's cheek. Then another and another, until she was totally overwhelmed with grief.

"You know you are," I said. "But being pretty isn't what matters to me. You are what matters to me—just you." I took Magda in my arms, expecting her to continue crying, but she shook loose of me.

"I'm so sorry," she said. "I don't know what came over me. That was such a stupid thing to do."

"It wasn't stupid, it was just—"

She waved my remarks away and set her jaw. "You are going to make it—you have to. I'm sorry about the hairdo thing. I—"

"It's okay. You are trying to cope with a very difficult situation."

"No, it's not okay. We need to focus on your survival."

I took Magda into my arms. "The next time I see you it will be in the States. Let's focus on that."

"Okay," she said with just the hint of a smile.

We stood and I pulled Magda to me, kissing her softly on the lips and exploring her mouth with my tongue. I ran my hand down her back, yearning to touch her buttocks. But I knew it might be more than I could handle, so I resisted the urge.

We drove back to base that night in a somber mood. The possibility of death hung over us like a shroud. I feared that if something went wrong, I'd never see my sweet Magda again. Magda sobbed quietly against my shoulder and held my hand so hard it hurt. I comforted her as best I could.

When we got back to base, we stepped out of the car and gave each other a long hug. I was surprised to see tears glisten in Sergio's eyes. He patted me on the back, reminding me of my father. "We will pray for you."

"Thanks, I'll need it." I was happy for all the prayers I could get.

I lifted Magda's chin with my finger and gave her a long kiss in front of her father. He looked on and smiled slightly. He didn't seem to mind. I waved goodbye as they got back into the car. Magda stuck her head out the window, her hand outstretched to me as her father started the engine.

"See you in America," she mouthed silently. I nodded and opened the door to the base.

Manny and Lazo were all over me when I saw them, wanting to know all about the meeting with Cuni.

"Tell us what happened," said Lazo.

"It went well. I can't give you any details, but I'm going to leave."

"I think you're crazy," said Manny. "What if you get caught? A military tribunal is not like a civilian court. You could get life in prison as a traitor. Torture. Death. They could brand you. Nothing is worth it."

"Magda is worth it."

Lazo looked dismayed. "Can't Magda wait until you get out of the army? Doesn't she know the danger she's putting you in?"

"It's not Magda's fault. Other factors are involved. Don't ask." Lazo and Manny looked at each other, their faces telegraphing alarm.

"Is Magda pregnant?" asked Manny.

I shook my head. "No. We haven't had sex."

Lazo looked perplexed. "Then give me one good reason why you have to leave."

I straightened my back. "Trust me. I have to do this. And I'm going to need you to cover my back. Are you game?"

Manny shrugged. "I'm game." He thought for a moment. "I take it you're bringing your machine gun with you."

"No, I'm not."

Manny looked horrified. "Are you out of your mind? You are going out there without your gun? You know they'll go after you. What if you get cornered and you don't have a weapon?"

"If I take my gun and something goes wrong, I'll be hunted down as an armed fugitive."

"What difference does it make? If you don't take it, you may be dead."

"And if I do take it, I could kill someone. Think about it, Manny."

"I have thought about it. And if I ever leave, I'm bringing a 57-millimeter cannon with me—the hell with the machine gun."

"That doesn't sound like you, Manny."

"Well, I guess Brown is turning me into a real soldier."

We all laughed in spite of ourselves.

With my escape only twenty days away, Estel set out to sell the family's possessions before the CDRs came to take inventory. She earmarked money from the sale to pay for my escape. I felt at once grateful and guilty for the family's generosity, knowing I would have never been able to pay Cuni without them.

The Hernándezes' house contained a wealth of paintings, antiques, silver, china, porcelains, and rugs. Quietly and discreetly, Estel informed her network of friends and associates to come to the house to buy what they wanted at a fraction of its worth. She even offered her jewelry for sale—pearls, diamond broaches, gold earrings. I tried to convince her to keep those items for herself, but she would not hear of it.

A steady procession of people stopped by the house to purchase precious objects. Some were happy to get the bargains. Others came because they loved the family and wanted to help. Estel told people to come alone or with just one friend so as not to attract attention.

People left with single items, sometimes stuffed in their pockets, sometimes hidden under their clothing, sometimes wrapped in brown paper and twine. Larger items were disposed of at night until only the rugs, bedding, and heavy furniture remained. Estel sold the family's treasures with the organization and discipline of a general. She did it quickly and efficiently, without obvious regret or complaint.

• • •

The next Sunday I could not get away from the unit, so Sergio met with Cuni to finalize the escape plans. When I called Magda from the phone booth in Santa Maria, Sergio told me that I was to take the bus from Guanabacoa to Cojimar and meet Cuni at La Terraza at eight p.m. Sergio would make payment in full to Cuni two days before the planned escape.

Lazo switched guard duty with one of the men from the 57-millimeter cannon units to provide me with cover on the night in question. He unlocked the gate for me. I thanked him before bidding him a hasty goodbye.

I was going to miss Lazo, Manny, and Lieutenant Brown, and my heart felt heavy with loss. I walked to Santa Maria where Sergio picked me up and took me to the bus stop in Guanabacoa.

I boarded the bus in my army uniform and settled myself in a window seat. The springs creaked as I sat down. I felt nervous and jittery, having spent a lot of time over the past two weeks considering what could go wrong. I rehearsed in my mind how to handle various scenarios. My stomach churned and a light perspiration slicked my face. I couldn't imagine that things would go smoothly.

The bus was old and cantankerous, emitting gray puffs of smoke and stalling occasionally at red lights. It lumbered along with its dusty windows and worn tires, stopping intermittently for people to get on and off. I thought about what I should do and where I would stay once I got to Florida. I had been too focused on my escape to think about it before.

Not coming up with any concrete ideas, I decided to wait until I got there to figure it out. Besides, the problem at hand was big enough to fully occupy my mind.

When the bus pulled up to La Terraza, there was a big commotion near the marina. I sat up in my seat and peered out my window to see a large crowd milling about. It was very noisy with much pushing and screaming. People's eyes reflected fear. For a few minutes it was unclear to me what was happening. The military police and army personnel were out in full force. Several people were being led away in handcuffs.

I scanned the crowd for Cuni. He was standing on the curb of the sidewalk with a look of alarm on his face. He locked his eyes on mine and shook his head ever so slightly, indicating that I was not to get off the bus.

I knew something had gone terribly wrong and it was incumbent upon me to stay put. A few people disembarked, and I leaned back in my seat, feeling grateful to have avoided disaster. The bus driver turned to me and asked, "Are you getting off?"

"No. I forgot something in Guanabacoa. I need to go back home."

"Suit yourself," said the driver. He put the bus in gear. A cloud of exhaust smoke filled the air. We waited a few minutes for the traffic to clear before moving on.

When I got off the bus in Guanabacoa, I went immediately to Magda's house. I was emotionally exhausted and full of angst. I banged on the door repeatedly, but no one answered. I realized the family had probably gone to Sophia and Rigo's house for the evening, so I waited for them in the park. I checked every fifteen minutes to see whether they had returned.

Magda and her parents arrived home around ten thirty p.m., totally amazed to see me.

"*Dios mio!* What happened?" asked Sergio.

"There was a problem in Cojimar. It looked like people were caught trying to escape. There was a big ruckus. The police and soldiers were there. They were leading people away in handcuffs."

Magda covered her mouth with her hand and emitted a noise from deep in her throat. I had never heard her make such an awful sound before. She ran to me and threw her arms around my neck. Her eyes were red and puffy as if she'd been crying.

"Thank God, you're all right."

Sergio regarded me with paternal concern. He was full of misgivings. "Did you see Cuni?"

"Yes, but just out the bus window. He shook his head at me. It was obvious that he wanted me to stay on."

"Thank God!" said Sergio. "Are you okay with this?"

"Okay with what?"

"With everything that's happened?"

"I guess," I said, still unsure of Sergio's meaning.

Sensing my confusion, he clarified his question. "Are you willing to give it another try?"

I took Magda's hand in mine. She squeezed it hard and smiled at me. I opened my eyes wide, anticipating her response. She nodded.

"We'll give it another try. See what Cuni has to say."

"Okay," said Sergio. "Now let's get you back to the army."

Sergio drove me back to Santa Maria, and I practically ran back to base. I asked the guard on duty to radio Lazo, who came to open the gate to let me in. Lazo was stunned. He looked at me quizzically, turned to the guard, and said sternly, "This never happened, do you hear?"

The guard regarded us with suspicion. He narrowed his eyes and looked at me closely. I held my breath for a long, agonizing moment. A lot depended on this young man's response. I wondered if this would be the end for me. If he reported my transgression, there would be hell to pay.

I looked at the soldier pleadingly, and he looked back at me with more understanding than I ever would've expected. He hesitated a moment, making up his mind about something that had nothing to do with me.

Then he looked me straight in the eye and said, "I understand. Okay."

CHAPTER 27

After my foiled escape attempt, Lazo decided to form a basketball team to provide me with cover should I need time to make arrangements for my next "trip." Highly organized and very persuasive, he told Lieutenant Brown that we needed some extracurricular activities to boost morale and to build a relationship between the army and the civilian population.

Brown agreed, and Lazo recruited enough men to form a special forces basketball team to compete against local schools. The team came together quickly.

At first we played Santa Maria High School and the school in Guanabacoa. Many of the men knew each other from their former neighborhoods. The games were greeted with much enthusiasm.

Lieutenants Brown and Pino attended these events, cheering us on from the sidelines. But when the number of games increased and we had to travel farther to get to them, the lieutenants decided they had better ways to spend their time.

Lazo benched me for most games. He built a lot of leeway into the schedule, so I could get away to talk to Sergio or meet with Cuni without being missed.

With the last attempted escape having come to ruin, Cuni was more cautious than ever in making his plans. He was suspicious about who had tipped off the authorities on the last go-round and wary about whom he could trust. He refused to employ any fisherman he didn't know personally, limiting the number of boats he could use to take people out of Cuba.

Weather was also a major concern. Hurricane season extended through late September, making it more difficult for anyone who wanted to leave Cuba. Storms were also common in October. We waited and waited, but no opportunities presented themselves for escape. My chances for anything happening in 1965 grew slimmer by the week.

Magda and I saw each other during my monthly leaves. I continued to strengthen my relationship with Lieutenant Brown and my fellow soldiers. I improved my military skills, played basketball, and bided my time.

In November, the CDRs took their inventory of the Hernándezes' home. They questioned the family regarding their lack of possessions and were suspicious that things had been sold. But they had no proof of transgressions. The months dragged on with the Hernándezes getting increasingly nervous about getting out of Cuba before Rigo turned fifteen. They had not yet been granted a visa.

By now a fresh group of recruits had entered the force, and Manny, Lazo, and I were looked up to as veterans. The new soldiers seemed very green to us, and we were chagrined to think we had once looked and acted the way they did. There were too many new soldiers for me to get to know them all. It would take a while.

My relationship with Pino continued to be strained, and I knew he was looking for any excuse to nail me for even the slightest infraction. I tried to remain deferential toward him, but I still spoke my mind on occasion, which he found infuriating. What's more, many of the other soldiers still challenged him politically. He blamed their defiance on me.

But I had managed to cultivate a good relationship with Mikhail, the Russian commander who had taught us many technical aspects of the ATGMs. As I got to know him, I realized he was more like us than I would have imagined.

A man about thirty-five, he had been forced to leave his country and family to come to Cuba. His parents were farmers, and he had grown up knowing the shame and pain of deprivation. He was married, had three children, and was eager to get home.

He often shared meals with Manny, Lazo, and me, and we spent a lot of time together talking about sports and the differences in our respective cultures. He was no more enamored with communism than were we.

In early March of 1966, Cuni informed Sergio that he was planning another "trip," and Sergio and I needed to meet with him—soon. Lazo scheduled a basketball game on the day in question so I could leave to see Cuni without raising suspicions. We met at the park in Guanabacoa.

"I have a fisherman who can take you and two others," Cuni informed me.

I started to ask a question and Cuni held up a hand for me to stop. "I know and trust the man."

"Good. When?"

"March twentieth. There's a small bar at the far end of *El Malecón*, a short way from the coast guard station in Cojimar. Meet me there at eight p.m."

I nodded, shook his hand, and made my way quickly back to the basketball game.

Built in 1646, the coast guard station was located in a beautiful Spanish fort called *El Torreón de Cojimar* that once was the pride of Cuba. A gray stone, turreted building overlooking the harbor, it was a lively tourist attraction before the days of Fidel. It now served as a checkpoint for boats leaving and entering the harbor. It was heavily guarded and impossible to avoid. Every boat going in and out of the harbor had to stop there for inspection.

My escape was to take place the Sunday night of my regularly scheduled leave. I savored the weekend, thinking it might be the last one I'd spend with Magda and my family for a very long time. Possibly ever. I spent Friday night with my family and the remainder of the weekend with Magda.

I kissed her every chance I could, and I told her how much I loved her. I was bereft at the thought of leaving her. Once again, we talked about our promise not to doubt each other's love—no matter what. On Sunday night, I bid Magda and her family a tender goodbye, and Sergio drove me to my meeting place with Cuni.

The night was dark with gathering storm clouds. I studied the sky for a moment, a little concerned with what I saw. I got out of the car and shut the door quietly. As soon as I saw Cuni, he lifted his eyebrows and turned his back on me. I wasn't alarmed. I knew what he was doing. He whistled softly as a signal for me to follow him. I walked behind him, sure to keep a safe distance.

We walked about a block and a half to an old, run-down bar. A small wooden sign declaring its name dangled from a rusted pipe. It rattled against the brisk wind. Rawness seeped into the air, and a chill whipped my shoulders. There were very few patrons, only three old men smoking cigarettes and sipping beers and a young man drinking jiggers of rum. Cuni nodded for me to follow him through a side door that led to the basement.

We walked down a narrow staircase with cracked plaster walls and holes in the ceiling. Mouse droppings covered an uneven mud floor, and a bare lightbulb cast an eerie glow on two boys. Cuni introduced them to me as Joey and Pedro Lopez. Joey was thirteen and Pedro was fifteen, although Joey was bigger and looked slightly older than his brother.

We shook hands, and Cuni made a small joke about us "all being in the same boat." I wondered what they were doing there before I realized that these frightened boys were to be my traveling companions.

Cuni told me their father had owned the candy factory in Cojimar that Fidel had seized several years before. I remembered Abuelo buying me candy from there when I was a child. It was always a special treat. Once a large and successful business, the building that housed it lay abandoned, its equipment stolen, its windows shattered. Pigeons perched on its windowsills, its sole inhabitants.

After talking for a few minutes, Cuni took us outside to the edge of the water. There was no beach, only sharp ragged rocks that jutted at dangerous angles like giant slabs of Arctic ice, rocks that could slice your feet or cause you to break a leg or to sprain an ankle. It would have been difficult enough to navigate them during the day, but at night it would be an exercise in balance and agility. I hoped the boys were careful enough to make it safely over this rough terrain.

I assumed this was our place of departure, that a boat would be along soon to pick us up. Cuni pointed to a light bobbing on the horizon. It looked like a beacon or lantern of some kind, but I wasn't sure. Although I didn't have any equipment with me to measure distance, I reckoned it to be about a mile out.

"Do you see the light in that fishing boat?"

"Yes," I said, glad that Cuni had told me what it was.

"That boat will take you to a larger one, which will take you into international waters."

I nodded my understanding. "How long before it comes to pick us up?" I was hoping it would arrive shortly. I was cold and apprehensive and wanted to get started as soon as possible.

"The boat can't come in here. It's too rocky," explained Cuni. "The fisherman doesn't want to chance wrecking his boat."

"How do we get to it then?"

"You'll have to swim."

"All of us?"

"All of you. I remember you said you were a strong swimmer."

"I am," I said, feeling suddenly apprehensive. "But what about the kids?"

"Their father says they can swim. I take him at his word."

My eyes widened. I looked at the boys in alarm, unsure of what to do. They didn't look very strong. I doubted they could make it.

I leaned down to talk to them. "Do you think you can swim that far?" They both nodded yes. The younger boy seemed more certain than his brother. I just shook my head. "You can back out if you want. There's no shame in it."

"No, we want to go," insisted Pedro. He hesitated a moment. "We promised our father."

"And you, Joey?"

"I go wherever Pedro goes," he said matter-of-factly. The boys looked at me expectantly. I was surprised at myself for feeling so paternal. They were very charming kids. I was thinking of my own brothers and how they would react in such a situation.

"Okay. You'll need to swim quietly. No talking or splashing around. You hear?"

The boys nodded. I took off my shoes and instructed the boys to do likewise. They looked very somber. We walked carefully over the rocks and lowered ourselves slowly into the water. It was bracingly cold, and a shiver ran through my body. I looked back to see how the boys were faring. Pedro was up to his waist in the coal-black water. Joey was close behind him.

I started doing the breaststroke as quietly as I could, and the boys followed suit. We had not removed our clothes, and they weighed heavily upon our bodies. I heard the steady strokes of the boys and was heartened that they seemed to be good swimmers. Still, the boat was a long way out to sea. About halfway there, the wind picked up and the waves started splashing our faces. I kept a close watch on the boys. None of us said a word. We needed to conserve our energy.

Every so often I heard one of the boys cough. It was a sharp, rasping sound that quickly disappeared into the night air. The sea was choppy and the boys were having difficulty keeping their heads above water. I was trying not to think what would happen if one of them got into trouble.

The boat was getting closer, and I hoped Joey and Pedro would make it. Pedro was struggling. I called to him to keep going. He looked like he could use some encouragement. The fisherman held up a lantern to help us see.

Suddenly, a large wave caught us off guard and smacked us all square in the face. Joey and I were able to handle it, but Pedro swallowed a mouthful of water. He cried out in fear. He was losing control, flailing his arms, and splashing helplessly against the white-capped waves.

"Hold on, Pedro. I'm coming," I screamed.

I swam as fast as I could toward Pedro, fighting the turbulent sea. I grabbed him by the hair and wrapped my arm around his chest, doing the sidestroke while I pulled him along. He was choking and sputtering, but luckily he didn't fight me, a common reaction of a person who's drowning.

I could barely see Joey in the darkness. He looked afraid. I wiped water from my eyes. "Tread water for as long as you can," I hollered. "I'll come back for you soon."

"I'm okay," he said. He appeared stronger than I would've expected. "Just take care of Pedro." His voice was thin and tinny and was soon swallowed by the wind.

I swam away slowly, dragging Pedro along with me. I was fighting the waves every stroke of the way. The water was getting rougher, slapping my face and forcing its way up my nose. I worked to blow the water out of my nostrils without using my hands. My calf suddenly cramped, and I fought hard against the pain.

When we got to the boat the fisherman helped pull Pedro out of the water. Pedro moaned, and his legs thumped against the bottom of the boat. He scrambled to right his body. A moment later I heard the pitiful sound of retching. The fisherman held his hand on Pedro's back to comfort him, while I hung on to the side of the boat for a minute, kneading the muscles in my right leg, and catching my breath before swimming back for Joey. I just hoped the wind hadn't made the water too choppy for me to save him.

I pushed off from the boat with my feet and swam toward the boy who was struggling to stay afloat. "Hurry," screamed Joey. His voice was ragged. He looked like he had not an ounce of energy left.

"I'm coming," I said. "Just don't fight me when I get to you."

I grabbed Joey around his chest—the way I had his brother. White foam capped the black water. I inched Joey toward the boat. The fisherman had started his small outboard motor and was heading our way. Within a few minutes he was alongside us.

He took the motor out of gear and idled it before lifting Joey out of the water. Pedro helped pull his brother aboard and I waited, holding onto the rail, exhausted. I lifted my one leg over the side of the boat and pulled myself in. My clothes clung to my body and water ran in rivulets down my hands and feet. My arms and legs ached and my head was pounding. I worked to catch my breath.

The fisherman blew out the lantern, and we sat in silence for a minute, trying to regain our composure. The boys had wrapped their arms around themselves. Their bodies were shaking and their teeth were chattering from cold and fright. The wind whistled and blew a cold drizzle around us. Pedro and Joey huddled close together for warmth. They looked to me for solace, but I had little energy left to give them.

"It's going to be okay," I said. "You were both very brave."

Joey and Pedro glanced up at me and nodded. Joey was blinking, his eyes wide with fright. There was no reason to smile.

The boat was only thirteen feet long, and it took water over its sides with every crashing wave. I looked around, found a pail, and started to bail. Joey stood shakily, grabbed an old rusted coffee can and began bailing beside me. I was very glad for his help.

Without saying a word, the fisherman steered the boat away from land. It slapped against the waves and pitched against the wind, its motor lurching and struggling. We fought the wind for more than two hours, bailing, battling the waves, and inching our way toward the Straits of Florida.

The boat we met was not much bigger than the one we were on—only twenty-feet long. We made the transfer successfully, and the smaller boat headed back to Cuba. We listened to the hum of its motor as it disappeared into the distance. The wind finally consumed its drone. The evaporation of the sound into the night was eerie.

The boys and I were freezing, and I was afraid we were all suffering from hypothermia. We sat shivering and looking up at lightning, which zigzagged across the sky, revealing fast-moving clouds. The wind picked up. Thunder boomed its arrival like a large kettledrum. Rain would soon follow.

Our clothes were sopping wet, and I wasn't sure whether we'd be better off with or without them. Pedro's lips were turning blue. Joey looked terrified. Suddenly, the captain, a big man nicknamed Macho, cut off the motor. We sat in silence, listening to the waves whipping the sides of the boat. We were all only one large wave away from death.

"Why are you stopping?" I asked.

"I'm waiting for the patrol boats to cross."

At least Macho sounded like he knew what he was doing.

I looked to the horizon and saw the patrol boats in the distance. I remembered Ralph cautioning me that this would be the most dangerous part of the journey. I sucked in my breath in apprehension. I could see a large ship much farther out, my ticket to Magda, and I longed for its safety and shelter.

Suddenly, the skies opened up and pelted our faces with a stinging rain. It came sideways like crystal needles, pounding our shoulders and rocking the boat. I was afraid we were about to turn over. Joey began to cry and Pedro admonished him to be quiet. Joey bit his lip and stopped sobbing. I was amazed at his bravery.

Macho struggled with the steering wheel, trying to turn the boat around. The motor was straining. Pedro and Joey clung to each other like Siamese twins, looking forlorn and helpless.

The waves knocked us from side to side and, for a moment, the motor sputtered. Another wave hit us, and Joey was thrown to the side of the boat. He had lost his balance and was about to go over. I lunged for him, grabbed him by the back of his shirt and steadied him until he regained his footing. I turned around and looked at Macho.

"What are you doing?" I screamed.

Macho hollered back against the howling wind. "We'll never make it. The storm is too bad. I'm taking us back."

I quickly assessed the situation and knew he was right. The patrol boats crisscrossed every half hour, and we could never make it into international waters in time. We would surely be apprehended. There was no time for escape and no time to wallow in disappointment.

Macho worked to keep the boat from capsizing, while I tried to comfort the boys. I was praying the motor would hold. Otherwise, we would be all lost at sea. The wind whipped the waves to new heights. They blasted the sides of the boat with such force I feared the wood would crack. The howl of the wind bellowed in fits like a wounded animal caught in a trap.

We clawed our way through the choppy seas for two hours before we spotted the lights of Cojimar. The water calmed considerably and the rain slacked off as we approached the port. We were headed for the coast guard station where the boat would be inspected for escapees like us. Joey and Pedro exchanged frightened looks. They knew the danger we faced.

"You'll all have to hide," hollered Macho.

"I know. Where?"

"Put the boys on the side of the boat under the ropes."

Pedro and Joey scrambled to hide where they were told. They were as quiet as cats stalking mice.

"You," said Macho, looking directly at me. "Get under here and don't make a sound."

He pointed to a compartment on the floor, directly under the steering wheel. I bent down to enter the cramped and foul-smelling space. I wiggled my body to find a comfortable position, but it was no use. I just wanted to be able to curl up without pain. I managed to get into a position where my legs were turned to the side. I was facing upward.

Slits in the floorboards enabled me to see the yellow light from the inspector's flashlight as he walked back and forth on the deck of the boat, checking for fish and anything else he might find. Macho did his best to distract him by talking. Another guard stood on the dock, overseeing the inspection.

"So how's your family?" asked Macho. I was impressed with his feigned nonchalance.

"Don't worry about them," said the inspector. "I want to know how many tunas you brought me."

"None this time," said Macho with a sigh. He chuckled. "Hell, I brought you a bunch of fish the last time I went out. I must've given you enough for a week."

"Well, a man has to eat."

"Sorry, it was terrible out there. I couldn't even fish for the waves and the rain."

"Is that so? It wasn't bad here."

"Take my word for it. It was like a hurricane. Thunder, lightning, the works."

I heard the guard walking back and forth as he shot the breeze with Macho. The hold was full of gasoline, kerosene, and tar that clung to my clothes, my skin and my hair. The fumes were making my eyes water. I was hoping against hope I wouldn't sneeze. If I did, it would be death—for all of us.

"I'll tell you what," said Macho. "I'll bring you twice the number of tunas next time I'm out. How's that?"

"All right, just make sure I'm on duty when you come in." The inspector shook hands with Macho and climbed out of the boat to open the way for us to pass.

When we pulled into the dock, Macho took his time cleaning the boat and putting things away, while I remained hidden in the hold. I didn't know whether he didn't want to appear to be in a hurry or whether he was waiting for prying eyes to depart. After forty-five minutes, he opened the hatch to let me out. I was covered from head to toe in vile odors and substances. I feared I'd never be able to remove them.

The boys and I walked back to the bar and Macho arranged for the boys' father to come and pick them up. I found a blanket in the basement and threw it over their shoulders to keep them warm. Pedro was shaking violently, and Joey's eyes were full of fright. He stood and gave me a hug. I tried to comfort him as best I could.

The boys' father arrived to get them. His face was ashen as he scooped them into his arms, telling them that everything was going to be okay. Señor Lopez nodded to me briefly before he left, obviously more concerned about his sons' welfare than in talking with us. I watched in sympathy as he led his boys down the path.

I was wondering what I would do next when Macho turned to me and said, "You can come back to my house for the night. I don't live far—just up the hill." It was about three in the morning, and I was glad to have a place nearby to stay.

We walked through the rain to his small cinderblock house that butted up against the street. Three steps lead up to the doorway. It was dank and dark inside. I could hear the muffled sounds of children sleeping. A light rain pattered the windows and palm fronds lightly whipped the side of the house. I removed my wet clothes, and Macho switched on the light and opened the door to the bathroom. It was small and dimly lit. A rubber duck sat on the ledge of the tub.

"You can take a shower in here," he said, picking his children's socks off the linoleum floor. "I'm sorry I don't have any soap. What with the rationing and all—"

"No problem. I understand. The shower will be fine."

"I'll leave a change of clothes on the chair."

"Thanks," I said, feeling grateful for the hospitality. "Where do you want me to sleep?"

"My kids sleep in the other bedroom, so you'll have to sleep on the floor in the room with my wife, Ana, and me. You can sleep on the throw rug. It won't be too comfortable. I hope you don't mind."

"No apology needed. Any port in a storm." We both smiled briefly.

Macho got me a blanket and pillow from an old wooden chest, and I put on the clothes he had given me—a Hawaiian shirt with big yellow flowers and pants too short to cover my ankles. But at least they were clothes. I was grateful I wouldn't have to sleep naked in somebody else's house.

Macho turned and looked at me. "One thing," he said before he climbed into bed.

"Yes?" I said. All I wanted was for him to turn off the light so I could go to sleep. I felt like I could not keep my eyes open one minute longer.

"My wife and I have to leave early in the morning. We have some business to conduct in Cojimar—fishing affairs. I'd like you to get out of the house before my kids get up. My little boy frightens easily."

"I'll do my best. Right now I'm just dog tired."

Macho nodded. "Please do. It's important."

"Okay. How many kids do you have?" I asked, although I was just being polite. I was far too tired to care.

"Three. One son and two daughters."

"That's nice," I mumbled. My eyelids were very heavy.

I buttoned my shirt, adjusted my pillow, and fell immediately into a deep, dreamless sleep.

CHAPTER 28

I woke up the next morning with the nagging feeling that something was wrong. I had been dreaming of the day I first saw Fidel and how my grandfather had shielded me with his body. Only this time Fidel was a monster, his eyes fiery red, and his body covered in fish scales.

Macho and his wife's bed sat empty, their bedclothes tangled in a messy pile. I could hear a great deal of commotion outside. Sunshine warmed the bedroom floor and the curtains billowed in. When I turned toward the window, I could see faces of people peering inside. I stood up, rubbing sleep from my eyes. Drowsy and disoriented, I stumbled toward the living room.

The front door was open and Macho's four-year-old son was standing on the sidewalk in his cotton pajamas. He was holding a tattered brown teddy bear and sobbing to a crowd of about thirty people that a stranger was in his house. He said his parents were missing, and he thought I had killed them. A woman stroked his forehead in an effort to soothe him. As soon as he saw me, he clutched his bear to his chest, pointed a small finger at me, and began to cry harder.

In this neighborhood, like others in Cuba, people knew who lived among them. I was a stranger and many of them assumed I was something worse—a criminal.

There was no back door to the house. The only way out was straight through the crowd. I was unfamiliar with the neighborhood, which would lessen my chances to make a getaway. I walked out the front door, hoping to talk my way out of the situation. The crowd began mumbling among themselves, pushing and pointing at me.

"There he is. Get him before he escapes," shouted an old woman wearing pink plastic curlers and a flowered blue housedress. She was waving a crooked, arthritic finger in my direction. It was just the kind of gesture that could spark trouble.

"He's the one the boy described," shouted a man.

Before I could make a move, the crowd pulled back and the director of the coast guard station and one of his guards pushed their way toward me. The director was carrying a pistol. They both were toting machine guns.

"What's going on here?" thundered the guard.

"That man's a criminal," bellowed a short young man with thick, horn-rimmed glasses. It struck me that he was trying to impress the young woman standing next to him with his machismo.

"Stay where you are," ordered the director. "Put your hands up. Make a move and I'll shoot."

I wondered what I had gotten myself into. He was a beefy man, about forty-five, with a stubbly gray beard and several missing teeth. His face was pocked from acne and his black eyes blazed. Bushy eyebrows nearly covered his eyes. He was one of the fiercest men I had ever seen. I tried to maintain my composure while my mind raced to figure out what to tell him.

"What the hell are you doing here?" His voice was low and threatening.

"What are *you* doing here?" I countered in a feeble attempt to buy some time. Adrenalin was coursing through my bloodstream, but I was still half asleep. I needed a moment to think.

"I'll ask you once more," hissed the man. His body was close to mine. He was poking me in the chest with a thick, dirty finger.

"I'm a friend of Macho's," I said. "We stayed out late drinking last night, and he asked me to sleep over."

The man stepped forward, his eyes blazing. I was wondering what I had said that made him so angry. "Liar!" he screamed. "Bastard!" He grabbed the front of my shirt. "Now are you going to tell me what you're doing here, or am I going to have to show you who's boss?"

I took a step backward. "I'm a friend of Macho's," I repeated. I had no desire to get into a fight with this guy—and certainly not under these circumstances. But I would do what I had to.

"You are a lying son of a bitch," he said in a menacing voice. "How do you know I'm not a friend of his?"

I knew I could take this man if need be.

"Because I know all of Macho's friends, and you're no friend of his."

"So you know *all* of Macho's friends?" I was looking him over, measuring his body for where to aim a blow. "Exactly how is that?"

"You stupid jerk," he roared. He grabbed me by the arm and pulled me into the house. I had no idea why. "Look, asshole, do you see that picture?"

A portrait hung slightly askew on the wall above the living room couch. It showed a family of six. The man talking to me was in the middle of the picture. "That's how I know his friends. I'm Gerardo, Macho's brother. I know everyone he knows. So you better come up with another story—and fast."

I winced, knowing I'd have to change tactics. I broke the man's grip, and the way I did it made him take notice. He glared at me sideways, regarding me with more respect. I looked him straight in the eye and said in quiet, controlled voice, "You know, you are absolutely right, Gerardo. Macho is not a friend of mine. I just met him last night. And we didn't have drinks together. In fact, I paid your brother to take me out of Cuba, and it didn't go well. So he brought me here. I haven't murdered him, his wife, or his children. And, by the way, if you poke me in the chest one more time, I will kill you."

"What?" sputtered Gerardo. His voice rose an octave and then cracked. He suddenly looked confused.

"You heard me," I said. "And one more thing. What we did last night was illegal—and you know it. Me, I'm just a kid. The authorities will give me five years—max. But your brother? He's an adult. They'll shoot him on sight. And you being so close to your brother—knowing all his friends as well as you do—they'll figure you were in on it, too. No doubt they'll shoot you along with Macho. So if you want to take me in, do it. But I suggest you use your head. Just let me walk out of here nice and easy like. And you'll never see or hear from me again. Understand?"

The man's body deflated like an old used tire. His shoulders collapsed and his face turned the color of putty. He hesitated for just a moment and then walked with me to the door. The throng was cheering, "Get him. Get the criminal."

Gerardo raised his hand, palm out, to quiet the crowd. "Hey, it's not a problem," he said. "It was all a mistake. This guy's a friend of Macho's. It's just a big misunderstanding."

The crowd muttered and began to disperse. They seemed disappointed. I squeezed between Gerardo and the wall and started walking outside. I figured Macho's brother wouldn't have the nerve to shoot me in front of everyone—but I couldn't be sure. I began walking down the street in my yellow Hawaiian shirt as if I had not a care in the world. A hundred eyes drilled my back.

As I approached the bus stop a couple of blocks from Macho's house, a car pulled up beside me. In it was Cuni.

"I hear you had quite a night," he said.

"Not one I'd care to repeat."

"Where can I drop you?" He reached across to open the passenger door. I slipped into the front seat, practically embedding myself into the upholstery.

"Just take me to Guanabacoa. I'll figure it out from there."

When I got to Guanabacoa, I stopped at my parents' house to change into my extra army uniform. My father was home. He was astonished to see me.

"What are you doing home, and why are you wearing those clothes?"

"I can't explain, and I don't have much time. I have to get back to base before they come looking for me."

My father regarded me carefully. He shook his head. "You tried to escape, didn't you, Frankie?"

I couldn't lie to him. "Yes."

"And you failed?"

"Obviously."

"So you were going to leave without telling me? Your own father?"

"I'm sorry. I wanted to. But if I did, I could've put you all in jeopardy."

My father sighed. I had heard that sigh before. It was his signature sound, an expression of his weariness in waging a war against the inevitable—something my father had done his entire life. I thought he would be angry with me, but I didn't get the sense that he was.

I felt an overwhelming understanding and tenderness for this man who had worked so long and hard in a very difficult job to raise me. He was a kind man and a good father. I was going to miss him.

"It's ironic," he said. "I was going to urge you to leave Cuba anyway."

I looked at him, surprised. "You were?"

"Yes, it's not going to get any better. Your grandfather thinks the Americans will come and save us, but I think that time has passed. It's just going to get worse from here on out."

"You think I should leave?"

"I think you should do what you must to make a life for yourself. I was going to have a long talk with you about it. But now it's not necessary."

"I'm sorry."

"Don't be, Frankie. It's just the way it is. But you should know I'm going to urge your brothers to leave also—when the time is right."

"The time is never right. But you have to keep trying."

My father's eyes conveyed a new respect for me. "What can I do for you, my son?"

"I could use something to get this grease off. After that, I'll need a taxi to take me back to base. I've got some big problems to deal with there."

When I got back to base, a new recruit was on guard, someone I didn't know. It was early afternoon, and I was supposed to have reported back to base by eight o'clock the previous evening.

The guard looked skeptical.

"Do you have a pass?"

"No," I said. I was just about to ask him to call Lazo to let me in when Pino drove down the road in a jeep.

"What's this all about?" he demanded. The suspicion in his eyes was as bright as gilt.

"This man just got back to base," explained the guard. "He was due in last night, and he doesn't have a pass."

"What's going on, Mederos?" asked Pino.

"I'm sorry I'm late. I had a rough night."

"Rough night?"

"Yeah, I went drinking with my friends, and we all fell asleep in the park. Then I had to go home on the bus and get changed and—"

Pino's eyes narrowed and he made a sniffing noise. "What's that I smell on you?"

"I don't know," I lied. "I don't smell anything."

"Well, I'll tell you one thing, it's not alcohol," he said as if relishing this conclusion. Pino turned to the guard. "Take this man to a holding cell. I want him to appear before a military tribunal. I'll be there shortly to question him."

The guard pushed me forward while I tried to think of a way to contact Manny and Lazo. They probably believed I was in the States by now—a depressing thought.

I waited in the cold, dank cell for about an hour before Pino appeared. He looked very smug. I couldn't tell whether he was angry that I was late or delighted to finally have me where he wanted. I stood at attention, and he moved very close to me, positioning his face against mine. It was a method he used to intimidate people. Knowing I was about to get the third degree, I stifled my impulse to turn away and steeled myself for the grilling.

"What did you do last night?" he demanded.

"I told you, I was out with my friends."

"What friends?"

"Friends from Guanabacoa."

"Anyone from here?"

"No, sir."

"What are their names?"

"It doesn't matter. Just friends."

"What were you doing?"

"Drinking."

"You weren't trying to escape?"

"No, why would I do that?"

"Because you're a troublemaker, that's why."

"Well, I wasn't."

"Do you take me for a fool, Mederos?"

"No, sir."

"Then tell me again what you were doing."

"Drinking."

"What's that I smell on your hair?"

"Alcohol, sir."

"You got alcohol on your hair?"

"It's not on my hair. It's on my breath, sir."

"You said it was on your hair."

"With all due respect, sir, *you* said it was on my hair."

"You know what I think?"

"No, sir."

"I think I smell gasoline. Gasoline from a boat. A boat you were on to try to escape. Only it didn't work. Isn't that right, Mederos?"

"No, sir."

"Where did you get the gasoline then?"

"It's not gasoline. It's alcohol, sir."

The questioning went on for five hours, but I stuck to my story. No matter what Pino asked me—or how he framed his questions—I simply told him I had been out drinking with friends. No more, no less. As time went on, his eyes turned feral and his face bloomed red in frustration.

Finally, one of the guards went off duty, and I knew the soldier who came on. He alerted Lazo that I was in a holding cell. Lazo immediately informed Lieutenant Brown who hurried down to the cell to find me. He burst in upon the scene, furious with Pino.

"What the hell are you doing? You have one of my men in a holding cell and you haven't told me?"

"That's right, I do." Pino turned to look at me with contempt. "Mederos tried to escape last night."

"Has he confessed to that?"

"Not yet."

"How long have you held him here?"

"Five hours."

"Five hours and you haven't bothered to inform me?"

"It's none of your business. Mederos is under my authority."

"The hell he is."

"This is a political matter."

"Not if he hasn't confessed."

"I smelled gasoline on him. He claims it's alcohol, but I know better."

"You're an expert on odors?"

"I'm not an expert, but I know the difference between alcohol and gasoline. I'm not an idiot."

"I'm not sure you *do* know the difference," said Brown.

"Are you challenging my authority, Lieutenant?"

"No, you are challenging mine. You've overstepped your bounds, Lieutenant."

"But this is a political issue."

"It's not a political issue just because you say so. You have no proof that this man was trying to escape. You've been itching to find a way to get Mederos for months. Now let my man out of that cell, or I'll report you to the base commander immediately."

The two men glared at each other for what seemed like an eternity while I stood watching. Pino's eyes bulged and his mouth contorted with rage. His nostrils opened slightly as he blew out his frustration. Finally, he turned to the guard and gave the order for my release. The guard unlocked the cell door. Brown nodded to me.

"Clean yourself up and report to my office," he said. I looked at the lieutenant in gratitude and headed toward the bathroom. I took a long, hot shower and scrubbed my skin, my hair, my arms, my legs. I worked to get the remnants of filth from beneath my fingernails and to remove the patches of grease from the back of my legs. When I finished, my skin shone pink.

I dressed in a fresh uniform and went to see Lieutenant Brown. When I entered his office, he looked at me skeptically. He shook his head slightly and pressed his lips together. I wondered where this conversation would take us.

"Are you going to give me the same cockamamie story you gave Pino?"

"What do you want me to say?"

"Tell me where you were last night, Frankie." His voice was soft, almost paternal. His eyes were full of sympathy. I looked at him and I knew I couldn't possibly admit what I had done. It would put him in a terrible position.

"I was out drinking," I said in a low, unconvincing voice.

"Is that the truth?"

"That's the truth."

I felt sad to be lying to him, but I suspected he already knew what had transpired. I looked at him and a faint smile played on my lips.

He returned my stare and the corners of his lips lifted ever so slightly. "Uh-huh," he said. "Get back to your troops."

When the base commander heard what had happened, there was hell to pay. Pino was reprimanded for not informing Brown that he had put me in a holding cell, and Brown was reprimanded for yelling at Pino in front of one of the troops. The men were livid with each other.

Although Brown's authority over his men had been reaffirmed, Pino was not about to forget what had transpired. He had a long and vicious memory.

CHAPTER 29

In certain circles in Cojimar, I had become a bit of a cause célèbre. Macho had told Cuni how I risked my life to save Joey and Pedro, two kids I didn't even know. Cuni couldn't believe what had happened—he never thought the boys would get so tired they would almost drown.

To Señor Lopez I was nothing less than a hero. He was so impressed with my actions that he told the story to many people involved in clandestine operations in Cuba. That one action enabled me to gain a reputation as someone who could be trusted. He told Cuni he was willing to do anything possible to help me, including providing me with whatever money I might need to escape.

In August of 1966, the government granted Magda's family their visas. Sophia and Rigo's home had already been inventoried, and they were anxiously awaiting issuance of their own visas.

With our days together quickly drawing to a close, Magda and I again discussed getting married in the States. We wanted to marry in a Catholic church sooner rather than later. It was an exciting yet difficult time, full of conflicting emotions and passions. I kissed Magda and her family a teary goodbye in mid-September.

With Magda's father gone, Rigo and Sophia were my only link to Cuni. Fortunately, Cuni had taken a keen interest in me and kept Rigo well informed about upcoming plans.

Ever aware of the dangers involved, Cuni requested I name a couple of people whom I could trust if things got dicey.

My choice was Uncle Luis whom I had not seen in a year but who had consistently voiced anticommunist sentiments. He lived a couple of miles from my home in Guanabacoa. Cuni suggested I visit him on my next leave to see whether his political views had changed. I stopped by on a pleasant Sunday afternoon. After dinner we went out to his backyard.

His property was surrounded by a cinder-block wall, seven-feet-high on the sides and four-feet-high in back. An old wooden outhouse listed behind some weeds, despite the fact that the house now had indoor plumbing. I had used the outhouse when I was a kid, and it provided Luis and me with an opportunity to reminisce about the good old days. Rosa, his wife, had asked Luis to fill it in many times over the years, but Luis kept it as a backup in case there was ever a problem with the toilet in the house.

We opened the door to the outhouse and watched three brown rats scurry down the hole, breaking the cobwebs that laced it. The stench took our breath away. It was so intense it made my eyes water. My hand flew to my nose to ward off the smell. I closed the door and stepped away from the odor.

Beyond the back wall was an empty lot where Uncle Luis grew corn and kept a cow and some chickens.

"So, how's the army treating you?" asked Luis.

I shrugged. "It's the army, what can I say? How's it going for you?"

Luis sighed. "Not very well. Since I lost my job at the Coca-Cola factory, I can hardly make ends meet. Luckily, we've got the cow and chickens for milk and eggs. It keeps us going for now, but there's no light at the end of the tunnel."

"I'm sorry things are so tough."

"It's bad, Frankie. I can't find a job—there's just no work to be had." He hesitated a moment, thinking and shaking his head in frustration. "Fidel is the worst leader we've ever had—even worse than that crook, Batista."

"Yeah, but he's smarter than Batista," I said, trying to keep the conversation on the topic of Fidel.

"Smart enough to ruin the country. Cuba will never be the same." He hesitated for a moment and lowered his voice. "To tell you the truth, I can't take it anymore, Frankie. I'm thinking about leaving Cuba. I'd like to get my whole family out."

I looked at my uncle, surprised. "Do you have a plan?"

"I'm working on it. I'll just take some time."

"They sure don't make it easy to leave."

"Not easy at all."

The conversation continued. I left convinced that I could still trust my uncle.

When I got back to the barracks, Lieutenant Brown lined up the troops and told us that we would be participating in the Multiprovince Military Exercises to be held in Las Villas, a couple of hours' drive from base.

This was to be the largest military exhibition ever held in Cuba. The exercises would include the infantry division, the 57-millimeter cannon division, and three rocket operators, including myself, Lazo, and Manny. And that was just the troops from our base. All told, more than a thousand army personnel would participate in the event and thousands of people would attend.

Due to my experience and past performance, Brown again chose me to demonstrate the ATGMs. Once more the top military brass would be on hand to witness the event, only this time it would be attended by both Castro brothers: Raúl and Fidel.

Since so many military units would be involved, we were informed that we had to leave base around November 20, 1966, to practice for more than a month with units from various provinces throughout the country. The exact date of our departure was still undetermined.

Pino was none too pleased that I was again to demonstrate the rockets. His demeanor toward me was icy. He routinely reviewed my file for the slightest transgressions and scrutinized the files of my friends Lazo and Manny. He watched us like a hawk, ready to pounce on any infraction of the rules, any sign of subversion.

On November fifteenth, one of the guards at the base notified me that I had an unexpected visitor: Magda's Aunt Sophia. She had told the guard that my mother was gravely ill, and she needed to talk to me. Brown issued me an hour-long pass. I climbed into Sophia's car and we drove to Santa Maria to talk.

We sat in the car by the side of the road. Sophia had taken her usual care with her clothing and was impeccably dressed, high heels and all.

"What's so important that you'd risk your life to come here?" I asked. I was worried that something really had happened to my mother. That thought was almost more than I could bear.

"I have news from Cuni," said Sophia. She kept her voice low, even though we were in the privacy of the car. She fixed her eyes on mine. "He's gotten a reliable boat and is planning a 'trip' for you and nine other army personnel."

This was unexpected and welcome news. I let out a sigh of relief. Maybe this was finally my break. "When?"

"Late November, early December. The exact date depends on the weather. You know the drill."

I felt suddenly confused, panicky. "Christ, that's when I'm supposed to be in Las Villas, practicing for military exercises."

"Can't you get out of it?"

"Impossible. I'm in charge of launching the rocket. It's a big deal— the highlight of the event. Everyone will be there, including Fidel. It's a command performance."

Sophia sucked in her breath. "Well, Cuni says you need to leave base within the next few days—no matter what's going on. So you'll have to leave before the exercises take place. That's all there is to it. Rigo and I can help."

"Do you know what you're saying? As soon as they discover me missing, they'll launch the biggest manhunt in the history of the country."

"That doesn't surprise me. But Cuni says this might be the last boat out. He's taking a big chance with the weather on this trip, and he can't guarantee any others. It's an opportunity you can't pass up."

I looked at Sophia with renewed respect. This was one courageous lady.

"I'm not the only one taking a chance here," I said. "As soon as they discover me missing, they'll come looking for you. You and your entire family will be under suspicion. They'll question you—and God knows what else. What will you do?"

Sophia reached for my hand. "I'll deny knowing anything about it. I don't owe those people a thing. I have no qualms about lying to save you."

"Well, the guard saw you today so they know who you are and what you look like. It won't be difficult to make the connection. You'll be taking a very big risk. Are you sure you're up for it?"

"If you aren't taking risks, you aren't living life. And from what Cuni has told us about what you did the last time you tried to escape, I figure you're a pretty good bet."

"This won't be like last time. Last time I was lucky. This time Pino has me under a microscope. He already has his suspicions about me. And believe me, his pride will demand that he bring me to justice if I cause any trouble."

Sophia thought for a moment. "Why does he hate you so much?"

I sighed wearily. "We got off on the wrong foot a long time ago. He thinks I'm the reason so many of the men challenge him—and he's right."

"I see."

"Besides, if I don't show up for the exercises, he's going to be in big trouble himself. He may lose his job—and perhaps worse. He has a lot at stake. As do Lieutenant Brown and the base commander. So they'll pull out all the stops to get me back. They'll do anything to avoid embarrassment and disgrace."

Sophia's face suddenly looked tired and drawn. Yet there was a determination in the set of her jaw and the muscles around her eyes that I had never seen. I understood how she could have founded and run a school. She was kind, bright, and extremely determined.

"I have no sympathy for those people," she said. "They are grown men. They are a big part of the problem in this country. They can fend for themselves."

I locked eyes with Sophia. I wanted to reiterate the implications of what she was proposing. I had to make sure no doubt existed in her mind regarding the possible consequences of her actions.

"Once I leave, I can't come back to base under any circumstances—whether the 'trip' materializes or not. If I defect, Pino will do everything possible to find and kill me. Guaranteed. And that may involve you. When that happens, I cannot—and will not—surrender."

"Nor should you." Sophia nodded. It was a sage nod, more like she was acknowledging my motives and character than agreeing with my reasoning.

"It may mean they'll put you and your whole family in jail. It may mean torture. Even death. Are you getting the picture?"

"I understand. But we can't just sit by and let Fidel run roughshod over everyone." She considered for just the slightest moment before saying, "It's a big risk, but one I'm willing to take."

I shook my head in amazement. "But I'm not even related to you."

Sophia smiled and squeezed my hand. "You are now," she said. "And some day you will be officially part of the family. We're all in this together."

A tear appeared in the corner of my eye. "Then we agree?"

"You bet," said Sophia as if she were leading a pep rally. I could hardly believe my good fortune of having this remarkable woman on my side. "When you escape, you'll come to my house. Cuni will know what to do from there."

Sophia reached over and hugged me. I was wordless, in awe of her courage. I embraced her long and hard before she drove me back to base.

The next morning Pino lined up the troops to tell us about the upcoming event.

"Soon, you will participate in the most important military exercises in the history of the country," he said. "Your performance will be witnessed by Fidel and Raúl Castro as well as top representatives from the Soviet Union, Hungary, Czechoslovakia, Poland, and Vietnam."

Just the mention of all of this gave me a headache. Sweat gathered in my armpits. I adjusted my body slightly while I remained at attention.

"As you know, Cuba has the strongest army in all Latin America. These exercises will demonstrate our military power to the world, especially to the Americans. We need to scare them, to show them what we can do if necessary. Even though no American officials will attend the event, they will know our capabilities. Word spreads in the intelligence community. Am I making myself clear?"

"Yes, sir."

"We will move out on November twenty-sixth or twenty-seventh. Until then, Lieutenant Brown will exercise the troops extra hours every day. You are to remain sharp and focused."

"Yes, sir."

"To make the best possible impression, you will all be issued new military uniforms and helmets made by our comrades in communist China. Pack your uniforms, clean your machine guns, and be ready to go.

"We will depart at two a.m. so as not to disturb the civilian population. That way we will travel through the cities in the middle of the night while people are asleep. I'm counting on you to make these the most successful military exercises Cuba has ever held. Any questions?"

"No, sir."

"Dismissed, men."

It was time to inform Manny and Lazo about my plans. Not the details, but the general outline. They were horrified.

"This is the worst possible time for you to leave," warned Lazo. "The entire world is watching, and when you don't show up, they'll come looking for you. You can bank on it."

"The timing can't be helped. I've put my trust in a good man who can get me out now—and I'm going with that."

"Christ almighty!" said Lazo. "This is the most ridiculous idea I've ever heard. The first time we were able to cover for you. And last time you got lucky that Brown came to your defense. But if you let down the chain of command at the exercises, no one can help you. Not Brown, not Manny, not me."

"I know the problems involved."

Manny looked at me in dismay. "You know what will happen? They'll post your picture on TV and on telephone poles all over the country. The police, the militia, and every CDR in every neighborhood in Cuba will be on the lookout for you. It will be a manhunt the likes of which the country has never seen."

"I know."

"Then use the good sense God gave you." I nodded my head back and forth and Manny looked exasperated. "Can't you at least wait until after the exercises?"

"No. If I don't do this now, I have no idea when—or if—I'll get another chance to escape. Fewer and fewer fishermen are willing to risk it. Too many people have died. My window of opportunity is now, and I have to take it."

Manny put his head in his hands and grumbled. "Then promise me you'll take your machine gun and enough ammunition to defend yourself. If you don't use it, you can throw it into the ocean. But you've got to have it—just in case."

Lazo looked thoughtful. "Maybe that's not the right strategy," he said.

"What are you talking about? How could he possibly benefit by not being armed?" Manny's voice was harsh and filled with conviction.

Lazo paused for a moment and looked at Manny as if he had given this some thought. "The first thing they'll do when Frankie doesn't show up is to search his cubbyhole. If his weapon is missing, they'll go after him immediately. But if his gun is still there, we could stall them—say he went to see his girlfriend or something. It might buy him a few hours."

I was grateful for Lazo's clear thinking. "He's right," I said. "A few hours could make a world of difference."

Manny sighed heavily and adjusted his shoulders. A look of sadness crossed his eyes before he pulled me into an embrace. When he finished hugging me, he said, "When?"

"Late tonight, after everything has quieted down. That way they won't miss me until morning."

I left under the cover of darkness with the help of Manny and Lazo. A slight breeze whipped the air and a steady rain slicked the streets. Rain beaded my hair and eyebrows. Branches of trees were reflected in black puddles like long slithering snakes. I ran all the way to Santa Maria, called Sophia to pick me up at our arranged meeting place, and then flattened my body against an ocher-colored building, nervously awaiting her arrival.

Sophia and Rigo arrived in short order and drove me to their house. The sun was just cresting the horizon. I stripped off my military clothes, including my underwear, rolled them into a ball, and stuffed them in an old linen bag for disposal.

I put on civilian clothes but carried nothing that would identify me: no license, no wallet, not even a toothbrush. Sophia had arranged for my clothes to be disposed of safely so I would leave nothing incriminating behind.

I ate a quick breakfast and prepared myself psychologically for my departure. Cuni had already arranged with Sophia and Rigo to drop me at the home of Señor Lopez. As part of Havana's underground, his home would serve as my hiding place until the boat left. I was eager to get there. The less time Sophia and Rigo spent with me the better.

The couple climbed into the front seat of their 1957 Chevy Bel Air. I lay down in the back seat so I couldn't be seen. Rigo was very nervous about transporting a fugitive, and the poor man kept lifting his shoulders toward his ears, blinking his eyes, and wiping his chin in anxiety. He was driving very cautiously, obeying the speed limit with the utmost care. The last thing he needed was to be stopped by the police for speeding.

Sophia began talking to me from the front seat, as much to distract us from a very nerve-racking situation as to impart information.

"I talked with the family the other day. Everyone is okay in the States."

"How's Magda?"

"Fine. She's missing you."

"Good. Did you tell her I love her?"

"I told her as much as I could without mentioning your name. I always speak in vague terms in case the authorities are listening in on our conversation. You can't be too careful."

"I understand. Does she know about my situation?"

"I told her someone she knew was going 'to party' today or

tomorrow. I'm sure she understood. She said to tell you to be careful and to have a very good time."

I smiled and leaned back down against the seat, thinking about how wonderful it would be to see Magda again. I could picture her face, her smile, her hair. When I thought about the last time I kissed her, I could practically taste her lips on mine. Our life together was going to be great. I just needed to get through the next couple of days in hiding and then survive the trip to the States.

I closed my eyes for a minute, listening to the sounds of the city. A band was practicing in the distance, probably a high school band. They weren't very good. I was trying to figure out the song they were playing.

When we turned onto one of the main streets in Havana, jack-hammers blasted the air. I sat up a little and peered over the front seat to see what was happening.

"Watch out, men are working over there," warned Sophia in a high-pitched voice. We were a couple hundred feet from the police station, and several policemen were milling around outside.

"Oh, my God!" Rigo turned around to look at me. "Get down. Hide!" His face was red and contorted in panic. He began talking to himself under his breath: "What should I do? What will become of us?"

"Watch where you're going," screamed Sophia. Her hands flew to her face and she leaned back in her seat, her right foot braced firmly against the dashboard. "What the hell is wrong with you, Rigo?"

Rigo swerved the car, but not fast enough to avoid crashing through a barrier and sinking the right front tire into a deep pothole. The car stopped with a thump, the tire suspended in air, spinning use-lessly. The boards of a sawhorse littered the street and a red lantern lay crushed on its side. Glass shattered into a thousand shards that sparkled in the light. For a moment we sat in stunned silence. I looked out the window to see a policeman coming toward us.

"Christ, what do we do now?" moaned Rigo.

"Just stay calm. I'll take care of it."

I got out of the car and opened the front door for Sophia. She stood tall in her black pumps. "Talk to Rigo," I said softly. "Just keep him busy until I straighten things out."

I walked toward the policemen very casually. "We've run into a little problem," I said with a smile. I was hoping my face wouldn't betray my emotions.

"Looks like it," he said.

"Would you mind giving me a hand? It's not a very deep hole. I think we can push the car out of it without much trouble. I'd really appreciate it."

"I think we can help," he said. He turned and waved to his buddies who were smoking cigarettes outside the station.

"Help me get this guy out of this pothole," he hollered.

The men grumbled a little, took a final puff on their cigarettes, and snuffed them out beneath their shoes before walking our way. One of them looked me up and down. The others didn't bother.

Four policemen pushed the back of the car while I worked the steering wheel. We soon extracted the vehicle from the hole. The entire operation took less than five minutes.

I shook the hands of all the men, thanking them profusely.

A policeman looked at me. "Maybe you should drive, instead of him," he joked, pointing at Rigo. We chuckled. The last thing I needed was to get behind the wheel where I could be seen by every passerby. But I couldn't say so. Sophia piped up.

"He would drive, but it's not his car," she explained. She winked at the men. "You know how you men are about letting other people drive your cars." The men laughed at themselves and nodded. Rigo, Sophia, and I got back into the car, and the men waved us on while I pretended not to be as relieved as I was.

Shortly thereafter we pulled up to a lovely home with a stone pathway bordered with marigolds. Señor Lopez stood outside, chatting with a couple of neighbors. Sophia and Rigo stayed in the car while I got out. I turned and casually waved goodbye as if I would see them again very soon.

When Señor Lopez saw me, he excused himself from his friends, opened the door, and waved me in. He was a tall man, especially for a Cuban, about six foot one. He had a pleasant face and wore beautifully tailored clothes, although his collar and cuffs were frayed. Like the rest of us, it had been years since he had bought any new clothes. He shook my hand vigorously. He was an ebullient, welcoming man.

Señor Lopez ushered me into the foyer. He, his wife, Maria, and their two sons lived on the first floor of this elegant house, and their daughter, Esme, occupied the second floor. Señor Lopez explained that Esme's husband had been sent to prison for "subversive activity." She lived upstairs to be near her family.

"Cuni has told me so much about you," said Lopez. "I'm honored to have you in my home."

"I'm happy to be here."

Señor Lopez looked at me wistfully. "I can't thank you enough for saving my boys." He took his wife's hand. The look that passed between them was one of pure love. "You were truly heroic. My family is forever indebted to you."

"That's kind of you to say. And it's very generous of you to put me up. I know it's risky."

"It's the least I can do. I've worked with Cuni for a long time. He's a good and honorable man. He's done a lot for people. I've told him that I'm here for anything you need. Anything. "

"Thanks. That means so much to me."

The boys burst into the room and ran over to hug me. They were jumping around like small children. They were in much better spirits than when I last saw them.

Joey looked up at me shyly. "Thank you so much for saving us. If it weren't for you, my brother and I would be dead. I pray for you every night."

I stooped to be at eye level with them. "Thank you, Joey. But that's what a man does. I'm sure you would do the same thing if you were in my position."

Joey and Pedro smiled and extended their hands for me to shake. "Well, thanks anyway," said Pedro.

Señor Lopez smiled. "Cuni has told everyone in the underground about what you did. The soldiers who are going with you on the trip have all heard about you. They're eager to meet you."

"I'm eager to meet them, too. But tell me, Señor, what's your involvement in all of this?"

"I provide funds where needed."

"Why, may I ask?"

"I hate Fidel. And when an ordinary citizen escapes to safety, it's a blow to him. But when a soldier escapes to the United States, it undermines his entire regime. It's my way of helping to get rid of him. It's very important to me."

"What about your boys? Why aren't they going?"

"This trip is only for soldiers. The boys will go at a later date."

I knew enough not to ask more questions.

"Let's get you settled," said Maria. She handed me a pillow and sheets and said she'd be back in a minute. She returned with clean underwear, a comb, a toothbrush, and pajamas.

"You can stay with us as long as you need," she said. "But for your sake, we hope it's only for a couple of days."

I took the nightclothes from her, but I knew I'd be too nervous to use them. I bedded down in my street clothes and kept my shoes on in case I had to leave in a hurry.

Both of the boys came in to hug me goodnight. Joey leaned over and kissed me on the forehead. It felt great to be appreciated. I hugged him and thought about how nice it would be have sons like Pedro and Joey one day.

I slept very lightly.

CHAPTER 30

As usual, Lazo got the troops up around five a.m. for a long run, and they returned to the mess hall around seven for breakfast. No one had missed me yet. At ten a.m. everyone gathered to leave for Las Villas. This was the first time Pino noticed my absence.

Pino called Brown into his office for questioning. Brown reported that Lazo had told him I was sick. He suggested that they send one of the troops to check the latrines. When it was reported that I wasn't there, Pino informed the base commander that a man was missing.

Captain Martinez sounded the alarm and questioned the guard who was on duty the previous night. But he claimed no knowledge of the situation.

If I were to miss military exercises, Pino and Brown would have a lot of explaining to do to Raúl Castro. I can only surmise what transpired.

"What's your gut feeling on this?" asked Pino.

"The last time he was late he went out drinking, but he did report back," said Brown.

"Well, I never believed that story."

"Believe what you want."

"He knows how important these exercises are, and he knows not to miss them."

"Yes, but if he's going to be away for more than a month, he probably wanted to see his girlfriend before he left. He's pretty lovesick."

"I don't want to report a man missing if we don't have to," said Pino.

"What do you suggest?"

Pino thought for a moment. "Get Lazo and Manny in here."

Manny and Lazo arrived in Pino's office, trying to conceal their anxiety. They pretended that they were completely dumbfounded that I was missing.

"Do you know where Mederos is?" Pino asked Lazo.

"No, sir."

"I must warn you, there will be severe repercussions if you lie. Are you sure?"

"Yes, sir."

"Was he at breakfast this morning?"

"No, sir. I haven't seen him all morning. He didn't look well yesterday. I understood he was sick."

"Was anything unusual going on with him?"

"What do you mean, sir?"

"To your knowledge, did he have any problems? Was he depressed?"

"No, sir."

Pino sighed. "It's imperative that he demonstrate the rocket at military exercises. We need to find him —soon. Had he mentioned that he was planning to escape?"

A muscle in Lazo's cheek jumped involuntarily, but Pino failed to notice. "No, sir, he never said anything like that."

"Manny?"

"I never heard him speak of it."

Pino hesitated for a moment, thinking. "Was something bothering him?"

"Not that I know of," said Manny. "Except—"

"Except what?"

"Except yesterday he said he wasn't feeling well."

"That's all?"

"That's all he said."

"What about the girlfriend? Do you think he went to see her?"

"I have no idea," said Manny.

"Lazo?"

"He didn't say anything like that to me."

"But it's a possibility?"

"Anything's possible."

"Do you know where she lives?"

"I have no idea," lied Manny. "Every time we've seen her, it's been at the beach."

"You know her name, don't you?"

"It's Magda," said Manny, trying to appear helpful. "Magda Hernández."

"Too bad it's such a common name," interjected Brown.

"Do you know where she goes to school?"

"In Guanabacoa, I believe," said Lazo.

Pino stood to indicate the interview was over. "That's all for now, men. If you think of anything else, notify us immediately."

Manny and Lazo saluted and left. They said not a word, but exchanged worried glances as they walked down the hall.

Lieutenants Pino and Brown had a window of twenty-four hours before they had to leave for Las Villas. They had wanted to get an early start so they'd have more time to practice on location for military exercises. But, if necessary, they could postpone departure until the following day. The troops were well trained, and the delay probably wouldn't make much difference to their performance. They'd prefer to postpone the unit's arrival for a day rather than to show up without me—and have to explain my absence.

Giving me the benefit of the doubt, the two lieutenants decided the best course of action was to keep things as quiet as possible and try to find me on their own. They immediately left for the high school in Guanabacoa and obtained Magda's address from the school's secretary. For whatever reason, however, she failed to mention that Magda had not been in school for more than a month.

When the lieutenants arrived at Magda's house, they found it abandoned with a sign posted outside that read, "Do Not Enter. House Inventoried." Pino and Brown walked around the neighborhood, inquiring about the family's whereabouts. No one knew where the Hernándezes had gone.

Finally, one woman told them that she had not seen anyone come or go from the house for weeks. Pino checked with a member of the local CDR and his suspicions were confirmed. The family had been issued visas and was thought to be in the States.

Pino turned to Brown and said, "This man had a girlfriend whose family was anticommunist, and you didn't know it? What's wrong with you?"

"It's not my job to know the political sympathies of all of my men," retorted Brown. "That's your department."

"With the amount of time you spend with your troops, I'd expect you to know these things. If you had paid the slightest attention to what was going on with your men, we wouldn't be in this mess."

"You want me to grill every soldier about the political leanings of every single person they know?"

"It wouldn't be a bad idea."

Brown shook his head. "It would be a total waste of time. If a man's family was anticommunist, do you think he'd tell me?"

"There are ways."

"It doesn't matter," snapped Brown. "We must find Mederos before we leave for Las Villas."

"I don't like this at all," Pino told Mikhail when he returned to base. "Mederos didn't go to see his girlfriend. She left the country more than a month ago. I'm willing to give him a few more hours because he's our best man—and we need him. But my guess is he's trying to escape."

"Maybe he missed his girlfriend so much he went crazy," offered the commander. "Maybe he shot himself, hung himself—who knows?"

"Not Mederos. That's not his style. He's one of the coolest men I've ever known. Christ, he could launch those rockets without blinking an eye. The guy has nerves of steel. Besides, he didn't take his gun."

"True," said Mikhail.

"We have to face reality. A key man in the force has defected, and we must leave no stone unturned to find him."

"It's not going to be easy. He's not only good at what he does, he's smart as a whip."

"He may be smarter than any one of us, but he's not smarter than all of us," said Pino.

Mikhail raised an eyebrow. "What do you mean?"

"Never mind," said Pino. He walked out of the office without shutting the door.

CHAPTER 31

I could not have been more grateful for the hospitality of the Lopez family. Although I was very nervous, I felt like I had found a safe haven from the authorities—at least for a few days.

Señor Lopez and his wife treated me with the utmost care and respect, and Pedro and Joey seemed thrilled to have me around. The second night I was there, I helped the boys with their math home-work. Joey had a test the next day, and he came home after school, proudly displaying an *A*. His parents praised him, but he graciously gave most of the credit to me.

Joey was an earnest, ambitious young man. He showed me his baseball card collection and some coins his grandfather had given him. He stored them carefully in a cigar box, each one wrapped in a small scrap of cloth so they wouldn't get scratched. He impressed me by knowing all the dates of the coins and which country they came from. He was obviously interested in history.

After dinner, Joey and I played gin rummy. He told me he played a lot of cards with his friends—and it showed. He quickly won the first two games. I prevailed in the second two and he won the last. I congratulated him, but he modestly said it was just good luck. I think he felt uncomfortable beating me. He reminded me quite a bit of my-self at his age. His brother wandered into the room when the game was finished, and the three of us talked about getting together in America.

Maria's cooking was a highlight of my stay. The first night she pre-pared lemon chicken with beans, rice, and fried plantains. She served

a chocolate cake for dessert. It was a rare and wonderful treat. I had
no idea where she managed to get chocolate, and I wasn't about to
ask. It had been a long time since I'd had a home-cooked meal.

Suddenly, a wave of nostalgia washed over me. I missed my own
family. I thought about the times we had shared in the past and the
times we'd be unable to share in the future.

I wasn't sure whether my father had told my mother about me
trying to escape. I tried not to think about it. If she knew, she'd be
worried and unable to sleep. I could imagine her lighting a candle in
church for me, making a novena, and pacing the floor with her rosary
beads after the family had gone to bed. I hoped my father had spared
her this news, at least for a while.

On my third day with the Lopezes, I wandered into the living room
with a cup of coffee. The curtains were closely drawn for security reasons and the lamp on the end table was turned down low. I grabbed
a coaster and placed my coffee cup on it so as not to leave a mark on
the table. I was feeling a little drowsy and hoping the coffee would
keep me awake.

The boys were at school and Señor Lopez and his wife were at
work. I had the house to myself. I tried my best to relax. I sat on the
sofa to watch the news, hoping my picture wasn't being splashed across
every television screen in the country.

To my surprise, there was no mention of me. Instead, there was
an episode of the television series *Zorro*. I was so engrossed in the adventures of the masked swordsman that, for a moment, I forgot about
my situation.

The door creaked open. I looked up to see Esme, a startlingly
beautiful woman in her early twenties. She had flawless skin, a finely
chiseled nose, and full lips dressed in pink lipstick. Long eyelashes
fringed her brown eyes and large, round breasts strained the bodice of
her red dress. Silk stockings accentuated shapely legs that ended in
black high heels.

Her slender waist was cinched in a wide leather belt. Pearl earrings dangled almost to her collarbone, and a matching pearl bracelet encircled her wrist. It was not the kind of attire I was used to seeing women wear, especially during the day. I felt a surge of adrenalin as I stood to greet her.

"Please, sit down," Esme said. Her wide smile revealed a set of perfect white teeth. She brushed a strand of wavy black hair away from her face.

"I heard the television and wondered if you might like some company." She nodded toward the television set. "Do you mind?"

"No, please. Turn it off, I'd love to have some company." Esme walked to the other side of the room and switched off the TV. She sat down on the couch next to me, crossed her legs, and began tapping her foot nervously. I studied her slender ankles with interest.

She smiled and nodded. "My parents call you their hero."

"That's overstating it. But thanks anyway."

Esme sensed that I didn't know what to say, so she took the lead in the conversation. "I don't mean to be nosy, but how long do you think you'll be staying with us?"

"I'm not sure. I could be here a week or so—or I could leave today. It's out of my control."

Esme took my hand. "It must be difficult. My father told me how you saved my brothers."

I pulled my hand away from hers and smiled. "It was my honor. Pedro and Joey are very special people."

"Joey said you helped him with his homework. Are you a teacher?"

"No, I'm just good at math."

"I'm terrible at math." Esme inched closer to me and pressed the length of her leg against mine. I felt myself getting aroused.

I took a deep breath. "Tell me about your husband," I said, hoping to steer the conversation in a different direction.

Esme sighed and waved her hand dismissively. "He's in prison. He's been gone for a very long time—and he's got a lot more time to serve. I'm very lonely and bored without him."

"How long is his term?" I asked, wanting to keep the conversation focused on her husband.

"Six years. More than four to go."

"I'm sorry."

"What about you? Are you married?"

"Not yet, but I have a girlfriend. She's already left for the States."

"So you must be lonely, too."

"I miss her, but I've been very busy."

Esme snuggled against me. I could feel the heat of her body against mine. I closed my eyes for a minute, enjoying the sensation. She put her hand on my thigh, and I looked up at her, startled. I let her hand linger for a minute before I placed it back on her lap. She frowned.

Provocative cologne scented the young woman's skin, and I was beginning to feel a little disoriented. My body urged me to surrender to temptation, but my mind warned against it.

I was in a safe house, fleeing for my life. Being so powerfully attracted to a woman was the last thing I expected to happen. My heart was racing. I was trying to quell my urge to take Esme in my arms, to run my hands over her breasts, and to insert my tongue into her mouth. *Christ!* I thought. *Have you lost your marbles?*

Esme interrupted my reverie. "It seems like we're in the same boat," she said in a low, husky voice.

"What do you mean?"

"You're missing your girlfriend, and I'm missing my husband. We're both very lonely."

"Uh-huh," I said. I didn't want to insult her, but I didn't want to encourage her either. What if her parents came home and found us doing something improper? I shuddered to think of the consequences.

Esme draped her arm around my shoulder, pressing her firm breasts against my side. She began kissing my ear, darting her tongue in and out and nibbling my earlobe. I sighed and moved slightly away from her. I broke out in a cold sweat—it was all I could do to resist her.

"What's the matter? Don't you like me?"

"Of course, I like you. Who wouldn't like you?"

"I don't know. You seem—"

"What?"

"Reluctant."

I sat up straight and moved my body a few inches away. "I have a girlfriend," I said. "And you have a husband."

"Why should that matter? Neither one of them are here, are they? Let's just relax and have fun." She ran her hands over my chest and undid the top button on my shirt. "They'll never know. We wouldn't be hurting anyone."

I took a long look at Esme. What she was saying sounded like something a man would say to a woman, not the reverse. I considered her proposal for a minute. She *was* alluring.

I took a deep breath. I needed to keep my wits about me. As much as I wanted her, I knew it would be folly to follow my instincts. I tried to focus on my goal of escaping. I hadn't come this far to lose everything over the need for a woman.

Suddenly the image of Magda flashed through my mind, and I imagined the guilt I'd feel if I betrayed her. I was just about to say something when the front door burst open, and Esme's mother walked in carrying a bag of groceries. She headed straight for the kitchen, barely giving us a glance. I got up from the couch, fastened my button, and took the bag from Maria. I set it down on the kitchen table.

"I hope you're hungry," Maria said cheerfully. "I've got food for dinner." She looked at me, and said, "I hope it's enough for a young soldier."

"And a hungry one at that," I said. I smiled at Maria, and she patted me on the back. Esme stood up and unpacked the bag. And I went down the hall to use the bathroom.

·　·　·

Right after dinner, Señor Lopez took me aside and said, "Cuni is coming tonight to take you to a different location."

"Where?" I asked, both sad and relieved to be leaving this house.

"He's contacted your Uncle Luis, and your uncle's willing to put you up for a while. Cuni thinks it's too dangerous for you to stay here much longer. I'm too well known for helping people out."

"But my uncle lives right in the center of Guanabacoa. That's where I grew up. My parents live there. It's the first place they'd look."

"That's why Cuni wants you to go there. He believes it'll be the last place the authorities will search. He says they'll figure you're too smart to be hiding in the most likely of places."

"Reverse psychology?"

"Something like that."

"What do you think I should do?"

"Cuni has a lot of experience in these matters. You should trust his judgment."

"All right," I said. But I wasn't totally convinced of the wisdom of this decision.

That night around ten, I was welcomed into the home of my uncle, his wife, Rosa, and my cousins, Magali and Marisol. The girls were seven and eight. Cuni came in to talk with Luis for a while before he left.

"Frankie will be here with you for about ten days," he said. "It may be a few days more or less, depending on how soon I can get a boat."

"I understand," said my uncle. "My nephew is welcome to stay here as long as necessary."

Cuni nodded. "This is a very dangerous situation, and I want you to understand what's required."

"Shoot," said my uncle.

"The most important thing is to keep everything looking normal. Do the same chores, talk to the same people, keep your regular routine. Don't do anything unusual or anything that will draw attention."

My uncle grew silent for a moment. Something was obviously bothering him. "We usually keep the front door open during the day," he said in a concerned tone. "What should we do about that?"

"If that's what you do, then do it," said Cuni. Luis and I looked at each other quizzically. Luis seemed puzzled as if wondering how this could be accomplished.

"Let me look around," said Cuni.

Cuni surveyed the house. The rooms ran one behind the other from front to back: living room, master bedroom, girls' bedroom, and kitchen. A small hallway led to the backyard. Cuni examined the closets and the backyard. Rosa made us some coffee, and we sat down at the kitchen table to talk.

"Frankie will have to hide under the bed in your bedroom during the day," Cuni told my uncle.

"All right," said Luis tentatively.

Cuni thought for a moment. "What time do you usually close your door at night?"

"When it gets dark—eight thirty to nine."

Cuni looked at me. "Then you'll have to stay under the bed all day, every day, until you leave. Lie face down so you can see people's feet in case someone comes into the house. Eat lunch under the bed. The way the house is laid out, you can scoot to the bathroom without being seen. Wait until it's dark to come out for exercise and dinner. You can sleep on the couch at night—as long as the door is closed and the shades are drawn."

"All right," I said, feeling nervous about the prospect of doing this.

"I'm sorry, Frankie, I know this will be uncomfortable, but it's necessary to ensure your safety."

"It's not a problem."

Cuni turned to Luis. "Are you sure you're okay with this? You're taking a big risk."

"I'm glad to do it," said Luis. "I have only one request." He hesitated.

"Which is?"

"That I be permitted to go with Frankie when he leaves."

Cuni looked momentarily perplexed, as if he wasn't sure what he heard. I was also surprised at the pronouncement.

"You want to escape, too?" asked Cuni.

"I do."

"What about your family?"

"I'll claim them once I get to the States. But I have to get myself out first. I've wanted to do this for a very long time. I just haven't been able to figure out how. This is a chance of a lifetime."

Cuni let out a whistle and leaned back in his chair. He looked up at the ceiling as if he were thinking, counting. A couple of minutes elapsed.

Finally, he said, "All right. I can make room for one more man. Are you sure you want to do this?"

"I am."

"What about the money?" I asked, knowing full well how much the fishermen charged.

Luis suddenly looked stricken. "I didn't know I had to pay. How much money do I need?"

"Don't worry about it," said Cuni. "I'll talk to Lopez. I'm sure he'll cover your expenses."

Luis and Rosa instructed their girls not to say anything to anyone about me being in the house. The next morning Magali and Marisol went to school as usual. Rosa opened the front door as usual while I hid under the bed.

The bed was covered with sheets and a yellow chenille bedspread that hung about an inch from the floor. Rosa tuned the radio to her usual station, and she chatted outside her house with the same neighbors—as always.

When the girls got home from school, they played with their friends, running in and out of the house as children do. Sometimes they'd come into the room and jump on the bed. Depending on how hard they jumped, the springs would press on my back. But, to my relief, Rosa would always scold them and scoot them away. Often a ball would land near the bed, and I'd knock it away with the back of my hand without being noticed.

I used the bathroom and ate breakfast early in the morning while it was still dark and the door was still closed. When no one was looking, Rosa would slide me a plate of food under the bed for lunch.

The most difficult thing was staying still for so long. I was in very good shape and my body ached for exercise. When my leg muscles cramped, I had to work through the pain in my mind, since I was unable to reach down to knead them.

Although I could hear noises and activity all around me, it often felt like I was in solitary confinement. Sometimes I dozed off to sleep during the day, but I tried not to, afraid I might draw attention to myself by snoring.

I watched patterns of sunlight shift on the floor as I waited for dusk. I thought about Lazo and Manny and what had likely transpired at military exercises. I went over in my mind the tactics Pino might use to catch me and what I could do to thwart them. By now I figured the CDRs had plastered my picture on walls and telephone poles all over the country.

Expectantly, I listened for Rosa to close the front door at night so I could eat, exercise, and get some fresh air. After that, I liked to spend time sitting in my uncle's backyard, studying the stars like Abuelo had taught me and thinking about my future with Magda.

CHAPTER 32

The military exercises were a huge success. Pino decided that the best course of action was to report that I was unable to perform my duties due to illness. This allowed him to avoid the repercussions of having a man gone AWOL under his command during such a sensitive time, while still giving him time to find me.

Lazo launched the rocket in my place, and he did an exemplary job. He hit the target on his second attempt and was rewarded with kudos from the two Castros and with wild cheering from the crowd. As soon as the men returned to base, however, Pino announced that his top priority was to find me.

I was considered a grave security risk due to my deep knowledge of Cuba's military secrets and weapons. Pino's biggest fear was that I would get to the States and divulge what I knew to the enemy. He was equally concerned that he would have to face the wrath of Raúl Castro for losing a man of such importance to national security. The consequences of that would be dire.

Upon returning to base, Pino established a command center to locate me, complete with maps of Guanabacoa and other areas. He affixed colored pushpins to the maps that identified places where I'd most likely hide and from which I'd most likely try to escape. He called a meeting with all the officers of the unit, including Lieutenant Brown and Commander Martinez to discuss how to approach the matter.

"I've given a lot of thought to Mederos," he said. "I believe he's still in the country, and I want your input as to the best way to get him."

"You don't think he's left already?" asked the base commander.

"No, do you?"

"I don't think he's trying to escape the country," said Martinez. "He's no fool. He knows the risks involved. But we need to get him back to base as soon as possible. The longer this thing drags on, the more problems we'll have."

Pino looked nonplussed. He turned to Lieutenant Brown. "Your thoughts?"

"My guess is that he got Magda pregnant during their last days together, and he is beside himself trying to figure out what to do. I think if you leave him alone, he'll come back by himself."

Pino shot Brown a look of disdain. "That's bosh! Poppycock! Mederos was a worm. He knew his girlfriend was leaving the country and he planned to join her. It was an act of treason—pure and simple. You're a fool not to think so."

"So what are you going to do about it?" asked Brown.

"I'd like this to remain an internal issue for the time being. I don't want word about his defection to get out. There's no use causing un- necessary embarrassment for ourselves."

Martinez shook his head. "If you really want Mederos back, you should notify the police, the local CDRs, and the militia. Give them his description and his picture, and they'll take it from there. You'll have thousands of eyes looking for him. Then it's no longer our concern."

"And look like fools in front of Raúl? I don't think so," said Pino. "I'm confident we can bring him in. Let's do it my way for now."

The next order of business was to backtrack my activities. The records showed that Sophia was the the last civilian to see me. Pino went to the CDRs and obtained her address without disclosing the reason for the inquiry.

Lieutenants Brown and Pino arrived at Sophia's home looking very official, their army uniforms laden with ribbons and medals. The entire family was watching television when Sophia answered the door.

"Frankie Mederos has left the army base and hasn't been heard from since," said Brown. "We were hoping you could shed some light on the situation."

Sophia took a step backward and swept her hair away from her face with her long, slender hand. "Well, I went to the base to let him know his mother was sick and his girlfriend was leaving the country," she said. "He seemed fine at the time."

"Has he come to your house since you last saw him?" asked Pino.

"No," lied Sophia.

"Do you have any idea where he may be?" asked Brown.

"No, did you try his house?"

"Not yet," said Brown.

Pino looked around and saw that the house had been inventoried. "Are you leaving the country?"

"Yes," said Sophia, without explanation.

Pino turned his attention to Rigo, Jr. "Is this your boy?"

Rigo looked fearful. "Yes," said Sophia.

"How old is he?"

"That's none of your business," said Sophia.

"Fourteen," volunteered Rigo.

Pino nodded and a smile of satisfaction crossed his face. "I assume you don't want him to go into the army, am I correct?"

Sophia sighed and nodded slightly. She didn't want her voice to betray her emotions.

Pino smirked and handed Sophia his card. "If you see or hear from Mederos, be sure to call me."

"I will," said Sophia before quickly shutting the door.

Pino looked at Brown as they walked away. "I don't think she's telling the truth," he said. "My gut says Mederos is hiding in there. Have the men surround the house and wait to see if he leaves so we can pick him up without drawing too much attention to ourselves. If he doesn't come out within a couple of hours, we'll search the premises."

"I think you're making a mistake," said Brown. "That woman was telling the truth. It would be a waste of time to take this any further. You're not going to flush Mederos out. Just let her be."

"I didn't ask your opinion," snapped Pino.

"Then do it your way. You never listen to me anyway."

Pino posted soldiers at strategic spots around the property and instructed them to wait the requisite amount of time. When I didn't appear, he ordered a thorough search of Sophia's home. But I was not to be found. Convinced that Sophia was lying, Pino interrogated her again. Only this time, he wasn't so nice.

"Lady, I don't believe a word you said about Mederos. You were the last one to see him. I know you are involved in this matter."

"I have no idea what you're talking about."

"Let me put it this way. It is of vital importance to national security that we find Mederos." Pino glanced at Rigo, Jr. "If this search goes on for any length of time, you might not be able to obtain your visas before your son turns fifteen." He hesitated as if to lend weight to his statement. "There are ways to delay visas, sometimes for months, sometimes for years. And I know them all."

"I'm sure you do," said Sophia. "But I have nothing to say. And I don't appreciate you threatening us."

Pino straightened his shoulders. "We have no reason to believe Mederos has left Cuba. For your information, we can and will find him," he said in a tone that made Sophia shudder. "And once he confesses, you and your entire family will have a price to pay. You will be charged with conspiracy and treason. And the consequences will not be pretty."

Sophia looked Pino straight in the eyes. "I told you I don't know where he is."

"Think about it," said Pino. "Talk it over with your husband and your son. If anything comes to mind, contact me at base. You know where it is."

"I do. Thank you for stopping by again," said Sophia curtly.

Without telling them what it would be used for, Pino obtained a list from the local CDRs of all the people they had on file who knew me. The list included my parents and grandparents as well as many of my aunts, uncles, cousins, and friends. For some reason Uncle Luis and Aunt Rosa—as well as a few other relatives—were not on the list.

With this information in hand, Pino called on my parents, greatly upsetting them by telling them that my chances for escape were nil. He outlined the penalties for harboring a fugitive or for withholding information regarding my whereabouts. He told them about conditions in Cuban jails—of cement beds, of roach-infested food, of cells called "drawers" where women lived in constant darkness and were raped and beaten by wardens.

But my parents were brave. They said they had no idea where I was or how I could be reached. They insisted they had not heard from me. They promised to call the base if they did.

Pino received the same response from my other relatives. His men ransacked the home of my grandfather, but Abuelo claimed total ignorance of my intentions or whereabouts. No matter what they did to him, I knew Abuelo would never betray me.

He also went to the houses of my cousins Gilbert, Tato, and Pipi and talked to several of my parents' siblings—to no avail. Having exhausted all his leads, Pino had soldiers disguise themselves as candy vendors in Guanabacoa to see if they could overhear any conversations that might lead to my apprehension.

The lieutenant had come to a dead end in his search when he came across one of my relatives at a chance meeting of the high army command in Havana. The man was an ardent communist who had fought the Americans during the Bay of Pigs.

Pino informed him about my disappearance and gave him the list of names supplied by the CDRs. My cousin checked the list and provided Pino with additional information, including the names and address of my Aunt Rosa and Uncle Luis.

When I woke up the next morning, my uncle informed me of the bad news over coffee.

"Frankie, Cuni told me the army's been looking for you at the homes of your relatives. They've ransacked fifteen houses so far."

"Jesus! Did anyone say anything?"

"Not that I know of, but Cuni believes it's no longer safe for you to stay here. They are on your trail, and it won't be long before they come here to find you."

"It's all right," I said, trying to tame my uncle's fears. "I've thought about what to do if it came to this."

"What?"

Luis was biting his lower lip and twisting his wedding band on his finger. I felt sorry to be such a burden on him and his family.

"I'll hide in the outhouse."

My uncle's eyes grew wide. "Christ, Frankie, the stench in there is unbearable."

"It's my only option."

"That's hardly a plan. They're likely to look there, too." My uncle began blinking rapidly.

I chortled. "They won't look where I'll be hiding."

My uncle wrinkled his nose. "You mean—?"

"I'll stand on the ledge inside the outhouse for as long as I think it's safe. But if I hear the soldiers coming, I'll hide in the hole."

"Christ almighty," said Luis. He bunched his shoulders and shivered. "You're one crazy hombre!"

"I've done more difficult things. How bad could it be?"

I spent the next three days in the outhouse, standing on a foot-wide ledge. There was no ventilation and no way to avoid the stink. It was not something you got used to. Rats scampered around my feet, nibbled at the toes of my shoes and scratched my legs, causing them to bleed. The silence was broken by the buzz of a legion of horseflies that bit my arms, legs, and face. The only good thing was that I didn't have to leave my hiding place to use the bathroom.

I left the outhouse late at night to eat some dinner and to get much-needed fresh air. Not knowing when the soldiers would arrive, I no longer slept on the sofa—it was far too dangerous.

Under the cover of darkness, I stretched out to try to get some rest in front of the outhouse. I slept against the outhouse door, leaving it open so I could quickly jump inside if I heard anyone approach. I hardly slept for three nights.

Late in the morning of my fourth day in the outhouse, I heard a big commotion outside. I could tell from the voices that at least half a dozen soldiers had arrived.

Recognizing Pino's voice, I lifted the outhouse seat and lowered myself into the hole. I sank into the muck, making sure to keep my eyes closed until I was submerged up to my shoulders. I was afraid of getting something in my eyes and being unable to remove it.

I moved my body to the right and positioned my head far enough from the hole to not be seen. I thought about Abuelo's advice about always doing more than your best when it comes to matters of love. I smiled, knowing I was doing more than my best.

The soldiers entered my uncle's house from both the front and the back doors and then stood at attention while Pino approached Rosa. She had just finished doing the dishes and was scouring the kitchen sink. Unnerved at the sight of the soldiers, she tried to remain calm.

Pino walked toward her, withdrew a picture of me from his chest pocket, and held it up for her to see. "This man is a fugitive from justice. Have you seen him?"

Rosa took the picture from Pino, examined it, and handed it back.

Her neck had broken out in a fine pink rash. "He's my nephew, but I haven't seen him for quite a while," she lied.

Pino's eyes grew flinty. "Mederos has defected from the army. Harboring a fugitive is punishable by death. Are you aware of this penalty?"

Rosa nodded yes.

"I will ask you again. Are you sure you haven't seen him?" Rosa took a sharp intake of breath. This was the most difficult decision she had ever faced—whether to protect me or to save herself from prosecution. She certainly didn't want to die in a Cuban prison. She had heard what went on there—fingernails ripped out, eyes burned with cigarette butts, years of solitary confinement. She thought about the torture. She thought about the pain. She thought about how her husband and daughters would cope without her.

Then she thought about what Fidel had done to the Cuban people. And what she wanted for her children. She hesitated for a moment and said, "I haven't seen Frankie for a long time."

"How long?"

"Months."

Pino put my picture back in his pocket and ordered his men to search the house from top to bottom.

The soldiers started ransacking her home, upending the sofa, looking in the closets and under the beds. They were searching for me or for any evidence that I had been there. But all I had were the clothes on my back. I had left no incriminating evidence.

The soldiers started pulling out Rosa's dresser drawers, dumping her underwear and nightgowns onto the floor. My aunt protested vehemently, scolding them for touching her private garments. She grabbed her delicate things off the floor and pulled them to her bosom before demanding that the soldiers leave her house.

Pino was having none of it. He ordered the soldiers outside to search the backyard and the outhouse, saying he was sure I was in it.

Two soldiers started walking toward the outhouse, grumbling to each other as they approached. My heart beat a staccato rhythm. They pulled on the old wooden door. It opened slowly, reluctantly, creaking on its rusty hinges.

"Phew!" said one of the soldiers. "It smells god-awful in here." The soldier sneezed and the door banged shut.

"You didn't even look," a second voice scolded.

"It smells so bad it could make you gag," said the first soldier. "I'm not looking again. If you want to be a hero, be my guest."

The second soldier groused a bit and opened the door a little farther. Two rats ran out of the outhouse and the soldier let out a yelp. Another rat scurried down the hole and jumped on my shoulder. My nerves were so raw it was all I could do not to scream.

"Christ, you're right," said the soldier. "That place should've been knocked down years ago. There's nothing in there but spiders and rats."

The door banged shut again, and I heard Pino's voice in the distance. "Any luck, men?"

"No one out here."

"All right," said Pino. His voice leaked grave disappointment. I smiled slightly. "We've got work to do. Let's move on out."

CHAPTER 33

It had been more than a month since I'd left the base. Informing the CDRs, the police, and the militia about my disappearance was becoming increasingly problematic for Pino, since it would raise difficult questions about the timing of my escape. The authorities would ask why they had not been informed immediately regarding the situation—and Pino had no good answer.

So Pino kept the search an internal matter, while Brown and Martinez continued to urge him to involve the CDRs, the police, and the local militias.

"If you don't do that, you'll never find him," warned Brown.

"How so?"

"I trained the man. He's the best I've ever seen. He's slippery as soapsuds. He knows every place to hide in the area, both in Cojimar and Guanabacoa. And don't forget, he stayed in the mountains three different times in his life. He even knows hiding places there. Mark my word, you're setting yourself up for failure."

Pino shot Brown a withering glance. He had given the matter much thought in the previous weeks. Those who saw him would've thought he was brooding. No longer able to tolerate the criticism, he decided to take a new approach to the problem. He said something totally unexpected.

"You have it wrong, Lieutenant Brown. *We* aren't going to find Mederos. *You* are."

"What?"

"You heard me."

"I don't understand."

"It's simple," said Pino. "I want you to mobilize the entire Elite Counterattack Force to find Mederos. You taught him. No one is better prepared to find him than you. I want the force to make it their mission to bring the worm in."

Brown was flabbergasted. Involving the entire force in such a search was unheard of, unprecedented.

"The force is here to protect the citizens against attack," said Brown. "We can't mobilize the entire force just to go after one man."

"We can and we will," retorted Pino.

"On whose authority?"

"On my authority. This is an emergency situation. A political matter. A matter of national security. You are now under my command, Lieutenant Brown. You now report to me."

Brown was horrified. It was impossible for him to believe that anyone—including myself—could escape the concerted efforts of the special forces. He was torn between his concern for me and his need to perform his duty. Making it worse, he remembered Pino's words, "He may be smarter than one of us, but he is not smarter than all of us."

"Who do you want me to include?" asked Brown.

"Everyone except the older men who know Mederos and might be loyal to him," said Pino. "But include Manny and Lazo. They know best how he thinks, and you may be able to pressure them into assistance. Mobilize the infantry, the men from the 57-millimeter cannons, and all the new recruits. That's an order."

Brown snapped to attention. "Yes, sir."

Pino thought for a moment, smugness filling his voice, "Exactly how many men is that?"

"Around three hundred," replied Brown.

A faint smiled danced on Pino's lips. "That ought to do it."

Christmas Day dawned crisp and clear with a hint of spring in the air. In Cuba the birth of Christ was traditionally a two-day celebration filled with the camaraderie of family and friends. The exchange of gifts occurred on January sixth—the Feast of the Epiphany—so December twenty-fourth and twenty-fifth were set aside for worship, socialization, and fun.

Every year my aunt and uncle held an open house for family, friends, neighbors, and anyone else who cared to drop by. My aunt decorated her home with greenery and hibiscus blooms, festooned the house with lights, and hung a wreath of silver bells on the front door.

Rosa's table creaked under the weight of food brought by friends and neighbors—roasted pig and fruits like mangoes, mamey, and papayas. The aroma of *moros y cristianos*, a rice and beans dish, filled the air. Rosa spent days before Christmas preparing desserts, and I looked forward to eating my favorite, *buñuelos*—fried sweet dough with powdered sugar and syrup.

Since Fidel had declared Cuba to be an atheist nation in 1962, Rosa did not display her wooden crèche, but set up a table for those wanting to play dominoes instead. She removed a record from its jacket to place on her small record player. The needle jumped on the groove for a minute, making a sharp, cackling sound before Paul Anka's voice filled the air. I was startled at how sad the words made me feel.

I'm just a lonely boy,
Lonely and blue . . .

The music filled me with such longing it brought tears to my eyes. I remembered holding Magda in my arms, her cheek close to mine as we danced to this song in her parents' living room. It seemed like I was a different person then.

One of the problems with hiding under the bed was that it not only deprived me of freedom of movement, it deprived me of freedom of expression. Suddenly, it felt more restrictive than ever. I had an overwhelming desire to stand on my own two feet, hug my relatives, and wish them a Merry Christmas. I longed to talk, to laugh, to interact.

I wanted to be who I was, who I used to be. And more than anything, I wanted to sing along with this song. But I couldn't. And I didn't.

Rosa didn't own many records so she played what she had over and over—but no one seemed to mind. At first, she was nervous about me being under the bed with company around but, after a while, she began to relax. I could tell from the tone of her voice. The sound of laughter rang out, and the floor vibrated with the footfalls of dancing.

On both days, I stayed hidden until the front door closed in the evening. From my position flat under the bed, I watched the feet of people coming and going to use the bathroom. When no one was watching, my cousins would slip me some fried plantains or a glass of Cuban cider under the bed and whisper *Feliz Navidad*.

Since I had no contact with Sophia and Rigo, I had no idea how Magda was doing. I was thinking about her all of the time, missing her terribly, and hoping she was singing Christmas carols and sipping *crème de vié* somewhere sunny and nice.

I wondered whether she was still wearing the ring I had given her. And I wished from the bottom of my heart that I could give her a gift.

CHAPTER 34

On December twenty-eighth, Cuni came by to cut my hair and to tell me that the trip he had originally planned had been cancelled. I could hardly believe my ears. It had been a long and nerve-racking wait, far too long to have my hopes dashed at this late date. I felt angry, deflated, and curious about what had gone wrong.

"What in God's name happened?" I asked, incredulous. I tried to mask the disappointment in my voice, but it was impossible. Whatever had transpired, I knew it wasn't Cuni's fault, and I didn't want to take it out on him. Still, the news was disheartening.

"Macho had arranged for a big boat to take people out, but he's backed off," said Cuni. He looked somewhat relieved.

I took a deep breath. "What was the problem?"

"Macho's older brother got wind of it, and he pressured him to cancel the operation. Macho decided it would be safer to lay low for a while."

My heart dropped at the news. I didn't know how much longer I could impose upon Luis and Rosa, or how much longer I could hide under the bed without being discovered. The sands in the hourglass were running low. I tried to corral my emotions. Cuni studied my reaction.

Surprisingly, he said, "There's another opportunity you might find of interest." I looked up, amazed. The timing could not have been better.

"What's that?" I said, afraid I had misheard him.

"I got a message from Señor Lopez that he has a trusted friend who's taking Joey and Pedro out of the country on Tuesday. Would you want to join them?"

"Tell me more about it," I said, although I had to admit the plan sounded promising.

"It's a good-size boat and seven or eight boys are going, including his sons. He's willing to pay the passage for your uncle."

I canted my head, thinking. "That's very generous of him. Let me talk it over with Luis."

Cuni nodded. "Fine with me. I want some time to ask around, make sure everything's on the up-and-up. Let's talk again on Saturday."

Luis was excited about the proposed trip, especially since Lopez believed it was safe enough for his own children. He thought Lopez would be extra careful after his boys nearly died during the last trip. Besides, Luis was eager to make a move before something happened to any—or all—of us.

When I informed Cuni of our decision on Saturday, he sighed. His expression gave me pause. Something was wrong.

"What is it?" I asked, perplexed. Cuni looked like he wanted to tell me something, but he didn't know how.

He swallowed hard. "I trust Lopez. I think he's a great guy. He's helped a lot of people." A moment of silence elapsed.

"But?" I prompted, concerned about the direction of the conversation.

Cuni hesitated a moment. "I guess I just need to come out and say it. I don't want you to go on this trip."

"What?" My voice betrayed my dismay. "Why?" Since Cuni had suggested this trip in the first place, I wanted to know why he had changed his mind. I felt exasperated.

Cuni shook his head. "I don't know this friend of his. And I haven't been able to learn anything about him, including what precautions he's taken. I'm a little leery of the situation. I don't want to chance it."

"What is your concern?"

"Too many people are involved," said Cuni as if he were thinking out loud. "There's a real chance for trouble. I'm afraid word might leak out."

"But Lopez is letting his kids go. Surely he's looked into this. He must think it's safe."

"I hope so," said Cuni. "But nothing in this business is guaranteed. And I don't have a good feeling about it." He placed his hand on my shoulder and said in a hoarse voice, "I hate to do this to you, Frankie, but let me tell Lopez you won't be going."

I faced Cuni. This was the first time he had ever called me Frankie. I knew in my gut that he cared about me. The look on Cuni's face and the tension in his voice were enough to make me agree not to go.

"All right, if that's what you think. But please thank Señor Lopez for his generosity and tell him how sorry my uncle and I are that we won't be joining his sons."

Cuni patted me on the back and sighed. "It may not seem like it right now, Frankie. But I think you'll look back on this as a good decision."

"I hope not," I said.

Cuni looked momentarily confused. But as soon as he processed my implication he nodded.

"I understand. You're just hoping nothing goes wrong for the boys."

"For them and for everyone else."

Cuni was silent for a moment. He shook his head slightly and draped his arm around my shoulder.

"I don't know when or how, Frankie, but I promise someday I'll get you safely out of the country."

"Thanks," I said. "I sure hope so."

• • •

The fate of the Lopez boys had occupied my mind all weekend. After our previous harrowing experience, I was praying this trip would go smoothly—for everyone. The fact that Cuni had reservations about it made me nervous, very nervous.

Tuesday night I could hardly sleep for worry. I tossed and turned and finally got up and drank a glass of milk. I looked out the window at the night sky. I was hoping for calm weather and that a safe boat headed for the States would take everyone aboard. If not—I rotated my head and breathed deeply. My skin turned to gooseflesh just thinking about it.

Wednesday morning broke warm and sunny and, as usual, I spent the entire day under the bed. After the sun went down Wednesday night, someone knocked on the front door. My uncle answered it, and Cuni came in looking somber and shaken. I was outside in the dark doing push-ups when Rosa called me into the house in a voice full of angst. I scoured her face for clues as to what might have happened.

I looked at Cuni and walked toward him. He was slump shouldered and sad, and I knew something was wrong. I took a deep breath and a step backward.

"I'm so sorry," said Cuni, extending a hand toward me. I looked at him, confused. My eyes widened, fearing he was bringing me very bad news. My mouth went dry not knowing what to think. He put his hand on my shoulder and shook his head.

I looked into his ghostly eyes and asked, "What is it?"

"You'd better sit down," he said, pointing to the sofa.

"I'm fine," I replied swiftly. "Just tell me."

Cuni cleared his throat. "I have news from the underground."

"The boys?"

Cuni sighed. "Yes."

I scrutinized his face. It took me a moment to focus. His hair was askew and his chin was blue with stubble.

"What happened?"

"Joey—" He stopped speaking as tears filled his eyes. His voice was rough and strangled.

"What, *what?*"

"I was so afraid of this. Someone talked, I'm sure of it."

"Tell me."

"The boys were right at the edge of the beach in Cojimar. They were just past the mango trees when they were surrounded by dozens of soldiers. When the soldiers screamed for the boys to stop, they all ran in different directions."

"And?"

"The soldiers let loose with gunfire. Six boys died."

"Joey?"

"Joey was shot dead in the back. He was covered in blood and lying face down in the sand. He never had a chance."

The muscles in my cheeks wilted, and my hand flew to my mouth. I looked at Cuni who was visibly upset.

"Dear God in heaven."

My emotions suddenly became ungovernable. I needed a moment to calm them. I closed my eyes and pinched my nose with my thumb and forefinger. All I could think of was how happy I was that Joey had won our last game of gin rummy. I remembered him looking at me with a gleaming smile and eyes crinkled with delight.

"And Pedro?"

"He was beside himself with grief, holding on to Joey. The soldiers had to drag him away from his brother."

"Where is he now?"

"He's been taken into custody. Since he's a minor, he'll get five years in jail."

"Five years," I repeated, thinking out loud. Pedro would be twenty before he got out of prison. Those were pretty important years of your life to miss. And then he'd be regarded with suspicion for the rest of his life.

"Is Señor Lopez all right?"

"The soldiers found out from someone involved in the operation that Lopez had funded the escape. The army went to his home and arrested him for subversive activity. Maria was sobbing uncontrollably when they led him away. She was inconsolable. He won't even be allowed to attend his son's funeral."

"Christ," I said. I stood silent for a moment in shock. "And his sentence?"

"Seven years."

I looked at Cuni. I had no words, either for the death of Joey or the arrest of Pedro and Señor Lopez. The things they did to prisoners flashed through my mind. Señor Lopez might be able to survive it, but the effects would follow Pedro forever. I opened my arms and hugged Cuni. Sweat ran from my forehead to my jowl. He embraced me and patted me on the back.

"It's a disaster for the whole Lopez family," he said softly. "Everyone is devastated."

"I can only imagine. Maria and Esme—" I looked at my uncle who would have also been killed if we had gone on the trip. I thought about what that would have meant for him and his family. Rosa would be a widow and the girls would be fatherless. And if I had gone, chances are I'd also be dead.

My bottom lip quivered and my hands began to tremble. I slipped them into my pockets so Cuni wouldn't notice. Fidel's face flashed through my mind. I imagined him brandishing his rifle.

"Young boys, for Christ's sake. What chance did they have? They—"

I was so full of grief and rage, I couldn't finish my sentence.

CHAPTER 35

A couple of weeks elapsed before I heard from Cuni again. Since our last conversation, I had hoped he would come up with something for me sooner rather than later. I knew much of what went into planning such a trip was out of his control. But my patience was stretched paper thin. He arrived at my uncle's house late one night, relaxed and in good spirits.

"We're getting ready for the next trip," he said. He appeared more confident about this trip than he had about the last one.

"Who's going?" I asked.

"Same as last time. Nine army men. They all think you walk on water."

"Only because you told them so."

Cuni chuckled. "They think of you as a hero—seven feet tall with arms of steel."

I waved my hand in dismissal. "I'm feeling more like a bedbug than a hero right now. Who's the captain?"

"Macho."

I leaned back and closed my eyes for a moment, thinking about Pedro and Joey. A small tear formed at the corner of my eye. I wiped it away with my knuckle.

"I hope it goes better than it did last time."

"It'll be different this time," said Cuni. "Macho's taking his whole family with him—his wife and three children."

I was very surprised at this news. "They're leaving the country, too?"

"Yes, all of them."

"When?"

"February or March—weather permitting."

I sighed heavily. "It can't be too soon for me."

Under Lieutenant Brown's direction, the army revisited all my relatives to make sure I wasn't hiding in their homes. Every method was being used to bring me in.

Rigo and Sophia remained the main suspects associated with my escape and for several weeks the army followed them wherever they went. Sophia did her best to shake them—and sometimes she did. In an effort to keep them in the country—and thereby involved in the investigation—Pino filed paperwork to revoke their visas. Fortunately, his timing was just one day off.

On February 15, 1967, visas were issued for Magda's Aunt Sophia, Uncle Rigo, and Rigo, Jr. Their bags were packed, and they were ready to leave for the airport the minute they received the documents.

Luckily, their airplane lifted off the runway only hours before Pino came to their home to arrest them. I was unable to speak to them before they left. But Luis heard through the grapevine that they made it safely to Florida. I couldn't have been happier at the news.

My extended stay at her home was beginning to wear on Rosa. A high-strung, fearful person, she was looking for a way to calm her nerves. Like several of her friends, she occasionally frequented a fortune-teller by the name of Balbina. Several of Balbina's predictions had come true in the past, and Rosa put a lot of stock in what she had to say.

Unbeknownst to Luis and me, Rosa decided to pay her a visit. Rosa came home that night visibly shaken. She was distracted when she made dinner, spilling boiling water all over the floor and mumbling incoherently while she cleaned it up.

After we ate dinner and I finished doing my exercises, she sat down with Luis and me to tell us what she had learned. Her face was drawn and ashen as we took our seats at the kitchen table.

"Balbina gave me bad news today," she reported. I sucked in my breath involuntarily.

"What did she say?" asked Luis. He seemed detached and depressed, and from the sound of his voice, I knew he was only feigning interest.

"She said someone close to me was trying to do something illegal and blood would be shed."

"And?" said Luis.

"And he wouldn't accomplish it," said Rosa. "She said he'd get shot."

I pursed my lips and glanced over at Luis. "Anything else?"

Rosa looked down and began wringing her hands.

"What?" demanded Luis.

She looked at me almost accusingly—or perhaps it was just my imagination. "She said someone else close to me would die, and there would be grave consequences for me and my family."

I felt a sudden stab of guilt, wondering what I had gotten my relatives into. Luis didn't respond. He heaved a sigh and got up and walked outside, leaving the back door wide open behind him. I knew the burden of what we were about to do was weighing heavily on his mind.

I squeezed Rosa's hand for a moment, got up, and followed Luis into the backyard. We sat on the ground, and Luis removed a pack of cigarettes from his shirt pocket. He offered me one, but I declined. Luis lit his cigarette and inhaled deeply. A sprinkling of stars winked overhead. I looked over and saw the cow standing in the moonlight. We sat quietly for a few minutes and then I said, "I think this wait is actually more difficult on you than it is on me."

Luis shrugged and opened his hands in a gesture of resignation. "It's just a terrible situation." His tone was sad and weary.

"It's hard to believe that one man could make so many people so miserable," I said.

"Damn Fidel!" said Luis.

"Damn them all!"

We sat looking up at the sky without speaking. We both needed a few minutes to calm our nerves. When Rosa told me what Balbina had said, the specter of death felt suddenly very close. Balbina's prediction made me feel vulnerable in a way I had never felt before. It also made me more conscious of my responsibility toward Rosa, Luis, Marisol, and Magali. These were people who were literally risking their lives for me.

"What do you think about what the fortune-teller said?"

"I don't know," said Luis. "I don't put much faith in those things, but it's unnerving to hear—and it makes Rosa crazy."

"Are you sure you want to try to escape?"

Luis sighed. "I don't know, Frankie. How can you be sure of something when the possible consequences are so horrific?"

"You can't."

"And what happened to Joey and Pedro brings everything closer to home. I keep seeing the body of that poor dead boy in my mind."

I shivered. "I can't talk about it right now. I can't get my head around what happened—the loss is too fresh."

"Those poor kids." Luis shook his head despondently. His cigarette ash had grown long and curly, and he tapped it off with his forefinger. It was spent and loamy. I watched it float aimlessly to the ground.

I nodded my agreement, and we sat for a moment in silence. "What has you most concerned?"

"Rosa and the girls, of course. I worry about what will happen to them if I die."

My uncle echoed my thoughts exactly. I patted Luis on the back. "Of course, it's only natural," was all I could manage to say.

•   •   •

That night I had a dream about Lieutenant Pino. He was as tall as a sycamore tree with arms that branched for miles. I was hiding in a dark box that was floating in water. His arms were drifting toward the box, getting closer by the minute.

Suddenly, they reached the box and broke it open. Icy water began rushing over me. I could hardly breathe. I felt cold, sad, and out of control. When the water reached my shoulders, I woke with a start. I lay in my bed staring up at shadows that dappled the ceiling.

The future that had always seemed so certain to me suddenly loomed as muddy and fragmented as this dance of light. A new species of fear invaded my soul, one far more powerful than I had ever felt. If I didn't succeed in my escape, my loved ones would pay a very high price. I stood and rolled my head in a circle, hoping to relieve my anxiety.

Rosa kept an altar in her living room that displayed statues of Christ, the Virgin Mary, and the Virgin of the Seas. White votive candles were nestled in front of the altar, and a small pillow invited you to kneel. I approached the altar, lit several candles, and dropped to my knees.

This was the first time I had seriously considered the possibility of being caught—or shot—while trying to escape. Up to this point, I had felt somehow invincible—a conceit of youth. But with the death of Joey and the arrests of Pedro and Señor Lopez, reality had set in. My cloak of denial had been rudely ripped away.

Tears flooded my eyes and streamed down my face like raindrops on a windowpane. I let them flow freely. I longed for Magda, her laugh, her warmth, her smile. I wanted to touch her and hold her in my arms, but more than that, I just wanted to talk to her, to smell her skin, to hear her voice.

I tried to focus on what it would be like to be married to her. I imagined coming home to her after a long day's work, eating dinner with her at the kitchen table, and making love to her into the wee hours of the morning. If only I could get to her. But, with all that had happened, I felt like my chances of escape were becoming more of a pipe dream than a possibility.

I tried to imagine Magda's life in America, but I was having a difficult time picturing it. My uncle had learned that she lived in Union City, New Jersey, but I knew nothing about that place. I envisioned her sitting in her pink bathing suit, laughing and sipping lemonade by the side of a pool, flowers blooming and royal palms swaying in the breeze. Did they even have palm trees in New Jersey? Who knew?

With the financial and other pressures facing new immigrants, I figured this was a highly unlikely and romantic scenario—but it was a comforting thought. For a brief moment the idea of Magda dating American boys flashed through my mind. I knew they would find her attractive and would be eager to date her. But remembering the promise I had made to never doubt her love, I banished the thought. Besides, the idea that she was seeing someone else would have driven me crazy.

Still, I had the terrible feeling that Magda was impossibly far away and I feared I would not be strong enough—or smart enough—to elude my captors and find her. The worst part was that she'd never know how hard I tried to get to her or whatever became of me. My mother once told me that not knowing what happened to someone you love is the greatest anguish anyone can experience. More than anything, I wanted to spare Magda that pain.

I rested my head on the altar and began to nod off to sleep. As I did, an image of a gas stove rose in my mind. Its burners were lit and red-and-blue flames leapt into the air. My hands gripped the metal grates surrounding the burners. I was playing them as if they were a musical instrument. Although discordant notes issued forth, I was desperate to finish my piece. I opened my eyes and focused on the image. *What did it mean?*

I thought for a moment and then it came to me. I was playing with fire. The question was how long could I do so before getting burned? It was beginning to feel too much to handle.

Something moved me to make an offering to the Virgin Mary. I cast my eyes about the room for an item to place before her, but I had no flowers, no trinkets, nothing of any value. I went to the kitchen sink and turned on the faucet. I opened the cabinet door, removed a tall glass, and filled it to the brim with water. I brought it back to the living room, careful not to spill any on the floor. I placed the water before the statue, hoping Mary might appreciate this simple gesture.

I bent my chin to my chest, covered my face with my hands, and prayed. *"Dear Mary, give me your help and guidance in this endeavor. Grant me the wisdom and strength to do what must be done to keep people safe."* I pulled out my handkerchief and blew my nose softly so as not to wake the family.

"Help me make the right decisions for myself and others. Please let Luis bring his family to freedom. And please look after us and bless us on this long and dangerous journey."

I lifted the rosary that was sitting on the altar. I fingered the crystal beads in my hands, kissed the crucifix, and made a sign of the cross. I said the Apostles' Creed, an Our Father, and three Hail Marys. I offered up another Our Father and started to recite the five Sorrowful Mysteries of the rosary.

The beads slipped through my fingers as melted wax pooled around the wicks of the candles. One after another, they crackled briefly and then flickered out, leaving an igneous spark and a brief trail of smoke.

I no longer knew whether I was capable of doing what was required to get to Magda. I no longer knew whether I had the strength to go on. I was beginning to doubt my abilities. I was thinking I had been delusional in believing I could outsmart the force and escape to freedom. It had been a very long fight, and I was very tired. I wiped the tears from my eyes with my knuckles.

I remained on my knees for almost two hours, feeling more alone and depressed than I had ever felt in my life.

CHAPTER 36

While hiding under the bed the next day, I developed a terrible cramp in my leg. I needed to stand and put some pressure on it to relieve the pain, so I came out from under the bed without my usual signal from Rosa. It was just getting dark and no one was home. I figured it would be safe for me to go outside to exercise.

When I opened the back door, I found a young boy standing right in front of me. I was so startled, I almost knocked him over. He was about nine years old with piercing blue eyes and fine blond hair. He was barefoot and was wearing bib overalls, clothes not usually worn by boys in Cuba.

The boy seemed as unsettled to see me as I was to see him. Not knowing who he was or who might be with him, I quickly closed the door, went back inside, and hid under the bed. Then I laughed at myself for hiding from such a young boy. After all I'd been through, it seemed very foolish. But it alerted me to just how keyed up and attuned to danger I was. And it did make me wonder—about myself and about the boy.

I described the boy to Luis, but he said he didn't know anyone who fit that description.

The next night when I went out to exercise, I saw the same kid in the cornfield about a hundred yards from the back of the house. His body was backlit by an outside light from the neighbor's farm. He looked at me and waved. I didn't wave back. I just continued to do my exercises.

Meanwhile, Luis had talked to the neighbors about the boy, but no one knew who he was. That in itself was very strange, since every-one knew everyone else in the neighborhood. The next night I saw the boy walking near the back of my uncle's property. He waved at me and I chased him, but he jumped over the wall and got away.

The boy appeared every night thereafter, sometimes walking, sometimes sitting on an overturned aluminum pail. Whenever I told Luis to look for him, the boy mysteriously disappeared—like he had melted into thin air. Yet he continued to wave to me whenever I saw him. The whole thing was beginning to unnerve me.

Luis began to think the boy was a figment of my imagination. He told me he feared the stress of hiding for so long was beginning to af-fect my mind. Luis discussed the matter with Cuni. The next time he visited, he asked me about it.

"Luis tells me you often see a boy in the backyard," he said.

"I do."

"Does he talk to you?"

"No, he never says anything, but he always waves."

"Has he threatened you in any way?"

"Actually, he seems quite friendly."

"Who do you think he is?"

"I have no idea. At first I thought he must be a neighbor's child, but Luis has asked around, and no one seems to know him."

Cuni thought for a moment. "Do you believe in ghosts?"

I laughed. "No. This kid is as real as you are. He's not a ghost."

"I'm a little worried about you, Frankie. Are you feeling all right?"

"I'm feeling fine."

"Are you sleeping well?"

"As well as I can under the circumstances."

"Luis says he's never seen this boy, even though he's looked for him many times. He's worried that you might need some medication or something."

"I'm fine. The kid is very elusive. But I'm not losing my mind, if that's what you're suggesting."

"I'm not suggesting anything," said Cuni. "Just let me know if I can do anything for you."

I was annoyed at Cuni's implication, but I knew he had good reason to be concerned. Due to the nature of what he did, he had to be very cautious about safety. The last thing he needed was for me to have a nervous breakdown.

"I will," I said. "Thanks."

Late the next night I saw the blue-eyed boy again. He waved at me from the cornfield, and for the first time I waved back. I didn't know what to make of the situation, and I was beginning not to care.

The following day Cuni came to see me again, obviously concerned about my mental health.

"Have you seen that boy?" he asked.

I smiled. "Yes, last night. I know you think he's an apparition or something, but I'm telling you he's real."

"All right, Frankie. I'm just worried you're going to crack on me."

I laughed. "It's been nerve-racking, but I'm not going to crack. At least not over a nine-year-old boy."

Cuni studied me for a minute while I looked out the window. It was dark outside. "I've been thinking—" he said.

"Yes?"

"The lights in Havana go out every night for forty-five minutes between eight and nine."

"Uh-huh."

"It would give me an opportunity to bring someone to see you with less risk than usual."

"What are you thinking?"

"I was wondering if you'd like me to bring your parents to see you before you leave. Maybe even your brother George."

I was flabbergasted. This was an unnecessary risk and completely out of character for Cuni. "Why would you do that? Do you think it will help me from going mad?"

Cuni laughed, but I knew that's what he was thinking. "Of course, I'd love to see them." I said. "But what about the risk? They might be followed. I don't want to take any chances with my family."

"There are ways to do it," Cuni reassured me. He patted me on the back. "Don't worry. Just give me some time to arrange it."

The more I thought about it, the more excited I became about seeing my family. I knew Cuni had two motives for arranging our meeting. He didn't want me to go crazy, and he knew it might be the last time I'd ever see my family—whether I made it out safely or not. With the future so uncertain, the only thing any of us really had was *now.*

A couple of days later, around eight thirty p.m., Cuni walked in the door with my father. Without saying a word, my father reached for me. We stood hugging each other for a long time.

Finally, he pulled away and held me at arm's length. "It's so good to see you again." His face was cut with lines of fatigue and worry.

"It's good to see you, too."

My father gave me a long, careful look. "I'm so proud of you, Frankie," he said in a voice choked with emotion. "You are following your dream."

"I'm doing what must be done."

"You are doing more than that. You're the first one to go. You'll be the first Mederos to make it to freedom."

"I hope so," I said. My father nodded as if my escape were a fait accompli. We walked to the sofa and sat down while Cuni walked toward the door, saying he'd be back in half an hour.

"After you make it, your brothers will follow," said my father. His voice cracked slightly. "My one wish in life is that the whole family gets to America."

I reached for my father's hand. "Don't worry. I'm going to make it."

"I think you will, Frankie. I have great faith in you. But if for any reason you don't, eventually your brother, George, will try. And if he doesn't make it, Raúl and Carlos will try. I know if one of you makes it, we will all be free some day."

"Freedom." I rolled the word around in my mouth feeling profound apprehension about what it would take to achieve it. For a brief moment my vision grayed out.

My father shook his head. "I don't want my children to grow up in this country. It's too hard—it's no way to live."

"And I don't want my children to grow up here either," I said. We sat quietly for a moment, considering how different life would be in America.

"What's going on at home?"

"It's been tough," my father said wearily. "Your mother is worried sick about you. Soldiers with machine guns roam the streets day and night looking for you. They've been to the house three times."

"Have they said anything? Given you any clue as to what they might do?"

"They're too cagey for that." My father thought for a moment. "The first time a couple of officers came by and questioned your mother and me about your whereabouts. That was a while ago now."

"That would be Lieutenants Pino and Brown." My father nodded.

"The second time a bunch of soldiers ransacked the house, looking everywhere for you. They were very rough, hollering and breaking up the furniture. They even threatened your mother."

"I'm so sorry." My father waved my comment away as if it didn't matter.

"The last time one of the soldiers told me you shouldn't bother to turn yourself in because if you did, they wouldn't hold a trial. They'd just shoot you on sight."

I shrugged. "It doesn't matter. I'm not about to turn myself in. It's all or nothing now. There's no going back."

"I wasn't suggesting you do. I was just telling you what they said."

"I understand."

Suddenly, I thought of Jabao. I don't know why, nothing had prompted it. Like many of my boyhood friends, Jabao had never gone beyond fifth grade. I wondered how he was making a living. I was just about to ask my father about him when he interrupted my thoughts.

"Your brother George would like to come to see you. Would that be okay?"

"Of course. As long as I'm still here and Cuni can arrange it, I'd love to see him."

My father rubbed his forehead. "I've talked to George about leaving the country. And I'm sure he'd like your advice."

"I'll do anything to help."

"Have you thought about what you'll do when you get to the States?"

I smiled slightly. "Whoa! One problem at a time. Right now I have my hands full just trying to stay a step ahead of the authorities. I'll figure out what to do when I get to America."

When Cuni came back, my father stood and embraced me. He held me tightly and his eyes grew red with tears. He closed them for a moment while he wiped away the moisture. With a hitch in his voice he said, "Good luck, my son. Be careful! And be brave!"

"I will," I said. "Thanks."

My father took a couple of steps toward the door and then turned around. He walked back, slipped some folded bills into my hand, and hugged me once more.

"I love you," he said. His voice was dry, almost a whisper. He pushed my hair back from my face with a trembling hand. He looked at me with insufferable sorrow and hope in his eyes.

"I love you, too," I said.

My father cleared his throat, patted me on the back, and walked out the door without looking back. Our visit was far too short.

I never saw my father again.

CHAPTER 37

My interaction with the blue-eyed boy was turning into a kind of dance, with him advancing and me retreating. I had seen him every night for a couple of weeks and every time he saw me he waved. He became a shadow figure, mimicking me when I did my exercises, doing push-ups and jumping jacks in sync with me. But he always kept his distance. My uncle never laid eyes on him, despite several more attempts to do so.

On February 28—my mother's birthday—Cuni brought her to see me. When I looked at her, my heart almost broke. How much she had missed me was written in the wrinkles etching her face. Her eyes were puffy and gray threaded her hair. I could hardly imagine what she was going through. Now I had this precious slice of time to be with her, and I wanted to make the most of it.

My eyes searched her face. I wanted to imprint her features in my memory so I would never forget them. In the future, I would need to be able to picture her eyes, her hands, her hair. I remembered her reading stories to me as a child. Suddenly my ears were hungry for the sweetness, the cadence, the rhythm of her voice.

"Talk to me, Mima."

My mother looked at me, confused. "What should I say, Frankie?"

"It doesn't matter. I just want to hear your voice. Say what you used to say when you called me for dinner when I was a boy. Do you remember?"

Of course," she said. "Come for dinner, my little chickadee."

"Why did you call me 'chickadee'?"

"I don't know. I started to call you that as a baby."

I sighed and tears welled in my eyes. "Thanks for saying that."

I took my mother in my arms and held her tightly. "Oh, Frankie," she said. "I just can't believe that you're a fugitive and all those men are after you. They're out to kill you. I never would have thought that people would be trying to kill my son. What will happen if—?"

"Shush," I said. "Everything will be okay. I've made it so far, haven't I?"

"Yes, but—"

I looked into her sad eyes and said, "I know it must be terrible for you. But you must believe in me. I've been trained by the best. I can do this. I'll make it." It suddenly occurred to me that I was saying this more to convince myself than to convince her.

"I remember when you were a little boy. I had such hopes, such dreams for you, for college—"

"Hush, Mima. Your dreams will come true. And so will mine. It's just a matter of time. When I get to the States, I'll find a way to let you know I'm safe."

"I hope it all works," said my mother fretfully. "I pray for you every day. Everyone I know is saying rosaries and novenas for you. Everyone. And we will all keep on praying."

"I know you will, Mima. And I will pray for you, too. Don't worry. We'll see each other again someday."

Mima and I exchanged rueful smiles before I gently kissed her goodbye.

My visit with George was no less sentimental. We talked about the family and my life in the army. We had never really had much time to bond in our lives, and I told him how sorry I was for not being able to be a real big brother to him. I think we both felt robbed because of that. I know I did.

But soon our talk turned to more practical matters. He asked me for names of people who could possibly help him and ideas on how to get out of Cuba. I gave him Cuni's name but made him promise never to disclose it—to anyone.

I told him about my experiences so far in trying to escape, and I warned him about the dangers and difficulties involved. I impressed upon him the perils in approaching international waters and how frequently the patrol boats went by.

He was listening intently, taking mental notes. He was a very bright young man and as passionate as I was about not living his life under Fidel.

I hoped someday we would be reunited in America.

CHAPTER 38

Something was terribly wrong. The blue-eyed boy was out back while I was doing my exercises, but he was not behaving in his usual manner. He was not his shy, elusive self. Rather, he was gesticulating wildly, marching back and forth at the perimeter of the property and beating his pail with a stick.

I was dressed in my workout clothes: sneakers, shorts, and a short-sleeve shirt. Having just completed one hundred push-ups, I looked at the moon for a minute before doing my sit-ups. Large clouds scudded across it, occasionally hiding it from view. I turned my focus again on the boy. He was trying to draw attention to himself, but I couldn't figure out why. His behavior was filling me with a deep sense of dread.

Suddenly, a group of twenty-some soldiers climbed over both sides of the walls surrounding Luis's property. They advanced quickly, crouched low to avoid detection. They were carrying machine guns pointed downward. I looked at them in alarm, grateful that the boy had given me a moment of warning. I drew in my breath, frantically trying to figure out what to do.

The boy pounded on his pail louder and faster, doing everything possible to distract the soldiers. I ran into the house to warn Rosa and Luis. When I entered the kitchen, I heard blunt pounding on the front door. *"Get out of here!"* said Luis. His eyes were filled with fear and his voice was urgent and intentionally low, too low for the soldiers to overhear. Rosa held the back door open for me.

•   •   •

"Open up in there," called a soldier. "Do it *now,* or I'll break down the door." *Christ,* I thought, *what should I do?*

I ran out the back door and mounted the wall near the rear of house. From there I scrambled up to the brown-tiled roof. I looked back to see some of the soldiers following the boy. I was concerned and puzzled. I had no idea what to make of this.

Why would the boy try to warn me? And why would he risk his own life by trying to draw attention away from me? His behavior could be considered aiding a fugitive. He could be arrested. Maybe he didn't know that—or maybe he didn't care. The boy had been a mystery to me from the first time I saw him. But I had no time to think about him now.

From my perch atop the roof, I could see the tops of the soldiers' heads. I recognized some of them. They had divided themselves into small groups and had occupied the entire street. Several military trucks were parked at the end of the road. Soldiers were conducting a house-to-house search. From their behavior I knew they had not specifically targeted my uncle's house, but were executing a general reconnaissance of the neighborhood.

I tiptoed across the roof, careful not to dislodge any tiles. I didn't need tiles crashing to the ground and alerting the soldiers to my whereabouts. I leapt the five-foot distance to the roof of the neighbor's house, bent low so as not to be seen. I could hear the rumble of military vehicles close by.

I crept over the roofs of four more houses and, having run out of structures, slipped quietly down a telephone pole and onto the sidewalk. Sweat galloped down my back and my heart beat wildly, partly from exertion and partly from fear.

I knew if I ran, I would attract attention to myself, so I calmly walked down the street as if I were just a neighborhood guy out for a stroll. A stray dog hobbled along the road, limping and yelping intermittently as if he were hurt. He was a small dog—some kind of a mutt—and, under different circumstances, I would have stopped to pet him.

Behind me I could hear the trucks revving up. Then Pino screamed, "Over there! That's him! That's our man! Get him!"

I looked back and saw three trucks following me. They were loaded with armed soldiers. My mind was working furiously, thinking of ways to outsmart them. Everything Brown had ever taught me flashed through my mind.

To my chagrin, two more trucks appeared on the other side of the street, trapping me right in the middle. Fear gained a foothold in the pit of my stomach, and my wits sharpened. I ran like the wind for three or four blocks with the trucks quickly gaining on me. I zig-zagged to make it more difficult for the soldiers to shoot me.

Suddenly, I was faced with a six-foot wall of sisal—a tropical plant used to make rope. Sisal three rows deep sat atop a berm used to fence a farm. The plant erupted in spiky, sharp spears that fanned out in various directions. Fierce thorns populated both sides of the blades. Sisal grew wild in Cuba and, when the plants grew back-to-back, they formed an almost impenetrable barrier. I was familiar with how much damage the thorns could inflict on skin. My legs had made the acquaintance of sisal when I was a boy, and they had oozed icky, yellow pus for days.

The trucks stopped about a half block from the berm, and Pino jumped out with a spring in his step. He started walking toward me with a chilling, satisfied grin, delighted to have finally cornered his quarry. Brown followed, looking less than pleased at the whole situation. Behind them Manny, Lazo, and my entire platoon looked on in horror.

Pino took out his pistol and pointed it at me. He grinned like a Cheshire cat.

"Put your hands up, Mederos."

I raised my hands in the air in a deliberate motion, palms out. My mind was racing, searching for my next move. "Now walk toward me slowly."

I kept my hands in the air and started walking in Pino's direction.

As I did, he began taunting me. After having waited for such a long time to catch me, he was enjoying every minute of this drama. My mind was laser focused.

"Here he is, men. Here's the worm that ran away. This is the guy who thinks he's smarter than all of us. Take a good look at him because this may be the last time you'll ever see him alive."

I continued walking in the lieutenant's direction. Pino looked right at me, savoring my predicament. He appeared to be simultaneously giddy and filled with staunch resolve—an odd combination.

"Hey, Mederos, how does it feel to be trapped like a dog?" he hollered. "What are you going to do now?"

I just stared at him and continued walking. My adrenalin was flowing. I felt like a racehorse at the starting gate.

Pino turned to Brown and said with relish, "So, here's your wonder boy, Lieutenant. Let's see him escape. Let's see how your training gets him out of this one."

Brown was eyeing me closely, curious to see how I'd respond. He was not as convinced as Pino that this game was over. While Pino was talking, I sauntered toward him slowly and calmly. Brown had taught me self-control. I was a model of obsequiousness and compliance.

I knew Pino might shoot me right then and there, but I thought it would be too quick for him—too easy. I figured he'd rather have the satisfaction of taking me in. After he made an example of me, he could do with me as he wished. What's more, he might think that killing me in front of the troops would damage morale, but I couldn't be sure. His anger made him unpredictable.

I kept walking until I got where I wanted to be. I had judged the distance I needed carefully. Without any warning, I turned on a dime and ran like a jackrabbit straight for the berm. The distance gave me the momentum I needed to scale it. The move startled Pino, and it took him a second to recover.

I was prepared—every muscle in my body was working in unison.

I jumped as high as I could and hurled my body at an angle that would roll the sisal aside so it would do the least amount of damage to my skin. I screamed in pain as sharp thorns pierced my body, dragging ragged bits of flesh along with them. I felt like a thousand bees had stung me, but I kept going.

I landed on the other side of the berm, bruised and bleeding. I rolled as soon as I hit the ground. Pino began shooting. He couldn't see me through the thicket, so he was shooting blindly. He let loose with several rounds of ammunition. I heard him order the other soldiers to follow suit. He sounded almost frantic in his desire to have them obey his command. As soon as he did, Brown countermanded his order, screaming, "No, shooting, damn it. No shooting."

Despite Brown's order, several shots rang out, probably from Pino's own gun. But I managed to avoid them. I crawled on my hands and knees for a distance to move out of the range of fire. Pino ordered the soldiers to push forward, but I knew it would be impossible for the trucks to penetrate the trees and thicket. The soldiers would have to circle the berm—about eight blocks around—to try to find me. I calculated it would take them nine or ten minutes.

Along with the thorns, several sisal tips had embedded themselves in my arms and legs, and I winced when I removed them. Adrenalin was still pumping through my veins, somewhat masking the pain. Blood streamed down my limbs, and I knew I'd have to find a way to stanch its flow so I couldn't be followed. If they used dogs to find me, I would be easy prey.

I clawed through the weeds, brambles, and vines until I hit soil and then rubbed dirt on my arms, legs, and face to stop the bleeding. The dirt was dry and pebbled with small stones. It was counterintuitive to throw dirt on a wound, but it absorbed my blood.

The good thing was that I had explored this area as a kid. I knew where I was. I had hunted here with a bow and arrow with my childhood playmates. I took a minute to get my bearings. I inspected the star-rich sky with an eye for direction. The Big Dipper informed me which way was north. My legs and hips were bruised and smarting so I couldn't run at top speed.

I limped along as well as I could in the direction of a cave I used to hide in with Jabao. I wiped my forehead with my shirtsleeve. I just hoped I could stay one step ahead of my stalkers. Blue-gray clouds covered the moon, and the hoot of an owl heralded my arrival.

Ceiba and jacaranda trees I remembered as a boy were still standing. I recalled cooling myself beneath their branches and regarded them as old friends. They served as landmarks for the location of caves.

I scrambled around in the brush for a while before locating the cave I sought. It was not a large cave, only big enough for two or three people. When we played in this vicinity as children, we all had our own cave. This one was Jabao's. Gilbert's was not far away, in the direction of the *Rio Lajas.* So was mine.

I stooped, gathered some sticks and broke them into small twigs. They snapped cleanly, sharply, piercing the air with a crackle. I also gathered some jaundiced weeds to obscure the mouth of the cave.

I knew how to arrange the twig and weed cover so the entrance of the cave would blend with the terrain. I wriggled myself into the cave and affixed the twig cover from the inside out. Once it was in place, the cave was pitch-dark.

It was difficult for me to be there without thinking of my youth which, at the moment, seemed like eons ago. The caves that had once served as a fond childhood memory would now be forever associated in my mind with running for my life.

Damn Fidel! He was not only making me fight for a future, he was robbing me of my past. Still, I was happy for the shelter. I sat with my knees pulled up to my chin for a very long time, catching my breath and waiting for my heart to regain its normal rhythm.

It was so dark in the cave, it didn't matter whether my eyes were open or shut. I kept them open just because it felt more natural. My right leg cramped for a minute, and I shook out the pain. I could hear the sounds of trucks and voices in the distance. At one point, they came closer and then faded away.

Every part of my body grew quiet, as if I were in hibernation. As I thought about what the next day might bring, fear descended upon me like a leaden cloak. Bile rose from my stomach and burned the back of my throat, but I worked to suppress the desire to cough, fearing it might reveal my location to the soldiers.

The cave was damp and moist, filled with the acrid smell of guano. Flies buzzed my ears, and I waved them away. I was very thirsty, and I licked my lips to moisten them. The mud on my arms and legs was beginning to dry and crack. It was starting to itch, but I resisted the urge to scratch. I distracted myself with the whistling sound made by the wings of mourning doves as they landed nearby.

A spider marched across my hand, its delicate legs tickling my skin. I impatiently slapped it away. It didn't feel like a tarantula, but it could've been. They were common enough in these parts. I wondered what other creatures might be in the cave with me. For a moment I thought I saw the bright, eerie eyes of a wild cat, but when I looked again it had vanished.

With each passing hour I felt a little safer. After a while, I let my muscles relax almost to the point of drifting off to sleep. I yawned deeply. I was bone tired, but I caught myself each time my eyelids began drooping and my chin started resting on my chest. I needed to remain alert for any indication that the soldiers were approaching.

I stayed up all night, listening for threatening sounds and hoping they wouldn't put dogs on my trail in the morning. Although I was well trained in escape tactics, being in the cave had triggered memories of a childhood trick that might serve me well. Under the circumstances, it was better than anything Lieutenant Brown had drilled into me—it could even save my life.

I soothed myself with that thought and with memories of kissing

Magda. My recollection of the last time our lips had met remained as fresh in my mind as white linen.

Despite my fatigue, I left the cave well before daybreak to head for the river.

CHAPTER 39

Not finding me in the darkness, Pino suspended the search until morning. The soldiers set up a tent so the officers could sleep on the bridge overlooking the *Rio Lajas,* while they made camp on the river banks. Pino had cordoned off all the roads leading out of the area and had ordered the trucks to take positions on both sides of the river. He was taking no chances that I would elude him.

Early the following morning, the soldiers fanned out across the area, a jungle-like terrain thick with vines and branches jutting every which way. They systematically plowed the fields, poking walls of brush and bushes with their machine guns. Some soldiers stood atop one another and peered through binoculars. They faced a tedious, time-consuming task, but they were determined to find me.

An hour before most of the soldiers arose I exited the cave and made my way through the area, stopping briefly at Gilbert's cave to rest. I inched toward the riverbank on my belly, across the briars, the wild blackberry, and the root-rich ground, hardly feeling the toll it was taking on my body. I moved quietly and slowly through the brush, fearing any quick movement—any snap of a twig—could give me away.

As I approached the river, someone called to Lieutenant Pino. I could hear them talking, arguing. As soon as they turned their backs on me, I slithered into the water like a crocodile off a steep riverbank. The river had a very swift current, and I knew which way it ran. Flowers and reeds lined the sides of the river and floated atop the surface of the water, forming a tangle of cover. These were the same hollow reeds my cousins and I used to play hide-and-seek with when we were kids.

I plucked a long reed and placed my lips around it, sinking quietly, stealthily beneath the surface of the water. The reed enabled me to breathe without being detected, and I made my way quickly, cautiously, downstream. I swam right under the bridge where the soldiers were positioned. I could hear the strum of their voices through the water. I swam a little faster. This was not a place I cared to linger.

Although the *Rio Lajas* was not very wide, it was deep, deep enough to enable me to swim quite a distance without being detected. I swam about a mile downstream before I saw the sun begin to filter through the water. I listened carefully for the voices of soldiers. They were intermittent and growing less distinct. After a while, they faded into silence. Thinking it safe, I raised my head above the water and looked around. I judged the coast to be clear and let out a sigh of relief.

I clawed my way up the bank of the river and hid behind a tree, catching my breath while getting my bearings. A startled animal raced from behind a rock and plunged into the underbrush. The warm sun was working its way up the sky and a large cornfield stretched before me. I stripped my wet clothes from my body, glad to feel the sunshine on my skin. I washed my clothes in the river as best as I could and then flattened them out on a rock to dry.

The mud had long since washed off my body, and I could clearly see my cuts and bruises. Several lacerations on my legs were red and angry, a sure sign of infection. I sat naked for a short time waiting for my clothes to dry, enjoying the soft caress of the breeze, and planning what to do next.

I knew Pino would be furious. I figured our game of cat and mouse had long since morphed from an obligation into an obsession with him. He was not a man who often tasted failure, and he would not want to make a feast of it now.

Rather than reveal the facts of the situation, Pino had lied to the head of the local militia the previous night. He said he needed help finding an escaped rapist and murderer. Pino supplied him with my description, telling him I was a dangerous criminal—and I might be wounded. He insisted he wanted me dead or alive.

Twenty members of the militia met to devise a plan to flush me out. The head of the militia was not well educated, having little appreciation for the nuances and complexities of military command. But he seemed industrious and competent, showing a keen interest in the assignment, and Pino was confident in his ability to carry it out. Pino had neither given him my name nor shown him my picture.

Distraught over my disappearance, Luis had gone to my father's house to tell him what had happened. "Frankie's in trouble. We've got to do something to help."

My mother closed her eyes and started to cry. My father turned to comfort her before facing Luis.

"What happened?" he asked.

"Soldiers came to my house and Frank somehow escaped. I have no idea where he went. Word on the street is that the army and the town's militia are out to get him."

Without skipping a beat, my father called my brother George into the room. "Who's in charge of the militia?" he asked.

"Jabao," said George.

"Jabao?"

"Frankie's old friend."

My father took my mother's hand. "Don't worry, Frankie's going to be all right."

Suddenly, the rumble of trucks filled the air. My mother pushed the curtains aside and peered out the window to see what was happening. Her hand flew to her mouth. Soldiers were everywhere, making their way down the street armed with machine guns.

My father turned to George. "Go tell Jabao he's not looking for a criminal. He's looking for Frankie. Let him know what's really going on." As George was going out the door, my father said, "Be quick and be careful."

George nodded, knowing full well the gravity of his mission. He reconnoitered the neighborhood, ducking in and out of doorways to avoid the soldiers. He was very nervous. When he finally found Jabao, he pulled him aside, his face flushed, his voice low.

"What are you doing here?" asked Jabao. He looked stunned to see him. George hesitated a moment, catching his breath.

"Do you know who you're looking for?" asked George, trying to quiet his panting.

"A rapist and murderer," said Jabao. But a quick perusal of George's face led him to believe he might be wrong.

"It's not a rapist. It's Frankie."

A soft whistle escaped Jabao's lips. "Whoa! Frankie? Your brother, Frankie? They didn't tell me that."

"Well, it's true."

"You're sure?"

"Very sure. He's trying to escape the country. He's left the army, and they're after him."

"Christ almighty!" Jabao turned and waved his men in. "We need to suspend the operation," he said in a voice filled with authority. "They lied to us. It's not a rapist we're after, it's Frankie Mederos." Since most of the men knew me from town, there was no resistance.

Jabao was furious, and when he got that way, there was no stopping him. Disregarding possible consequences, he marched straight to the bridge and confronted Pino.

"I thought you were looking for a goddamn criminal," he charged.

"We are—a murderer. Is that criminal enough for you?" Pino looked at Jabao as if he were a creature lower than a slug. He had neither time nor patience for such nonsense.

"You lied to me, you bastard. And I don't like being lied to."

"What are you talking about?" snapped Pino.

"You aren't looking for a murderer. You're looking for an old friend of mine."

"How do you know that?"

"Trust me, I know it," retorted Jabao. "I know Frankie Mederos and he's no criminal."

"You don't know what you're talking about," sneered Pino. Frustration had seeped into every line of his face. "We're after a criminal—and we're going to get him."

Jabao looked at the water and laughed. "I've got news for you, buddy. If it's Frankie you're after, you're *never* going to get him. He knows this area like the back of his hand. You're wasting your time."

Pino glared at Jabao, enraged. "What are you talking about? Do you know something you're not telling me?"

"I sure do," said Jabao. "Frankie was here—right under your nose—and you missed him. You think you're so smart, but you have no idea how to catch him."

"What do you mean, I missed him?" demanded Pino. He was seething at the gall of this man for speaking to him this way.

Jabao laughed, hesitating to tell Pino exactly what he knew had happened. Instead, he said, "Do you think you're going to find Mederos here? On his own turf? Impossible."

"We'll see about that," said Pino. "I've got men on both sides of the river and more on the bridge. And at this very moment soldiers are scouring the fields. We've got him trapped. There's no way he can escape."

Jabao threw back his head and laughed. "Do you think Frankie would wait for daylight to escape? He's already gone. He left under the cover of darkness—he's miles away from here by now."

Lieutenant Brown looked down at the flowers and reeds in the water, and it suddenly dawned on him what had happened. A faint smile of pride danced on his lips.

"Then you're going to help me find him," said Pino.

"Don't count on it," said Jabao.

Pino started to threaten and protest. But Jabao just shook his head. He raised his chin, set his jaw, and with a steady gait walked away from the lieutenant.

Once my clothes were dry, I decided my best plan of action was to head to Macho's house in Cojimar. Going back to my parents was too risky. I thought Macho's place was my safest bet, especially since I believed the boat was leaving in just a few days. I was sure Macho would welcome me, and I figured if I stayed there we could all leave for the States together.

I followed the path of the river and stopped at tunnels and caves I knew along the way, biding my time until it got dark. For obvious reasons, I didn't want to arrive in the daylight. I was keenly aware of all the pitfalls, all the places I would most likely be apprehended. I moved quickly, stealthily.

When I burst into Macho's front door, his eyes widened and he almost collapsed. "Jesus, Mary, and Joseph! What the hell are you doing here? The whole army is looking for you. How in God's name did you escape?"

"It's a long story," I said.

Macho looked me up and down. "My God, you're all cut up. What happened to you?"

"It's nothing."

"Well, it looks pretty bad to me."

Macho called his wife, Ana, to help me. I sat at their kitchen table as she plucked the thorns and burrs with a pair of tweezers, clucking in admonishment as she worked. I had removed as many as I could, but several burrs were still firmly attached to my back—well beyond my reach. Ana twisted them gently to extract them, and I winced in pain. She then applied iodine to my sores, wrapped the deeper wounds in gauze, and secured her work with adhesive tape. I thanked her with my eyes.

Macho shook his head at me. "You never cease to amaze me."

"Well, I'm pretty damn tired of being amazing," I said. All I wanted was a meal and a bed.

"I bet you are," said Macho.

Ana offered to make me something to eat, which I eagerly accepted. I was ravenous.

"I just want to get to the States and have this whole thing over," I said. "I miss Magda terribly."

"You'll get there," said Macho. I wolfed down a sandwich and up-ended a bottle of orange soda. I was so thirsty I gulped it all down at once. I wiped my face on a thin paper napkin, careful not to disturb my sores.

"Can I stay here until the boat goes out?"

"I'd like to put you up, but I can't," said Macho. "The schedule for the trip is a little uncertain—it could be a couple of weeks, maybe longer. My brother Gerardo is likely to come by in the meantime. He knows who you are. It's too dangerous for you to stay here."

"Why can't we leave sooner?" I asked. My patience was at its end.

"The damn motor on my boat gave out. I'm buying a used one. It's the only thing I can get my hands on. The blockade has made things impossible."

"I understand," I said in a voice that telegraphed my unhappiness.

"Once I get it, I'll have to take the boat out a couple of times to test the motor—make sure it's okay. I can't take us out to sea and have it conk out."

"I know it's important," I said. My mind harkened back to what happened on our last trip. If the motor had died, we would have all perished—that was for sure.

"The timing on the trip is still unclear," said Macho. "I also have problems with Gerardo. He takes his job at the coast guard station very seriously—I guess they didn't make him director for nothing. He's very suspicious about what I'm up to. He needs to see me go back and forth from fishing a few times to relieve his mind."

I grunted my dissatisfaction. "What do you recommend I do in the meantime?" I asked. I was trying not to be too short with Macho, but I was fed up. The fact that I was facing yet another delay was sending me over the edge.

"Let me get Cuni," he said. "He'll know what to do."

Macho turned to his wife and asked her to run to Cuni's house to tell him where I was. Within thirty minutes Ana and Cuni arrived in Macho's driveway. When Cuni saw me, his handshake soon gave way to a hug. When he pulled back, he shook his head.

"How the—"

"I know," I said and waved him off. I was too tired to provide him with the details of my escape.

"Everyone's looking for you."

"So I hear. Sorry to have caused so much trouble. I—"

"Can you get him out of here—now?" interrupted Macho. He was obviously nervous. "I'll feel a lot better once he's gone."

Cuni turned his attention to Macho. "Just a couple of things," he said. "Did you get the boat?"

"The boat's all lined up," said Macho. "The problem's the motor."

"Well, hurry it up," said Cuni. "You're giving me a heart attack with all these delays."

"I have to get the motor and test it—and I have some issues with my brother," explained Macho.

"Then figure them out," snapped Cuni. "This can't go on any longer. It's gotten too dangerous. You've got to leave within a couple of days—no matter what."

"I'll do my best," said Macho, looking simultaneously concerned and annoyed. The two men glared at each other. I cleared my throat.

"In the meantime, what should we do with Frankie?" said Macho.

"Don't worry about him," said Cuni. "Worry about your own part of this operation. I'll take care of him." He nodded at me. "Let's go, the car's outside."

Cuni and I bid Macho goodbye, and we clambered into the car. I slid down on the seat to avoid detection. Cuni put the key in the ignition and the car roared to a start. He stretched out his arm and adjusted his rearview mirror.

"Where are we going?" I asked.

"You don't want to know," said Cuni as he backed out of the driveway.

"Well, you might as well tell me. I'll find out soon enough."

Cuni was silent for a moment. "Where's the last place Pino would look for you?"

I sighed and shook my head. By now I knew the way Cuni's mind operated. I thought for a moment and then it occurred to me.

"No," I moaned.

"Yes," said Cuni. My heart lurched like a train off its tracks. I had gone full circle.

Cuni drove me back to Luis's house. I was right back where I had started.

CHAPTER 40

Luis was both flabbergasted and delighted to see me. Although Rosa was very nervous, he willingly agreed to hide me again, despite the heightened danger. Cuni told him what had happened and assured him it would be only a couple of days before we'd be able to board a boat for the States.

On April 11, 1967, Cuni informed Luis and me that the boat was leaving that very night. Finally! Luis and I could not have been more thrilled. When his girls got home from school, Luis took them separately onto his lap. He told them he loved them and would miss them dearly, but that this was something he had to do for them all to "live happily ever after."

They were too young to understand the full implications of what he was saying, but they understood the storybook analogy, listened attentively and assured him in small brave voices that they would all be okay until he could arrange for the family to join him. I followed suit and bid Rosa and the girls a sad—but hopeful—goodbye.

To lessen our chances for apprehension, the launch was scheduled to take place in a little-traveled area south of the harbor—a place that was sheltered and out of the way. In addition to me, the group would consist of the nine soldiers and my Uncle Luis.

Joining us were Macho and his family—his wife and three young children, including the boy who had proclaimed me to be a murderer. Macho would serve as the captain, and another fisherman would serve as his mate. A total of seventeen people would try to escape in one small boat.

Cuni informed us that Macho's boat would pick us up at nine p.m. He wanted us to be on the shore two hours earlier, awaiting its arrival. I thought this was too much time to hang around. I was very aware of the danger involved, and the very thought of apprehension gave me the willies. Not wanting to be a sitting duck, I postponed our leave-taking until eight p.m., figuring we would still have plenty of time to get to our destination.

We called a taxi and, in an effort to avoid suspicion, asked the driver to drop us off at the Cultural Center—not far from our place of departure. I figured this would be an innocent enough looking place to wait.

I was thinking about all the things that could possibly go wrong with so many people involved when the taxi driver—a friendly black man with a Louis Armstrong smile—interrupted my thoughts.

"It's very strange," he said.

"What's that?"

"I've had three other fares tonight, and they all wanted me to drop them off at the same place."

"What's strange about it?"

"The thing is," said the driver dryly, "there aren't any events taking place at the center tonight."

"Just a coincidence, I guess," I said, shrugging nonchalantly.

"I guess," said the driver, but he didn't look convinced.

Luis and I exchanged concerned glances. My antennae were up for something that might be wrong. As we passed the Cultural Center, I saw a group of people sitting on the limestone stairs: two pregnant women; two old men; some people in their sixties; and several families, including young children. The ages of the people and the looks of anxiety etched on their faces gave me pause.

"Driver," I said, "I've changed my mind. Why don't you drop us off a block or so down the road."

"Are you sure? There's nothing there."

"Yes. We just want to take a walk and look at the ocean for a while before we meet our friends."

"Suit yourself." The driver shrugged and pulled up to the curb. I got out and paid him the fare with some of the money my father had slipped me the last time I saw him. I gave him a generous tip, knowing my pesos would be worthless once I left Cuba. I had five American dollars left in my pocket. It was going to have to suffice for whatever eventualities lay ahead. The taxi driver thanked me, smiled, and then drove away slowly in his big, black Cadillac.

I stood for a couple of minutes on the side of the road, mulling over the situation. There were too many people at the Cultural Center on an eventless night to be a coincidence. My stomach felt queasy. "Something's not right," I said to Luis. He looked at me in alarm.

"What are you thinking?"

"I don't have a good feeling about this. We might be better off if we don't go near those people."

"Whatever you say," said Luis. He looked worried too.

"Let's take the back streets that lead to the coast," I said. "I think it will be safer."

Having thoroughly searched the area, Pino figured I must be leaving Cuba from the port of Cojimar. Various places were commonly used for departure—places near the fort and on the ocean side of Havana.

Pino mobilized the force to Cojimar and went to talk to Macho's brother, Gerardo, who was in charge of the coast guard station. This was the same man who had accosted me outside of Macho's house the day after my aborted escape with Pedro and Joey. The lieutenant informed him that he was conducting a high-security operation, and he would need to set up a command center at the fort to carry it out.

Pino then ordered the troops to search all the docks in the area and to look for me in every single fisherman's boat—he wanted no rock left unturned. The search was conducted quickly, thoroughly, and

efficiently. Brown had done a fine job training his troops in search tactics. Their performance was exemplary. Fortunately, they were looking
in all the wrong places.

When we arrived at the shoreline, there was a group of people sitting
on a spit of land full of large ragged rocks tilted at various angles like
crushed metal. This was the same place of our planned departure. I
had envisioned us being here alone, and I found sharing this space to
be unnerving. Waiting with an assemblage of strangers was the last
thing I had expected. It made me hyperalert, edgy, uneasy.

As we got closer, I recognized them as the same people who'd
been waiting on the steps of the Cultural Center. I sidled up to a middle-aged man and asked him what they were doing. After hedging a
bit, he told me they were waiting for a boat that would take them to
the States.

"When is it coming?" I asked.

"It should be here within a half hour. You're leaving, too, I pre-
sume."

It was obvious what we were doing, so I nodded my agreement.

I scanned the heavens and wondered whether Magda was looking
at the stars and thinking about me, too. It wouldn't be much longer
until I saw her. My mind drifted for a moment imagining our reunion,
and then I quickly regained my focus. I couldn't think about *mi novia*
now. I had to concentrate on the task at hand.

I inspected the horizon, hoping to see Macho's boat coming toward us. There was no sign of it, but it was still a little early.

I caught something out of the corner of my eye and saw nine
strapping young men approaching. These were the soldiers who were
to accompany us on our journey. We made our introductions. They
all seemed quite friendly. I got the feeling my presence provided them
with a sense of leadership and security.

Macho's wife and children soon arrived, and I settled them down next to me on the rocks. I thanked Ana again for taking care of me the last time I saw her. Fortunately, her little boy had lost his fear of me.

To my left a frail old man was holding the arm of a younger man. He had a dry, rasping cough and looked like he might be fighting the flu.

Another elderly man sat next to a woman whom I assumed was his daughter. She had the same high cheekbones and aquiline nose. He seemed very nervous, and she was trying to calm him by talking softly. His face was heavily lined and sprinkled with age spots. He was spry for his age. I judged him to be well over eighty.

I introduced myself, and he said his name was Miguel. He seemed sweet-natured, and I took an immediate shine to him. We struck up a short conversation. He told me his wife was deceased. He had eight children and forty grandchildren. Under different circumstances he might have shown me their pictures.

Behind us, lounging on a rock and smoking a cigarette, its incandescent tip glowing orange in the dark, was the taxi driver, the same one who had just delivered Luis and me to our destination.

"What are you doing here?" I said.

"I've always wanted to leave Cuba. When I saw all the people at the center, I was suspicious. When they left, I decided to follow them."

"So you hadn't planned to go?" I asked, amazed. After all I had been through to try to escape, it seemed like such a quick decision. I felt a little envious.

"No, I just figured I'd take advantage of the situation." He uttered this as casually as if he had decided to suddenly drop in at a neighborhood bar.

"Where's your car?"

"The Cadillac? I left it by the side of the road." He said it like it was a wad of tobacco he had spit on the sidewalk.

"Pretty nice car to abandon."

"Who cares about a car? Freedom is what matters." He hesitated for a moment. "I left the keys in the ignition—someone might be able to use it."

"Good thinking." He beamed at the compliment.

I started to count the people in the other party—fourteen in all. I wondered about the size of their boat. I figured it must be big.

It was a little after nine p.m., and I still hadn't seen any sign of Macho's boat. I took a deep breath and looked at my uncle. He was chain smoking and making a clicking sound with his tongue that indicated he was even more nervous than I.

I sat down next to him, considering what might lie ahead. Some Cuban land crabs crawled sideways between the rocks in search of food and each other. I was thinking about how often my escape had taken the same sideways direction, and I hoped this was the night when my luck would change.

I was wondering about what role the soldiers might play in case of an emergency when I felt someone tap me hard on the shoulder. I turned around and saw Macho standing behind me, accompanied by his friend, the fisherman who was going to serve as his mate. At first my mind couldn't comprehend his presence. It took me a minute to take it in.

"Christ, Macho, what are you doing here? You're supposed to be picking us up in your boat."

"There's no time to talk," whispered Macho. He was red in the face and very agitated. "We've got to get out of here."

"Whoa! Not so fast. Where's the boat?"

"I couldn't get the motor started," he confessed. He looked scared, defeated, and eager to leave.

His buddy confirmed his story. "He gave it his best shot. He tried and tried, but the motor just wouldn't turn over."

As we were speaking, the people around us started standing up, grabbing their children and readying themselves for departure. I looked out to sea and saw their boat coming toward us. It was about seventy-five feet from shore, not a large boat, but it looked sturdy enough.

When the boat got nearer, people started stampeding, splashing and jumping through the water like bluefish. "Come on, we've got to get outta here," urged Macho. "If they get caught, we could be arrested, too."

The soldiers came toward me, looking for some kind of direction. I had to make a split-second decision. Macho was hollering for us all to leave, but I had other ideas. I held up my hand and said, "No, we aren't going back. We are *all* going to Florida tonight."

"What? All of us?"

"Yes, all of us."

"But—" started Macho.

"Don't give me a hard time, Macho. Just shut the hell up and get in the boat."

I grabbed Macho's daughters—one in each arm—and headed straight for the vessel. Pandemonium broke loose with everyone scrambling to get on board. The boat was tilting back and forth. Water that had dripped off people's clothing settled in the bottom of the boat. Luis trembled, hesitated. He wasn't a good swimmer.

"C'mon," I shouted. "This is our last chance. We've got to go *now*. We can't wait any longer."

It was a mad rush to the boat, with people falling into the water, children wailing and scrambling to get on board. The captain of the boat was beside himself.

"What the hell are you doing?" he bellowed. "Get out of my boat."

He started pushing people off the sides of the boat with his paddle.

"We're all going to Florida," I hollered. "Let us in."

"You're not part of the group. You haven't paid your passage. It's too dangerous. The boat's too small. I can't take you all."

Ignoring his protests, I climbed aboard the boat and placed Macho's two daughters on a seat next to their mother. Ana gathered them onto her lap and pulled their heads to her bosom. They clung to her neck, crying in terror.

The soldiers followed my lead and climbed in after me. Luis followed suit. Macho carried his little boy on board, and I immediately ordered the pregnant women and the old men to sit down. The boat was far too crowded. It was rocking dangerously from side to side.

People were pushing for a place to sit. The younger children were perched on their parents' laps, their arms clutching their necks and backs for dear life.

When the last person was finally aboard, I screamed at the captain, "Go! Now. Get this damn thing outta here." The fisherman grumbled but did as he was told, knowing full well that between me and the other soldiers he had lost control of his boat.

The motor sputtered to a start and began to strain, working well beyond its capacity. The boat struggled to overcome the roll of the water. Unfortunately, I could see bigger, white-tipped waves in the distance.

"There are too many people. We'll all drown," warned the fisherman. "It's too much weight for the motor."

"Just move the boat out," I shouted. "Once we get offshore, we'll decide what to do."

The boat was sitting low in the water. It chugged forward, the motor whining, straining. I looked up at the stars again, a reflexive move to make sure of my bearings.

Once we got offshore a short distance, everyone calmed down a little. Emotions were generally spent and most people were either too tired or too scared to squabble. Many sat in a state of shock while others sat tight lipped, their faces and postures betraying their emotions. Although no one uttered the words aloud, there was only one thought uppermost in everyone's mind: how in God's name will we ever make it to freedom without dying?

Clouds covered the sliver of moon, and a tense, eerie silence descended over the small vessel.

CHAPTER 41

With our combined weight, the boat sat so deep in the water that waves crested over its sides. We were all sopping wet and up to our ankles in water. The soldiers and I were bailing, working furiously to keep us afloat. I was thankful to have so many able-bodied men in our midst, but I was concerned about how long we could survive with the boat so overloaded.

The children were cold and terrified of being out at sea in the dark—it was even frightening and disorienting for the adults. Conditions were already deteriorating, and several people were of the opinion that we should return to Cuba. To my dismay, Macho was one of them.

"It's no use, Frankie," he whined. "We should go back and turn ourselves in. Beg the government for mercy. If we do, we could get several years in jail, but at least we'll still be alive."

I turned and glared at him—after all we had been through together, I couldn't believe what I was hearing.

"I won't be alive," I snapped, knowing full well I'd be shot on sight. "And get it straight, Macho, once you leave Cuba, there *is* no mercy. We've come this far, and we're not going back. We're *all* going to Florida."

Macho grunted, knowing what I said was true. I thought the issue was settled when my uncle interjected, "But we'll surely die out here. Drowning is such a horrible death. What will happen to Rosa and my girls?" His voice began to crack, and I was afraid he was going to become hysterical.

"I don't want to die," he cried.

"You're not going to die." My voice brimmed with frustration. "We've got a lot of work to do. Now shut up, damn it. Both of you."

The others in the boat started mumbling among themselves, talking about the danger. Many of the original passengers resented our presence. One man in particular was vehement in his opinion that we had no right being in their boat in the first place. Others grumbled their accord. I knew if I let this continue, things would quickly get out of hand.

I could count on the soldiers to keep order, but there was another problem that needed to be solved. All of us could never make the ninety-mile journey in this small boat. I needed to take action—and fast.

I turned to the captain and ordered, "Shut off the motor." The captain looked at me in disbelief.

"Have you gone stark raving mad? Why?"

"To save gas. Now do it."

"No, I'm turning back," he responded defiantly.

"No, you're turning off the motor," I said in a steely voice. The captain shot me a look of contempt, and the passengers cowered in their places, fearing a fight would break out. The soldiers stared at me, willing to back up any decision I made.

"This is *my* boat," said the captain. "And I'll do what *I* think best."

"This is *not* your boat anymore," I thundered. "This is *our* boat. And you can either follow orders, or you can jump overboard and swim to shore by yourself. But no one will help you, and we're *not* turning back."

The captain sat fuming. I gave him a minute to calm down. The only sounds were the waves splashing the sides of the boat and a child's whimpering. I watched as the moon seeped between shredded clouds, casting a silver glow onto the water.

"What are you proposing we do?" he demanded.

I looked at the soldiers. "We're going to wait here until we see another boat either this size or larger. And then we're going to take it."

At first the captain looked astonished, but then the muscles in his face relaxed slightly and his breathing became easier. He knew what I said made sense. He didn't say another word. Neither did I. Nor did anyone else.

He reached over and turned off the motor.

We sat in the darkness for several hours, waiting, praying, and drifting with the movement of the waves. The boat rocked back and forth, sometimes lurching violently. Almost everyone was nauseous. With no food or water, people were becoming dehydrated.

A thick mist settled over the boat, adding to our discomfort. One of the old men was shaking, tears drifting down his thin, parched skin. I grabbed a rubber-lined sack to cover him, hoping it would ward off hypothermia. He looked at me with gratitude and a terrible fear in his eyes.

A young woman was vomiting, and her husband was trying to comfort her. She was eight months pregnant and afraid she would go into labor in the boat. She was holding her belly and crying that she didn't want to deliver her baby at sea—with so many people watching. She feared she and her baby would die. Her husband urged her to be brave, and he promised to get her to a hospital as soon as we reached the States.

Occasionally, someone would mutter something about going back, but these comments went almost unnoticed—and definitely un-heeded. By this time, everyone seemed resigned to their fate, silently bemoaning the fact that they had lost control over their destiny.

After a while, the fog lifted and we spotted the lights of a boat headed our way. The mood lifted in the boat, but I instructed the cap-tain not to start the motor until it got closer. I wanted to save as much gas as possible. The passengers who were awake were nudging those who had fallen asleep. They were very excited.

Unfortunately, as the boat got nearer, I could see it was even smaller than the one we were on. It just wouldn't do. A collective groan rose from the throats of the passengers, and the boat grew heavy with disappointment.

About a half hour later, another boat appeared in the distance. It looked big enough, so I told the captain to start the engine and head toward it. Some passengers were hopeful. The more sanguine were relieved.

When we got closer, however, I could see that another fishing boat sat alongside it. I was afraid they would defend one another. Even if we could overtake two boats, it would make things too complicated. The passengers grumbled in resignation. A few started weeping. Dreams were turning into desperation.

"Just hang on. The right boat will come along soon," I said. I didn't want people to abandon hope. Another hour elapsed before I spied a third boat. It was just the right size and appeared to have three men on board. The outlines of their hunched bodies were black against the midnight-blue sky. With all the soldiers at my disposal, I figured it would be a cinch to overtake them.

"That's it. That's our boat," I screamed to the captain. I was both excited and relieved at the sighting. People started sitting up straighter and looking around expectantly. A couple of people pointed in the direction of the boat.

"Crank up the motor," I ordered.

"It's no use," said the captain. "It's too far away. Our boat is too heavy. We can't go that fast. We'll never catch up."

"Just do what I say, damn it. Do it anyway." I was desperate not to miss this opportunity.

The captain started the motor and we inched toward the boat in the distance. It was about four miles out at sea. The men aboard it were fishing. We traveled at a sluggish pace. Still, we were moving and they were sitting still. We were gaining on them, slowly but surely.

"Just keep going," I said. "We'll make it. How's the gas holding out?"

"We're still okay," reported the captain.

I motioned to one of the soldiers to come and talk to me. "When we get there, I want the soldiers to commandeer the boat." I handed him a circle of rope.

"Tie and gag whoever is on it, and then we'll redistribute the people to balance the weight. Do whatever you have to, but take that boat." I looked at the young soldier and said, "Just watch out; the fishermen may have knives." The soldier nodded and passed the order along to the other men.

I leaned over to speak to Macho. He was looking more hopeful. "Once we take the boat, I want you to drive it. As soon as the soldiers secure it, we'll tie the two boats together so they won't drift apart. It's not going to be easy. Have your friend serve as your mate." Macho silently nodded.

With our plan in place, I watched as we drew closer to the boat. It seemed like an eternity. But little by little we were catching up. Conditions in our boat were becoming increasingly difficult, and I hoped against hope for success.

As we approached the boat, I called for our captain to kill the motor. We slid next to the boat, and I used an oar to keep the two boats from ramming into each other. Once the boats slowed down, I reached out to the other boat to steady us.

Before the three men in the second boat knew what was happening, six soldiers jumped into their vessel and grabbed them. They struggled, but were soon overpowered.

The soldiers bound their hands and feet, but I instructed them not to gag the men until I had a chance to speak with them.

"Who are you and what are you doing out here?" I asked.

The first man spoke in an outraged voice as if he were king of the sea. "I'm director of the fishermen's cooperative," he said, looking as if I should be impressed with his credentials. He was so supercilious, he made my flesh crawl. He nodded toward the younger man sitting next to him, a man with kind eyes who looked to be about thirty. He regarded the man with contempt. "This worm tried to escape the country and was sent to jail for five years."

"Uh-huh," I said, shooting the young man a sympathetic look.

"This is the first time he has gone fishing since his release. We've accompanied him as part of his probation. We wanted to talk to him to make sure he was rehabilitated—that he had learned his lesson in jail."

"What lesson is that?"

"That he needs to remain loyal to the Party."

"What has the Party ever done for him except rob him of his freedoms?"

The man looked astonished at the audacity of the question. He did not reply.

"Who are you?" I demanded, turning my attention to the second man.

He was a thin, intense man with dark, beady eyes. "I'm a member of the Communist Central Party," he said proudly. "I'm here to do my duty."

"Good for you," I said, sarcastically.

I turned to the man who had tried to escape Cuba.

"And you?"

"I'm nobody—just a guy trying to live his life."

"Well, it may be your lucky day," I said. "Because we're all on our way to Florida."

"What—?" started the director. I didn't wait for him to finish his sentence before ordering the soldiers to gag the three men so they couldn't cry out.

The soldiers and I redistributed the people so there were slightly fewer than twenty in each boat. I ordered the pregnant women and the old men to remain in the boat with me. We tied the two boats together—one behind the other—and resumed our journey.

We traveled for a couple of hours with me periodically adjusting our course by reading the stars. The wind was picking up, but with what Abuelo had taught me, I knew how to compensate for it, calculating how far north I needed to travel to reach the Florida Keys.

I wondered whether my grandfather ever anticipated something like this. I guessed he had. I remembered him saying, "Mark my words, Frankie, someday this knowledge will come in handy." I smiled thinking about him.

Knowing we were approaching the danger zone—the area of the patrol boats—I ordered the two captains to cut their motors. I remembered Ralph saying the patrol boats could pick up an engine on radar. I ordered everyone to be quiet.

We sat in silence while waves sloshed over the sides of the boat, occasionally splashing someone in the face. It was still very dark and the slap of cold water always came as an unwelcome surprise. It was just another assault on the nerves of people who were close to the breaking point.

After what seemed like a lifetime of waiting, the passengers began to grumble. Several people had urinated in the boat and vomit was clinging to clothing and skin. The stench was horrific. Everyone was hungry, thirsty and, most of all, very afraid of dying.

One man became hysterical, accusing me of waiting for nothing. No one was thinking clearly. People began doubting that the patrol boats actually existed—they even started accusing me of making up the need to patiently sit and wait. Why, I could not imagine—other than the fact that they were operating on pure emotion. But, without a doubt, two groups of people knew the value of waiting: the fishermen and the soldiers.

Because the patrol boats traveled without lights, I knew they'd be difficult to spot in the distance. I kept a careful lookout and insisted we stay put, while trying to quell a near mutiny. People were pushing and fighting, and I was afraid we'd soon have a man overboard. The soldiers worked relentlessly to nip arguments in the bud and to calm people down.

Suddenly, we heard a din in the distance. It soon became a hideous, thunderous roar. All arguments ceased and voices grew silent. Some people covered their ears, and children scrambled onto the laps of their parents for protection. The adults strained their eyes to see a patrol boat approaching.

It looked like a black leviathan, a large, threatening, and ominous presence. The adults sat in stunned silence as my heart constricted in fear. This was the moment of truth. I blessed myself and whispered a short prayer to the Virgin Mary that we wouldn't be apprehended.

Then I spotted another patrol boat coming the other way. Both were heavily armed military boats with guns pointed outward. The passengers had never seen anything like them before—no one could believe their power and size. They totally dwarfed us. Our small boats looked like toys beside them. We watched in awe as the behemoths crossed in front of each other. Their horns boomed in the distance, producing a solitary, preternatural moan in the darkness.

Once they passed completely out of sight, I gave the captains the signal. "Go, go, go!" I hollered, as if screaming would make the boats go faster. I was filled with a sublime excitement and a boatful of apprehension. The captains revved up their engines, and I readjusted our course to compensate for the drift the boats had taken while we were waiting.

I looked up at what had turned into a crystalline, star-sprinkled sky and hoped it wouldn't be long now until we all tasted freedom. I held my breath as we slowly crossed into international waters.

CHAPTER 42

Believing that our biggest challenges were now behind us, my muscles relaxed, and I drifted into a deep sleep. I dreamt of Magda wearing a white lace blouse, her hair pulled back and fastened with a blood-red rose. She was unspeakably beautiful, standing on a red, white, and blue balcony, her smile broad, her arms outstretched. I was running toward her, my fingertips straining to touch hers. I was just about there, but I couldn't reach her. She was dissolving into nothingness, slipping away. It was at once a soothing and unnerving dream, the kind I had grown used to in recent months.

A breeze kicked up, and I struggled to lift my eyelids. When I opened my eyes, the water was pink. Red. Orange. Purple. A Crayola splash of storybook colors. The sky boasted long slivers of deep crimson that melded into scalloped gunmetal gray, creating mysterious shapes that hung as low as an old rope swing and then slowly burst into bubble-gum pink.

The sun exploded through thick bunches of moving whirls that twisted back and forth upon themselves and then morphed into faces of dolphins, mermaids, and cats with long wondrous tails. A pyrotechnic display of smoldering embers under lit clouds of violet blue.

The sun crested the horizon, trumpeting its arrival with blinding rays that shattered into a million gold discs that floated like water lilies atop a pond. The incandescent ball was radiant in its triumphant ascension, its rays shooting across the horizon as if blessing the ends of the earth.

The boats rocked gently in the deep-blue water as the sun moved higher in the sky. It was an achingly profound and wordless moment. We sat in awe, some people crying softly, some nodding their heads, some closing their eyes in silent prayer. Mothers drew their children to them, holding their heads in the palms of their hands and thinking of how they would raise their offspring in a land of freedom. Fathers regarded their wives and children with renewed hope for their futures.

I searched all the passengers' faces, thinking of what this moment meant to them—and to generations to come. I thought about Magda and how I would someday tell my children and grandchildren how this all came to happen.

Never was there a more glorious sunrise.

Once the moment passed, the mood in the boats became almost celebratory. Although many of us were sick, the sun promised to both warm our bodies and to dry our clothes, and that alone was enough to make us feel better. The icing on the cake was that we were now free people, no longer suffering under the tyranny of Fidel. And, after our harrowing experience, we were now well on our way to the United States.

I calculated that we had enough gas to make it to Florida. The bigger problem was that almost everyone was in need of medical assistance—some more than others. Our throats were parched. Our stomachs were empty. Many of us were suffering from either dehydration or hypothermia—or both. The children, the elderly, and the pregnant women were in the worst shape, but their spirits were buoyed by having crossed into international waters.

We made our way toward Florida for about an hour before I spotted a massive ship in the distance. Russian cargo ships often plied international waters and, given the Soviet Union's close ties to Cuba, they were known to pick up Cuban refugees and return them to their native land for prosecution. Apart from your boat being shot out of the sea, this was an escapee's worst nightmare.

I hollered to Macho who was driving the other boat. "What do we have out there?"

"I don't know, but it's damn big."

"Russian?"

"Christ, I hope not."

"It's white. Russian ships are always white," I said. A feeling of dread was beginning to bind my throat. I didn't want to believe this was happening.

"Yes, but so are a lot of other ships," returned Macho. He sounded more sanguine than I, and the tone of his voice lifted my spirits.

As the ship moved closer, it was evident that those aboard had spied us. Several men were hanging over the rails of the boat, waving their arms wildly and hollering something to us. But I couldn't tell what they were saying—or whether their movements were friendly or hostile.

"Can you read the lettering on the boat?" shouted Macho.

"Not from here, can you?"

"No. What do you want to do?"

"There's not much we *can* do. If it's a Russian ship, they'll have guns, artillery. There's no way to escape them."

Back in Cojimar, Gerardo was manning the radio, listening to the open airwaves for any information regarding my disappearance. Lazo, Manny, and several other soldiers were standing by, examining maps of the area that were spread on an old wooden table.

Lieutenant Brown looked on almost casually, knowing full well that Pino was not thinking the way I would. Not being a military strategist, he had made many tactical errors in his attempt to find me. And Brown was content to let him continue to make them.

Since their thorough search of the docks and the fishermen's boats had yielded nothing, Pino was eager for any scrap of news. He glanced at Manny and Lazo who were talking softly to each other. He strained to overhear their conversation. He still suspected they knew more about my disappearance then they had let on.

Suddenly, a grin crossed Gerardo's face and he turned toward Pino.

"I've got a report that a ship is approaching what's believed to be two boats of Cuban refugees needing medical assistance."

The soldiers looked up expectantly. A broad smile crossed Pino's face. He was almost salivating. "That's him." He grabbed Macho's brother by the arm excitedly. "That's my man."

"It could very well be," said Gerardo levelly, although he found Pino's excitement about this development annoying. His back stiffened and he looked at the lieutenant with an astringent eye.

"What are they saying?" demanded Pino.

"I can't quite make it out," said Gerardo. "It's an SOS, but they aren't talking directly to us. I'm only intercepting this."

A heavy mist blew in as we drew closer to the boat, making it impossible to make out the name of the ship. It had reduced its speed and was heading our way. A man was leaning over the side of the ship photographing us.

It didn't seem typical of Russian behavior, but I couldn't be sure. Perhaps they were refugee sympathizers documenting our escape for history. Or perhaps they were Russian communists gathering evidence for a trial. There were no tracks in the snow for me to follow, and I didn't want to take any chances.

People in our two boats began arguing among themselves about what we should do. Some believed it was a friendly ship that would provide us with much-needed medical attention.

Others thought we should refuse to step on board. They wanted us to take our chances getting to Florida on our own. I was besieged by doubts about what action to take. I didn't have enough information on which to base such a momentous decision. I was in desperate need of something—or someone—to guide me.

The soldiers remained calm, quiet, and alert, confident in my ability to handle the situation.

Manny and Lazo looked on anxiously as Pino pushed Gerardo aside, attempting to preempt his actions.

"Give me that radio. I'm taking over now," he said.

"No, you're not," said Gerardo, pushing him back. "This is my job. I'm in charge here."

"Damn it, I want the coast guard to go after those worms and pick them up immediately," barked Pino.

"But if it isn't a Russian ship, it could turn into an international incident," said Gerardo. "We've got to be careful. I could lose my head over something like this."

Pino scowled at him and let loose with a colorful string of expletives before saying, "You're making too much of this. Just do as I say. Send out the coast guard. We need to get to these fugitives before the Americans claim them."

Gerardo eyed him warily. "I need more information," he said, trying to keep his resentment from showing. "I've seen this kind of thing before. It can get very complicated very quickly, and then we'll have Fidel down our throats. I'm not chancing it. I'm going by the book."

Pino mumbled something incomprehensible, and all eyes turned back toward Gerardo. He looked the lieutenant up and down. Neither man appeared ready to back off. Pino glared at Gerardo while Gerardo thought for a moment. There was a long, pregnant pause. Everyone in the room stood somber and silent. Finally, Gerardo told Pino that he was not turning this situation over to him without knowing exactly who he was after.

"I need the name and description of the man for my records," he said.

Pino heaved a heavy sigh, exasperated at Gerardo's intransigence. He glanced at his watch impatiently. He drew a picture of me from his chest pocket, angrily slapping it down on the desk. "That's him: Frankie Mederos. Are you satisfied now? That's the guy I'm after."

Gerardo picked up the picture and examined it closely. The man in the photograph looked somehow familiar, and he was feeling a vague sense of unease. Then it struck him who I was. While he didn't know my name, he knew my face from the night of our confrontation in Macho's home. It suddenly dawned on him that I was the man his brother had tried to help escape.

The muscles in his face began twitching, alerting him to danger. His eyes moved back and forth as his mind raced to make a connection. It occurred to him that if I had left the country, Macho might be with me. And so might his nieces and nephew.

His mind returned to the morning his nephew stood among the crowd, hugging his teddy bear for comfort and protection. He pictured the boy's small hands, his narrow shoulders, and his shy, timid smile. Then he thought of how his nieces always greeted him with hugs and laughter. As tough as Gerardo was, he couldn't bear the thought of them all being killed.

Not hesitating a moment, he threw the photo down on the table and flew out the door before Pino could react or object. He was mumbling something about urgent business, leaving the lieutenant standing confused and speechless. Manny and Lazo watched him in amazement. The door banged shut behind him, punctuating his departure like an exclamation point.

Gerardo ran up the hill to Macho's house, hoping against hope to find him there. He raced up the front steps and rapped repeatedly on the front door. No answer. He frantically tried to turn the knob, but the door was locked, something Macho and his wife never did.

He cupped his hands against the reflection as he peered through the living room window. The interior of the house was oddly dark and lifeless—no cooking smells, no radio playing, no children laughing. His heart sank like a boulder when he realized the house was empty. He drew in a deep breath, knowing for certain that Macho and his whole family were with me.

CHAPTER 43

The captain of the *Gran Lempira*, a Guatemalan freighter, was hauling cargo to Canada when he spotted two boats filled to capacity and struggling to make their way to America. Suspecting we were Cuban refugees, he immediately radioed the United States Coast Guard.

"I've got two small boats full of people in my line of sight," he reported.

"What's your determination?" inquired the American officer.

"Best guess: Cuban refugees."

"Number?"

"Thirty to thirty-five."

"Destination?"

"On course for the Florida Keys."

The captain had dealt with refugees from this large Caribbean island before, and he knew that few boats came across the bow of his ship without passengers in need of immediate medical attention. Sympathetic to the fact that refugees risked their lives for freedom, he was eager to get us to safety as quickly as possible.

"Request permission to take them aboard."

"Permission granted. I'm notifying the Guard in Key West—a boat will be on its way shortly."

Having returned to his post at the fort, Gerardo picked up the American rescue order on the airwaves.

"What have you got?" demanded Pino. Gerardo glanced at Manny and Lazo who were listening intently. Thinking Macho and his family were safe, Gerardo told Pino, "The United States Coast Guard has been alerted. The Americans are coming to rescue the refugees now."

Manny, Lazo, and Lieutenant Brown looked at each other. They stifled smiles while Pino fumed. They had never seen him so angry. Eyes ablaze, he stood up abruptly and kicked over a chair. "The hell they are," he roared.

Alarmed, Gerardo could only stare. This was not behavior he expected from a military officer. This lieutenant was clearly overwrought. He seemed to have lost his ability to reason. This was a potentially explosive situation that could quickly spin out of control.

"Dispatch two Cuban boats to arrest them," ordered Pino, his voice coarse with rage. "They may still be closer to Cuba than to the United States. Hurry, damn it, while there's still a chance to bring them in."

Gerardo knew better than to confront the Americans, and he wanted to get that point across to Pino without engaging him in a violent confrontation. This was a tall order, since he himself was seething, none too happy that the lieutenant was throwing his weight around. He tried to siphon the anger from his voice.

"I don't think that's wise," he said through clenched teeth.

"It's wise if I say so." Pino was not about to have his authority challenged by Gerardo.

This guy is loco, thought Gerardo. He regarded the lieutenant with disdain. He knew the personality type. Calm to the point where he exploded in anger. And if you challenged him, it was curtains—maybe not immediately, but eventually. The man was relentless.

Gerardo paused, assessing the situation while growing more anxious by the moment. It was the height of the Cold War, and people were trigger-happy.

He looked at Pino. "Do you remember the Missile Crisis, Lieutenant?"

"Of course," said Pino.

"Well, maybe you don't remember very well." He hesitated. "Or maybe you've never seen pictures of the victims of Hiroshima."

"I don't need you to talk to me about Hiroshima."

"Damn it, I'm going to talk about it," said Gerardo. "In case you've forgotten, the whole island of Cuba could be incinerated with the touch of a nuclear button. We could be on the brink of triggering the largest disaster this country has ever seen. I consider myself to be a tough guy, but I'm not stupid."

"What exactly are you getting at?"

Gerardo glared at the lieutenant. "I'm trying to keep you from starting a goddamn war. And if you keep up this behavior, that's exactly what will happen."

"I'll do what I damn well please," responded Pino. "I'm not going to start a war, and I'm not about to have my career ruined over the likes of you."

Pino pushed Gerardo roughly aside and issued an order for the Cuban coast guard to bring us back—dead or alive.

I stared up at the ship, desperately trying to figure out what to do. Although I couldn't see them clearly, the people on the ship gave every indication of being friendly. But it could all be a trick. I had been through too much not to be careful, not to be suspicious.

I turned and looked at the passengers in my boat and then at those in Macho's boat. A small boy was asleep on his mother's lap, exhausted and oblivious to his surroundings. Mucus caked his nostrils and his breathing was ragged. He looked like he was running a fever.

I stared at the two pregnant women, both sitting with their hands folded neatly beneath their stomachs, and thought about their babies. It was almost too much to take in. The lives of thirty-one people—as well as two unborn children—were in my hands. I had to make the right decision.

I turned and looked at Miguel. For an old man, he was hardy and alert. Out of the blue, a thought occurred to me. I climbed over several people and moved my body next to his. Many of the passengers were studying me. Suddenly, a stark silence descended over the boat. The only sound was the raspy breathing of a sick child. It felt like the moment before the heavy velvet drapes rise at a theatrical performance. Everyone was watching.

"Miguel," I said, "I need to talk to you." He looked at me curiously, sensing that I was about to ask him an important question. I cleared my throat and narrowed my eyes.

"How old are you, Miguel?" I asked bluntly. There was no time for further preamble.

"Eighty-three."

"Have you had a good life?"

"Good enough."

I waited a moment. "Well, you have already lived your life. I know you would like to live a few years longer but, under the circumstances, would you be willing to do something for the lives of others?"

Miguel sat up straighter and shifted his weight. He looked at me respectfully. "I would," he declared like a true Cuban gentleman.

"Good."

"What do you want me to do?"

I took his hand in mine. "Look at me. I want you to be the first one to go onto the ship—like a canary in the mine shaft. If everything is on the up-and-up, walk to the back of the ship and give me a signal—wave to me that it's okay. If it's a Russian ship, don't come out—even if they pressure you, even if they threaten to kill you. You must be willing to die rather than betray us. Will you do that for us, Miguel?"

The old man hesitated for just a moment as if trying to absorb what I was asking him. Then his eyes cleared of confusion and a sense of purpose eclipsed his fear.

I studied Miguel carefully. He had been suddenly gripped with a sense of honor and purpose. He was welcoming the challenge.

"Yes, I will do it. I will not betray you. I will die if I have to." He pointed to his fellow passengers. "I will do it for you and for all of them."

"Good, Miguel. Good," I said.

Miguel looked at me and smiled. I sighed in relief now that a plan was in place. A few people clapped in recognition of Miguel's bravery, and he smiled proudly.

Picking up the order that two Cuban boats were being sent to arrest us, the American Coast Guard officer called for a second boat and two helicopters to be dispatched to the area in case of a conflict. He radioed the captain to inform him about the situation.

"Two Cuban coast guard boats are heading straight toward you," he said. We are sending air cover. Under no circumstances are you to turn the refugees over to anyone. Do you read me?"

"Sí, claro," replied the captain.

I waved to the ship's captain and got his attention. "We have an old man who wants to come aboard," I said. "He needs to talk to you."

The captain nodded. He turned to order his men to help Miguel up the ladder and onto the boat. Several men shook Miguel's hand before he disappeared from view. Knowing it would take a few minutes for the situation to resolve itself, I sat down beside one of the soldiers. His name was Eduardo. He told me his two older brothers had died—drowned—trying to leave Cuba, but he was sure we would make it. "We have to," he said in a determined voice. Eduardo said he'd been learning English. He wanted to become a doctor once he got to America. I wished him luck.

A young mother stood up for a moment and then inadvertently sat on her daughter's doll. The child—who looked to be about four— began to whimper, working to retrieve it from beneath her mother's thigh. The girl had a head full of dark, springy curls that bounced as she pulled on her toy. Her mother lifted her leg, and the child yanked the doll free, ripping out some of its hair in the process.

"You sat on my dolly. That was stupid. Now she's ruined."

Her father looked at her crossly. "Gina, don't you *ever* call your mother stupid." Gina stretched out her arms and held the doll before her. She looked the doll in its glass brown eyes and said in a small, serious voice, "Don't worry, dolly, we're going to MerryCa. And there you can say whatever you want."

The passengers laughed, relieving some of the tension suffusing the boat.

Fifteen minutes elapsed, and Miguel had still not returned. I was becoming anxious. I turned my head toward the soldier and heaved a weary sigh.

"What do you think is going on?" he asked.

"I'm not sure," I said. "Maybe they're questioning him—or giving him something to eat."

"Perhaps. Or perhaps they are Russians, figuring out what to do with us. Maybe we should get out of here while the getting is good."

"It's possible," I said, trying not to sound as alarmed as I felt. "But I don't want to leave Miguel—not yet. Let's give it a few more minutes."

Ten more minutes elapsed with still no sign of Miguel. I felt as tense as a father awaiting the birth of his baby. And with every passing minute, I felt more guilty for having sent an old man on such a dangerous mission.

I looked around. A middle-aged woman was furiously fingering rosary beads, her mouth working silently, her eyes half closed. A father was talking quietly to his son. A nine-year-old girl repeatedly made the sign of the cross, saying "God help us!" under her breath.

Finally, a murmur ran through the group, and people started elbowing each other. I looked up to see Miguel standing at the back of the ship. He was cloaked in a gray wool blanket and smiling broadly. Two men stood beside him and another stood squarely behind him.

"It's okay," Miguel hollered. He waved for us to approach. Everyone in both boats started screaming and hugging each other, delirious with joy. Husbands were wrapping their arms around their wives and parents were embracing their children, laughing.

The soldiers scoured my face for confirmation while the captains of our small boats awaited the go-ahead order. I looked again at Miguel. I wasn't completely certain that it was okay to proceed. I still had a lingering doubt. Maybe my mind just couldn't take in that my ordeal was finally over—or maybe it was something else. But it was certainly no time for rash decisions.

I looked more closely at the man standing behind Miguel. He was tall and husky, a burly man who looked like he could wrestle alligators. His eyes were fixed straight ahead as if he were under strict orders. The thought crossed my mind that he might be holding a knife—or a gun—to the old man's back.

I hesitated for a moment, thinking. The passengers looked at me, gauging my reaction. Seeing the look on my face, their mood suddenly changed. They looked around, confused. They grew silent and serious, taking their cue from me.

I whispered a prayer for guidance. This was neither a time for hesitation nor a time for hastiness. I looked up at Miguel. He was standing straight with his shoulders thrown back, happily waving us in. I blinked my eyes, not believing what I was seeing. I closed my eyes and opened them again. Only this time I was sure. My body relaxed and a broad smile crossed my face.

Standing next to Miguel was a young boy, the blue-eyed boy, the same one who had warned me about the soldiers coming over the wall surrounding my uncle's backyard. He was standing next to Miguel, clear as day and nodding to me. He smiled and mouthed only one word: "Come."

I immediately knew what to do. I looked at the captains of our two small boats and nodded to them. I snapped my fingers. "It's okay," I said. "Go!"

The passengers exuded excitement and relief as they gathered themselves up to board the ship. Several Guatemalans helped them aboard. The taxi driver was beaming from ear to ear, white teeth blazing against jet-black skin.

Macho and his mate said they would take our boats to Florida, and I bid them goodbye, watching their wake spin the blue water white as they sped away.

I turned to the young man who had tried before to escape Cuba. As soon as I removed the bandana that gagged him, he hollered to the communists, "I'm free, you bastards, I'm free." He looked proud and triumphant. I smiled, knowing exactly how he felt.

Once we came aboard, the captain introduced himself and greeted us with great enthusiasm, treating us like honored guests. Medical assistance was dispensed to those in need. Drinks were eagerly consumed and hot meals were served all around.

After I had had something to eat, the captain informed me that the American Coast Guard was on its way to take us to Florida. I smiled at the thought. Disturbingly, he added that two patrol boats from the Cuban coast guard were also headed in our direction. I looked out and spotted the Cuban boats in the distance. They looked threatening and ominous. My face blanched pale as milk. The captain looked at me, knowing full well what I was thinking.

"Can you get us safely out of here?" I asked.

"This is a Guatemalan ship, and I can't take you out of international waters or you will be classified as Guatemalan refugees," the captain informed me. I looked at him in alarm, not quite understanding what he was saying. My mind was too stressed to process this kind of information. To me, there was only one thing for certain: two Cuban boats were moving quickly toward us in one direction, and the Americans were advancing toward us in the other.

The captain watched as I clenched my jaw and rolled my head to relieve the tension. "Relax," he urged. "I'm not turning you and your people over to anyone but the Americans." I breathed a sigh of relief and the corners of my mouth drifted upward. But I still didn't feel safe.

We waited for what seemed like an eternity. Suddenly, I heard the howl of helicopters overhead. I looked up to see an American flag painted on the side of one of the choppers. The colors were vibrant, lacquered to a high gloss. A couple of minutes later an American boat appeared and circled the ship. The name *Cape Darby* was etched on its side. After surveying the situation, the boat pulled alongside the ship and the captain requested permission to board.

"Permission granted," shouted the captain of the *Gran Lempira*. He saluted smartly. I looked out and saw the American flag flapping tautly on the stern of the boat.

Gerardo intercepted the call that the Americans had left to go pick us up.

"It's over," he told Pino. "The Americans have taken control. We can't confront them or we'll have an international incident on our hands."

The planes in Pino's face collapsed and his mouth contorted in anger. His lips drooped, then contracted into a tight, wrinkled circle.

"The hell we can't," he bellowed. "I don't give a damn about the Americans. I'm not stopping until Mederos is dead. And that includes any other worms he has with him. Kill them all if you have to."

Manny and Lazo exchanged worried glances, wondering how Gerardo would react. Pino looked Gerardo straight in the eye and pounded his fist on the table.

"This is your problem and you've got to solve it," he thundered. "It's a matter of national security. Mederos is one of our top men. He knows all our military secrets, and he will give them up to the American imperialists. He's a menace, a traitor. Your head will be on the block if you don't bring him in."

Gerardo glared back at the lieutenant with cold, black eyes. He had never been a man to be toyed with, and he was not about to be toyed with now. To Pino's dismay, Gerardo said, "No, Lieutenant, it's not my head that will be on the block—it's yours. We are not confronting the Americans. And we are not killing any Cubans. My brother and his family are on one of those boats. There will be no bloodshed in international waters. Not on my watch."

Gerardo picked up the radio and countermanded Pino's order, telling the Cuban coast guard to return to port immediately.

An American Coast Guard officer of Spanish descent boarded the ship and walked briskly toward us, accompanied by three guards. He was a handsome man, trim, fit, and broad shouldered. He stood tall and saluted me and all the other soldiers. We returned the salute. He looked around at the passengers.

"Is everybody okay?" he asked in fluent Spanish. I was surprised he wasn't speaking English. Then it occurred to me that the Americans would give Spanish-speaking officers these kinds of assignments.

"We're all fine now," I said.

"We will escort you to Key West," he said surveying the crowd. "Is this everyone?"

"Yes," I said. I looked over at my fellow passengers. They were all huddled at the back of the boat, smiling. One of the children offered me a small wave. I nodded and waved back.

The officer turned to one of the guards who handed him a scroll wrapped around a stick about the thickness of your thumb. It looked very official, complete with gold finials and fringe. He nodded to the guards to run the American flag up the pole. It undulated in the wind alongside the Guatemalan flag. I looked at the striped flag with its patch of stars. I felt like we were all stars, each in our own way. I sat and stared at the flag in wonder—we all did.

The officer cleared his throat and plucked his eyeglasses from his shirt pocket. He worked the arms of his glasses around his ears until they settled in place and then he adjusted them on his nose with his forefinger.

He unrolled the scroll, and asked us to please stand. Words written in black calligraphy were inked on yellowed parchment. They looked elegant and very official. A gold seal was affixed to the bottom of the document with a ribbon adding a colorful flourish.

We scrambled to our feet, helping each other up. People were rearranging their blankets around their bodies. Miguel stood proudly beside me. The officer hesitated a moment, surveying the crowd. Tears sprang to my eyes as I looked at the other passengers nestled together. Some were beaming, some were crying, and some were still shivering, whether from cold or emotional trauma I could not determine.

I knew everyone had a story. I knew mine, but I didn't know theirs. But I did know that the genesis of everyone's journey was a thirst for freedom. I thought about all the people who, in one way or another, had helped me escape.

I pictured Sophia's face the night she visited the base. I thought about my relatives and Magda's relatives, about Manny and Lazo and Lieutenant Brown, about Ralph, Jabao, and Cuni. I thought about poor, fearful Rosa feeding me sandwiches under the bed, and my little cousins slipping me something to eat at Christmastime. I thought about Pedro, Señor Lopez, and Joey. And then I turned my head and looked into the eyes of Miguel. Brave, brave Miguel.

Suddenly, the words of the Cuban poet José Martí sprung to mind:

> *We are an army of light*
> *And nothing shall prevail against us*
> *And in those places where the sun is darkened*
> *It will overcome.*

The officer cleared his throat and began, "In the name of the president of the United States of America, I welcome you to freedom." His words took my breath away. I looked up at the American flag with tears dripping down my face. I wiped them away with my fingertips, unashamed of my feelings.

The officer continued, "In the name of the Congress of the United States of America, I welcome you to freedom." A breeze kicked up, and the American flag proudly unfurled, flapping noisily over the ocean.

I looked toward Cuba, thinking of all my loved ones whom I had left behind. For a moment an image of Abuelo standing in his boat flashed through my mind. I wondered whether I would ever see him again, or whether I would ever again put foot in the country Columbus had dubbed "the most beautiful land that human eyes have ever seen."

Then I looked in the direction of America and thought about Magda and the life that stretched before us. I thought about our unborn children, should we be fortunate enough to have them. But the best thing was that I knew in my heart that somewhere in America Magda was waiting for me. I had someone to go to. I had never doubted her love.

I looked up at the officer. He nodded to me, smiled warmly, and said as if his words were uttered for me and for me alone, "And in the name of the American people, I welcome you to freedom."

The men whose boat we had commandeered stared at the spectacle before them. The captain smiled in satisfaction. The passengers cheered and hugged one another, exultant, jubilant. Children looked at their parents and clapped their hands gleefully. The pregnant women beamed and patted their bellies. Miguel nodded and waved to the crowd, amazed that he had become a hero at his advanced age.

And I sat down on a chair, covered my face with my hands, and wept.

EPILOGUE

I had spent more than a year listening to Frank's story over glasses of wine and endless bags of corn chips and salsa in my home in Haddon Heights, New Jersey. During that time, Frank and I forged a strong friendship. By the time we finished, he said I knew his story better than anyone else in the world.

Frank was amazing. His patience in answering my numerous questions was remarkable and his recall of events that occurred decades ago was incredible. He even acted out scenes such as the time he escaped through the sisal by doing a somersault on my living room floor. His military background shows. He is still in great physical shape.

Frank had an uncanny knack of remembering exactly what was said in this story, and I often could not write fast enough to capture his dialogue. But he never jumped ahead of himself. He told me the story sequentially. This was often frustrating because time constraints would sometimes dictate that he leave me in the middle of an exciting scene.

For instance, I knew he was hiding in the outhouse and the soldiers were approaching, but Frank had to leave before telling me the outcome. I, dear reader, was just as eager to find out what happened as you.

When the coast guard picked Frank up at sea, my instincts told me that this was the perfect ending to his tale. Yet questions remained. I looked at Frank and asked, "What happened to Magda? What happened to your family?"

Silence.

"And what became of Manny, Lazo, and Lieutenant Pino?"

More silence.

Frank thought for a moment and then sighed. "It would take a whole other book to tell you."

I leaned back against the sofa and thought *I need to know what happened.* I would be taking another chance in writing a story without knowing its shape and ending. But Frank had established a track record with me, and I was willing to trust his instincts.

"Do you think your story is worthy of another book?"

Frank's eyes twinkled for a moment. "It's a very good story," he said. He is a master of understatement.

"Can you give me a hint of the plot?"

Frank laughed. "You know me," he said. "I need to tell it to you over time, just the way it happened."

"Not even a small clue?"

Frank considered for a moment. "Let me just say that I think a good title would be *Stalked.*"

I sipped a little wine as a smile formed on my lips. I knew I was in for another adventure.

"Same time, same place? Next week?" I asked.

Frank nodded. "See you on Tuesday." He opened the door, looked back at me, and said, "You will not be disappointed."

Following is an excerpt from the conclusion to
Frank Mederos's story of heroism.

Stalked:
The Boy Who Said No

Patti Sheehy continues Frank Mederos's true-
life story of romance, suspense, and intrigue in
Stalked: The Boy Who Said No. After
defecting from Cuba's Special Forces and
making a harrowing escape from his homeland,
Frank faces new challenges in America. With
five dollars in his pocket and a boatload of
determination, he sets his sights on achieving
the American dream.

ISBN: 978-1-60809-125-6

Illustration copyright © 2013 by Emily Baar

Published in the United States of America by Oceanview Publishing, Longboat Key, Florida

www.oceanviewpub.com

10 9 8 7 6 5 4 3 2 1

PRINTED IN THE UNITED STATES OF AMERICA

Stalked:
The Boy Who Said No

PREFACE

In *The Boy Who Said No: An Escape to Freedom* we follow the harrowing adventures of Frank Mederos, a member of Fidel Castro's Special Forces, as he defects from the army, spends five months on the run from his fellow soldiers, and makes a desperate escape by boat to Key West, Florida.

When Frank arrives in America his trials are far from over. While he works to make a life for himself, sinister forces in Cuba plot his destruction. This is his story; a tale of love, loss, courage, and friendship.

Stalked: The Boy Who Said No is based upon countless hours of interviews with Mr. Mederos. He was able to attest to the parts of the story that directly involve him. In many areas of this narrative, however, Frank knows what set events in motion and how they played out, but the details of what happened in between remain in shadow.

As a result, many scenes, descriptions, and dialogue have been written based on how Frank imagined them to have occurred knowing the characters, time frame, and history. Liberties were taken in creating material that Frank could only surmise, given the outcome of events. The experiences of Frank's former commanding officer, Pino, in the cane fields and in the Soviet Union as well as the interactions among the Cuban operatives are fictionalized.

Nonetheless, the skeleton of this story—Frank's attempted recruitment by the CIA, his relationship with Magda and Chris, his life as an immigrant, and his encounter with his friend Lazo and the Cuban operatives in the hills of north Jersey—are true. Thus, *Stalked: The Boy Who Said No* is called a true-life novel.

The names of some characters have been changed to protect the privacy of family members and those still residing in Cuba.

CHAPTER ONE

Lieutenant Pino picked up the phone. The forty-year-old Cuban military officer had one message for Commander Martinez, one sentence that would change the course of his life. He didn't bother to identify himself when the commander answered.

"It's over," he said. "The son of a bitch has escaped."

"Jesus Christ. When?"

"Just now!"

"How?"

"The American Coast Guard picked him up. We intercepted the radio transmission."

"Christ almighty, this is all I need!"

The lieutenant took an audible breath, but did not respond.

"I want you back at base, pronto, Lieutenant."

"Yes, sir."

"And you'd better have one hell of an explanation for this." The phone went dead. Pino lifted his chin as if he were preparing for a fight and signaled to his driver to start the engine.

CHAPTER TWO

Lieutenant Pino arrived at base at four p.m. Sensing his mood, his driver remained silent during the trip, regarding the lieutenant cautiously in the rearview mirror. The lieutenant seemed agitated, his hands fisted, his mouth twitching uncharacteristically. Thick blue veins throbbed at his temples, looking as if they were about to explode. He appeared shell-shocked and bone-tired.

The driver pulled into base and opened the door of the Russian-made jeep. Pino stepped out of the vehicle and straightened his back. He glanced at his watch, then at his driver. His eyes were hard as cement.

The base was unusually busy with men scurrying in different directions in frenzied activity. They saluted smartly when they saw the lieutenant, but Pino detected a trace of fear in their eyes. He found this unsettling. He knew it was going to be a long, trying day.

Before the lieutenant walked three feet, he was told to report to Commander Martinez's office. He tightened his shoulders and hastened down the hallway.

The commander stood against the open window, red-faced, nostrils flaring. Pino sucked in his breath. He had seen that expression on the commander's face before, and it never preceded anything good. Martinez stabbed Pino with his eyes, turned, and lowered his chin. A thin layer of fat settled above his collar.

"Shut the door, Lieutenant," he barked. The older man's eyes were flinty, his lips starched.

Pino turned slowly to close the door, hoping to buy a little time to think. He pivoted to face his commanding officer.

"So, we have a situation," Martinez said curtly.

Pino blinked, dreading this conversation. "A situation?" he countered. It was an instinctive reaction. He knew full well what the commander meant. He also knew this meeting would involve no fiery tango, no point-counterpoint. He could offer no real defense. He had gambled and lost. Now, there would be hell to pay.

"What situation?" mocked the commander. "You told me an hour ago that Mederos has escaped—picked up by the American Coast Guard. I'd call that a situation. Wouldn't you, Lieutenant?"

Pino bit his bottom lip, not wanting to respond. He hesitated a moment and looked at the ceiling. He needed a drink—a double scotch. Finally, he nodded and said in a strangled voice, "Yes, sir."

"Can't hear you, Lieutenant. Speak up!"

"Yes, sir."

Martinez shook his head in exasperation. "What do you have to say for yourself?"

Pino straightened his spine as his stomach dropped away. "Couldn't be helped, sir. We did everything possible to bring the worm in."

Pino's commanding officer looked incredulous, as if he were still trying to process what had happened. The air in the room grew as still as that preceding a tornado. Pino looked at the commander, and an image of a Cuban boa flashed before his eyes, its body coiled, its jaws unhinged to consume its prey. Like the rodents it attacked, Pino felt he was about to be asphyxiated, eaten alive.

"Everything possible, Lieutenant? Everything possible?" The commander paused, trying to quell the roar in his ears. "I'll tell you what was possible," he spat. "It was possible that we followed procedure in this situation. It was possible that we notified the police, the Committees for the Defense of the Revolution (CDR), the goddamn militia. It was possible that they would've posted Mederos's picture on every window and on every telephone pole in this goddamn city, in the goddamn country if necessary." He shook his head.

"It was possible that Mederos would've been arrested the day he defected." The commander's voice climbed an octave as he concluded his monologue. "It was possible that this whole damn fiasco could've been avoided, and Mederos would rot away in some rat-ridden jail." He hesitated a moment, giving his words gravitas. "For your information, Lieutenant, that's what was possible."

The commander exhaled loudly, eyes blazing. Pino stiffened. He felt like all the oxygen had been siphoned from the room, and he was gasping for breath. Only he wasn't. "But *you!* You, with your stubbornness, your willfulness, your know-it-all attitude, you made all of that *impossible.*"

Pino squeezed his lips together and lifted his chin, but said nothing. The room seemed suddenly hollow, devoid of power on both of their parts. The clip of boots hitting pavement drifted through the open window. The sun cast a puddle of yellow on the linoleum floor. When the commander spoke again, his voice was hoarse, almost a whisper.

"You and your damn arrogance will cost us plenty, Lieutenant. Both of us. Do you understand?"

Pino bit the inside of his cheek and returned the commander's glare. He felt a tickle at the back of his throat but resisted the urge to cough. *Bile*, he thought. The two men stood in silence.

"Make no mistake about it," said Martinez. "We're through with this little game of yours. Your so-called state of emergency at this base is officially over." He scoured the lieutenant's eyes. "I am in charge now. And, as your commanding officer, I'm placing you under house arrest."

Pino blanched. His body grew rigid, fear cramping his stomach. Small beads of perspiration dewed his hairline.

"I've notified the administrator at headquarters in Managua, and a delegation is on its way to deal with the issue," said Martinez. "They will arrive first thing tomorrow morning. Meanwhile, you are confined to base. You will not leave, you will not go home, you will not go anywhere until further notice. You know the drill. Am I making myself clear?"

Pino nodded. He opened his mouth to speak and then thought

better of it. The commander looked like he would brook no argument. Still, he felt he had to defend himself. Finally, he said, "How could you do this to me? You know how loyal I've been to the Party."

The commander's eyes widened. "Christ almighty, Lieutenant. You just don't get it, do you? This isn't about being a loyal communist. It isn't about being an educated Marxist. It isn't about being a good soldier. This is about being a total asshole!" He turned and pointed outside. "Do you see what's going on out there, Lieutenant?"

Pino looked out the window. He had been so self-absorbed that he had barely noticed what was happening around him. Now things were becoming clear.

"Mederos knew everything about our operation—Christ, nobody knows that better than you." Martinez shook his head in frustration. "He's probably spilling the beans to some eager little CIA officer right now. This is a matter of vital importance, Lieutenant. Even an imbecile like you knows that."

Pino took a step backward, watching the commander carefully as he crossed to the other side of the room. A couple of minutes elapsed before Martinez spoke again.

"I've ordered the men to take measures to protect us—Cuba—from the consequences of Mederos's treason. God knows what the imperialists will do with the information he provides them. They could attack at any time—take out our missiles before we have time to move them. That's why this base is in such an uproar."

Pino remained mute as a mime, knowing full well that Martinez spoke the truth. He exhaled loudly as the commander opened the door and signaled to the soldiers standing guard outside. They advanced quickly and surrounded the lieutenant, while he stood like a bronzed statue, his icy eyes staring straight ahead. To Pino's chagrin, Martinez ordered the soldiers to escort him to his office.

Pino walked stiffly down the hall while the soldiers held his arms. He could feel their condemnation. He could feel their hatred. Humiliation burned his cheeks.

He checked to make sure his shoulders were back and down. He didn't want to appear stressed in front of the men. Not now. He puffed his chest, trying to look less vulnerable. He worked to keep his breathing regular. He worked to control his rage. But he startled like a frightened alley cat when his thick office door slammed shut behind him.

Pino looked at his large mahogany desk, at his black telephone, at his gray filing cabinet. But in his mind's eye he saw a narrow cot, iron bars, and a pitted porcelain basin. *Is this my future? My life?*

He knew a similar crime in Russia would prompt a sentence of hard labor in the ice-laden camps of Siberia where your fingers, toes, and ears would blacken and wither from frostbite. Or you could be sent to work the uranium mines in the Urals where your teeth would rot from the roots from radiation and your hair would drop in clumps, leaving your scalp red, scaly, and exposed. At least there weren't any uranium mines in Cuba. And the country was warm. But Cuban jails were no picnic either.

Pino stomped around his office. "Damn Mederos!" he muttered. "Damn him! Damn him! Damn him!" He lifted his arm and threw his fist into the cinder block wall, leaving scraps of skin behind. He shook his hand to release the pain, and then drew it to his mouth to suck out the sting.

Years of work, years of study, years of kowtowing to the likes of Commander Martinez and to Lieutenant Brown and it's come to this? For what? For one little worm?

A shudder surged through the lieutenant's body. His stomach clenched as a headache bloomed behind his eyes. He sat down at his desk and shuffled a few papers. He signed some forms, wondering whether this would be the last time he ever conducted official business. It was too much for him. He dropped his pen and stared at the wall. *How could I, a person who drinks scotch from Waterford tumblers, ever survive some concrete cesspit? Besides, it wasn't my fault. I tried everything. I did my best.*

Pino rested his forehead on his fingertips while a fury as dark and black as lava churned his belly. He worked to control it, to harness it. As bad as things appeared right now, he knew he would be the victor. He would prevail. When he put his mind to something, he always did.

CHAPTER THREE

Accompanied by two soldiers, Pino headed back to his room in the officers' barracks, located in the imposing mansion once occupied by a wealthy Cuban landowner. It was just past eight p.m. He climbed the five marble steps and entered the commodious lobby filled with gilt-framed oil paintings and fine European antiques.

A Tabriz carpet covered the floor beneath a leather couch. The first movement of Mozart's Symphony no. 40 in G minor played softly in the background. Cuban military officers were treated well. Pino nodded to the sergeant on duty before ascending the wide interior staircase.

A soft breeze wafted through his bedroom window as Pino unbuttoned his shirt and removed his hat. His body was lean and muscular, and he worked to keep it that way. He fell to the floor and did a hundred push-ups before he removed his shoes and squared them at a right angle to the wall. Tomorrow morning he would set them outside his door to be polished.

The lieutenant performed his usual evening ritual of showering and brushing his teeth before he climbed into bed. The mattress was firm, effortlessly supporting his back and weight. He set a glass of water on a cherry-veneer bed stand, anticipating a long night ahead.

Tomorrow the brass from headquarters would arrive, throwing their weight around, asking a million questions. He could picture their faces, stern and ruthless, their mouths tight wads of condemnation, their eyes stony and accusing.

He could hardly believe it had come to this. *If only that imbecile at the Coast Guard station had followed my orders, this never would've happened. That's always the way, isn't it? You give some miserable peasant a little power and it goes to his head. Hell, if the Cuban Coast Guard had done what I ordered, we would've gotten Mederos before the Americans did. All that babble about triggering an international incident was just stupid talk.*

Suddenly, Pino felt hot and sticky. The paddle fan twirled overhead, but the room was closing in on him. He sipped some water, kicked off his upper sheet, and banged his feet against the mattress. *How could Mederos elude me for so long? He must've had help. He wasn't smart enough to pull this off alone. But who?*

Pino ran through the possibilities in his mind. *Manny? Lazo? Lieutenant Brown?*

Nah, Brown was too smart for that. He was far too fond of Mederos, but he wouldn't actually help him escape. That would be treason. He would be executed for such behavior. And he knew it. He'd never risk it. But the other two? They were always palling around with Mederos. Thick as thieves. They'd do anything for each other. That's the way it is with the Special Forces.

Pino rubbed his forehead with the palm of his hand, trying to soothe his pounding headache. *What difference does it make now? Any way you look at it, my goose is cooked. Still, it would help to point a finger at someone else when the hard questions are asked.*

Suddenly, he remembered the smirk on Jabao's face the night Mederos vanished into thin air. *What did he say?* He tried to recall the exact words. *"Do you think you are going to find Mederos here? On his own turf? Impossible."* He sighed. *Maybe it was inevitable. Fate. Destiny. Whatever you want to call it. Christ. What am I thinking? Something like this wasn't meant to be. Mederos was a menace, a wart on the face of communism. A cancer that needed to be excised, removed forever.*

Pino sat up in his bed. His vision blurred for a moment before the face of Frankie Mederos pirouetted before his eyes. It was as if he were right there in the room with him. "You stinking bastard. You've screwed up everything. My whole damn life is ruined because of you." It barely registered to Pino that he was talking to himself.

The lieutenant slammed his right fist into his left palm, feeling the force of his self-inflicted pain. He stifled a scream, imagining his fist connecting with Mederos's jaw. He wanted to mangle his face, to bash in his brains.

"I'll get you, Mederos. I'll get you, Mederos. I'll get you, Mederos," he said in a voice loud enough to be heard through the walls. He repeated the oath like an ancient Buddhist chant sung in a monastery high in the Himalayas. The words looped round and round in his head and on and off his tongue until the morning light wedged itself through the shutters. Then he slowly lifted his body from the bed to face whatever the day might bring.

CPSIA information can be obtained at www.ICGtesting.com
Printed in the USA
LVOW08s0454300615

444314LV00002B/3/P